DEATH'S COLLECTOR: VOID WALKER

BILL MCCURRY

Infinite Monkeys Publishing LLC

Carrollton, TX

Bill-McCurry.com

Editing: Shayla Raquel, ShaylaRaquel.com

Cover Design: Mlblart, miblart.com

Interior Formatting: Vellum

ISBN-13 (Ebook): 979-8-9899343-3-1

ISBN-13 (Paperback): 979-8-9899343-4-8

ISBN-13 (Hardcover): 979-8-9899343-5-5

ACKNOWLEDGMENTS

I'd like to thank my wife for supporting my writing habit and for smiling patiently while I talked about made up people as if they'd be coming over for drinks later. I'd also like to thank my editor, Shayla Raquel, a wonderful partner who has moved on to much more important work.

Finally, I have to thank the reasons I fell in love with this genre: Leiber, Howard, Moorcock, Zelazny, Harrison, Heinlein, and many others. They built the town that I'm lucky enough to stomp around in.

ONE

A visit to the whorehouse would be better than splashing blood all over the dirt. I told myself that as I glanced at the glob of spit on my boot. The guard smirked at me and wiped his chin, careless of the four unprotected places I could ram my sword into his body before he shifted his feet.

Instead of murdering the man right that second, I grabbed the back of my belt with my sword hand. I was trying to uncomplicate my life, and killing a king's man is always a complicated business.

From behind me, Pil said, "I told you to go to the brothel and let me announce you."

I grunted but didn't come right out and agree that she was smarter than me.

The guard's eyes crinkled in his round, red face. "What would this ancient bastard do with a whore? I bet he's as limp as a cow's tit."

The man's three companions laughed, leaning on their spears behind him.

I let go of my belt. "That may be, son. But I've copulated so much with a limp willy I could row a boat with a rope. And satisfied women who wouldn't touch you if you were made of gold and candy."

Red Face squinted. I might have overwhelmed his vocabulary.

I sighed at myself. Comments like that were unlikely to simplify my life. The castle courtyard behind the guard was thrumming with busy people, and some would notice if I stabbed this man through the neck. I shuffled half a step back from him and the gate.

"Let's walk back down the hill, Bib," Pil said. She often spoke so quickly she sounded flustered, but she was as steady as bricks. "If you're just too good for the brothel, then we can go to the tavern, or the stable, or the blacksmith, and you could buy the king some nails and send them up as a gift tomorrow, with a note. A note that asks whether he's happy you didn't kill his stupidest, ugliest guard. Let's do that."

The guard flinched like he'd been hit. In the weeks Pil had traveled with me, I had concluded that her beauty was one of her less significant qualities, but she was still likely the prettiest girl in the city. It had to hurt the guard to hear words like that from her. But he straightened up and pointed his spear at me. "Get on out of here, you clump of dog shit! And take your bitch with you!"

I had been shoving down the urge to kill this bastard. Now that he had pointed his weapon at me, my urge bloomed into a hearty craving for his life. I called back to Pil, "Who is this surly pissant to threaten me, anyway? What gives him leave to insult my friends? And spit on my damn boot?"

I didn't add, *How dare he block my way when I have come to betray his king?*

It didn't seem that such betrayal would uncomplicate my life, but I owed debts to more important beings than kings. And I couldn't betray the king while standing out on this dusty road. I stepped forward, angling to walk around the guard's spear, my hand on my sword.

The guard shifted his feet, but before he moved, Pil raised both arms and called out, "Wait! He's bringing His Majesty a message from the Rocky Lizard People of the North, and I'm guarding it— and him. The old fart may die any minute, just look at him! I mean,

I had to carry him halfway here. Don't delay letting him see the king."

Red Face squinted at Pil as she babbled her lies, and I walked all the way around him. I ached to draw my sword and thrust it through his back and into his heart, but I forced my hand to be still. Then he spun and whipped out the butt of his spear to knock me off my feet. He executed the move with a hell of a lot of skill too, more skill than I expected. He almost caught me before I leaped away.

I drew my sword, and Red Face jumped back before thrusting his spear at me. I rushed him, knocked his weapon aside, and sliced his arm from shoulder to elbow. He dropped the spear and staggered away, cursing and clutching his bicep.

The other three guards had been laughing at me, the feeble old idiot. Now they pointed their spears at my chest and shuffled their feet as if they might lunge any second.

"Stop! Just stop it!" Pil bellowed, her hands in the air again as she stepped forward far enough for me to see her. She exuded enough confidence to stop everybody. She glanced at me and then stared at the now-motionless, wide-eyed guards. "Bib, make your kills clean this time. Don't maim them so that they take a month to die." She gave the guards a pointed look. "All right, go ahead."

The guards paused; I suppose to assess that new information. I bounded over and yanked one's spear out of the way with my free hand. I kicked its owner hard on the knee, and he stumbled as he shouted something bad about my sister. I pushed him toward his two comrades, who stepped high to get out of the man's path.

Half a dozen more guards were now sprinting from various parts of the courtyard. Some held spears, and two had drawn swords. One of the guards near me thrust his spear so hard that when I stepped aside, he slipped. I sliced his skin across the skull and forehead. He fell to his knees, howling, and his unwounded friend backed away toward the middle of the courtyard.

I should have killed all those guards, but I hesitated to slay the king's men right there in his own courtyard. After all, he was my friend. And despite Pil's bloodthirsty comments, I knew she'd be pleased if neither of us ever killed again.

To hell with that. I laughed at the guard backing away, at the one bleeding on the dirt near me, at the ones charging me, and at all their rat-snot, pissant friends inside this castle. Part of me knew I couldn't kill them all, but that knowledge was weak and pale.

The man I had pushed into his friends recovered and thrust low to cripple my leg. I sidestepped and stabbed him in the throat with a snap before whipping around to face the others.

Red Face, holding his mangled arm, shouted, "Shit-mouth bastard! Throw down that sword!"

His words couldn't strictly be considered a threat, but he might try to attack me again. Not today, but someday. I lunged and put six inches of my blade through his heart. When I withdrew, he stared at the wound in his chest, trying to pull open his shirt with his one good hand. Then he collapsed straight down like a load of loose sticks.

"Wait! Stop!" A skinny guard charged toward me from an outbuilding in the courtyard, waving his arms. "Wait, dammit! Stop! All of you, just wait!"

Everybody stopped and waited. Most people, even some soldiers, don't really want to kill another person, and they welcome a reason not to.

The man charged over as if he were fighting a fire. His whiny shout went up half an octave. "Stop it! Damn your dicks for dog turds!"

Now standing beside me, Pil muttered, "Do you know this crazy chicken man?"

I didn't look at her because I *did* know the man, and he *did* look like a chicken with his long, scrawny neck and sharp face. He arrived and jumped between the other guards and me. I said, "Hello, Stan."

Panting a little, Stan adjusted his helmet and poked a greasy lock of yellow hair back under it. "Gods damn it to my mother's twat, Bib, for the first time I'm glad to be stuck here as a stinking guard instead of out soldiering and crushing the king's foes. All these tit-suckers here would have got themselves killed fighting you, and I'd have to do all the guarding work alone."

A towering, bristly guard lowered his sword and stepped close to Stan. "Corporal, what in perdition is this? Who's this man? Tell him to surrender."

Stan turned to Bristle Face and waved his hands as he spoke. "Dammit, Sergeant, this is Bib! You know, Bib? Hell, I forgot, seven in ten of you weasel-dicks are new and don't know shit from a pork pie."

The sergeant puffed up. "Hold on, Corporal—"

Stan cut him off. "You goat-shaggers have just come as close to death as you've ever likely been, and you probably won't thank me for saving your asses, nor even buy me a drink, will you? Bib's the most dangerous man in the world."

Pil raised a skeptical eyebrow at me.

The guards all scrutinized me. None of them looked convinced.

Stan went on, warming to his audience. "First off, he's a sorcerer, and even amongst them, he's a nightmare. Just as deadly as a hundred wolves pissing fire. He slaughtered a thousand men and women in two minutes using horrible magic that would drive you or me insane if we heard even a word of it. It's true! I was told it by a pure woman who was there, and who's never told one single lie in her blessed life. And with my own eyes I saw him charm a water fairy, and her as naked as your nose. Beautiful too."

Some interested murmuring rose from the guards who had crowded around.

Stan was walking back and forth in front of his listeners, gesturing with gusto as he spoke. "He got both . . . I am not shitting . . . *both* his hands sliced right off, and he's grown 'em back again! And he killed that bucket of pus and doorknobs, Vintan Reth, who was the cruelest, smartest, most villainous vomit chunk of a sorcerer who ever lived. But Bib killed him deader than your daddy's dong. If I hadn't looked out here to see what the shouting was for, every one of you waddling bastards would be bleeding to death on this dirt right now!"

The guards grumbled and peered at me.

"Well, you're welcome!" Stan shouted. "Bib, I mean, Lord Bib, where do you want to go? I'll take you there as safe as babies so you don't have to dirty up your sword on any more of these boobs."

Stan escorted us past the guards, who didn't seem inclined to test me now.

At the keep itself, one of the main door guards remembered me from the year before. He smiled and winked at me, and I walked straight inside with Pil. I hoped I wouldn't have to kill him when it came time for betrayal.

"Thank you, Stan." The man had journeyed to the southlands and back with me almost two years ago, and I slapped him on the shoulder. "I'll find you later and buy you some drinks. So, you'd rather be a soldier than a guard?"

"I'd rather be an ass stain than a guard."

"All right, I'll fix it with the king."

Stan beamed, showing all the appalling teeth he had left. "Damn nice to see a friend. Figured you might be dead by now, like most everybody else from the old days."

"The old days were two years ago," I said.

"Happy to see you ain't forgot them." Stan trotted back toward the courtyard.

After Stan rounded the corner, Pil said, "I like your friend."

I laughed.

Pil glanced at the ceiling and sighed. "No, really. He's brave. He didn't have to run out in the middle of that fight, or what had been a fight and what might have become a fight again soon. And he seems honest."

This time I snorted.

Pil touched my arm. "Fine, maybe he got some details wrong—I wasn't there for all that—but I bet he told it exactly the way he understood it to be true, and that's more honesty than you find in most of us."

"Sure, he's a diamond in a world of horse turds. Please let me think now."

"If you haven't thought before now, I predict failure."

I saw her scowl before she looked away. It was a furious look, and I wondered when she'd get tired of following me around while I got us into trouble. A young sorcerer like Pil could sure as hell could find better things to do with her life.

During the short walk to His Majesty's study, I reviewed my plans. I had agreed to force war upon Glass, a war with great armies, and then make sure the kingdom lost. The God of Death required that of me. The prospect had shriveled me some when I made the deal, but it had been the best bargain I could get to save a lot of people who were innocent to varying degrees. Most importantly, it saved me.

Also, I had to fight in that war, far out in front of the army.

I had puzzled on this problem for several weeks, searching for a way to pay my debt to the gods without causing real harm to the kingdom, or the king. During my long ride south, I had stopped at the neighboring Kingdom of Eastgate, and I came up with a subtle scheme to solve everybody's problems.

Of course, I had never started a war before. Looking back now, maybe I shouldn't have tried to be quite so subtle.

"I never expected to meet a king," Pil said as we tramped down a hallway through Castle Glass. "Now I'm going to meet my second one."

"They're not so special. I never met a one who could whistle worth a damn."

A guard stood beside the closed door to the king's study. As I approached, the door was flung open with a crack and a blonde woman in her mid-thirties stamped out into the hallway. She noticed me, lurched to a stop, and stared.

"Ella?" I almost ran over and kissed her before I stopped myself. Such familiarity might have been unwelcome, considering the firm tone she had used when saying she didn't love me anymore.

Ella ran to me, though. Her hair straggled across her wide, blue eyes. Her cheeks were hollow, her lips were pale, and she was painfully beautiful. I held out my arms. She grabbed my shirt front with both hands, pulled me against her, and lay her head on my shoulder.

I embraced her, and we stood that way for a short while. At least it was short enough that nobody made any uncomfortable remarks. I didn't speak a word. I couldn't think of anything to say that would make things better than this.

At last, Ella pushed me back a couple of feet and looked down. I had a wisp of a notion that she was about to apologize to me for something. Instead, she stomped on my instep before wrenching away from me.

"Fingit stab it in the ass with fire!" I yelled, hopping on one foot.

"Where have you been?" Ella's eyes had gone deep blue and predatory. "You told me you would come, and I needed you. Pres refuses to help me. Desh has disappeared and is perhaps dead or abducted. Where were you, Bib?" She glared at Pil. "Off whoring with her?"

"Pil, this is Ella," I said, trying to smile.

Pil cocked her head at Ella for a moment before wrinkling her nose the way she might when playing with a child.

Ella ignored that and jumped at me. I winced, but she just grabbed me by the shirt front again. This time, she tried to shake me. "You should have been with us, but instead you galloped away on sabbatical, weeping about what a cruel killer you are."

I thought Ella was being pretty damn harsh, but her eyes were shiny with tears. "I'm sorry, Ella, but I didn't exactly promise to come . . ." I stopped when she glared at me. Then she looked down again.

"Something's wrong," she whispered.

I leaned my head close to hers and murmured, "What is it?"

"I don't know!" Ella shouted, flecks of spit flying. "I'd do something if I knew!" She lowered her voice to a whisper. "The king has become unpredictable and . . . harsh. We suffer bandits and angry nobles. And Desh has disappeared. I fear someone has taken him."

I couldn't help smiling, since Desh was a crafty sorcerer. "If somebody kidnapped Desh, you should feel sorry for them. When he escapes, none of them may survive."

Ella hauled off as if she might hit me, but she lay her palm on my chest instead.

"What about Limnad?" I asked. Limnad was a water spirit, and the last I knew, she was Desh's lover. If he had broken her heart, then she might have torn him to bits. She might have done it anyway if she didn't like something he said.

Ella stepped back and rubbed at her sallow cheek. "That crass, grasping trollop disappeared when Desh came to the city."

That made sense. A wild spirit creature like Limnad couldn't bear places where men built in straight lines, stone on stone. She wouldn't have been able to stay with Desh, no matter how much she loved him.

A tall, honey-haired boy of thirteen poked his head out through the study doorway. "If you're going to fight, either kill each other in the courtyard, or entertain me with it in here."

I bowed. "Your Majesty, I have some horrible news. There's war between Eastgate and your kingdom. They're marching right now, or at least soon. I heard the order given."

Ella gasped.

The king sagged. "You're right, that's pretty bad." Then he glared at me. "So, why were you there listening to orders being given?"

I set my jaw and tried to look noble. "That old fart, King Ert, summoned me to perform some shady task for him. Of course, I turned him down and came straight here to warn you."

Pres narrowed his eyes and examined me. Every one of my friends had looked at me that way at some point, as if they knew I was lying. My wife had done it too, and both my little girls. I glanced over at Ella, and she was staring at me that same way.

I almost choked out the truth, but of course that would be crazy.

"It was awfully darn lucky you were there, I suppose," Pres said. He still didn't look as if he believed me. "Not that I hate seeing you, Bib, but you came at an awful time. Well, come on in and join us. Then I'll decide what to do about you and your overheard orders."

TWO

I possess an ocean of faults. I've been told that spending a few hours with me will reveal a good number of them. Sometimes a few minutes is long enough. I admit to a smidge of vanity, and nobody would say that killing people is a good quality. I wouldn't.

When I walked into the king's study in Castle Glass, disloyalty and gross treachery had been added to my faults just recently. I would have preferred not to betray my friend, King Prestwick, but Harik, God of Death, had laid that burden on me.

This was the way things worked with sorcerers and the whiny, small-minded gods. Sorcerers had to bargain with gods for the power to use magic. In exchange, the gods demanded that sorcerers do horrible things, or give up fine things, or lose people they love. And the gods made sure a sorcerer kept his bargain, or suffered in ways devised by a god who has had an eternity to think about suffering.

Sorcerers ride this beast of hellish bargains until the weight of promises destroys them, or until something else kills them first. When I walked into Pres's castle that day, I carried with me four debts to the gods. I planned to pay off each obligation, never replace it with another, and so find some peace by poking the gods in the eyes.

It wasn't impossible. I had never heard of another sorcerer doing it, but that didn't mean it was impossible. I intended to reduce my complications one at a time, and the dim, nasty, tongue-dragging, self-worshiping gods could kiss each other's asses for eternity.

I first met King Prestwick of Glass when he was eleven years old. Now he wasn't yet fourteen, but one didn't screw around with kings no matter their age or disposition. Hard, careful work would be needed to betray him.

Two weeks ago, when I entered the Kingdom of Eastgate, I had purchased fine clothes right after I stole the gold I needed to pay for them. I then demanded that King Ert receive me. Introducing myself as an emissary from the King of Glass, I laid out a declaration of war backed by ornate, official-looking documents on stolen vellum.

I figured there was an even chance Ert would believe me because he and Prestwick's father had made war on each other every three or four years for decades. A few piddly hills stood on the border between them. Those hills were full of silver, and both kings wanted them.

Glass happened to own those hills just then. I claimed that King Pres of Glass, through me, proposed to make war on Ert and settle ownership for all time by single combat between the kings' champions.

King Ert had a ferocious monster of a champion, and everybody knew it, so I hoped he would agree. Ert could take over the hills if he won. If he lost, he could pretend the whole affair never happened and invade again in a few years.

The king surprised me by hesitating. He finally agreed, though, when I insulted his ancestors and told him his children looked fat and stupid.

After that, Ert smiled when I stipulated that he bring his army along to mark the glory of the event. If anything bad happened, his army would be close by.

Pil had asked me beforehand why the hell King Pres would ever agree to my proposal. I counted on three things for that. First, victory would give him some relief from Eastgate's harassment, at least for a few years. Second, if he lost the hills, just like Ert, he could conveniently forget all about it and fight for the hills again later. And third, he wasn't going to lose because I'd be his champion.

I needed Pres to agree for my plan to work, and he would agree. He would because he trusted me and believed in me.

However, I wouldn't tell Pres I was skilled enough to take a wound, make it seem debilitating, and surrender before I could be killed. When I did that, Glass would lose the war. Not a person would have to die, and that would be fine with me. Sure, I preferred killing, but in this case, I wanted to aggravate the God of Death by making sure not a single person died. We'd see how Harik, that pouch full of vulture scat, liked being cheated of all those deaths.

I felt bad about betraying Pres into defeat, but it would be defeat with as little pain as possible.

King Ert would march toward Glass soon. Maybe he was already marching. King Prestwick didn't realize it, but the war had already started.

Pres brought us into his big study to join some people. I knew a few of them well, including Pres, Ella, and Pil. I had only met Pres's mother, Queen Dall, a dozen times or so. She was a small, pale, straight woman, like a displeased icicle. When she saw me, she gritted her teeth and looked away.

"Hello there, Queen Dall!" I called to the other side of the room as I poured myself a glass of wine from a side table. "You're looking well, Your Majesty. Good color in your cheeks, which is healthy for sure." I dipped my head in her direction and then drained the glass. Dall muttered something as I reached for the bottle again.

A slim, fair young man with black hair stood beside Dall. He watched the room with relaxed eyes, tapping his fingers on the bookcase next to him. He might have been a soldier, but if so, he had not just arrived from the field. His boots were polished bright, and his cobalt blue shirt looked crisp. His sword rode easy on his hip. People who didn't wear swords could hardly imagine how awkward they were to carry around. Getting comfortable with them required several weeks of knocking over vases, whacking ladies in unfortunate places, and tripping over the damn things.

Another stranger stood by the wall to the king's right. His wooly brown head only came up to my chin, but his girth made up for his lack of height. He was so fat he looked as round as a ball wearing a bright red robe. I found it hard to guess his age. He stood without shifting, scrutinizing each person in the room and pursing his lips over and over as if he might spit out a grape seed.

My abstinence from drink had ended weeks ago, across the sea, during a boring convalescence. Throughout the long ride south to the Kingdom of Glass, I had practiced drinking at every opportunity, and by now, I had regained most of my former prowess. I tossed down a second glass and then offered the third glass to Pil. She shook her head, so I poured that one into myself too.

"Let us begin," the queen announced.

Pres clenched his teeth and stared at his mother until she looked away. He sighed and shook his head. "Of course, Mother." Then he made introductions all around. The young man I didn't recognize was Captain Parth, one of his officers. The king didn't introduce the man in red, or even look at him.

The king leaned his butt against the edge of the desk, and I realized he'd grown a few inches since I last saw him. "There are several things I don't understand," Pres said, "and I hope we have the right minds in the room to educate me. First, who destroyed the villages of Stitch and Bother? The bandits in the west have been subdued." He nodded at Parth, who nodded back. "These little places didn't even have much that was valuable. More bandits? Rebels? And who kidnapped Desh, if he is kidnapped? How did they accomplish that? And are they crazy?"

I spoke up. "Your Majesty, I hate to disturb this conference, which I'm sure will turn into a regular holiday soon, but who is that?" I nodded toward the tubby man in red.

The king glanced over at the man and twitched as if he hadn't known the fellow was there. "This is Dimore, my advisor. And my sorcerer."

I smiled. "It's a damn fine thing to have one's own sorcerer. Pleased to know you, Dimore."

The sorcerer smiled at me. "Same."

That was a disturbing revelation. Pres might think he had found a sorcerer to order around, but more likely, Dimore had discovered a king to exploit. Worse than that, Dimore might interfere with my pernicious plan.

Ella pushed past me. "I do not know the names of the criminals who destroyed the villages, but I know their sign, Your Majesty." She reached into her shirt and withdrew a big scrap of torn linen. On it, a brown circle was set against a silver field. Blood spattered the symbol.

Pres reached for the cloth and examined it. "How do you come to have this?"

Ella cleared her throat. "A friend in your army passed it to me. To bring to you."

"I don't like your having friends in my army I don't know about!" Pres barked.

Ella looked him in the eye. "I am endeavoring—"

"Never mind!" Pres cut her off, waving one hand. "Does anyone recognize this?"

Everybody shook their heads or otherwise expressed ignorance.

The king sighed and tossed the scrap onto the desk behind him. Dimore leaned to glance at it as the king went on. "Well, let's look at this other damned thing. It's clear King Ert wants the Flathead Hills, but why is he declaring war on me now? Does he have some advantage he thinks we can't know about? Is it that champion of his?" Pres gazed at me.

I dipped my head in the tiniest bow possible. "Well, Your Majesty, may I ask an important question before I tell you what I've seen and surmised?"

Pres drummed his fingers on the desk. "Go ahead."

"Are we having a meeting, or are we planning something?"

Ella hissed and dropped her head.

The king almost smiled. "Which would you prefer, Bib?"

"If it's a meeting, then likely no two of us will leave this room with the same idea of what we learned." I pointed around at everybody. "We'll have to have another meeting or two just to figure out what really happened in this meeting. But if we're planning something, when we walk out of here, we'll have a plan, and we can start doing shit that's in that plan."

Pres ignored a whispered curse from his mother. "Assume that we're planning something. But I may change my mind."

"I understand. Now, we don't know as much as a pinch of spit about these brown-circle boys, except for one thing." I glanced at Ella and took a step away from her so she'd have to move if she decided to whack me. "They burned some villages and may—*may*—have taken Desh prisoner. If they did, he'll know all about them once he's escaped. He may kill a good parcel of them too."

"Why do you feel certain that Desh will escape?" Parth asked. "He may be a wizard, but he's little more than a boy."

I grinned at him. Desh was only a few years younger than Parth. "Because Desh is a cold, sneaky bastard. Also, it's mighty rare that regular people can hold a sorcerer captive for long, even if they catch one. They don't think the situation through. Say they get lucky and capture a sorcerer, what do they have then? A pissed-off sorcerer they don't know what to do with. Who'll be mighty aggravated when he escapes."

Parth glanced at Queen Dall, who gave him a tiny "I told you so" look.

I went on. "So, we might know more and plan better once Desh returns."

Ella slapped her thigh with one hand. "Desh is your friend and may be dying. Nothing could be more important than that to the Bib I knew."

I could have counted off a dozen things more important to me than saving Desh. As sorcerers, we could have only the most tenuous of friendships, anyway. I expected Pil to leave and go her own way at any time. However, Ella wouldn't care about our pretentious sorcerer bullshit. Telling her the truth would only keep the arguments and threats coming, so I searched for a believable lie.

Pres saved me when he said, "Let's lay that aside for now. Bib, tell me about King Ert. Why did he declare war now? Has he gone mad? I think madness runs in his family. Is that right, Mother?"

Dall nodded. "His grandfather ran away into the woods and froze to death. His uncle crafted a suit of armor from burlap and tortoise shells, and he went to battle in it. There are more examples."

Parth looked up. "Was his uncle victorious in that war?"

"Well, yes. But it must have been luck."

I jumped in. "Your Majesty, I stood not thirty feet from Ert when he declared war on Glass. Now that I think of it, he was ranting a bit when he did it. He didn't say why, but he gave the order right there for his champion to sharpen his swords and axes. Ert is sending his champion south as soon as may be, along with his army to make things more festive. Then it will be single combat to decide ownership of the hills for all time.

"Of course, I left straightaway and wore out two horses getting here to warn you. I volunteer to fight as your champion, Your Majesty, if you'll allow it."

Parth laughed silently, but the king relaxed.

I continued. "Your Majesty, you should muster your army and march north right away. If Ert brings his force on through, he may decide to come attack you here unprepared, while your soldiers are still planting the fields."

Parth turned to me. "What if King Ert ignores your slaughter of his champion, and attacks?"

"Then I will fight in the front line." I would have to, since that was one of the conditions of my bargain.

"Front line is my division." Parth grinned and rubbed his jaw. "You'll be under my command, Bib."

"Beautiful, can't wait." I threw him an enormous smile and considered ways I might murder him.

Pres looked past me and said, "Young woman . . . Pil . . . you came here with Bib. What can you tell me?"

Pil was nineteen, but when she smiled, she looked like a carefree girl of fifteen. Now she smiled at the king. "I was there with Bib when King Ert declared war—that's the clear and flashing truth, Your Majesty, and I know that Bib can be . . . oblique to the truth sometimes, but I am not. I do promise that King Ert gave the command right there to march south and make war on you."

Pres gazed at Pil for a couple of seconds. Then he glanced at me, looked back at Pil, flicked his gaze to the ceiling, sighed, and stared at Pil until he started turning red. He picked up the brown-circle insignia to examine it again. "Thank you, Pil. That helps."

Ella touched my shoulder, smiling at Pres. She had raised the boy while Dall had been scheming and planning feasts. I guess I was the only one Ella could share her fond wishes for Pres with since Dall was as sour as a persimmon.

The king tossed the insignia back onto his desk. "Here's the plan. Hope you like it, Bib. Parth, take fifty men and accompany Ella to find these village-burners and rescue Desh. Or, if he doesn't need rescuing, and he probably won't, assess the situation and return here to report. We can decide then whether to muster the army to put down rebels, or criminals, or renegade priests, or . . . whatever."

Ella strode over to stand beside Parth. "Thank you, Your Majesty!"

"Bib and Pil, I invite you to accompany me north to meet King Ert," Pres said.

"Excellent choice, Your Majesty. Full of kingly wisdom and guile," I said.

"Don't bounce like a puppy yet." Pres sniffed. "I'm not taking the army north, and you will not be attending as my champion. I'll go with two hundred men and parley with Ert. I'm tired of this damned blood spilling over those hills every few years. I think I can talk him out of war and make a permanent arrangement we can both live with."

"No!" Dall and I said at the same time. When I realized she was on my side, I felt an instant of doubt.

I raised my voice over Dall. "Pres, that's just a shitty . . . well, reckless plan. If that maggot pie Ert has lost his mind, he could cut off your head and skin you."

"You cannot go without the army!" Dall walked right up to Pres. "It's unfair to your people. And to me."

The boy king laughed in his mother's face. "I am not taking the army north. If I do, I may as well cut half my soldiers' throats now, and Ert half of his. For what? But if I go unprepared for war, that will show my good intentions. Besides, we may need the army here, depending on what Parth learns about these brown-circle dogs."

Pres pointed toward the door. "I will prepare the army, though. Send word around to the counties so they'll be ready to form up. But I *do not* want to take them away from spring planting. I won't invite a famine."

"Your Majesty!" I held up both hands and tried to think of some profound argument that would make Pres do the stupid thing I wanted him to do.

The king smiled at me. "Bib, this is the plan. Now, go do the shit in the plan. Oh, I've had rooms prepared for you and Pil. Two rooms . . . is that right?"

Pil nodded. "That's right."

Pres smiled for an instant, and I saw that a boy was still inside him someplace. "Two rooms and baths. Take advantage of the baths. Right away. That's a royal decree." He hesitated. "Two baths, right?"

THREE

maid led Pil and me to our rooms, showed us the baths, and then left.

"I wonder whether I can get my clothes washed?" Pil said. "I look as if horses have been trotting on me for a week."

I jerked as the nausea slammed me first. That was unusual. Normally, the sensation of being stretched and pulled up through the top of my head arrived before the desire to vomit. That desire never lasted long, though. It always disappeared when I reached the Gods' Realm, cut off clean like a heel of bread sliced away, leaving no sense of sight, smell, or touch. The only sounds were what the gods wanted to say to me and what I might say in return.

"Awful," came the deep, smooth, careful voice of Harik, God of Death. "Simply pitiful. Any chimpanzee could have been more subtle. Any jellyfish more forceful."

"The war isn't over, Mighty Harik! By the way, how many jellyfish have died since the beginning of time? I have a bet with the king."

I drew my sword. Its single power was to let me see as the gods see, and as I swept the blade across me, it left behind a pale, flat light. I stood on the dirty patch sorcerers were confined to when they visited the gods to bargain for power and give away things that made life good.

After a moment, I examined the sky and found no sun. The light seemed to be everywhere, filling the spaces like air and throwing no shadows at all. I shuddered before turning to the three-level marble gazebo that dominated me and my bit of soil.

Harik—tall, pale, and so classically beautiful it was unoriginal— sat on the lowest level. His robe, blacker even than his hair, revealed one sinewy arm and shoulder. His outstretched legs were crossed at the ankles, and he smirked at me as if I were stupider than a jelly- fish. He said, "Fatuous. You have made a horrific beginning, Murderer. I frankly cannot conceive of a stratagem that might save you." Harik leaned forward. "That dreary boy may not hate you, but he does not trust you. A wise king."

"Mighty Harik, I can think of five different ways to pay my debt. But you've been so mean to me, I refuse to share them."

"We lack your confidence. Both of us, in fact." Harik leaned back again.

I knew he was talking about himself and Lutigan, God of War. They both owned pieces of my various debts. Sakaj, Goddess of the Unknowable, might own a bit too. That had been kept vague. "Mighty Harik, you ass-rubbing rodent of shame, no time limit was laid on me. And so that they don't get jealous, you can tell Lutigan he's a ripe pig's bladder that walks like a man, and Sakaj is a snot-streaming, over- priced harlot who is unskilled to the point of embarrassment."

When a sorcerer deals with beings of boundless power, it is crit- ical to show he doesn't give a shit about them. They don't believe it, of course, but without it, they never take the sorcerer seriously.

Harik looked away. I wondered whether he was grinning or maybe rolling his eyes. Then he said, "We have placed a time limit upon you now. And don't dare whimper about fairness. We are gods and care nothing for such human ideas. Be done with this war busi- ness within twenty-one days. By the twenty-first sunset from now."

"Don't you mean sunrise? That's what you usually say."

"It is not. You're just trying to gain half a day."

"All right," I said. "How about forty sunrises?"

Harik stood and boomed, "Do you think you can haggle with me?"

"It is the trading place."

"Ah. I suppose it is." He sat. "But no, it shall be twenty-one sunsets."

"Sunrises."

"Fine! Sunrises! See if that helps you." Harik smiled. I hated it when he smiled. "If you fail, I will increase the number of lives you owe me."

"Now wait—"

"Wait for what? For someone to make it fair? Just? That penalty will be on my behalf. For Lutigan, if you fail, you will betray the Knife at a time of Lutigan's choosing."

I felt disgusted. The Knife was the Gods' name for Pil. But disgust wouldn't help me trade, so I made my expression confident and saucy.

Harik went on. "And as punishment for your foul words to me, should you fail, the blonde woman will henceforth hate you."

I felt my eyes become less saucy. "Ella?"

"I suppose, yes. Who cares about her name?"

"She already hates me," I said.

"She will hate you more. She will revile you. She might try to murder you if you do not kill her first."

"You'll just wave your hand and make her hate me?"

"Of course not. Sakaj will do it."

"I'm not sure I believe you," I said slowly.

Harik launched me back into the world of man. I slammed into my body and staggered.

Pil steadied me with one hand. "Harik?"

"The ocean of ripe pus himself," I said.

She nodded, and I could see she wanted to ask about it. However, no sorcerer cares to share details of his deals with the gods, and it was ill-mannered for one sorcerer to push another about it. She turned toward one of the baths.

Instead of doing the same, I grasped Pil's hand and stepped into her room so we could talk.

Pil shook her head. "I think a blind opossum could have handled that better than us. The king is doing the right thing, based on everything he knows, but it's not the thing we want him to do."

I scratched my beard. Now that a bath was close, every itch hit me like a rock. "So, we need to change everything he knows. Would you like to guess how?"

"Um . . . bribe somebody to tell lies for us? Of course, we don't have a bit of gold, or anything else valuable, but we could walk back down to that brothel and see how much we can earn before sunrise." She raised her eyebrows.

"Let's make that our fallback plan. No, we're going to kidnap Queen Dall."

Pil's mouth fell open. Three seconds later, she started grinning. "And blame it on King Ert."

I created a kidnapping plan that nobody would call simple. I hated that, but we were short of time and resources. If my planning proved weak, audacity would have to fill the gaps.

Deep in the night, after my bath and a polite visit from Pres, Pil and I crept toward Dall's Tower. It wasn't as fancy as that name made it sound—only forty feet tall and thirty feet square. But Dall's husband had detailed his carpenters to build her a comfortable apartment on top. Maybe he did it out of love, or maybe he did it to get her the hell away from him, I don't know.

In the hours past midnight, only one guard attended the tower, walking up and down the stairs. Nobody was allowed to use the tower except Dall, so we had no concern for idle witnesses.

When the guard reached the bottom step, I pulled a tiny bit of my magical power out of the air. From the dimness across the hallway, I twirled the power toward a wall sconce on the first landing. The wooden torch rotted in the middle, snapped, and fell to the stone landing with a clatter and a puff of sparks.

Like any reasonable person, the guard turned, stared for a moment, and climbed back up the stairs. I rushed up and whacked him on the back of the head. He didn't collapse right off, so I hit him again and then dragged him thumping up the next set of steps while Pil fished in a bag for rope, a gag, and a blindfold.

We stowed the unconscious guard in a side room and crept to the top landing. I locked eyes with Pil, hoping she would review the plan in her mind just as I was doing.

We intended to rush in and surprise Dall as she slept, then disable and bind her. Pil had fashioned some nice masks so the queen wouldn't know us. It was a rush job, but I had never seen neater stitches.

Once Dall was helpless, I would drop a ransom note I had prepared on behalf of King Ert. Pil would tie off a rope long enough to reach the ground and toss it through a window. Then we'd ignore the damn thing.

I had earlier exercised some magic to convince two of the castle's horses to jump the fence and stand beside the tower until I needed them. While Pil hustled Dall down the stairs, I would convince those horses to neigh, scream, and bolt for the courtyard gate like Lutigan was chasing them with a barbed whip. They weren't to stop until they reached the river five miles away.

Earlier, when making our plans, Pil had asked, "What will we do with Dall then? I mean, we're not going to kill her, are we?" Her face showed lines of doubt, and she clenched one fist, which she held in a good position to punch me.

"No, we're not, although I'm sure that Dall, spiny lizard of a woman that she is, would kill me if she could. Once everybody charges out into the night to investigate the calamity, we'll drag Dall a hundred feet up the corridor into a side passage and stash her in one of the abandoned northern storerooms. All gagged and tied up, nobody will hear her or look for her there. They'll believe she's halfway to Eastgate."

Pil had squinted at me and shaken her head.

"It will work!" I said. "Pres will march his army north so I can do battle for him and his ma. You'll circle back and loosen Dall's bonds so she can work herself free in a few hours. But don't get caught. You'll break young Prestwick's heart. He's already in love with you."

Pil had wrinkled her nose and sighed. "I know how to deal with some boy who has a longing in his trousers, but not if he's a king."

"Like you would with any other lad, but don't kick him."

We had then parted to bathe and prepare.

As with most complicated plans, mine did not end up unfolding quite as intended.

On the highest landing of Queen Dall's Tower, I touched her door and nodded at Pil. She nodded back, holding up a gag, a sack, and bindings for the queen's hands and feet.

I pushed into the first room, quick but careful. It was devoid of queens. I moved on to the next room, expecting to find Dall asleep in bed. Instead, she sat scribbling at a desk with her back to a tall window. Fresh, chilly air blew in, and I saw the gibbous moon through it.

Dall craned her neck to see around the lantern on the desk between us. Before I reached her, she stood and flipped the desk over toward me.

The little desk was no obstacle, but the lantern broke at my feet. Flames jumped up toward my knees. That stopped me damn quick.

Most of the light died with the lantern. I skipped aside and slapped at my left trousers leg, which was smoldering. I could see the queen and Pil outlined in the moonlight. Dall rushed away from me, yelling, "Stop!" and almost ran into Pil.

I heard Dall draw a mighty breath to scream. Pil stepped in and punched the woman below the breastbone. By the sound, it knocked the wind out of Dall, and Pil whipped the sack over the queen's head. I glanced back at the door, suddenly sure that somebody must have heard us.

Dall tried to push Pil away, but it was like a feather pushing a chicken. The queen stumbled back, banging her calves against the windowsill.

I jumped toward the queen, but I was several steps away. Pil reached for Dall with both hands, but the older woman flailed, smacking against Pil's arms before teetering. Pil strained to grab her, but Dall tumbled backward out the window.

Hoping there was a ledge outside for Dall to land on, I poked my head and arms out. There was no ledge. I could just make out Dall's body on the ground forty feet below me. She never had screamed.

I grabbed Pil's arm and turned her toward me. Her eyes were glassy in the moonlight and her mouth was open, as if she had been punched in the stomach instead of Dall. I dropped the fake ransom note on the floor before twirling a yellow band of magic out to the horses, convincing them to raise hell and run. Then I pulled Pil back out into the hallway.

Halfway down the tower stairs, Pil said something, so I glanced back. She didn't speak again but instead made a soft keening like she was hurt. No tears or sign of pain were on her face, though. She met my eyes, went silent, and took a breath, as steady as the stone wall beside us.

I hurried on downstairs with Pil just behind me.

FOUR

The gods didn't love Pil and me, that's for certain. But they didn't take the opportunity to tangle our feet and toss guards in our way as we fled from Queen Dall's rooms. The gods were probably engaged in more interesting activities, such as attending some play they had written about themselves to celebrate their own divinity. It would include oratory, dancing, and sword fights that slaughtered different sorts of inferior beings in each performance. That's what I imagined, anyway.

I cursed myself for not leaving our masks behind on Dall's bedroom floor, or at least throwing them out the window after her. I stowed them in Pil's bag as we rushed along, but if a guard searched it, we'd face some sharp questions. Most everybody seemed to have run out toward the screaming horses, though, and the three people we passed in the halls hardly glanced at us.

When we reached our rooms, I guided Pil toward her chamber. She knocked my hands away, though, and marched into my room, flinging open the door. I followed her in and shut it behind me.

Pil stared at me, her face calm, and said, "Is this sorcery? Killing? Arrogance? Murdering innocent old women?"

I opened my mouth, but she cut me off.

"Or is it only your version of sorcery? Dixon was a scoundrel and a swindler, but he wasn't an outright killer like you. But then I only knew him for six months, and he might have ended up like you."

Dixon had been Pil's teacher when I met her, but he died soon after. About ten minutes after. And no, I didn't kill him. "Pil, Dixon was worse than you believe. You didn't know him years ago."

Pil stepped close and looked up at my face. "Hah! How many people do you think Dixon killed in all the months I knew him? Guess."

I didn't want to guess. I wanted to calm Pil down, but she wasn't stepping back. "If I'm required to guess, I will say he didn't kill anybody."

"That's right!" Pil snapped. "How many people have you killed in the months since we met? Do you even know?"

I felt a little nauseated, and my hands shook a bit. "Twenty-nine. I know how many."

Pil backed away. "Bib, do I have to become like you?" Her face looked like she might cry, but she snarled it away.

I shook my head. "Pil, you don't have to be like me, even a little bit. You make your own decisions. But I can tell you this. Whatever you want to be, that's not what you'll end up being. The gods will make sure of that."

Pil sat down on the edge of the bed and looked away. "It would be nicer if somebody asked us whether we wanted to be sorcerers, you know, instead of dumping it on us with no choice."

"You're right, that would be mighty nice."

She cleared her throat. "Aren't you going to say something cynical and sarcastic and heartbreaking and pretend you're just making a joke?"

"Nope. I'm going to ask whether you're staying." I stepped in front of the door, caught myself, and stepped away.

Pil stood, faced me square, gritted her teeth, and said, "Yes."

"I'm happy, but Fingit's belly button, why?"

"I don't know." She glared. "Half the time, I don't even like you."

I grinned. "That's normal. Most of the folks I've known felt like that."

Pil walked past me into the hallway. I closed the door behind her.

I sat on the bed and cut our masks into strips, which I wove into a rough necklace. I slipped the necklace over my head and hid it down my shirt before pulling off my boots and mussing my hair. Then I stepped into the hallway to shout random questions about the goddamn furor that was keeping me awake.

During the next half hour, I overheard different people proclaim that the queen had been murdered, that she had taken her own life, and that she'd gotten drunk and fallen out of her window.

When things had died down to a few maids running around and guards shouting ignorant questions, I pulled on my boots and knocked on Pil's door. She didn't answer. Well, she was a sorcerer and didn't need me to handle her affairs. I evaluated the situation and trotted to the king's chambers. By then, the current story was that an assassin had tried to push Dall out her window, but a maid had been wearing her nightgown, so Dall was still alive but in hiding for reasons that were vague.

A guard pointed me to the audience chamber, a bare room that Pres disliked. I realized that not kicking Pil's door until she answered had been a mistake. She was distressed about her part in the queen's death, and she might not put it in perspective the way a more experienced sorcerer would. I imagined her grabbing a guard and confessing to murder, and cold sweat popped up on my neck and back.

As I stood in the hallway along with three guards, Ella rushed around the corner toward me. Her eyes were puffy and her voice tight. "Someone has killed the queen."

"I've heard it from a dozen people. I expect it's true."

"They killed the queen," Ella said as if I hadn't spoken. "Here within the keep itself. I can't believe it."

I didn't reach out to pat her shoulder, but I wanted to. "It was an unlikely occurrence, sure."

"They must have used magic!" Ella glared at me. "They

employed magic, didn't they? The murderers used a magical disguise, such as the ones Desh once made for us. That must have been how they reached her. Do you agree?"

I nodded in a way I hoped looked wise but noncommittal. "It's possible. But this may have been done with skill, and no magic at all."

Ella turned away and pounded the wall with the heel of her fist. She must have liked Dall a lot better than I thought. Ella hadn't been this upset months ago when she thought I was dying. Of course, that was after she fell out of love with me.

The audience chamber door opened, and guards shooed us inside. At the other end of the big room, Pres sat above us on the throne, looking years older. He wore a dressing gown and held a sword across his knees. That disturbed me a little. When the king held his sword, he was ready to judge people and decide what would be done with them. Parth stood to Pres's left. The old general of the army, Pobla, stood on the other side of the king, and Dimore waited in a corner, solid and still. A dozen guards lined the walls, and six more stood between Pres and us. Two blocked the door, including Stan, whose eyes were as wide as pot lids.

Before Ella and I reached the middle of the room, two guards shoved Pil inside after us. They had evidently hauled her out of bed. She was barefoot, and I saw her chemise poking out from the neck of a brown threadbare robe somebody had given her.

A few seconds later, a guard escorted Sir Linkan into the room. He was a trim, older man with a highly civilized mustache, and he commanded the castle, its guards, and its servants. He glanced around and blinked a lot but otherwise seemed steady.

The guards lined up Ella, Linkan, Pil, and me in the center of the room.

"My mother has been murdered, as you must know." Pres stared at the floor as he said it, and his voice was an octave lower than it had been that morning.

Ella said, "Pres, I'm sorry—"

He raised a hand to cut her off. "It's not the time. Killers were in my home." Pres pointed at Linkan. "The home you are charged with protecting."

Linkan swallowed but didn't answer.

The king turned his glower toward me. "You. You are not the most dangerous man in the world. That's bullshit that scratches your ego."

"Well, I never called myself that." I met his eyes. "I am tolerably dangerous, though. I stand ready to do your enemies dirt and kick them in the nuts. And then slit the bastards' throats."

"Huh." Pres nodded toward Pil. "If I tell you to kill her, will you? Would you kill Ella for me?"

"What?" Ella squeaked.

Pres tightened his grip on the sword. "Bib, I cannot count you as loyal to me. You taught me that all existence turns, rises, and falls according to numbers. You arrived this morning, and Mother was thrown to her death this night. I don't believe in coincidences. They are improbable, statistically so."

The king turned to Ella. "I love you like a mother, and I always will. But a year ago, you left us to go away with Bib. You chose him over us. I can never trust you when it comes to him."

Beside me, Ella shook her head but didn't say anything.

I shrugged. "Hell, that's all done, Your Majesty. Ella thinks I'm worse than a damn snake now. You can trust her."

"Parth, if Bib speaks again, have the guards put him in irons and gag him." Pres didn't look away from Ella as he said it. Parth gave a smooth nod. General Pobla scowled at the captain before looking away.

I decided not to push the young king. Besides, Ella and Pil had both started spouting contradictory words at the boy. He was infuriated and grieving, but I figured he'd listen to Ella, who was like his mother, and to Pil, the girl who had made his brain flap like a rooster. I, the foul-mouthed, degenerate uncle, kept quiet.

Pres leaned back and waited until Pil and Ella stopped talking. "Don't do that again, ladies. Bib, did you kill my mother?"

"I did not, Your Majesty."

"Did you draw that circle on the wall beside the window?"

I tried not to look surprised. There sure as hell had been no circle on the wall when I left. "Not that, either, Your Majesty."

The king gritted like he was chewing brass. "Did Pil do those things for you?"

"No, I didn't!" Pil pulled her robe tighter.

I added, "That's right, I wouldn't ask her to do something like that."

Parth grinned and pointed at me. "Guards, bind him."

The king flapped a hand at Parth. "Forget that binding shit for now. I want answers." He glared at me. "True answers, not lies." He opened his mouth but then turned to Ella. "Did you . . . oh, Krak damn it, damn them, damn you, and damn me! You could all be lying! Or none of you!"

"I am not lying," Ella said. "And I don't believe that Bib and this woman are, either. We can aid you. Let us."

The king stared at the floor and sighed. "Guards, take Linkan. Put him in a cell. I'll think about what to do with him later."

A guard whispered something to Linkan, and the older man nodded. He walked out of the room, escorted by two guards at a respectful distance.

Pres met our eyes, each in turn. "I am gathering the army. When half has arrived here, it will march east in pursuit of those brown-circle villains and destroy them to the very last man."

I asked, "Did the murderer leave behind anything more articulate than the letter 'O' rubbed on the wall? Or scratched on or painted?"

"Drawn in blood," Pres said, his brow low.

"Well, of course." I nodded. "Why not be as ghoulish and theatrical as possible? Was there a note of any kind?"

Parth cocked his head. "There was no note. Why would you think there's a note?"

"It's another opportunity to write craziness in blood," I said.

Pres pounded his throne's arm with his fist. "There was no note!"

Whoever had drawn on the wall had also made away with my note. "Shit!" I whispered.

Pres nodded at me. "Yes, shit. Here is what we will do. General Pobla, you will muster the army right away. When half the levies have arrived, form them up and march east."

Pobla bowed, but I saw a flush of confusion on his face.

The king grimaced at Parth. "Captain, you take Ella and fifty men. Ride east to scout for the army. Search for Desh too. I'll travel north as planned to treat with King Ert. When I've dealt with Ert, I'll return here and take the rest of the army east to unite the two parts. When I find those who wear that symbol, I won't just defeat them. I will crush them so that no one ever remembers them."

Nobody said anything for a few seconds. Then Pobla cleared his throat. "About splitting your forces, Your Majesty—"

Pres cut him off with a chop of his hand. "I know what you're going to say, and I've already thought about it." He stared at me. "This is the plan."

I spoke up. "It's a hell of a plan. Nobody would ever predict it. There are risks, sure . . ." I wanted to tell Pres not to split his army, that it was a stupid goddamn thing to do. It would be the same as telling every groaning halfwit warlord in the east to come overwhelm him and kill everybody in sight.

However, the gods required that I betray Pres into defeat. Giving the boy helpful tactical advice wouldn't serve my ends.

The king stared at me. "Bib, you will scout for Captain Parth. You're a sorcerer, a cruel killer, and as you said, tolerably dangerous. Accompany Parth's force and be their eyes. Find the murderer and bring the army to him. Or fetch the murderer to me."

I opened my mouth to argue, but the king raised his voice. "Bib, if I find that you've lied, that you killed her, no sword or spell will protect you. I will spend the lives of every man and boy in this land to kill you if I must."

That was awkward as hell. I wanted to start a war, or at least a good fight. But Pres wanted to end the war with Ert before it was well started. That wouldn't help me, and I couldn't fix it by farting around with Parth in the east. I needed to ride north with Pres to poison his peace talks.

But if I defied the king, that would piss him off, and he was already angrier than I'd ever seen him. I had heard that his father had been a raging son of a bitch, and Pres might end up one as well. Maybe I could convince him that he needed my protection. I could say that he wouldn't be safe guarded by just two hundred horsemen—all of them heavy drinkers, and a fair number afflicted with diseases of the groin that might drive a man insane.

I dipped my head to the king. "Your Majesty, I was the first one who bowed to you as king, and I said I hoped you'd remember that when it came time to start throwing people in the dungeon. I regret that I have already made a commitment that takes me north. I'm bound to it, so I am sorry, but I can't scout for your grisly captain here."

Parth smiled and winked at me, which made me falter for a moment before going on. "Since I'm riding north, I suggest I accompany you. Which is what you laid out in yesterday's plan, so in a way, it's Your Majesty's idea."

Ella leaned in and whispered to me, "Bib, come east with us. Pres is clever and can make peace with King Ert. Whatever is in the east is the real peril. I can feel it."

I had often found Ella's hunches to be reliable. But sometimes they were based on her fiery need for the world to be the way she desired rather than the way it was. I couldn't risk pissing off Harik based on her speculations, so I shook my head without looking at her.

Pres stared at the sword on his lap, and he rolled the hilt in his palm. When he looked up, his face had gone bright red. He glowered at me and said in a tight voice, "I understand. You're a wizard and have far greater obligations than a friend and his family in some backwater kingdom. You're dismissed. Leave me. Be out of the city by sunset."

"Wait!" Parth shouted.

The king and Pobla gaped at the man as if he were running around the room waving his privates.

"Look at his leg." Parth pointed at me.

I managed not to look, but I realized what he had seen. My left trousers leg was scorched.

Parth said, "Someone set a fire in the queen's room when she was murdered. Her desk was singed." Everybody was staring at me, so none of them saw Parth smile one of the most purely joyful smiles I had ever seen. "He is the murderer."

I searched for any argument or lie that would prove the man wrong. It didn't matter that he really was wrong, at least technically. I was still thinking when the king said, "Take him."

I drew my sword as I spun toward the door. My only chance was to cut a path to the hallway and run. Then I'd find a horse and stay ahead of the pursuit until I could string them out and kill them a couple at a time.

Stan and another guard stood between me and the door. I darted in and stabbed the other guard in the belly just as Ella shouted, "Bib! Run!"

A swift guard from the side wall reached me. I ducked his cut and sliced open his thigh. Then I turned back to Stan, hoping I wouldn't have to kill him.

Stan wasn't attacking me, though. He had dropped his sword and was standing against the door with one hand clamped onto the latch and the other hand over his eyes.

I should have cut off his hand, snatched open the door, and sprinted away. Or I could have just killed him outright. I might have punched him silly and thrown him away from the door. To be frank, he had shocked me, and while I was trying to decide, another guard charged in and whacked me with the flat of his sword.

Pres shouted, "Don't kill Bib!"

I thought that was awfully nice of the king, considering everything. Meanwhile, four or maybe five more guards charged over and began smacking me with the flats of their blades. I dodged the first couple, but one connected with the back of my head and I fell to my hands and knees.

They must have hit me enough times to knock me out, because I woke up in a different place. I smelled fire, charcoal, and dirt. Men were holding me facedown with my arms pinned over my head. I looked up to see that I was in a smithy. My hands had been stretched out across a wooden board, and Pres stood over me with a big ax.

I spun one finger, pulled a blue band of power out of the air, and rotted the ax handle near the blade. The ax head fell and plopped onto the ground. Pres stared at the stump of the ax handle.

"Damn it!" Pres shouted. He walked away, calling over his shoulder, "Kick him, and keep kicking him!"

Somebody kicked me in the ribs. I pulled another blue band to rot part of the roof and drop it on the king's head, but when the next kick landed, I jerked and bobbled the power away. Pres came back with a thick iron bar as long as my forearm. That was unfortunate, since I had no power over things that had never been alive, except for natural effects like weather.

Kneeling, Pres smashed my right hand with the iron bar, and I howled as pain shot all the way up my arm. He hauled back and kept hitting that hand until he had crushed it all to hell with a total of eight blows. Pres had been a good student. Eight was an ill-omened number—two cubed.

During the beating, I kept pulling power, but I couldn't hold it while people kicked me and Pres smashed my hand over and over.

The king went ahead and mangled my left hand with eight more blows. That was to be expected. Then he leaned down close to my head and growled, "I know you can do magic with your feet." He pointed at somebody behind me. "Remove his boots!"

I had thought the destruction of my hands had hurt, but Pres's work on my feet redefined the king's skill as a torturer. I passed out before he finished with the second foot.

FIVE

When I opened my eyes, I seemed to be bouncing down a slope on my back. Then pain bit my hands and feet before chewing its way in toward my stomach. I endured that for a couple of breaths before realizing I wasn't on a slope. Some people were carrying me by my arms and legs along a corridor. I strained to break loose. That wasn't a good escape plan, unless flopping on the ground like a guppy counts as escape, so it was better that I failed.

"Stop wiggling," somebody said.

I raised my head and focused on the people carrying my legs.

Some guard had my left leg. Parth had my right and was smiling back at me. "I congratulate your optimism, although I will regret leaving you behind when we ride east. All your courage and verve will rot like a turd in the sun." He shrugged, stumbled, and ran my foot into the wall.

I screamed but didn't black out.

"That was rude of me," Parth said, now watching where he was going. "Sorry."

I gasped, "Go swallow glass and shit a wine bottle."

The man nodded but didn't look at me.

Parth and the guards carried me into a bare stone room and laid me on the floor. The guards trooped out. The king had followed us and now leaned over me. Parth stood behind the king's right shoulder.

Pres said, "Bib, I'll deal with you when I've handled things with King Ert. Who knows, maybe you stirred up the whole thing. I'll have to question Pil about that."

"Is she all right?" I asked.

Pres frowned.

"You let her escape! That was a mistake." I squeezed my eyes shut against the pain. "By the way, I didn't kill Dall."

"Bib, I don't think I've known you to go a day without lying to somebody. Very well, you were in her room when she died, that's clear. Who killed her if not you?"

I didn't intend to say that Pil did it, and I doubted Pres would accept that his mother threw herself out the window rather than look at me. I ached to accuse Parth of the murder, but the story wouldn't hold up. If he had killed her right in front of me, why didn't I report it? Or kill him myself? Or just stop him from doing it? Hell, Parth and the king might have been playing checkers when Dall died—the perfect alibi. So, I stayed quiet.

Pres nodded. "No fancy lies? Maybe it was Pil. Even if that's true, you're an accomplice and just as guilty." He looked away before regarding me again. "I didn't like doing that to your feet and hands."

"That's too bad, you have a knack for it." I kept my face blank, hoping to unnerve him.

"Maybe I do have a knack," he murmured. "But I can't hold you here if you're capable of magic, and if you're not here, I can't punish you."

"You mean chop off my head."

"Maybe not." Pres gave a tiny grin. "I may have you hanged." Then he swallowed and stared at his hands. "Maybe not even that. But you could have done this," he whispered. "I know you, Bib. And I know that you may escape no matter what I do. I should stab you in the heart right now, but . . . Krak, you could have killed her, but maybe you didn't. So, I won't rush into executing you."

I lifted my right hand, and the pain took away my breath. "That's . . . mighty goddamn merciful of Your Majesty, you pig's asshole with a crown."

Parth looked down, but Pres acted as if he hadn't heard me. "As I said, I didn't like crippling you, but I couldn't order somebody else to do it. If you live to take vengeance, you don't need to kill anybody but me."

I sneered. "Your mercy bewitches me. My nipples are as hard as diamonds."

The king stood while calling over his shoulder, "Replace this wooden door with an iron one. Take his clothes. Have a man bring food and water but in metal bowls. And the man must be naked too. No object enters this room unless it's made of metal or stone."

The king strode away without looking at me, and Parth followed. I heard Pres say from outside, "Call my physician to care for his hands and feet." The door slammed, and a bar dropped on the other side.

I lay on the cold stone, breathed through the pain, and tried to figure out whether I could have screwed all this up any worse. I was still figuring, without success, when the door opened for a skinny naked man with a heavy brown beard. I could see his ribs even through the weave of hair that covered most of his torso. He carried two copper bowls.

I shifted and struggled to sit up.

Walking toward me, the naked man said, "Oops," pretended to trip, and splashed water from one of the bowls all over me. "Sorry there. At least you got a bath." He dropped the water bowl, and it bounced across the floor, ringing. "You got some yummy bread and broth here, though. It's full of good stuff." He winked as he knelt in front of me.

The smug bastard plucked a soggy bite of dark bread out of the bowl. "Arvin was my chum, and you don't get to poke holes in my chums for free. Open." He pushed the bread against my lips. "I fixed this up just right for you."

I took the bread into my mouth, and when he pulled his hand away, I spit it into his face, where it bounced off with a soggy plop.

"Goddamn dog-knocker!" he bellowed as he stood, wiping his face with his sleeve. "I'll tear—"

I didn't learn what he intended to tear. He had stepped between my legs. I slammed them together, high and low, bellowing as my feet throbbed, and knocked him onto his back. He shook his head slowly as I rolled toward him like a wine barrel, my hands and feet screaming all the way.

The man's nose broke with a cheery crunch, like biting an apple, when I slammed my elbow into it. I aimed for his throat next, but he writhed and I hit his jaw instead. I felt tempted to go for a few teeth since my elbow was right there by his mouth, but I angled for his throat again. My next strike made him gag, but it didn't kill him. I paused to aim so I could slay the dripping asshole properly, but somebody kicked me in the back first and dragged me away.

A square-shaped, uniformed guard with calm eyes bent and punched me on the cheek, careful to stay away from my legs. "Settle down, son." He was at least ten years younger than me. He punched me on the side of the jaw. "Shh."

I nodded hard.

"Won't be no more food for you, I guess." He picked up both bowls and gestured toward the skinny man with one of them. "Get up! You ain't gonna die!"

The skinny fellow stumbled to his feet, a trail of blood dripping from his nose, and both men walked out of the room. The door slammed, and I heard the bar drop.

I scooched to the wall using my elbows until I could sit up against it. I spit a little blood and wondered whether it would have been better to be meek and make big eyes while I ate whatever horrible crap the bastard tried to feed me. Well, to hell with that. That skinny turd wouldn't be bold enough to idly poke at me again. Although, if I acted like I was whipped now, they might get saucy enough for me to murder one of them.

My hands and feet had begun to swell, so I set about trying to wiggle my fingers and toes one at a time. On my third busted-up finger, something inside me tried to lift itself up through the top of my head. It stretched me before my entire spirit was yanked out of my body, and that jolt of nausea came along to remind me I once had a physical stomach.

Some god was yanking me like a bug on a string, and whatever I wanted could go eat beans. The nausea soon dissolved when all physical sensations disappeared. I drifted in a void, with nothing to see or touch. All the pain had been left behind with my body.

During training, young sorcerers go with their teachers to trade with the gods. When students experience that lack of sensation, they always try to fart at some point, just to see whether it can be heard in the Void. I had never met a sorcerer who hadn't tried to do that.

But the gods don't live in the Void, not in the real Void I mean, which is a crazy stretch of emptiness between the world of man and the Gods' Realm. The gods have just created a trading place that seems like nothingness. There they can mock sorcerers, tell jokes, pick their teeth, and cheat like drug pushers in a rat-filled alley without sorcerers knowing.

I usually knew, but only because my sword allowed me to see through the nothingness and appreciate the gods in all their smug arrogance. But Pres, that son-of-a-she-goat-in-heat, had taken my sword when he captured me. Now I would be dealing with the gods blind.

I could say one thing for certain: Farts cannot be heard in the presence of the gods. Not by the one farting. But the gods can hear them just fine. There might have been a metaphor in there someplace, but I despised the gods too much to go looking for it.

"You continue to fail, Murderer. This has been a repellent beginning," the God of Death said from the nothingness. "I expected incompetence, but this reeks of a willful repudiation of our bargain."

"It shocks the hell out of me to hear you say that, Mighty Harik," I said. To my shame, I had to agree with him, but I couldn't admit it. "Don't tell me that I fooled you just like I fooled this boy king."

"You cannot deceive me any more than I could be deceived by a loaf of dough, which you now resemble, by the way." Harik sounded like he might be smiling. He probably thought he could trap me into some horrible deal. "Unless you exhibit some cleverness, you shall suffer all the penalties. Perhaps more."

"So I guess you know what I plan to do next, you smirking brother to Lutigan's nasty crotch."

Harik's voice dropped to a growl. "Murderer, are you ready for oblivion? You are idiotic to insult me in your situation."

I reconsidered my next insult, which involved doing something naughty with a whale. I have been accused of speaking out a bit too much sometimes. "Well, this has been edifying and just enjoyable as hell, Your Magnificence, but I need to get on with betraying the king." I pulled myself toward the world of man.

Harik yanked me back. "Cease posturing! I might, just perhaps, be willing to lift you out of your current helplessness in some minor way if you offer me a fair bargain."

"You mean if I give you my left testicle and polish your boots for eternity?" I sneered.

"At least I shall not require your first-born child," Harik snipped.

I couldn't clench my fists or bite my lip. As it was, nothing held me back from shouting, "Damn you, you rangy, void-sucking son of a bitch!" After a moment, I added, "Your Magnificence." For years, I had believed that Harik killed my first child. That hadn't turned out to be quite true, but the spot was still tender and Harik didn't hesitate to poke it.

"That insult sadly lacked imagination," Harik said. "I must have aggravated you a little. Come, this is where I ask what you want and then you, like a mewling infant, beg me to make the first offer. So . . . beg."

"Goodbye, Harik." I drew myself back toward the world of man.

Maybe I could find my own escape without the gods' help. Maybe I couldn't. But I'd be damned if I threw another debt onto the pile I already owed them. I had grown wary of complexity and how it stretched a man thin, and I intended to have no more of it.

"Wait!" Harik barked. He dragged me back toward him again,

and silence extended for several seconds. That meant another god was present and plotting with Harik in voices I couldn't hear.

I called out, "Mighty Lutigan, no matter what Harik is offering you, count your fingers afterward! And your toes. And check your drawers to make sure all the important things are still there."

I was guessing that the God of War was present, since he and Harik held my two most immediate debts. Lutigan expected me to fight in the front line in the coming war. Well, what he really expected me to do was get killed, since of all the gods, he hated me most.

After another long pause, Lutigan's harsh, rumbling voice said, "Murderer, just go start a war, stand up front, and die. How hard is that? Krak's blood and bile, you're taking for goddamn ever. Accept Harik's deal and get on with it, you floppy little feather!"

"No deal," I said.

"Then . . . how about something subtler?" Harik asked. "You have destroyed the Knife."

"Pil? What do you mean?"

"It's too soon," Lutigan said. "You pushed her into the uncaring murder of innocents too soon. She's not a natural at it like you."

"I am not a natural!"

Silence drew out for a full five seconds. That had popped out, a peculiar thing for me to say considering all my killings. At last, I said, "Go shit sand! Pil's all right, just a little shaken. She'll be fine."

"That's a roaring lie. She'll be dead within a month," Lutigan said. "She won't make it happen. But when it does, she'll think she deserves it."

"Bull!" I said, without much conviction.

"And it'll be your damn fault!" Lutigan roared. Even without a body, I wanted to flinch.

"Fortunately, I offer an elegant solution," Harik said. "Remove her memory of killing that stick of a woman. To be thorough, remove the Knife's memory of the whole night."

"That will protect her," Lutigan grated. "And it will protect you —she won't be able to confess or point a finger at you."

"So . . ." I heard Harik's smile again. "What do you offer in exchange for the Knife's existence?"

"Nothing." I didn't even pause to think about it. Whatever Harik demanded of me would be complicated and probably treacherous. Removing somebody's memories without their knowledge was always a perilous endeavor. "Goodbye, Your Magnificences. Although I doubt that immortal beings get tapeworms, I hope you get a couple strong enough to tow a boat."

I pulled myself toward my body, and this time, neither god hauled me back. I flopped into a world of dank air, cold stone, and throbbing pain.

SIX

Most people don't think about sorcerers much. In all their life, they never come close to seeing one.

Many of the people who do think about sorcerers believe that the gods watch over and protect us, ready to provide magical power and good luck. It's as if sorcerers are babies learning to walk, and the gods are fond parents standing right behind to catch us before we fall on our asses or do something irretrievably fatal.

That image contains a surprising amount of truth. The gods will help sorcerers who are in bad spots, if the sorcerers agree to pay. But the analogy would be more accurate if the parents slammed the baby against the wall a few times before standing it back up, or even snipped off a finger.

Also, the gods aren't even a little bit fond of sorcerers. Most sorcerers die before they're twenty-five. If people considered that, they'd understand that gods don't care to protect sorcerers. Or maybe they just do a shitty job of it.

I didn't desire to find out how many times Harik wanted to slam me against the wall to save me from my current folly. I wasn't helpless and, with a dab of luck, could still murder my enemies. And if I couldn't save myself before they killed me, at least I wouldn't goddamn whine about it.

I prodded all my fingers and toes, which were beginning to swell like sickly sausages. Pulling magical power and then directing it demands a good amount of dexterity. My smashed, split-open fingers and toes couldn't be described as nimble. They could hardly be described as fingers and toes.

My least-destroyed digit was my left big toe. Pres had whaled on my left foot last of all, and maybe his arm had gotten weary. Sitting on a throne isn't physically taxing. Although most sorcerers don't use their feet for magic, I had taught myself the knack and decided that with a little assistance, my toe might pull power and do something with it.

The bare room didn't contain much in the way of assistance, but I couldn't afford to wait for help to show up. The king's physician was coming, and if he bound my damaged hands and feet, I might not be able to move them at all. Also, somewhere an iron door was being prepared for this room, and currently the wooden door was the only weak point I saw.

Still sitting on the floor, I leaned forward, gritted my teeth, and touched my shattered forefingers to each side of my bruised and scraped big toe. I hoped to push a bit with my fingers to help my toe achieve a little better movement.

Five sweaty, groaning minutes later, I had pulled a little power six times and accomplished not a damn thing. My fumbling toe had let the power slip away every time. I leaned back against the cold wall, breathed deep through the pain, and tried to relax for a while. Then I stretched my fingers forward and guided my toe for half a minute until I had a perfectly healed right forefinger.

The finger still hurt, but not as much as it had. Healing transfers the pain to the healer, although the pain isn't as great. That's still true when a sorcerer heals himself. But the main thing was that I had one usable finger.

With one finger, I could heal my hands, feet, and every other wound in my body. With one finger, I could rot the wooden door, or even shatter it.

I was carrying a lot of magical power thanks to my onerous bargains with Harik and Lutigan. With one finger, I could call a storm and enough lightning to destroy a decent part of this castle. Or destroy the pissant king himself.

I had power and a means of using it. This was the perfect time to do something stupid and get recaptured or killed. Having all that power was a little like being drunk. There's a reason why sorcerers die young.

Despite being crammed full of rage and frustration, I calmed myself. I would let the physician bandage me, or dip my hands in buttermilk, or whatever ridiculous thing he decided to do. He probably wouldn't think much of one uncrushed finger, and he could report to Pres that I was as chewed up as if I had tried to catch a landslide.

Then I'd heal myself, deal with the wooden door in some way that didn't sound like an earthquake, steal some clothes, and find a weapon. Once I was free, I'd reassess and figure out how to locate Pil. Although, if Pres didn't already have her, I couldn't imagine she needed help.

The physician arrived maybe an hour later. For a man who looked at people naked, he seemed awfully uncomfortable with his own wrinkly nudity. An old fellow with shaky hands, he rubbed my wounds with some phenomenal healing agent he had devised, and he grinned when he shared that the secret ingredient was bull's piss. At least he had a gentle touch. The square guard who had punched me, now naked, watched all this.

When the physician pulled out some bandages, the guard took them away. "Nope, not unless you got some bindings made of steel in there." He patted the physician on the shoulder. Then he led the old man away and locked me in again.

As soon as the bar dropped, I started healing myself. The entire procedure required more than half an hour, but I didn't spend as much power as I had feared. My hands and feet were whole, although they still smarted sharply. That was the price paid for healing, even healing myself.

I felt it might be afternoon. Although I sure as hell couldn't look out a window, I had a decent sense of time. Escape might be easier after sunset, and if I waited long enough, somebody would remove the wooden door for me when they brought the iron door. But Pres was sure to send a lot of guards to watch me while they swapped doors.

The best time for my escape was now.

After considering the problem of noise, I concluded that pushing the wooden door out would be the best tactic. A guard or two must be standing on the other side. With luck, they'd be idling in front of the door and cushion its fall with their bodies.

I winced as I pressed my palms against the door, pulled a blue band of power, and rotted the edge of the door all the way around. Then I pushed hard. The wood groaned as the door fell away from me, and I laughed when it landed on something that cried out.

The square guard gaped at me as I charged through the doorway and ran across the door, which was tilted over some inattentive, cursing man. The blocky guard jumped away from my punch. I might have kicked him in the crotch, but I didn't want him to scream. Instead, I rushed him, grabbed his head, and smacked it against the stone wall, probably not hard enough to kill him. I ached to slay the man, but it wasn't my most pressing need. Maybe I could kill him another day. Or I might spare him. He hadn't been a bad jailer.

If his skinny friend was under the door, though, he'd be deader than hell in a minute.

Another guard charged up the hallway toward me with a raised cudgel. As I spun to face him, he dragged off his helmet with his free hand and a long tangle of black hair flew free. I watched Pil in a guard's uniform run past me, reach down, and whack the other guard as he tried to crawl out from under the door. She hit him again with the cudgel, this time on the forehead, and he went slack. I saw that he wasn't the skinny, shambling tower of ass hair that had tried to feed me.

Less than a minute later, I had the square guard's uniform, boots, and sword gathered into my hands, and I followed Pil at a run down the hallway. She led me around a corner and flung open a drab oaken door before waving me through.

The room was an office of some kind, with several bookcases and chests lining the walls. A young, handsome man sat at a desk facing away from the door, and he looked over his shoulder at me. "You don't have any clothes on," he said, raising his eyebrows.

I held out the guard's clothes as I walked across the room. "Help me put these on. Hurry!"

The young man shook his head as he stood, but he reached out to take the boots when I shoved them at him. A second later, I punched him in the jaw. He fell backward on top of his desk, and I punched him twice more to be sure he was out.

"Damn it," Pil said, rolling her eyes as she closed the door. "This room was empty ten minutes ago. I came to rescue you, but I guess I should have just gone to the inn and had a drink, or taken a nap until it was time to escape. You make it hard to be nice to you, did you know that?"

"Shit!" I had pulled the guard's shirt on. It was huge. I felt like a frog wearing a rain barrel, and the sleeves stretched six inches past my fingertips. "He didn't look that big."

"I'm not going back for the other one's clothes, and you'll never be pretty anyway." Pil cracked open the door and peeked out.

I yanked off the shirt and began stripping the young man on the desk, who was closer to my size. I assumed him to be some sort of clerk, based on his clothes, which were brown on brown, trimmed with uglier brown.

"Hurry up," Pil muttered.

I hauled on the guard's boots. "They fit better than my old ones."

"Fine, let's have a party and a dance on the village green. Here, trade swords with me." She drew my sword out of her scabbard and handed it to me.

I smiled and passed her the guard's sword. "I was wondering

where to go looking for this. You've saved me some time and aggravation. Thank you, Pil."

"Thank Ella. She didn't say how she stole it from the king, but she found me and brought it. She said . . ." Pil looked at the ceiling and cleared her throat. "She said, 'This weapon belongs to Bib and no other. That prevaricating son of the most vicious curs in the islands of Ir does not deserve it, but the gods do not care about my judgment in this matter.' Then she talked about your messy habits and your bad singing voice." She peered into the corridor again. "Hurry up!"

"I'm ready! Let's find Ella."

Pil closed the door and stared at me. "Why?"

I didn't have an answer to that. I stared back at Pil like a dim lizard.

Pil bit the inside of her cheek. "Don't you have tasks to perform for Harik and Lutigan? What does Ella have to do with them? She's going east and seems happy to go, but the king is going north where the war ought to be happening soon. We're still going to make sure the war happens, right? The queen already died for it."

That stopped me short. I opened my mouth but wasn't sure what to say to that.

"Don't weep over me, I make my own choices!" Pil scowled as she said it. "You didn't force me to do anything, and you couldn't if you tried, so let's not talk and talk about it until they come kill us." She opened the door and stepped into the hallway without waiting for me to answer, so I hurried after her.

We marched away from the shouts of angry jailors back at my cell, turned left at the next passageway, and nearly bounced off Dimore's enormous, red belly as he trotted toward the corner.

I kicked the sorcerer in the knee, and he squealed, so I punched him in the jaw. He staggered back with glassy eyes as I pulled my knife. But before I could kill him, he flapped both hands. He looked as inoffensive as a partridge.

"Wait!" Dimore puffed. "I don't have a bit of interest in hurting you."

"You're sweet, but that doesn't change things," I said.

Dimore peeked around me and raised his eyebrows at Pil. Her expression must have disappointed the man. He bit his lip. "I guess you're upset with the king. I don't think he'd be surprised to see you whole again. Or sad." He stared at the ceiling.

I worked hard not to glance up. I watched his hands. If I saw his fingers move to engage in magical nonsense, I'd stab him during the first wiggle.

At last, Dimore seemed to forget about the ceiling. "You may be planning to kill the king. I might be if I were you."

I realized that my vengeful thoughts hadn't run so far as the specifics of murdering Pres. They had stopped at a vague intention to drop something heavy like a castle on him, or be unconcerned with his safety when the war started. That sounded a bit weak to me. "Yes, I plan to stab the son of a bitch in every organ and twice in the liver."

"It's not his fault, you know. He's been charmed to behave like an awful tyrant these days." Dimore stepped back and pressed his fingers together in front of him where I could spot any movement.

Pil whispered, "Bib, somebody's going to wander by on the way to the privy and raise the alarm! Let's go!"

"Charmed by who?" I asked Dimore.

He hesitated. "Weldt."

"Oh. So, the God of Commerce appeared to Pres in the bath one day and said, 'You're charmed to be an asshole, now pass the soap,' eh?"

Dimore sighed. "It was more involved than that, you are correct. You can save him, though. Him, and everybody else he might terrorize."

I sneered. "You did this to him. You save him!"

"My days of galloping horses and wading through swamps are over," Dimore said.

At least the sorcerer hadn't denied his guilt. I said, "I am disinclined to help the little turd. His temperament is no care of mine." I stepped past Dimore, but he shifted in front of me, almost tripping.

"Help him even though you don't care." With big, tender eyes, Dimore said, "Do it because you don't care."

I smiled. "Hell, I was warned off such cheap philosophical arguments my first month at school. I'm surprised at you, Dimore." I didn't tell him that although his argument was cheap, it made me admit that I cared a little. But my caring was tiny, and my anger at Pres was prodigious.

The sorcerer relaxed. "Go east to save him."

"Go east? That's all?" Pil said.

"That excludes three-fourths of the entire world," Dimore said. "What more do you expect?" He pushed past us and trotted around the corner toward the cells.

"Go east to do what?" I called after him, but he didn't return.

Pil scowled. "That brought us two minutes closer to a good stretching on the rack. Follow me!"

"Wait!" I whispered. "They'll be looking for two people dressed as guards. Let's split up."

The young woman nodded. "I'll meet you at the stables."

"No! They'll expect us to go there. Meet me at the tavern. We'll steal somebody's horses while they're getting drunk."

Pil trotted off toward the keep's main entrance. I hiked toward a hidden sally port I knew from a year before when I had been the king's guest. He had honored me for saving his life and killing traitors who wanted his throne. Lives and thrones didn't seem to count for much in Glass these days.

I chuckled at myself and stopped whining, even in my thoughts. It was unbecoming of a sorcerer.

In the castle courtyard, the sun told me it was midafternoon. I traipsed toward the main gate, matching the speed of the people near me. I kept my head up, didn't meet anybody's eyes, and trusted the clerk's hat to cover most of my gray hair.

Nobody stopped me. I don't think anybody even looked at me.

Five minutes later, I walked up to the tavern to find Pil leaning against the corner. She nodded at two fine horses tied up beside a few nags. A powerful, impressively muscled black stallion stood closest.

"Mine," Pil said, pointing at the black creature. "You should've gotten here faster."

"Fine," I grumbled, but I wasn't unhappy at all. The other horse, a white gelding, sure wasn't the image of a perfect horse. It was a bit on the small side. Its short neck, big chest, and flat knees weren't pretty. But I judged he would still be running when the black beast had run his heart out and fallen down to die.

Stan stumbled around the corner of the tavern and dropped to his knees before puking. He looked up, almost fell over, and steadied himself with a hand on the wall. "Bib?" He peered at my face. "Glad you ain't dead. Thanks for not killing me."

"Thanks for not making me. We're in a hurry—"

"Wait! I got a reward for standing in your way. Do you want some?" He fumbled in a pouch and brought out some copper coins. A few fell in the dirt. "Huh. Didn't think I spent so much." He held out his hand.

I waved him away. "No, keep it and have a drink for me. We need to borrow these horses."

Stan's face had been green, but it turned white in an instant. "Don't do that. That black one's Captain Parth's horse. The other belongs to his slave. Don't take 'em."

"Really? Then these are the perfect horses for us!" I laughed and mounted the gelding while Pil climbed up on her tall horse.

Stan stood up, fell backward, and slid down the wall to sit on his butt. "Don't tell 'em I let you steal their horses. I served a lot of hard officers . . ." He shook his head.

"Don't worry, Stan. If we see them, I'll be too busy cutting out their hearts to chat." I pulled my horse's head around to ride down the hill.

"At last, thank Fingit's bloody anvil!" Pil said. "I didn't realize until today what a chatty old fart you are." She cantered her horse down the hill, and I followed.

Parth's voice rang out from behind us, "Bib! Damn you, bring back my horse. Capps, where's my bow?"

I looked back and saw Parth glaring at us as a substantial, square-headed man handed him a bow and then an arrow. I kicked the gelding into a gallop. I didn't feel that Parth would shoot at us with great intent and risk hitting his horse. He'd probably fire toward us out of frustration. But I didn't know how the man thought. He might kill twenty horses to put me in the ground.

Regardless of how murderous Parth might feel, pursuit would be just a few minutes behind us.

SEVEN

If Parth was a thoughtful type, he'd hold off pursuit until his fifty soldiers were assembled and then ride after us in force. No fifty men in history have gathered with much speed, even to drink and gamble, so Parth might need two hours or more to organize a pursuit. It might even be sunset before he rode out through the castle gates.

I couldn't count on him waiting to marshal his horsemen, though. His thirst for my life might have been so great that he rushed out and was destroying his horse to catch us. Pil and I rode east across the shallow summer hills, hard enough to make our mounts blow.

After half an hour, Pil angled away to the north. I had made a possibly foolish decision as we rode, so now I caught up to her and shouted, "Why are you riding toward Eastgate?"

"What?"

I slowed my mount to a trot, and she matched me. It wouldn't hurt to rest our horses for a minute or two. "Not north. We'll head east instead."

Pil looked at me like I'd suggested we tunnel back to Castle Glass and drink all the king's wine. "Just because that red blob

Dimore said go east? We don't know him from a hole in the ground."

"I agree that I don't trust Dimore farther than I can spit an anvil," I said.

She pointed north. "Well, the war's over that way, or it will be, if we do our jobs."

I shook my head hard. "No, we need to ride east, and it hasn't a blasted thing to do with Dimore. Come on, we don't have time to argue."

Pil halted and sat up high in the saddle. "That sounded like an order, Bib, and you've sounded that way a lot recently, an awful lot. I've been letting it pass, but . . . maybe I was wrong, maybe this is the time for us to part ways."

If I had been able to kick myself in the butt, I would have. "Damn me! Damn me for a stumbling bull! I'm sorry, Pil, I really am. I understand that I have no right to tell you what to do. I'll be better about it, I promise."

She scratched her ear and frowned. "Fine, all right, I guess I've already proven that I'll let you get me involved in stupid and reckless things, but I won't do crazy things, and not as your servant or as your little sister. You're more experienced than me, I admit that, but you're no better or smarter. So . . . why east? You haven't decided to rescue the king from his bad mood, have you? He doesn't have any daughters to reward you with."

"No, it's not that. Pres will never go to war the way I want unless he trusts me, and he'll never trust me until I bring him his mother's murderer."

Pil's jaw worked for a moment. "But I'm the murderer."

"Not even a little bit! It was an accident." I reached over and patted her shoulder. "These brown-circle types are obvious trouble-makers, what with burning villages and hanging sheep and all."

Pil squinted at me.

"Never mind." I waved my comments away. "They're bad, so we'll find one, bring him to Pres, and say he's the murderer."

"But he'll say he's innocent."

"What guilty murderer wouldn't?"

She leaned toward me. "What about evidence?"

I smiled. "We'll have the whole return journey to create some. When we're done, the evidence will convince a dozen horse traders and a twenty-bit whore."

Pil looked back toward the castle. "I think Parth drew that circle on the queen's wall."

"Maybe. Why do you think so?"

"Because . . . well, I guess because I don't like him."

"Me neither. Maybe we can figure a way to frame him for the murder. Sorcerer, I invite you to travel east with me to do bold and memorable things."

The young woman smiled and looked even younger. She jerked when tears started running down her cheeks. She rubbed them off, looked at her fingers, and said, "That's embarrassing." Pil cleared her throat and smiled at me again. "Bold things. That sounds delightful."

Pil turned east and urged her horse into a gallop, and I followed. We rode all night and well into the next morning with only short spells of walking to rest the horses. Stopping for meals was unnecessary because we didn't have a scrap of food or a spit worth of anything to drink.

Before noon, we neared a road running east-west. I shied away from it because I couldn't think of a single person we liked who could also be traveling that road. Ella might have been an exception. An hour later, we topped a hill and spotted a burned-out village on the near side of the road, a quarter mile away.

"I imagine that's one of the little towns that those brown-circle bastards destroyed," I said as we halted. "Let's investigate."

"Why?" Pil asked.

"So we can know things!" I snapped.

"Like what?" Pil said with big, innocent eyes.

"Like the best place to find a murderer!"

"We know they came from the east, and you said any old brown-circle thug will do to accuse of murder. Are we going to find something that makes us go in a different direction?"

I scowled. "Hell, there may be clues to more than that! Indications. Signs. Survivors!"

"Probably not survivors. This poor place was destroyed days ago, and as for signs . . . Really, do you think we'll find signs and clues so helpful that they're worth spending the rest of the day on a search? Let's ride east and say that's good enough."

"We might find beer, or water, or food."

Pil hesitated.

I grinned. A moment later, something whipped across my scalp, taking the clerk's homely brown hat with it.

"Run!" Pil shouted, and I kicked my horse. I dared a look over my shoulder but couldn't make out anything that might have plowed across my head that way. The hills were as treeless as the bottom of the ocean. I felt blood trickling down the side of my head and into my ear.

"What is it?" I yelled at Pil.

"It's them!"

I pictured Parth's arrow skimming through my hair, and I shuddered.

An earnest chase began then. At last, I made out Parth leading eight horsemen. I don't know where the other forty-two of the bastards were, nor where Ella might have been. Parth pushed hard, but we were better mounted, and by sunset, we had lost sight of him.

I considered an ambush, but fighting nine men in the dark sounded chancy. It wasn't the sort of thing that had allowed me to grow into a charming old drunkard. Before midnight, we reached a small, shallow river, and we stopped to water the horses and ourselves.

Pil peered both up and down the river. "North or south?"

"If any of them is much of a tracker, it won't matter. We won't fool them. We could keep riding east, I suppose, which they might find confusing, but that just feels lazy."

Pil waited for a second. "North or south?"

I nodded to the north and turned my horse into the shallow water.

By morning, I had spent most of two days in the saddle, apart from some choice minutes devoted to being imprisoned and getting crippled. As a younger man, I could have ridden one more day singing songs as I went. I wasn't young anymore, and I had to punch my leg to stay sharp as I rode. We left the river to ride east again, the sunrise stabbing through our eyes.

Before the sun had lifted its whole self over the horizon, I spotted a figure far ahead, walking in no hurry but likely to intercept us if we rode straight on. The terrain had become dry with tough, patchy grass. We could see to the horizon ahead of us. A sweet wind was blowing, and I expected a pretty day later on.

I pointed at the figure, and Pil shrugged. "We might as well talk to them," she said. "They may know something useful, and they're right in our path. It won't take a minute, and they don't look dangerous."

I winced when Pil said that. "What did I tell you about people who don't look dangerous?"

She nodded. "Right. They're the worst ones. I'll work on being more suspicious, like a nasty old sorcerer."

We loosened our swords as we rode to meet whoever was wandering the dry plains. Soon I made out that he was a small man, wearing a faded green fur coat and carrying a long staff over his shoulder. He didn't look at us.

I saw a six-foot-wide line scratched into the grass and earth ahead of us, cutting across our path. The line was simple and uneven, dug out the way a child might dig with a stick, if the child was two hundred feet tall. It ran as far as I could see both ways, and I drew rein before I reached it. The man was just arriving, anyway.

Now I saw that he stood as high as my chest and wasn't wearing a coat. He was clad all over in thick green fur. It even covered his face. I leaned back in my saddle. "Hello there, sir! I—"

The being stopped me with one hand but didn't look up. He jammed the staff into the ground, and within a few seconds, it sprouted into a twelve-foot-tall shade tree with pink blossoms. The creature sat down on a chair that I hadn't seen appear, leaned back, and raised a dark, ornate wooden mug that seemed to materialize in his hand. He finally looked at me, sipped, and in a nasal voice said, "Come on, bark it out while the day's young."

I tried to recall whether I had read about any magical spirits like this. I didn't think so. "Good spirit, may we cross this . . . demarcation and ride on?"

"No. You can't." His eyes gleamed pink at us.

"We're on an important, noble task," I said, "so is there any way you might allow us through, even if that's not the tradition?"

Pil nodded. "Important and noble."

The creature smiled a two-fanged grin at Pil before peering at me. "You're wasting your time, which is fine with me. I can smell your bodies rotting from here. You'll be dead in twenty or thirty years."

I forced a laugh. "Maybe we could perform a modest service? Or, oh, engage in a contest? Answer riddles?"

The spirit leaned back and stretched his legs. "*You* may be dead in twenty or thirty seconds, grampy." He winked over at Pil. "Maybe not you."

"I can weave beautiful grass wreaths if you want one, with flowers," Pil said. "I'll weave some of my hair into it."

"Aww . . ." The creature nodded at her and sniffed, sucking tufts of green hairs into his nose for a second. "Have you known the touch of a man?"

Pil glanced at me but didn't answer. She was pulling the spirit's leg, since she and I had never done more than lean against each other to keep from falling down drunk.

The spirit raised a bushy eyebrow. "Let's talk about that wreath later."

An orderly retreat might become necessary. If this being was a powerful spirit, he might kill us both between one breath and the next. Even if he was a minor spirit, defeating him would be a bloody, uncertain endeavor. I smiled my most affable smile. "I'm willing to be flexible and cooperate, good spirit. Riding around the border of your domain would delay us considerably."

"Hey," Pil muttered to me, "look at the blossoms."

I focused on the pink flowers and realized they were really tongues hanging all over the tree, probably hundreds of them.

The spirit opened his mouth, and a sound like tall, dry grass in a high wind came out. It kept going for at least ten seconds, and I realized he was laughing. "You jackasses! Nobody rides around. Nobody turns around. And as sure as farts stink, nobody crosses the line." He stood up and squeezed his left hand, making the mug disappear.

I concluded he was a wood spirit or maybe a grass spirit. In fact, the thing's hair was the exact color of the grass around us. I could exert strong magical influence over growing things, but I didn't know whether I could hurt this mystical creature. The odds were poor.

Pil's chances of striking a mighty blow were even worse. Over the weeks, she had enchanted for herself an unnaturally accurate bow, a sword that possessed an urge to protect her, a knife as sharp as glass, a cloak that shed water like a beaver, and boots that let her jump shockingly high but only twice a day. She'd require time to string her bow, so I didn't see how any of that could save our lives from a mystical being.

If the situation veered toward hopelessness, I would try to root the spirit to the earth before we fled. Magic is strongest when convincing something to do what it already wants to do, and being rooted is one of the things grass likes best.

The spirit flexed his fingers on both hands. He grew claws like black, eight-inch thorns.

I considered every object I had seen since we met the spirit. There weren't many, if I didn't count tongues. I whistled. "That was a beautiful mug! You probably crafted it yourself with unworldly skill."

The spirit shrugged. "What's it to you?"

"I bet that in five tries, I can guess what you were drinking from it."

"You must think I'm a goddamn moron!" The spirit laughed again. "And I suppose you want me to let you pass if you guess right."

I nodded. "That would be customary in these situations. I don't mean to offend you. I just thought it would be different—maybe something new."

Sorcerers know from dealing with the gods that an immortal being's worst enemy is boredom. Over the years, wise and studious sorcerers have concluded that spirits are not immortal. Their lifespans are limited to hundreds of years, or maybe thousands. They don't live forever, but after a few centuries, they must rarely run across something new.

The spirit snorted at me, which sounded like a tightly bundled sheaf of grass being broken. "Fressa's eyes and Effla's tits, you must think you're a clever puppy dog. Just how many people do you think have proposed to guess what I'm drinking? I can hardly count that high!"

"I understand. How many have offered to let you take one of their fingers for each wrong guess?" I glanced at Pil again, and she swallowed but nodded.

The spirit tilted his head at me and smiled. "Can't say I've heard that before."

I smiled back. "Good! I get five guesses, one for each finger on my left hand. If I guess wrong five times, we renegotiate. Maybe you'll want a chance at the fingers on my right hand. But if I'm correct, you let us pass."

"To hell with your nose-picking right hand. If you lose all the left fingers, I'll kill you both."

"But if I guess right, we pass unharmed."

"Sure, why not?" The spirit sat back down and restored his mug. "This may be fun."

I dismounted and handed the reins to Pil while giving her an urgent look. I hoped she recognized it as a plea for her to run like hell if I guessed wrong the fifth time. "All right, good spirit. My first answer is rainwater."

The spirit moved almost too fast for me to see. Pain convulsed my hand as he bit off my left thumb. When I opened my eyes, the entity was sitting again, poking a needle through my thumb to string it onto a twist of hemp. I forced myself to let my hand dangle at my side, as relaxed as if I were ordering a drink. That didn't stop a couple of tears from dripping down my cheeks.

Rainwater had been the most obvious choice and almost certainly wrong. But I couldn't ignore the obvious, even if it cost me a guess.

The spirit could be drinking sap, but that seemed close to cannibalism. I glanced at the tongues on the tree. "You're drinking blood."

The creature grinned. "You've got to be more specific than that, chappie."

"Why? I said blood. If it's blood—any kind of blood—I win!"

He stuck his green, reedy tongue out at me. "We didn't stipulate how detailed your guess needs to be. Not my fault if you make sloppy deals."

"Hell no." I crossed my arms. "I'm done with this contest and its cockeyed rules. It's over. Void. Consider it a bad dream."

"Go ahead and forfeit. I'll kill you both before you can fart." The spirit stood taller. Then he floated two feet above the grass. "You challenged the Spirit of the High Middle Plains. There's no walking away from that."

"Huh. I guess there's a Spirit of the Low Lower Plains then." I was just saying stupid things while I tried to think. "I believe I'd like to challenge him instead."

"It's a her, not a him, and you can't. Now guess!"

I couldn't fight him, run from him, buy him a drink, or sing him to sleep. "How about I trade—"

"Quiet!" the spirit bellowed, hurling dirt and loose grass into my face. That startled the horses, but Pil managed to control them. "If the next thing out of your nasty, moist, pink mouth isn't a guess, I'll pull you into strings, weave you into blankets, and send you home on the backs of your horses."

I held my breath for a few seconds. "Virgin's blood."

The spirit swept in, bit off my forefinger with a snap, and returned to its finger-stringing with a grin. "You're awful at this. You should have tried to stab me or run away. Wouldn't have helped . . ."

I shook my hand, and droplets of blood flew. I flexed my

remaining fingers. Did all magical creatures drink blood? What kind? I wished I had asked Limnad the river spirit about that. This foul bastard wouldn't be drinking from an animal. It had to be human blood of some kind. "Murderer's blood."

I grunted as my left middle finger was snapped off in the spirit's scratchy mouth.

Virtue didn't seem to make a difference. I hesitated, considered, looked at my boots, and hesitated again before deciding to trust my instincts. "King's blood."

This time, the spirit smacked into me as it grabbed my hand and bit down. I stumbled but caught myself.

The spirit dangled three of my fingers on the twine and held up the fourth. "One more guess, you thumping boob. You better get some inspiration fast."

Damn my instincts. I glanced up at Pil on her horse.

"No fair asking that slut for help!" the spirit yelled.

Pil had shaken her head at me, anyway.

Could it be priest's blood? That seemed as good a guess as any, meaning it was lousy. The spirit was nearly bouncing in his chair. He seemed to be enjoying himself to an almost embarrassing extent, which I supposed was nice for him.

I scanned the scene again, taking in the tongues and the spirit's fine necklace of my fingers. The one remaining finger on my left hand started itching. That was crazy. If I guessed wrong, I'd be dead before I felt the finger bitten off.

I glanced back at Pil, who was pale but sat her horse as still as a stump. She slipped her hand over toward her sword, and I noticed a streak of fresh blood staining her shirtsleeve at the elbow. I hadn't seen it earlier.

Well, the spirit was mighty swift. Maybe too swift for me to follow, and magical too.

I stared into the spirit's eyes as I pointed at Pil. "You're drinking her blood."

The hair covering the creature's body drooped. "How could you know that? You cheated, you damned, squeaking fart of a sorcerer!"

I heard Pil's breath catch.

I took a deep breath to steady myself. "Good spirit, please don't feel bitter about this. It was mostly luck." I held up my dripping left hand. "And you do get to keep the fingers."

He sat taller and examined his new finger necklace. "That's true. Well, go on before I decide to make you guess something else. But you'll only get three guesses this time." He glanced at my crotch.

I mounted, nodded to the spirit, and rode east.

The landscape changed the instant I crossed the line. We rode into an open forest of tall, narrow trees. Thick, bright green grass poked up through a carpet of fallen green and white leaves. The trees' white trunks shot up thirty feet before the first limbs branched out. It felt as cool as early spring. A narrow river lay to our right with otters scampering along the bank.

When I looked over my shoulder, the spirit had disappeared. Also, the forest stretched as far as I could see, with no sign of dry grass, plains, or big lines dug in the dirt.

I turned and rode back past where the line should have been, but I did not return to the dry plain.

"Where did we go? Did we go anyplace?" Pil looked at the sky with huge eyes.

I examined the sky with her and saw that the time of day hadn't changed when we rode across, even if the landscape had. I swung my head around to see the whole sky.

Pil was nodding. "I see it too. The clouds are the same, or they're close to it, just about the same as they were. Bib, what does it mean?"

The spirit's voice called from somewhere in the woods, "It means you should keep riding east, you idiots! I'll send word to my employer that you're coming to see him. And here's a little good advice: Think up something fun to do when you get there, but hurry. He gets grumpy when you make him wait."

EIGHT

I wondered whether some god was enjoying the foolish look on my face. The landscape had changed, but the sky had not. A god might have carried us off to a land much like our own, but I found that unlikely. Any god could accomplish it in a moment, of course, but none would want me to believe I was worth the effort.

Maybe nothing had changed, but we had been charmed by the spirit to see trees and leaves where none existed. That explanation seemed likelier.

"Pil, please fire an arrow into that tree." I pointed at one fifty feet away.

"You don't think it exists, do you? It's a phantom tree?" She dismounted and strung her bow. She put an arrow in the middle of the trunk at the height of my head. We trotted to the tree, and as I examined the trunk around the arrow, she said, "Do you want to kick it to be sure?"

I ignored that. I tried to ignore my throbbing hand too, but with less success. "I guess the trees are real, but maybe we're charmed to see no change in the sky."

"It's changing now. That cloud that looked like a nose is changing into a spoon."

The tree swayed as if a strong breeze was blowing, although the winds were light. Leaves showered us.

Pil and I stared at one another and then ran back to our horses, where I pulled a white band and investigated the tree from a distance. I learned that it was moving in ways a tree shouldn't move, but that was all I learned. I convinced it to hold still, although I had to pull a second band to do it. I gazed around at the other motionless trees, stunned by my monumental lack of knowledge.

I could have called Harik to ask for help, or beg advice, or just insult him, but I didn't. I felt weary thinking about it. "Pil, I don't believe I'll call on Harik unless the situation becomes grim."

"Oh, all right." Pil nodded. "When all the rest of your fingers have been bitten off for jewelry, would that be a grim situation in your opinion? Or do I need to give up my fingers too?" Her eyes twinkled as she said it. "If you won't ask for help, I guess I will."

She took a breath, looked up, closed her eyes, and opened them right up again. "That's strange, I heard Fingit calling to me, but I couldn't reach him and I don't think he could hear me, which is pretty darn unusual. Unusual, in the sense that it's never happened even once before. Not to me. Has it happened to you?"

"No, it sounds peculiar. Are you sure you were doing it right?"

Pil shook her head. "There aren't many ways to do it wrong. Lift yourself, call their name, get there. If they let you."

I raised myself and called for Harik, but I had no more luck than Pil. "It's a puzzle," I said, "but we can't just sit here on our horses crying about how the gods don't love us. That spirit said to travel east, so I'm sure as hell not going that way."

"What about healing your fingers?"

"Let's not stop for that yet. I've still got a palm. I can slap somebody if I need to." That was bravado, and I'm sure she knew it. If I slapped someone with that hand, I'd cry and I might pass out.

Pil grinned. "All right, not east, but let's not ride back west, either. The spirit may expect us to be scared and desperate to go back home."

I turned my horse north, and Pil didn't object. I shook my

chewed-up, aching left hand, which didn't soothe it any more than the previous hundred times I'd shaken it.

We rode north, pushing our horses hard. A stream came into view on our right, flowing back toward the river, and throughout the afternoon, it ran straight north without a bend. I followed it, and we never left the forest. In addition to otters, quite a few water creatures fled from us. The forest held no birds or wildlife that I could see. By midafternoon, the air had become still but chilly.

Pil and I dismounted by the stream to rest the horses. She stared into the water and even walked down to kneel at the water's edge.

"You might not want to drink," I squeaked through my dry throat. "You can be sure the horses are thirsty, but you don't see them drinking that enchanted water, do you? That says something, right?"

She trudged back to me. "I was just looking at my reflection. To see whether my hair's out of place."

"Well, that's a damn lie, and we both know it." Her hair couldn't have been more disarrayed if it had spent the last two days in an elephant's crotch. "If you're lying this much, then I'm a bad influence on you."

I reached to dig through Parth's saddlebags, and failed. I stared at my fingerless left hand and then laughed.

Pil wrinkled her nose. "If you think it's that entertaining, let's go back. I bet I can convince him to strip off your toes."

"Let's do it on the way home." I sat on the stream bank and pulled a green band to start restoring my fingers. My body already knew how fingers were built, so I didn't need to understand the details. I just needed to provide the power and push it at the right times.

Pil sat beside me. "Bib, what are we doing here? Is there a hidden army out here someplace for the king to fight?"

"Maybe. If you distract me, I'll have a permanent rude gesture on this hand." I kept working.

Pil gazed across the water. "Do you plan to do whatever Dimore wants done to save the king from whatever unspecified thing he needs saving from?"

"It's not my highest priority. I'd rather find some simpleton out here to be our murderer. It would be fine if he's one of those brown-circle rascals, since Pres knows them to be enemies. He'll want to believe they're guilty. That's a beautiful thumb, don't you think?"

"Breathtaking," she said without looking. "What's your main goal, Bib? Save the king, or frame a murderer, or scare up a hidden army? Or present yourself to that spirit's master, or employer, or . . . whatever it is that can hire spirits?"

I glanced at Pil. I didn't care to mention that I might have to betray her someday if I didn't make sure Pres lost his war by Harik's deadline. "Don't hold back, Pil—you can go ahead and ask me your real question, I'm not shy. Do you mean to say, 'Bib, how come you know so much about so much? Why are you so wise and handsome?'"

Pil sniffed. "Sometimes you are an ass, and not in a charming, eccentric old bastard kind of way. Just an ass." She sounded hurt for a moment. Or she might just have been sick of me. My history with women and just about everybody else suggested the latter.

I finished restoring my hand, which took me about a minute. I grinned at Pil. "Hell, I'm sorry for being such a harsh old bucket of saw blades. I have one main goal, Pil, and that is telling the gods to go slap each other for the rest of time. I'm done with them."

Pil watched me, her eyes widening.

"So, I need to retire my debts, starting with the war that Pres will lose, and I want to get it done with all speed. I am flexible with respect to methods. If I seize too hard upon one tactic, then I have only one path to victory. But if I relax and look around, I will see limitless options for success."

"What are you talking about?"

"We're hunting murderers!" I stood and walked back to the horses. "Bugger Dimore. He can drag his chunky ass out here to save the king if he thinks it's that important. Let's find some nitwit with a brown circle on his arm and gallop straight back to Glass."

Pil held up a hand. "Wait, go back a minute. You want to be free of debts? After all these years? Why now?"

I hadn't explained this clearly to myself yet, so I paused a long while before answering her. "Sorcery always takes more than it gives. Well, it's taken too much from me."

"Whose fault is that?" Pil said with no expression.

"Mine, but now I'm done with deals and gods. Or I will be soon." I opened one of Parth's saddlebags to dig through it.

As I pawed through the first one, cursing the whole time, Pil said, "I've searched every bag already, twice, and there's nothing to drink. Or eat."

"By all Krak's hairy places!" I pulled a magnificent blue silk cloak from one of Parth's bags. "Saving this for yourself?"

Pil turned red. "There wasn't one made of burlap and grease, so I didn't think you'd be interested."

I laughed. "You're right, I wouldn't be. You ought to wear this thing. You'd be everybody's idea of the ferocious, beautiful sorcerer ready to turn swords into sand and warriors into toads. People would piss themselves when you walked in the room."

Pil gave a weak grin. "I can put it on now."

"If you like. It feels chilly out." I tossed her the cloak and then mounted my homely horse. Parth was still chasing us, so sleep could wait until after dark.

The sun dropped to late afternoon, stealing away warmth as it fell. We pressed north, alternating pace as we went. Then the little stream curved hard to our left. Rather than turn back toward Glass, I kicked my horse to pick his way down the steep stream bank and across the shallow, quick current. But he shied away from the water and refused to set a hoof into it. He balked even when I dismounted and led him. Pil's stallion made such a definite objection she was almost thrown.

I examined the stream and might have seen glimmering on the streambed. The low sun didn't throw much light, though.

"I hate to spend power trying to force them across," I said. "The stream might curve back north again past the next tree. Who knows . . ."

Pil guided her horse around without answering and urged it up the bank. The next moment, she yelped and swayed in the saddle toward me, an arrow poking all the way through her left shoulder.

She grabbed the saddle to pull herself up, but the big horse bolted. Pil slammed to the ground like a sack of corn, and bounced.

I climbed up the bank, still holding my horse's reins. I grabbed Pil's ankle to pull her down the stream bank into cover. Several men and one woman were shouting out there. I saw at least ten horsemen and twice that many men afoot.

"Pil! Look at me!"

Her face was nearly as white as cotton, but she met my eyes.

"I'll mount and then pull you up!"

Based on her expression, she might have thought I said I'd fly over the battlefield and piss fire on our enemies, but she nodded.

"Don't hit my horse!" shouted a voice I recognized as Parth's.

"Mine neither!" yelled a gravelly voice I didn't recognize.

As I mounted, I glanced around to assess things. Somebody had told Parth exactly where and how to ambush us. Ten more horsemen were charging us from each direction along the stream bank, but we could still squeeze out of this ambush. I prepared to convince twenty horses to throw and stomp as many men as possible.

"Bib!" Ella yelled. I didn't see her. "Don't fight! Don't fight!" she shouted from someplace among the horsemen.

"Fight?" I bellowed. "How about run?"

Four more arrows whipped past, but none of them flew close. I pulled Pil up with one hand and used the other to start pulling bands of power. A little part of me felt smart that I had healed my hand before all this hell got stirred up. I whipped bands out to the horses south of us, and a few seconds later, they began rearing, bucking, and charging the dismounted bowmen.

I kicked my mount to gallop right between the crazed horses and the stream bank.

My horse screamed and heaved to the left. As he fell, I dragged Pil and myself off to the right. I rolled, but Pil landed on the arrow in her shoulder and screamed louder than my horse. She lay on her side panting, and any chance of her fleeing had just disappeared.

I knew I ought to surrender, but I was pissed off and hungry for these men's lives. I drew my sword and spotted Parth charging, but he slowed before he reached me. Ella galloped right past him to put herself between us.

"Don't fight!" Ella shouted before she leaned down and murmured to me, "I can negotiate our way to safety, but not while you're murdering the king's soldiers."

By then, Parth's force had drawn close and pointed about thirty of their swords at me. Parth raised his weapon and scratched his jaw with his other hand. His horse stamped as he gave me a crackling smile. "Drop your sword."

"Go to hell."

"We can kill you in ten seconds."

"I can kill you in five seconds, you waddling pile of turds. How did you get past the guardian, anyway? I thought you were too stupid to spit out hot coal."

"Oh, that!" Parth laid his sword over his shoulder. "It was simplicity. Once I swore to execute you, that grassy spirit allowed me to ride right through. He even revealed your location."

"Bullshit!" I said, pointing my blade at Parth's left eye. "I won't accept that you're that clever."

"Very well, you have found me out. It wasn't my idea. It was hers." Parth chuckled and pointed at Ella. She turned as red as a weeping eye.

NINE

I hadn't imagined that Ella would betray me. I knew she disapproved of me, and I had often been a pain in her ass. But she had never been a backstabber.

This was probably how Pres would feel when I engineered his army's defeat: angry and hopeless. It would be worse than a broken heart. His face would look as if I slammed him in the belly with a mallet. I smiled when I pictured it, although I kept my sword pointed at Parth's brown eye.

"You needn't smile," Parth said, laying his sword across his horse's neck. "I care nothing for your secret jokes. Lay down the sword and the knife as well."

If I could keep the man talking for fifteen seconds, I could convince the rest of the horses to go berserk. Then I'd call up a wind to fling the millions of leaves into the air. With everybody bumbling around blind, I'd grab a horse and flee south, away from the archers. I would be forced to fight a few dismounted men as I cut my way out, but it was my best chance to escape. I might not even get killed.

On the other hand, running wouldn't help Pil. She was rolling on the ground now with an arrow through her shoulder, her face gone gray.

"You promised me you wouldn't kill him!" Ella shouted.

"Wait!" I lowered my sword and stared at Ella. "You advised Parth that he should promise to kill me, and then you made him promise *not* to kill me? And he said yes?" I made a show of examining Parth. "Is he stupid?"

Parth gave me a wide smirk, but Ella cut in before he could speak. "It was my only means of preventing the spirit from destroying us all. That spirit reviles you, Bib. What did you do to it?"

"Put all that aside!" Parth pointed his sword at me. "I shall honor my word to that fuzzy spirit and kill you." He smiled with teeth so bright they nearly distracted me. "But to honor my word to the lady, I will forbear until I discuss it with the king. Unless you behave like an ass. I'll then be pleased to cut off your head and leave it under a bush."

The block-faced man who had handed Parth his bow back in Glass now stumped toward him. The fellow's jaw looked as wide as his forehead. He grumbled, "Can I see about my horse now, sir?" He glanced toward my gelding that I supposed had been his horse before I stole it. The poor animal lay with an arrow in its leg.

"Not yet, Capps. I may need you to slaughter someone first."

The man frowned but nodded, then glowered at me. "Hurry up with the surrendering. I don't want my horse to suffer no more."

Parth nodded at Capps and then yelled at me, "I will slice you into strips if you don't lay down your damn sword!"

I might not be able to trust Ella, but I knew I couldn't trust Parth. I lowered my sword and held it out to Ella.

Parth scowled. "Oh no——"

"I'm surrendering to her," I said as Ella accepted my blade. "You don't have a goddamn thing to do with it. Pretend you're not even here." I passed my knife to Ella too.

"It is out of my hands." Ella shrugged. "He capitulated to me, so I bear responsibility for his well-being." She glared at me. "And his good behavior."

"Absolutely," I said with big eyes. "I'll have so much good behavior you'll want to drink whiskey and race goats."

"What?" The captain winced.

Ella shook her head before lifting her chin at Parth. "I cannot with honor allow him to be harmed."

Parth had turned red, and his horse was stamping. Capps looked sideways at the captain and shuffled two steps away from him. But then Parth sniggered and started a deep belly laugh. Soon, he wept and got a little fit of the hiccups. He clamped his hand over his mouth and black mustache, but he kept laughing.

Everybody stared at the captain until he settled down to a giggle or two. "I should kill you now. A wise man would do that. Perhaps I shall, Mistress Ella's allowances notwithstanding. You men, hold him."

I noticed Stan for the first time as he backed away from me shaking his head, his brow drawn. Three other men stepped up to grab me. I threw one into Capps, and they both fell. I wrenched another's knee and broke a third's ribs.

Seven men tried me the second time. They sacrificed some blood and teeth before pinning me on the leafy forest floor.

Ella was shouting the whole time. "Captain, what of your honor? You promised not to kill him without the king's leave. And he surrendered to me! Will you smear my honor as well?"

Parth guffawed and then cleared his throat as he dismounted. "Mistress! Why should we be so operatic? I have counseled the king against such sentimentality more than once. We, too, should avoid it." He gestured toward me with a huge smile. "Men, kill him now."

I was prepared to call a wind that would astound and blind everybody nearby. But Ella charged into the soldiers holding me, swinging the hilt of my sword at them. She didn't stop until she stood over me knocking heads and elbows whenever Parth's men came close.

I sat up. Ella shoved me back down with her boot and growled, "Stay there!" She flipped her blonde braid back with her free hand and said, "This is unnecessary, Captain! Bind him tightly. He shall give me his parole, and he will not escape."

Still chuckling, Parth said, "He escaped from a locked cell in the middle of the castle! With his hands and feet destroyed! He is a sorcerer, and I should kill him now, this minute, else I may not live out the day tomorrow."

I eased my hand up, hoping Ella would pass me my sword if everything went even further to hell . . . if that was possible. I held four white bands in the other hand to call up the wind.

Parth sheathed his sword.

I raised the wind, and leaves whipped into the air, but Parth jumped toward Ella. He smacked her sword aside with one hand, drew a knife with the other, and slammed her down on top of me. He pressed his knife blade against her throat.

I had seen people with finer fighting skills than Parth, but I had never seen anybody as fast.

The captain bit off each word: "No magic. Stop it this moment, or she dies."

My next thought was reckless and insane. If Parth cut Ella's throat, I would have at least a few seconds to save her. Could I convince a horse to trot over and kick him in the head?

"Stop." Parth shifted his knife to Ella's face and mashed down on her throat with his other arm. "One thrust into her brain. It will be instant. So, stop."

I let the wind die. Leaves ruffled toward the ground. A dozen horses forgot why they were upset.

Parth smiled as if I were his favorite uncle. "Good! Now let us all stand up, step back, and breathe." Ella and I stood facing Parth and ten soldiers. Twenty more soldiers surrounded us. The captain went on: "I see that I might be required to sacrifice a quarter of my men—or more—in order to kill you. Ella would almost certainly die. My death is not an impossibility. My mission would be imperiled."

I showed my teeth. "I guarantee that you will die, you son of a bitch, even if everybody else lives to be one hundred."

"I suspect that great insights would be possible if we made the test, but let's put that aside. Here is the arrangement. We shall not attempt to kill you or disarm you. For the sake of all the gods, it would prove futile to bind you. However, you may not travel with us, nor may you interfere with our mission. If we never see you again, all will be well."

"Hell, is it my birthday?" I asked. "If you toss in a tavern and some gambling, it sounds like paradise. Give me my sword." I reached out to Ella for my blade. "Pil comes with me, and Ella if she wants to."

Parth nodded at Ella and grinned. "Of course. Mistress Ella, you may always come and go as you wish. Please accept my apologies for threatening your life. I hope that you understand that I was forced to that extremity."

Ella gave him a bright smile. "I understand. You are a smear of filth without honor, and the king shall know of this."

They might have kept bitching and talking bad about each other's ma, but I didn't hear it. I was scrambling over to Pil, where she lay stiff on her side, breathing fast and shallow. The wound had bled through her shirt and the silk cloak, but not so much as to threaten her life.

"Deep breaths, young woman," I said, kneeling. "You'll be up and beheading bears by sunrise tomorrow."

I hadn't thought it possible for her to get paler, but she did. She whispered, "Fingit's forty hammers, I must be dying. Whenever something's bad, you say that it's good, you liar."

"Normally true." I probed the wound, and she hissed. "Not this time. I will have to break it and pull it through, though."

She closed her eyes. "Can't . . . you soften the wood or something?"

"There are three reasons why that's a bad idea, but here's the best one. If I leave rotten wood behind in that wound, you really will be dead."

"Can you save her?" Parth asked from behind me.

"Why the hell would you care?"

"I have never witnessed a healing."

"Well, I expect I can. Nothing's certain with sorcery, of course. She'll need a healthy supply of wine or beer to take with us for her convalescence."

Pil widened her eyes at me, and I touched my finger to my lips.

From some distance away, I heard a galloping horse and Stan's irritable shout. "Captain! Captain!" He drew rein at the last second, almost bashing into Parth. "Captain, there's men out there! Little ones, like boys, just standing there looking at us. Four of 'em, standing there as still as my daddy's heart."

Parth stepped back from me. "They haven't said anything?"

"No, sir, they haven't even opened their lips to spit. We didn't seem 'em walk up. They were just standing there like they sprouted out of the ground. Whangs of the gods, maybe they did sprout up!"

Ella and I glanced at each other.

"Parth, you get your men ready to ride away fast," I said, breaking off the feathered end of the arrow. Pil yelped and then held her breath as I said, "Those sound like Hill People."

Parth rubbed his chin and looked in the direction Stan was pointing. "I have never encountered them. I know they're dangerous, but it's just four men."

Ella had cut off the loose end of her belt, and I slipped it into Pil's mouth. "Bite down," I murmured to her. "Parth, there may be a hundred you don't see."

"Where?" The captain looked around. "The trees are fifty yards apart!"

"Doesn't matter. You hid your men from me behind that brush and down the stream bank too, didn't you? A thousand Hill People are stealthier than three of your horses."

Closing her eyes, Pil nodded at me. I pulled the arrow through in a quick, smooth movement. She convulsed and went limp, panting.

I turned to Parth. "It also doesn't matter because four Hill People can kill half your men. Maybe more."

Parth frowned as if I had said four cranky pigs could kill half his men. "Our mission is scouting. These Hill Men may be the very thing we seek."

I almost pulled a green band to heal Pil, but I stopped. If the Hill People did attack, I couldn't afford to be slowed down by pain in my shoulder from healing her.

"Very well." Parth shook his head slowly. "This seems mad, but I shall give the order to mount."

Before any of us moved, a high-pitched but loud bellowing started in a strange language. I didn't understand it, but I recognized it as the speech of the Hill People.

"Too late to run," Parth said, brushing his hands together.

"No, it's not!" I said. "It's not late at all. It's the perfect time to run."

"Captain, it is a flaming good day to run away," Capps added.

"No, we must investigate. We should at least speak with them." Parth mounted and trotted his horse toward the shouting Hill Person.

I yelled after Parth, "This is a fine opportunity to count the number of your organs, Captain. It'll be easy, once the Hill People lay them on the ground in front of you." I turned to Ella. "Please watch over Pil."

Ella nodded and drew her sword.

Pil struggled to one knee and held her sword out to Ella. "Use mine. It's enchanted to protect you."

Ella pushed it away. "You have greater need of it than I."

If the Hill People could be defeated by stubbornness, Ella would sweep the field. I chased after Parth.

The Hill People stood apart from each other in a square fifty feet on each side. Stan had been incorrect in his count of four men. There were three men and one woman, each about five feet tall and medium brown. My skin was also brown, although lighter, but they would feel no kinship with me. In their eyes, the lowest Hill Person was superior to all other humans.

I joined Parth, Stan, and three dozen of the soldiers, some mounted, and we faced the Hill People from twenty paces away. The one yelling had moved on to groaning, whining, and whistling, but presently he stopped.

Like all Hill People, most of these weren't much above five feet tall. They appeared chunky with muscle, but that was deceptive. The typical Hill Person was faster than almost any Westerner, and they nurtured a long, profound fighting tradition among men and

78

women both. I had read of a Hill Person town attacked by slavers when almost all the adults were away at war. The children slaughtered most of them and tortured the rest.

These Hill People wore simple forest-colored clothing and sturdy boots. They carried short spears, long knives, and javelins on their backs. I couldn't examine their weapons, but Hill People usually crafted finer quality goods than found in other lands. They were not a backward people. They were an accomplished people who didn't care that outsiders couldn't understand their ideas and ways.

Silence stretched out for thirty seconds. I whispered to Parth, "You wanted to see them. There they are. Did you have a plan for what you'd do next?"

"I planned to speak with them."

"Allow me to toss in a fact or two," I said. "It would be bad manners for them to speak first, since we're such inferior specimens. Also, Hill People do things for reasons. They're not just out for a jaunt in the country. They're here to accomplish something."

Parth nodded, raised his hand, and called out, "Greetings. I am Captain Parth. I serve the King of Glass."

The closest man on the left, with a skinny neck and long arms, said, "What kind of demon are you?"

Parth opened his mouth and closed it. Then he glanced at me.

I stepped forward. "We're the worst kind of demon." None of them reacted. "We have only one power. We use the truth to make people suffer."

"What the hell are you talking about?" Parth whispered.

I ignored him and waited for Skinny Neck to answer, but he just stared at me. I looked over at the Hill Man who had made all the noise. "I appreciated your song."

Skinny Neck twitched. Nobody else moved. They probably didn't know our language.

I went on: "My friend, Larripet, was a Hill Man. He let me listen when he sang."

"I do not know anyone like that," Skinny Neck said. "You are probably lying."

That was a shame. I had hoped to trade on Larripet's friendship like I was a crooked rug merchant, but that had been crude optimism. I didn't want to agree with this man that I was a liar, but I didn't want to call him a liar, either. "You express things very clearly."

The Hill Man frowned, and his skinny neck bobbed as he swallowed. "Where is your master?"

Parth pointed back toward Glass, but I slapped his boot and cleared my throat before he said anything.

"Our master is on the other side of this stream," I said.

"That is a lie. The Gar-chap-gar is on the other side."

"I'm sorry, the what?" I figured it was some sort of Hill Person name.

"Why are you here, demon?"

I raised my eyes to the clouds in a way I hoped they'd think was reverent. "We're here to honor our dead."

The Hill Man's eyes flicked back and forth between Parth and me for several seconds. "That is not a good joke."

Parth cleared his throat, but I ignored him. "I'm busy honoring my dead children. I can stop long enough to talk to you, though."

The Hill Man spoke to the Hill Woman fifty feet away from him. She didn't sound happy when she answered. He examined me as if waiting for me to sprout some extra legs and dance. "Demon, it may be right for you to bring the spirits of your demon children to these lands. I am not an expert on demon habits. If demons grieve, go do it now. Then you can go."

I nodded and stepped back.

"We will kill all these others now," the Hill Man said, digging his toe into the ground.

The woman beside him threw her shoulders back. A soldier far to my right cried out, and one far to my left cursed. I glanced both ways and saw that each man had a javelin in his chest, maybe in the exact center, although it was hard to be sure.

While I had been glancing, the four Hill People had charged us, dodging as they came. Five soldiers shot arrows at point-blank range and missed their zig-zagging targets by at least three feet.

I cursed and drew my sword, and the singer changed angle to

charge me. He feinted at my head with his spear, cut at my knees, and came in to slice my belly on the return stroke, ferocious as a windstorm. I blocked and used my reach advantage to thrust at his chest. He turned aside to dodge the thrust, countered by stabbing at my eyes, and tried to kick my knee when I blocked the counter. Then he sprang back out of the way when I swung to cut off his foot.

Parth's big, roan horse hit the ground neighing and nearly rolled on me. I heard Parth shouting enraged profanities. From all sides, yelling, cursing, and crying whirled around me, but I didn't have time to look.

The Hill Man stalked toward me, testing with his spear. I feinted low and thrust high, and he guided my blade just past his temple before thrusting at my throat. I dodged and then ducked his next thrust before stepping back and pretending to slip on the leaves. When he jumped in to kill my clumsy, off-balance demon ass, I slipped aside and thrust into his neck. I followed that by stabbing him in the heart before I turned around.

A Hill Man who wasn't one of the original four was pressing Parth hard, and I saw him slice Parth's arm. I ran three steps and thrust into the Hill Man's back, then twice more to put the man on the ground while Parth caught his balance.

A quick scan showed that at least thirty soldiers were down. Only four or five Hill Men seemed to be leaping and tearing through the soldiers, leaving blood, moans, and bodies behind. Some must have attacked from the lakeshore unseen—they had surrounded us, and we'd been ignorant of it, like a bunny in a snare. Ella and Pil stood together. They seemed to be alone for the moment.

I would have loved to call down some fearful, decisive magic at that moment. For the past half hour, I had been dallying with the idea of filling the air with dead leaves. However, the Hill People were probably a damn shot better at fighting blind than Parth's soldiers.

The drawback of Caller magic like mine is that most of it requires time and the right conditions. I couldn't call together a thunderstorm in an instant. I couldn't make trees grow and bend to whack an enemy a hundred feet away. I couldn't even require a horse to do what I wanted without a few seconds to work up to it. While I was farting around with that, some Hill Man could slaughter me five times over.

I followed Parth, getting excited by the prospect of killing some more of these ferocious bastards. We reached four soldiers, who stood fencing with one Hill Man. One soldier's off arm had been mangled. The Hill Man facing them threw five furious attacks in five seconds, thrust into the wounded man's chest, and whacked another on the head, stunning him. The surviving soldiers avoided death by a finger's width every time. They never answered with an attack of their own.

Parth and I ran to help the soldiers who still lived. The Hill Man lasted ten seconds against us and then fifteen, but at last, Parth sliced his neck deep enough to slay him. My disappointment was as sharp as getting kicked, so I spun to find somebody else to kill.

Then the sounds of fighting stopped dead, leaving scattered moans and cries. It looked as if the Hill People hadn't allowed many of Parth's men to live. I didn't know how many Hill People were left alive, but they had all disengaged and drifted away at the same time, leaving behind four of their dead friends. Within ten seconds, all of them had disappeared.

I looked across the field and sprinted when I saw both Ella and Pil on the ground. Pil sat with Ella's head in her lap. Somebody had sliced Ella across the chest, and her shirt was soaking up blood. She was panting, but her color was good.

I knelt and probed the wound. "I swear I'm not touching you in a frisky fashion. In fact, I'm not enjoying this at all, so don't break my arm."

Ella chuckled, winced, and chuckled some more.

I hummed for a moment. "It's a deep, bloody scratch, but not bad. I bet the scar won't be more than four inches wide."

Ella glared up at me. "You bastard, you said it's just a scratch."

I almost patted her cheek but stopped myself. "Rest a minute. I'll come back."

Pil said, "Bib! Those two men fought alongside us." She pointed at two bodies twenty feet away. "Your friend and the grouchy one, and without them, we'd probably have died."

Stan lay on his back with an appalling wound in his belly. I suspected that only his hands were keeping his bowels inside him. He was moaning, but his eyes were closed.

The other man was Capps. He lay on his back, writhing and holding a wound almost identical to Stan's. He met my eyes, but he didn't say anything.

If I hurried, I could save Stan's life.

"Will they return?" Parth asked me.

"Hell, I don't know. If they come back, ask them why."

I knelt over Stan, commenced pulling green bands, and put him back together over the next five minutes. When I was done, my belly felt as if a bad-tempered blacksmith was dragging a hot, barbed sword back and forth across it.

"I have heard about things such as this. Curing wounds," Parth said from behind me. "But I've never seen it until today."

"The world is full of improbable things," I said, drawing my sword. "You should watch me throw dice sometime. Probability can kiss my ass." I stood over Capps, saw that he still lived, and marked his heart with the tip of my sword.

"Wait!" Parth shouted, and he grabbed my arm before I killed the man. "Repair him too."

I laughed. "That's a foolish statement. He'll just help you try to kill me later on. You might as well tell me to raise all these Hill People from the dead." I couldn't do any such thing, but it wouldn't hurt for Parth to think I could.

Parth pointed at Stan. "You healed him."

"He's my friend, which sounds unlikely, but life is full of whimsy."

"Capps is my servant. I'll pay you to heal him," Parth said, his voice low and threatening.

"You don't know what it would cost me. I guarantee you can't pay enough." I watched Parth. I couldn't tell whether he was worried about Capps or angry about my defying him. "I'll make a bargain with you. If you let me kill Capps, I'll heal your cut-up arm. But if you insist that I heal Capps, then I'll cut off your arm before it putrefies and kills you."

"Kill him," Parth said without hesitating.

Capps hissed and closed his eyes.

"Bib," Ella said, standing beside Pil and nodding at Capps. "That man preserved us from death. However great the cost to save his life, I will pay it if I can."

I stared at her for a few seconds. "That's as honorable as hell, isn't it? I don't find honor to be of much use, as you have pointed out to me on occasion. But I'll go ahead and save him just because you asked."

I knelt to work on that miserable thug, glanced back at Ella, and was shocked to find tears in my eyes. I told myself it was a reaction to the battle, although I had never done that after any other fight. Within five minutes, Capps was whole again.

"Get up and walk around," I said, still kneeling. I felt like I was being cut in half. "Take Parth with you. You can celebrate your return from the ass-edge of death."

I wavered on whether to heal Parth. It would be ridiculous to help him since the man had threatened to kill me. If anything, I should murder him without delay, while he was wounded. But I had made the bargain to heal him, and when a sorcerer starts breaking bargains, he's asking to be destroyed. Besides, I didn't want to squander a strong fighter like Parth when every tree might conceal an angry Hill Person. I decided to put the decision aside for a bit.

I beckoned to Stan, who was checking on his fellow soldiers. Most of them were probably dead. The Hill People were thorough.

Stan trotted over and stood beside me as I knelt. "Thanks, Bib, for stuffing my guts back in me—that was a friendly thing. They feel fine, so I guess you got them back in the right place, tight and tidy as a nun's knickers."

"That's fine," I said. "You can do me a favor then by helping me." I glanced at Parth, who was giving orders to the survivors. I winced as pain dragged through my belly. "I can't stand up by myself, and I don't want that stack of crusty turds to know it."

TEN

I finally became convinced that we were no longer traveling through the normal world when I flopped into a stream full of magical succoring fish. The sky, water, and trees looked the same as ours, but tiny differences had been bothering me. Some weren't so tiny. We still hadn't spotted an animal in the forest or a bird in the air.

Other points didn't mean much to me until I added them up. We had moist, cool morning air without any dew. The breeze and the lake's surface moved in slightly different directions. Uncounted leaves covered the ground, but none were dead. They all looked as if they had fallen this morning, and the trees were still thick with them. I had never seen that type of tree before, either, even though I'd traveled all over the continent.

After Stan helped me stand, I had him bring Parth to me. I made the captain wait while I healed Pil's shoulder. Then I gritted my teeth and healed the man's arm, hoping he wouldn't use it to kill me someday. Ella refused to let me heal her wound, saying she knew what it would cost me. She couldn't know, of course, but it was a charitable sentiment. Then, bent over the furious pain in my belly, I hobbled to one of the dead soldier's horses. Stan helped me onto its back.

Parth flushed red and near choked getting the words out, but he asked me to stay with his group, at least until the Hill People threat had passed. I made him ask three times before I agreed.

I immediately made Parth wish he hadn't asked me to stay. He ordered two of the six remaining soldiers to return the way they came, find the army, and report on what waited ahead of them.

"Why do you hate these unfortunate boys so much, Parth?" I pointed at the two soldiers and then wished I hadn't when pain bounced around in my belly. "Did they spit in your beer? Most of the Hill People are waiting back there for us."

The captain glared at me. "I should send you then, but I fear I would become morose without the prospect of killing you at a more auspicious time. Are there not Hill People awaiting us upstream as well?"

"Maybe one or two, but after we suffered this slaughter, they'll expect us to gallop home." I pretended to gaze that direction with great wisdom while I bit back some whimpering. "If we run the other direction, they'll likely hesitate to fight us until their whole force catches up. Then they can wipe us out at leisure, bragging to each other about their sweethearts as they go."

"Very well." Parth's eyes twinkled, and he sounded excited. "You are less trustworthy than a frayed rope, but I do not believe you would sacrifice your life to spite me." He called out, "Follow me and don't fall behind. I might not turn back to save you."

The devastated company rode away from the battle with the Hill People, traveling in fear of another four, or eight, or forty Hill People catching up with us. Parth and Capps rode in front. Stan and three soldiers followed them, while Pil, Ella, and I rode behind. Two soldiers trailed us all.

Parth set a hard pace. It was the right thing, but it tortured me. Pain slammed through my arm, shoulder, and guts every time my horse put a hoof on the ground. Soon, the stream bent back around to the north.

Just before sunset, the mare Parth had given me was running

along the stream's edge when she stepped in a hole. She staggered, and I tumbled sideways out of the saddle into two feet of water.

That shock distracted me from the pain. I stood up and saw something sticking out from my face. I pulled a small yellow fish off my right cheek, another off my forehead, and a third off my nose. They were as long as my hand. Looking down, I realized that dozens of these fish had clamped onto me with their mouths. I looked like a fishy hedgehog.

Ella had trotted back, leading my horse, and she laughed down at me. I kept on yanking fish off myself, but when I got down to my waist, I realized that all the pain had disappeared. I patted my shoulder, arm, and belly like some wheezy street performer before I accepted that the fish really had removed the pain.

"Ella! Come here!" I said.

She leaned back in the saddle. "I think not."

"Jump in! Trust me!" I beckoned.

She gaped. "What did you say? Did you just utter the words, 'Trust me'? You, the very spirit of mendacity?"

"Uh-huh." I slogged out of the water, bowlegged because of the fish still clinging to the insides of my thighs. When I reached land, I held out my hand to her.

After a few seconds, she dismounted and took my hand. "I have lost every damned wit I ever possessed," she muttered.

"Dive on in," I said, but she was already jumping. She came up covered in yellow fish, just like me. When I told her to check her wound, it had been healed without even a scar.

By that time, Parth had galloped back to us. "You two, mount. Ride. Or die." Ella started to speak, but Parth jumped in. "I don't care if you're the king's mother, sister, and paternal grandmother all in one. Ride."

"May we de-fish ourselves first?" I asked.

He gritted his teeth. "Hurry up!"

Ella and I began plucking the fish off each other, and halfway through, we went crazy and had to start laughing. We couldn't stop laughing, either. Parth had been slapping his thigh over and over as he ground his teeth at us, but then he started laughing as well.

"Well, that was diverting!" Parth said, catching his breath as we climbed out of the water. "You're more amusing than kittens. Perhaps the king will tell me not to kill you after all." He hinted at a smile.

As we mounted, Parth said, "Where are Abrim and Gale? I didn't pass them."

We rode back along our trail for a minute searching for them, but the two soldiers at the rear of the column had disappeared. Parth called off the brief search, and we encouraged our horses with the reins to gain a few strides while galloping to catch the others.

Parth led us on into the night. I was anxious to escape the Hill People but fearful of riding into a nighttime ambush. After some contemplation, I shouted "Wait!" at Parth. He slowed his horse to a trot.

I called out, "If we could see the Hill People coming, it would be smarter to stay put for the night instead of galloping on blind. Do you agree?"

"Of course, but we cannot see them. I can hardly see you!"

"Maybe we can hear them coming. Stop for five minutes."

I feared that Parth wouldn't heed a man whose crotch had so recently bristled with fish, but he agreed to wait.

My scheme would require that I burn through a lot of power. But I wouldn't need that power later if a Hill Man's spear was in my heart. I pulled band after band, whipping one out to each of the trees within half a mile.

I had never done this before, and if it didn't work, we would all look mighty foolish scattered around dead. "Parth, you dripping hyena, have a man hustle over to one of those trees."

"Your five minutes ended ten minutes ago, but very well. John, run to that tree and stand there."

John, a tall young man with a thick beard, sprinted toward the tree as if his lover lay naked under it. When he reached the trunk, loud creaking and grinding sounds came from high among the branches.

"Run to another tree!" I called.

"Right!" John yelled, then he raced to the next tree trunk.

One of the other soldiers, Bimmit, held a hand in front of his baby face and muttered, "Ass-kisser." Dern, his big, scarred friend, chuckled down at him.

The first tree fell silent when John left it. The second tree popped and creaked when he arrived.

"Well, damn my wife five times," Parth said.

"A fine sentiment." I nodded. "Each tree will sound off when somebody walks under it, and they'll do it pretty far off. Far enough to warn us so we can mount and flee."

Parth scratched his hair. "All right, I heard it, so I suppose I shall believe it. Everyone, dismount and rest yourselves. Do not unsaddle your mounts." He grinned at me. "You are inordinately useful! I take back one or two of the horrible things I said about you."

I ignored that.

A minute later, Pil sidled up to me and whispered, "I know it's wrong of me to ask, and I won't feel hurt if you tell me to go straight to hell, but how did you do that?"

Even though asking another sorcerer about his magic and his deals was one of the rudest things a sorcerer could do, I didn't mind Pil inquiring. I might need to ask her a similar question someday, and I could hold this over her head.

I said, "The basic spell isn't too hard. Trees sense heat, even the heat of a person. Also, they can make their branches bend and twist by expanding one side or the other, and that makes noise. Putting the two together is simple. The hard part is keeping it going all night. You go get some rest on my behalf, because I'll be awake speaking sweet nothings to trees."

Pil looked as if she wanted to ask another question, but instead she squeezed my arm and walked away.

Before dawn, a tree to our south sounded off. A second one joined the first. By the time a third tree was groaning, we all were in the saddle and galloping north. The fourth tree went off due west of us. We had almost been surrounded again.

When the first shreds of light began showing me the world beyond the nearest rider, I realized that the stream was widening into a great pond. Then it became a small lake, and soon a lake too wide to see across. Parth never slowed down, and I didn't know what useful thing I might say if he did.

Within an hour, we spotted a small cluster of brilliant white buildings. The morning air was clear and chill, and we could make out the place from over a mile away. I smelled lilacs, and I soon saw them growing around the building. We approached at a trot, weapons drawn, but nobody met us. If fact, not a single person stood in sight.

The seven cottages and the big boathouse were all as finely built as any structure I had ever seen, even in the wealthy parts of the Empire. The little ghost village unsettled me. It was too nice to be anything besides a trap. When I dismounted, I pulled some more bands and charmed a semicircle of trees to stand watch a quarter mile inland. They need only be active for a short while, so the cost in power wouldn't be high.

We searched the cottages and found not one person. Every building lacked furniture, food, and goods too. The walls inside had been painted the same aggressive white as the outside.

"No person has lived in this place." Parth smiled as he swung a door open and closed. "I wish we could investigate it. I believe it might teach us something momentous."

"I agree," Pil said, "except for the part about investigating and the part about something momentous. And the teaching part too. But yes, nobody has lived here."

Parth grinned at her, but before he said anything, Stan shouted, "Hey, come look at this big, purple, rat-humping boat!"

A forty-foot longboat filled the boathouse. It had five benches and five banks of oars lying inboard, but it wasn't rigged for sail. The inside was natural wood, but the hull had been painted the color of a lacquered plum.

"That's a trap," I said.

Parth nodded. "Trap."

"Indeed," Ella said.

Pil stepped to the side to get a better look.

"Nah, it's just a boat," Capps said.

Stan whacked Capps on the shoulder. "You heard all of them sorcerers and the captain say it's a trap, didn't you? Who the hell are you to say it's a boat and not a trap? You drop-assed idiot!"

Capps shouted back, "What makes a trap, eh? What?"

"Look at how shiny it is!" Stan yelled, pointing at the longboat. "Mouse-brain, you don't go climbing inside of shiny things! You just don't! How did you ever live to get so old?"

Stan's explanation contained a little truth, if freely interpreted and allowed a couple of metaphors.

One of my trees sounded south of us.

Parth jerked his head in that direction. "If someone wants us to flee in this boat, they can swim to perdition. Come on." We trailed him back to our horses at a run, but before we mounted, a tree northward sounded off. Just a second later, I heard one to the west.

"Damn it," Parth said, one foot in the stirrup.

Bimmit struggled with his side-stepping horse, which smacked into Dern's horse. They cursed each other, two geysers of profanity.

"We can penetrate their line if we hasten." Ella was in the saddle and wheeled her horse.

At least six more trees in all directions groaned and creaked. There might have been more. The sounds ran together.

"They can be here in a minute, or at most two," I said. "I don't think we can defeat eight or ten Hill People. No, I'm damn sure we can't."

Parth nodded at the forest. "So, It seems we have certain death . . ." He nodded back at the boathouse. "Or probable death." One second later, he sprinted toward the boathouse with Capps just behind him.

I was right behind Capps.

When I skidded into the boathouse, I saw Parth start unmooring the boat with professional skill.

"I'll slow them down!" I shouted.

"Yes, proceed. Do that." Parth didn't look up from his work.

"Ella, don't let him leave without me." I drew my sword and was nearly trampled by Stan and the three other soldiers as they raced into the boathouse.

Pil stepped up beside me and began stringing her bow with smooth, certain movements. "Do you have a plan?"

"Not a good one. You kill as many as you can. I'll whack the others with whatever I can find."

"No fine strategies for complementing our skills, then? That's disappointing, I was hoping to learn something from you since you're such a wise, old, very old sorcerer."

I glanced at Pil and saw her face sweating, and she had paled to almost white. But her voice and hands were steady, and I would never have guessed that she was fearful.

Half a minute later, a Hill Man poked his head up from the other side of a house's roof. Pil put an arrow in his forehead.

"Damn nice to have a magic bow, eh?" I said.

Pil nocked another arrow. "Do you want me to make one for you, a long, scarred-up magic bow that creaks every time you draw it?"

Any noise the Hill People might have been making was smothered by Pil's sarcasm.

Two more Hill People charged around that same house, one on each side. Pil shot one in the chest, and he fell. The second was halfway to us when she killed him.

"Scoot back, back, back!" I snapped. Pil and I hurried forty feet along the wooden walkway toward the boathouse door. Only the lake and some wooden posts lay beneath us. On the way, I pulled four red bands of power. Five Hill People ran around and between two houses, and I cursed as I pulled four more bands.

"Get down and look away!" I yelled, and I flung the bands at the front walls of the two houses. It cost a ridiculous amount of power, compressing the wood a hundredfold in an instant. I looked away as the walls exploded in every direction. The concussion slapped me, and splinters were hurled against my body. A couple were big enough to stab through my clothes, but not enough to give me more than shallow punctures.

I peered at the destruction. Three Hill People lay on the dirt, and only one was moving. Another had fallen to his knees and was swaying with a big splinter through his arm. A fifth shook his head and sprinted toward us. Pil stood up and killed him as he reached the walkway.

"Run to the boat!" I said.

Pil nocked another arrow.

"Fine, stand there and give them two targets!" I knelt as seven more Hill People loped toward us from around the houses. They scanned side to side as they came. One pointed at us and shouted, but the others kept gazing around. I guess they thought we couldn't have created that much hell by ourselves.

Their dawdling gave me time to pull three blue bands, smack my palm against the wooden walkway, and rot twenty-five feet of it between us and the land. Pil had already shot an arrow into another Hill Man, another perfect kill. The next man dashed onto the walkway toward us, broke through the rotten wood, and plunged right into the lake.

"Go!" I shouted.

I followed Pil into the boathouse at a run. Hill Men yelled what I imagined to be the dirtiest curses in their language, and a javelin clattered off the doorframe as I hustled through it. The longboat had been pushed out of the slip, and everybody sat at oars except Ella and Parth. Ella had drawn her sword and was blocking Parth's way to the boat as she screamed abuse at him.

"Board!" I yelled. "Board now!"

Ella and Parth jumped in the boat, and it listed. Pil followed, and I almost knocked her into the bottom of the boat as I leaped in.

"Pull! Pull hard!" I stood up in the stern where I could watch the Hill Men when we cleared the boathouse. The boat crawled at first, but after three oar strokes, we gained speed.

"Go! Go! Go!" Dern yelled until John whacked him.

The first javelin would have landed on the middle bench, but I had some blue bands ready. I rotted the wooden shaft just behind the flying javelin's head. It slammed into Stan's chest, and he yelped, but when the shaft fell apart, it had wobbled in the air and lost a lot of its force. I did the same to three more javelins. Two of them landed in the bottom of the boat, and Parth twisted so that the third hit him on the cheek instead of the eye.

Then we rowed out of range.

About half a mile from shore, Parth halted the rowers. By that point, Pil and I were manning oars too. Nobody spoke for five seconds before Capps said, "What the hell do we do now, huh? I mean, Captain?"

"I think I'll enjoy my ability to breathe," I said. "You can do the same, and you might show a little gratitude, you grimy snot stain."

"Settle yourselves," Parth said. "Our mission remains the same. We're scouting."

Pil sat up straight. "It seems pretty hard to scout when we've lost our horses and food, doesn't it? It's not so much scouting as it is strolling around looking at things, or rowing around, I guess."

"There's no need to be a defeatist," Parth said.

"So, you call what happened back there a victory? If I ever need to hire a soldier, I hope I find one better than you." Pil's chin was up and her face heated.

"I will not force you to come with us. You can stay here." Parth nodded at the water. "If you want."

I was ready to help Pil against this jaw-grinder of a soldier, but I couldn't tell what she was trying to accomplish.

"Oh, I'll come along for the pleasure cruise," Pil said. "But you shouldn't overestimate the importance of your mission and then expect your captives—I said, *your* captives, *us*—to save your oh-so-elevated ass in one battle after another."

Parth cocked his head at Pil for two seconds. Then he gave her a wry smile. "Don't worry, Pil. I won't."

Pil sighed and then looked at the bottom of the boat. Or maybe she was looking at her hands, which were shaking.

I felt embarrassed that Parth had understood why Pil was pissed sooner than I had. Pil hadn't hesitated to kill those Hill Men. But now she had time to think about it.

"We have a choice," Parth said. "Thoughts about rowing straight across the lake?"

I stood on the bench and peered across the water. "This lake is at least twelve miles wide."

"Is that a guess?" Parth said from the bench behind me. "Or do you have some special knowledge?"

I made my eyes as innocent as a puppy's. "Well . . . I am a sorcerer."

Actually, I knew for a fact that I was correct. I couldn't see the far shore even though my eyes were hale enough to make out a shore about twelve miles away in good conditions, if it existed.

The soldiers were whispering among themselves. Capps turned his back to them, and Parth ignored them. The captain scratched his jaw and examined the near shoreline. "If we row along the coast, we're inviting the Hill People to follow us. So, we'll go straight across the lake."

I raised my hand. "Hold on. I said the lake's wider than twelve miles. That means it could be a hundred miles or a thousand."

Parth glanced at the sun. It was still early morning. "We shall row across the lake until midday. If the far shore fails to appear by then, we'll return here and follow the coast northward. Perhaps the Hill People will have chosen to go kill someone other than us."

So, we rowed toward the middle of the unnamed lake of unknown size. The sun seemed brighter and warmer out on the water. By late morning, sunburn plagued everybody's face but mine, which was brown to start with and weathered like a boot.

About the time I thought we might turn around, Parth said, "I believe I see the shore. Starboard bow."

I clambered forward and edged John off his bench so I could stand on it. "Well, it's shore if you mean there's water touching the land. But it's not a long shore. It's either an island or a peninsula poking out into the lake."

Parth stood as if that would help him see the land. "We should scout it."

"Hell, don't do that!" I said.

Parth shook his head. "We must determine what is there. Perhaps water or food."

"And there may be poisonous plants and serpents big enough to eat us, or monsters, or cruel sorcerers," said Pil.

Ella said, "Parth, if our force was intact, I would concur, but with these few remaining—" She jerked. "Did you hear that?"

"No, pray what did it sound like?" Parth asked.

"A voice."

"Man? Woman? Parrot?" Parth said.

"I couldn't tell, just a—" Ella whipped her head around, searching. "Once again . . ."

"What in the flaming frog farts did it say?" Stan yelled. Everybody looked at him. "What? Is it the wrong question? Should I have asked about her kittens back home?" Dern encouraged him with a slap on the back.

"It . . . it said, 'Gruesome whore.' I think that was it." Ella gazed at the barely visible land. "No one else heard it?"

We all professed not to have heard the 'Gruesome whore' comment.

"Perhaps it was intended for me alone," Ella said. "I think we must investigate."

"We must row the hell away from here and tell the voice to kiss our asses." I cupped my hand and bellowed toward the shore, "Kiss our asses!" in a fine, seagoing voice.

"It must be gar-gar," Parth said, standing to examine the land. When Ella and Capps gave him blank looks, he added, "Perhaps it's *the* gar-gar that the Hill Man mentioned. The one living beyond the stream. We should give it a significant berth. Row on."

Parth and Ella fell into a disciplined but nasty argument about the gar-gar. I had been thinking about this subject ever since I saw the land, and damn Parth's eyes and elbows for mentioning it. The Hill Man had called it the Gar-chap-gar. I didn't know what that meant, but if it had run up against the Hill People and lived, not much good could come from visiting it.

Besides, scouting this place and meeting the Gar-chap-gar wouldn't help me finish my tasks. This was a distraction, maybe a fatal one, and definitely an aggravating one.

As I leaned over to join the argument, Pil touched my arm. "I need to see this Gar-chap-gar, whatever it is, or he is, or whatever.

All these people died to get me here for some reason, and that reason's not to sit my ass in a boat. Please help me."

I almost told her that all those people sure as hell hadn't died for her, and that going ashore for such a reason was a stupid thing to do. But maybe it was only stupid for me to do it. Maybe it was her goddamn destiny. Some sorcerers claimed that every one of us has a destiny. I doubted it, unless our destiny is to be dead. Either way, I couldn't make that decision for her. "You'll try even if it means you kill more people today? Or get killed?" I asked.

She swallowed and nodded.

I felt certain that landing would be a foolish thing for me. I opened my mouth to tell Pil she'd need to find other allies, but I found myself saying, "Hell, I've done more ridiculous things for people I hated. And I don't hate you too much." I patted Pil's hand and glanced at Parth, who had just called Ella a stumbling, tight-assed cow. "Parth, all the rest of us intend to land on that shore."

"I don't," Capps grumped.

"Shut up," I told him. "So, Captain, unless you want to cut out all our hearts with a knife and mean words, we're landing this boat."

Parth sneered at me, paused, and then smiled. Then he laughed hard, a pure and happy sound. "I yield. If we make this foray all together, it cannot fail to meet a joyful end." Still sitting, he bowed to Ella, "I apologize, Mistress. My bovine remark was churlish and uncalled for."

Ella said, "That is—" She held her breath, turned, and stared at the shore with raised eyebrows. "You are forgiven, Parth. Your comment was genteel compared to the one I just heard."

ELEVEN

The shore Parth had spotted was a little island, about two miles across. We grounded the longboat on a narrow, pale beach. A meadow of tall grass and wildflowers covered the whole island. Stepping from the boat onto the beach was like walking from late spring straight into midsummer. A breeze set the tall grass, weeds, and sunflowers waving everywhere. It smelled green and dusty.

Clouds of butterflies pocked the meadow, flapping so close that I could reach out at any time and almost touch two or three. Some were the size of my thumbnail, and a few grew as big as my hand. I needed a moment to make sense of all the colors and patterns. It was a charming scene, except for the squatty black stone tower in the middle of the island.

When confronted by such a structure, the smart choice is to turn around and go elsewhere, to have a drink if possible. But Pil was already striding toward the building, saying, "I guess we'll either investigate that monstrous thing or get back in the boat, because there's nothing else interesting around here."

I drew my sword. Ella raised an eyebrow at me and then drew

hers. We followed Pil, and when I glanced back, everybody else was following us.

That tower seemed to be the only man-built thing on the island. No person was working near it, chatting around it, or lounging on top of it. In fact, I couldn't see a single man or woman on the entire island. Pil hiked across the meadow toward the tower, holding out her hands so butterflies could float past them. I flanked her, hoping to spot anything deadly in time to do something useful about it. Bimmit flanked me, waving his hands around to shoo butterflies.

The square tower measured about twenty feet on each side and twenty feet high. When Pil reached it, she stood with her arms crossed, tapping one shoulder, as she examined the closest wall of black stone blocks. I scooted back a bit to keep the whole scene in view.

Parth stood beside me. "I see no doors or windows." He craned his head.

"We'll guard the perimeter, Captain," Bimmit said, his eyes big and locked on the tower.

Parth nodded. Dern and Bimmit ran, having decided that the "perimeter" lay fifty paces behind us toward the boat. John stood behind Parth and two steps to his left.

Ella and Stan had begun walking around the tower, searching the walls and ground. "Nothing on the other sides," Ella called out.

"No tunnels, neither!" When Stan came back around the tower, he was jumping up and down every few steps.

"Do you think there's a magical entrance?" Pil murmured to me.

"Maybe. Or maybe somebody made a bad enemy and got bricked up in there. I wonder what's on the roof?"

Pil nodded at me, walked up to the tower wall, and jumped.

"Good goddamn!" John yelped, and the other soldiers shouted similar profanity.

Pil's enchanted boots didn't lift her high enough to land on her feet, but she caught the edge of the roof with her arms and elbows. She pulled herself up and over onto the top.

"See? See?" Stan bellowed at the soldiers standing far back

toward the boat. "I told you she's a sorcerer! If you still want to try a sly grope, Bimmit, you go right on and do that. I promise to bury your tongue and your willy, because that's all that'll be left of you. So, you mind whatever shitty baboon manners you have and put it out of your head that she's the prettiest girl you ever saw. And don't call her a sorceress, neither, it's disrespectful! They're all sorcerers, woman or man, and that's what's what."

Off to the side, Capps gave Stan a slow clap.

Stan scowled. "Oh, shut it, or I'll break those hands off and make two back scratchers."

If Pil heard any of Stan's lecture, she didn't show it when she looked down at us a minute later. "There's nothing up here—not a door, or a hole, or a pipe, or a bump, nothing. Maybe this is just a block of rocks and we leave it alone."

Parth frowned. "Bib, this enchanting, soul-shriveling sort of business is along your line of expertise. What should we do? And whatever it is, you go first."

"I think we should declare that we've done a manly job of scouting, get back in the boat, and row away from here." I stared up at Pil and raised my voice. "This pile is made of black rocks with no way in or out. Does somebody need to paint EVIL TOWER— BEWARE! on the wall for you?"

Parth said, "As for me, they emphatically do not. I can recommend that we leave this island undisturbed." He turned toward Bimmit and spun his hand in the air, one finger up. Bimmit nodded and trotted off toward the boat with Dern.

Pil jumped down and staggered but didn't fall. "I'm not finished." She closed her eyes and pressed her hand against one of the black stones for most of a minute while we all watched. Five butterflies landed on her, including a deep blue beast the size of both my hands together. At last, she said, "I think I can break in if I get a big enough rock, enchant it, and then beat the wall with it. Help me find a rock, melon-size." She wandered into the tall grass with John and Stan following like helpful puppies.

"Wait!" I yelled. "Do you really want to hit an evil tower with a magic rock?" Experience told me that such actions ended badly. Or maybe fear was telling me that.

It didn't matter. Nobody waited.

I shouted, "At least tell me what you learned by groping that awful thing!"

Without looking back, Pil called out, "Help me find a rock!"

I didn't want to touch the nasty, wicked tower, but my mouth puckered at the sound of Pil giving me orders. I settled my thoughts and then brushed the black wall with my fingertips.

The tower collapsed.

Ella screamed my name, and I heard others shouting. I should have been killed, but the stones dropped and clattered in a circle around me. Not one of them touched me. After fifteen seconds of tumult, the last stone came to rest. A tiny copper cup landed at my feet with a tinkling sound. I picked it up and saw a full-leafed tree engraved on the side.

I looked up when a stone shifted on the great pile where the tower had stood, and I saw a woman standing on top. She was naked and blue-skinned, with an inhumanly perfect form and an impatient look on her face.

"Limnad?" I said. "Are you all right?"

Limnad, the Spirit of the Blue River, had once hated me, then pitied me, and then gotten damned tired of me pitying myself. She blinked and smiled. "Yes, I am better now. Thank you for freeing me, Bib. Is the swishing, port-town harlot here?"

"Well . . . Ella's here."

"Vile betrayer of the innocent," Ella said through clenched teeth. "Have you broken Desh's heart and destroyed him yet?"

"I don't know where Desh is." Limnad sounded like she might cry. "I lost him—"

I jumped in. "Limnad, please look at me. Was that you calling to Ella?"

"Yes, it was me. I'm sorry if I hurt your feelings by not calling to you, Bib, but blistering hatred carries farther than love. Well, fond respect."

"Limnad . . ." I paused to weigh my next question, but while I was still weighing, Limnad's face went slack and she paled three shades.

Springing down the pile of stones with otherworldly grace, Limnad placed her hand on my chest and whispered, "Bib . . . run!"

The spirit swirled around me like water rushing down a hillside, and she ran at a shocking pace. Within a few seconds, she had fled the island and disappeared into the lake.

I almost ran too, but I didn't know what from or why, and ignorance rooted me. I locked eyes with Ella. "Did she tell you what was so terrifying here?"

Ella shook her head. "She told me to climb up my own nether place with a shovel. Nothing else."

"She was getting boring," a man's lazy voice said from beside Pil, who jumped and stared at her arm.

Several dozen butterflies flapped and fluttered around us, but the enormous blue one on Pil's arm caught my eye. I got the sense that I had caught its eye too, since it fluttered up to float right above me.

I had witnessed a dog talk in the recent past, so a talking butterfly didn't seem unfeasible.

"That river spirit?" I said. "Boring? That's unlikely. I have always found her clever and challenging. She knows some good games." I prepared to pull a few white bands. If things went too badly, I wanted to call a wind that was stiff enough to blow a butterfly ten miles.

"Does anyone know a good joke?" the butterfly asked in a voice that sounded like he might start yawning.

Capps pointed at Stan. "He's funny-looking."

"That's not amusing," the butterfly said. "It's really rather pitiful. Anyone else?" It flapped ten feet away.

Parth's mouth had been hanging open, but now he grinned at the butterfly. "How many sorcerers does it take to build a fire?" He held his breath as if he'd just told his sweetheart she had a gray hair.

The butterfly shaded to a brighter blue. "Ooh, how many?"

"Three." Parth smiled, but not with his eyes. "They're small, but they burn really well."

"I've heard it before." I don't know if all butterflies can sigh, but it sounded like this one did. "Only it was Denzmen, or husbands, or sailors, or . . . you see."

Parth shrugged. "I am known not to be a humorous person."

"No, you are hardly a person at all . . . anybody else?"

Pil blurted, "Are you the Gar-chap-gar?"

"Yes." The butterfly flapped upward. "But don't tell anybody."

I said, "Is there something we can call you besides Gar-chap-gar? It's a beautiful name, of course, but awkward in conversation."

The butterfly stopped flapping and hung in midair. "Dabbs. That will be fun." It fluttered in a circle between Pil and me. "You're an interesting pair. She doesn't fear me but seems nervous. You act calm but are so terrified you're about to make urine."

Dabbs was right. I hadn't felt so petrified since the God of War had threatened to obliterate me. My mouth felt like a sandy hole. I swallowed twice and said, "I've always harbored a powerful dread of butterflies. It's held me back in my profession."

"I'm sure." Dabbs flapped higher.

I recalled reading hoary old books and conversing with hoary old sorcerers, but I couldn't recall anything like Dabbs the butterfly. Flapping around and joking seemed out of character for sorcerers. Dabbs might be a spirit of some sort, but Limnad wouldn't be so scared of another spirit. She'd be respectful toward the greatest spirits but not afraid. I dreaded to think Dabbs might be a demigod. I had killed one of them a few months ago, and the others might feel snippy about it.

I hoped to Krak and his dozen dimwit offspring that Dabbs wasn't one of the gods in disguise. Such manifestations were rare, but they happened.

When I was a young sorcerer, a stray mongrel adopted me. The next day, I left him alone. He destroyed all my clothing and buried my spare weapons. He chewed off the table legs, carried them outside, and tried to drag the four-foot-wide tabletop out a three-foot door. Then he carried my pouch of money off and gave it to a man I hated. Finally, he bit every person who lived nearby, crapped all over my house, and ran away.

Gorlana told me later that Lutigan had manifested as my mongrel to give me hell. It was because Gorlana had angered him and I belonged to her. Of course, neither of them cared whether or not I suffered. Hurting me was just a way for Lutigan to mock her.

These are the beings that control the universe. It explains a lot.

If Dabbs was a god, then he might want to trade, and I'd be even deeper in debt to them. I nearly sagged just thinking about it.

Still, I might be able to tweeze some helpful knowledge about this butterfly out of Harik. I knew the god's weaknesses, and I could say no better than a mean banker. I lifted my spirit out of my body and called for Harik, heading for the place where sorcerers made trades that ruined their lives. I didn't reach it, though. I seemed to be stuck between it and the world of man. I called for Harik again, and I might have heard him answer from far away. It was too faint for me to be certain.

When I dropped back into my body, no time had passed in the world of man.

Dabbs flapped hard and fluttered just over my head. "Bad sorcerer. So, so rude. This is a god-free territory." Pain slammed from my scalp all the way to my toes like two jagged spears of lava throbbing along with my heartbeat. It took my breath and sight away. When they returned, I was on my knees with my sword lying on the grass in front of me.

Pil and Ella helped me to stand. I coughed and said, "I didn't realize gods are forbidden. I approve of the policy, of course." I rubbed my eyes.

"Your words make no sense on the surface," Dabbs said, "but they're true deeper down."

Pil cleared her throat. "Dabbs, I feel silly saying this, but I had a strong urge to come to this island, I guess to meet you. Can you tell me why this is happening to me?"

"Oh? That was entirely a mistake. You're not nearly as interesting as I thought you'd be. I'm sorry for the error, Pilithis."

Pil jumped back a step and stared at Dabbs. He must have just spoken her real name, which was a terrible thing for other sorcerers to know. Now that I knew her name, I could bind her, attach bad luck to her, and do quite a few other unpleasant things. If she was smart, she would protect herself by killing me as soon as possible.

"Damn it to Krak and Lutigan on a pony!" Parth's voice was tight but steady. "Bib, since you are my expert on things that cannot be rationally explained, tell me what this is." He was pointing at Dabbs.

"Dabbs is our host, Parth. We should be polite guests." I didn't add, *Or he'll blind us all with pain.*

"You don't have to shout," Dabbs said, fluttering above Parth. "I do believe this is the rudest realm I've visited in a long time."

My heart galloped, and I took a deep breath. "That's interesting, Dabbs. In a thousand years?"

"More like three." Dabbs fluttered through a perfect loop.

Parth grabbed my arm. "I believe we're finished here. I certainly am. If you aren't, then you may remain here with this being."

"Wait," I whispered, not that I gave a damn whether Parth waited, ran, or sank into the earth. I wanted everything to stop while I struggled with the idea that Dabbs was a Void Walker. I couldn't say it out loud, but I was almost positive.

Void Walkers were unaccountable, solitary beings that walked across the Void and between realms as easily as I could walk across this island. The world of man was a realm, and the Gods' Realm was another. At least one more existed, but sorcerers couldn't agree on what it was or how many more lurked out in the Void.

Two Void Walkers were known to have visited the world of man in the past century. One created a land of magical whimsy and random terror for almost fifty years before it disappeared while reciting a birthday poem. The other appeared one morning in the Kingdom of Paster, turned every adult into a golden daffodil, and departed before lunchtime.

I tried to smile at the Void Walker. "Well, Dabbs, we should be going. Thanks for the hospitality." I backed away. "Come on, everybody, we have to catch up to Bimmit and Dern before they row off and maroon us."

"Oh, don't go yet." Dabbs sounded as if he could be sad if he worked up to it.

Pil glanced at me and back at the butterfly. "I'm sorry, really sorry, but we have to go because we're hunting the queen's murderer."

"But you murdered her," Dabbs said.

Nobody spoke or moved.

Dabbs hovered. "That should make your task easier. Right?"

Parth shouted at Pil, "You killed her?"

Ella stepped close to me. "I wondered whether you had done it."

"Sorceress, did you murder Queen Dall?" Parth growled, raising his sword.

"No!" Pil fingered the hilt of her own sword. "Not technically."

I stepped between Pil and Parth. A scuffle sounded from behind me, but I didn't turn to look.

"Have I created a problem?" Dabbs asked. For the first time, he didn't sound as if he needed a nap. "I despise untidiness."

"Move, Bib!" Parth said. "I must place her under arrest, and you must swear not to free her. If you don't agree, I must kill her here." Parth tried to walk around me one direction and signaled John to circle me the other way. I shifted to block Parth. Pil could handle John. As I moved, I saw that Ella had pinned Stan facedown with an excruciating joint lock.

"Sorry about all this bother, Pilithis," Dabbs said. "Here." Dabbs zipped in a straight line, the way no butterfly in history has done, and hovered above Parth's head. A moment later, Parth was crushed downward, as if an invisible barrel containing a mountain had fallen on his head. In a heartbeat, Parth had become a smashed and mangled body at the bottom of a two-foot-deep, perfectly round hole.

Staring, Pil opened her mouth and made a noise like a baby chick.

Dabbs said, "You're welcome."

TWELVE

Pil knelt beside the shallow hole that Parth's corpse lay in, if the broken and squashed pile of human parts could be called a corpse. She rocked back and forth for a couple of seconds before straightening and looking up at Dabbs. Her face was stony, but one eyelid was trembling. "I didn't want you to kill him."

Dabbs fluttered through a gentle swoop. "Did I kill the wrong one? People are difficult to understand sometimes. Do you want me to kill the old one here?"

"No!" Pil and I shouted at the same time.

The butterfly sighed. "Well, what do you want?"

Pil stood and yelled, "I didn't want you to kill him!"

I stood back but whispered, "Pil, shh."

"I don't know why you want him. He's awful," Dabbs said. "You can have him back if you'd like, but not as a gift given for nothing. If I give you a life, you give me one too."

"Just leave it be, Pil!" Ella's voice shook as she stared at Dabbs.

I added, "I wouldn't give a split walnut shell for that bastard. Leave him in the hole."

Pil glanced over at Stan. "He's your leader, so what do you say about it?"

Stan scrunched his face in thought. "He's the captain, and he could give orders and such if he was alive, and that's good from an army way of thinking. But raising dead folks is unnatural and most likely evil, especially when they're all crunched up like that, so a priest might say to leave him lie." He smiled as if he had answered everyone's questions.

Pil looked up at Dabbs. "What kind of life do you want?"

"The fairest sort, of course. I want you to appreciate that, because fairness is the rarest of qualities in this existence. I'll create some for you right now. His death is as much your fault as mine. If I give him his life back now, you must give him his life too, sometime in the future."

"Shit!" I stepped up beside Pil. "I suggest you not do it. Strongly. Really damn strongly. Hell, one of us might have to kill him, but you'd be forced to jump in and save his life. Even worse, if he tries to kill you, you'll have to let him!"

Pil grabbed my upper arm hard. "I know, everything you're saying is right, but I need to do it. He's dead because I killed Queen Dall, and I couldn't save the queen, but I can save him. And don't say it's your fault! You didn't force me up those stairs!"

"So angry at the old man," Dabbs said from above us. "So afraid. Are you sure you don't want me to kill him too? As sort of an apology?"

"No, don't. I am not afraid of him." Pil didn't quite meet my eyes.

"Yes, yes, you are. I can feel it." Dabbs flew in a circle above Pil's head.

Pil shouted, "Then tell me his real name! You told him mine."

I held my breath.

Dabbs kept circling Pil's head. "Of course, I'm happy to. You! Old man! Tell us your name."

I wiped my palms on my trousers. "I regret to say that I prefer not to share it promiscuously."

"Hmph. I'm sorry, Pilithis, I tried."

Pil threw up both hands. "Why do you know my name and not his?"

"I am in your head, but I'm not in his." The butterfly flapped up to a height of ten feet. Glowing specks of varied colors appeared on the ends of Dabbs's antennae and legs. Several more specks bloomed around the edges of his wings.

I said, "Those are just beautiful. Exquisite. I'd appreciate them more if I could see closer."

Dabbs zoomed down and hovered a few inches in front of my face.

I scrutinized the specks. No two were the same shape, but they all seemed familiar.

"I don't understand," Pil said.

"You don't understand?" Ella growled. She and John stood huddled thirty feet away. Ella was pale, and John's legs were shaking. Ella went on: "I don't understand why you're having a cheery conversation with an insect . . . that murdered Captain Parth!"

Pil's face sagged and a tear fell.

I said, "You're right, Ella, this sorcerer crap must seem callous."

Pil spoke up. "Dabbs, I accept your deal. Bring Captain Parth back."

"Dandy! Something different!" Dabbs circled Parth's body, which quivered as a tiny crackling noise rose from it. Then his parts jumped, popped, and jumped twice more. Within a few seconds, Parth's head began re-forming with wet, crunching sounds. The man's mouth and eyelids stretched open, and his eyes dashed back and forth. His neck reassembled itself to the sounds of gagging and strangling.

Parth whipped his head from side to side as the smashed-up segments of his arms stacked themselves back together. His torso reinflated like a bullfrog's neck, hissing and snapping as it grew, until his pelvis sat on the ground atop his crushed legs.

I didn't hear the noises Parth's legs made as they pulled themselves back into line and lifted his body. Once his torso had returned, Parth began shrieking with his arms covering his head, and I couldn't recall hearing any person in more pain. When at last his body appeared to be complete, Parth collapsed back into the hole, trembling and moaning.

"Thank you," Pil whispered, and she ran to Parth.

"Yes, thank you, Dabbs," I said. "Meeting you was one of the most astounding events of my life, maybe the most marvelous of all, but we need to continue our journey."

"Wonderful. Where's my present?"

"I . . . didn't know to bring one, Dabbs. I'm sorry about that. I'll be happy to go find one and deliver it someplace."

"I don't like to wait. It's boring." Dabbs sounded like he'd be bored with anything I offered him.

Pil looked up from Parth. "I have these enchanted boots." She pointed at one foot.

"Really? Really?" Dabbs waggled his insect legs. "They don't suit my sense of fashion. Old man, I do quite like your weapon." Dabbs landed on the hilt of my sword. "It's nice. Tingly."

"Dabbs, it would tickle me to give you almost any nice thing I own, but this sword was a gift from the Father of the Gods. I can't just hand it to somebody."

"Krak gave it to you? That makes me want it even more. Does it have a name?"

I cleared my throat. "Yes, it does, but the name's so damn pretentious I can hardly say it without getting hives."

"Oh, say it." Dabbs fluttered up and landed on my head. "Say it to make me happy."

I held unnaturally still and tried not to imagine getting crushed. "The Blade of Obdurate Mercy. Krak will tear me into bits finer than flour if I lose this weapon."

"That doesn't sound like my problem." Dabbs's voice dropped almost to a growl. "Does it?"

If Dabbs didn't want Pil's magic boots, he sure as hell wouldn't want any of my nasty things, except for the sword. I could offer to assist him somehow, although I hated to go chasing off on some intricate task for this murderous creature. But I hated even more the idea of losing the sword.

If I didn't do something, Dabbs might smash me to bits and pluck the sword out of my remains. I opened my mouth, but an avalanche fatigue made me close it again. I almost told Dabbs to do me a favor and take the awful sword. Life would be a damn sight easier without it, and maybe Krak wouldn't mind too much. I enjoyed that thought for a second, and then I tried to smile with more vigor than I had left in me. I had been awake for most of two days.

Before my mind drifted further, I said, "Let me do a service for you, Dabbs, by way of a gift."

"Something I can't do for myself?" The butterfly flapped up and circled twenty feet above us. "I can do anything worth doing, anything at all."

"How about something that's beneath you?"

"Almost everything is . . ."

I kept quiet.

Dabbs said, "Well, I permitted a man to enter my territory. He dug things out of the ground, shot arrows into animals and people, danced, and engaged in a shocking amount of fornication. It was all diverting for a while."

"But not anymore," Pil said. She had Parth sitting up, but his head was hanging. John and Stan were helping her.

"No, not anymore."

Pil grimaced at the butterfly. "When did you give this tavern ape permission to do all those nasty things?"

"Just about 197,602,400 wing flaps ago."

"Ah." Pil examined the toes of her boots. "Around two hundred and eighty days, then?"

I swear the damned butterfly purred. "Yes!"

Pil stared at the Void Walker with no expression. "That sounds like a long time. Are you sure he's hasn't been randomly killed?" She wasn't wholly successful at keeping the sarcasm out of her voice.

"Probably not," Dabbs said, giving a nice impression of shrugging when he didn't have shoulders. "I've never known reality to be that accommodating."

I cut in. "What should we do to this dirt-digging fornicator? Kill him? Make him eat soap?"

"As long as he never comes near my lands again, I'll be satisfied."

"I'm anxious to do this service for you," I said. "Excited, really I am, but I can't help asking . . . you can probably wave a wing and make this fellow's head fly off. Why are you having us do this?"

"I hate to rescind an invitation. It's untidy."

"Of course," I said. "Where do we find this newly boring individual?"

"North. He and his people live to the north atop a big, knobby hill, with a nice cliff beside a river. Three hundred feet high. He was terribly proud of that. He mentioned it five times in twenty-three minutes. That's 0.217 times a minute. He was wretchedly proud of it. It's mystifying."

Ella nudged my arm and pointed at the air around us. A sparse cloud of small silver butterflies had gathered.

I held up one hand. When a butterfly landed on it, I saw a brown circle on each wing. I whistled silently. Existence hates a coincidence. If the brown-circle hooligans belonged to the Void Walker, we'd be wise to leave them be. Or sing them songs.

Dabbs fluttered in a disorderly circle. "I don't think you're paying attention."

I glanced up with my mouth open.

"How many people are around this grunting bastard?" Stan asked. Ella and I stared at the soldier while I waited for us to get squashed to death. Stan shrugged his trembling shoulders. "Good to know in case we have to fight 'em, right? Well, you weren't paying attention!"

"Two thousand two hundred and nine," Dabbs said. "You must hurry."

"Is time a factor? Is he planning something?" Ella asked.

"No, I'm just telling you to hurry. I'm tired of you. Hurry on before I decide your presence is worse than this idiot's arrows and dancing."

I helped Stan pick up Parth by the arms, and we ran, half dragging the captain with us. I hoped that everybody was right behind me, but I didn't look back to be sure.

Bimmit and Dern had not rowed off without us. When I considered it, I realized that I had been foolish to talk about them marooning us. I'm sure they would have been pleased to leave us, but with only two men rowing, the longboat would move like a crippled duck.

When I halted, Dern said, "We positioned ourselves to guard the boat."

"Sure, that was a wise and daring move," I said.

Bimmit quirked his lips. "It might have been stolen by ruffians. Or pirates."

I nodded. "Or a million butterflies might have carried it off into the clouds."

Dern squinted at me, maybe wondering if I was serious. "What's wrong with the captain?"

"He pissed off a bug, and it stomped on him," I said. "Help him into the boat."

Parth still wasn't talking and wouldn't meet anybody's eyes.

"Bib, you needn't be so harsh." Ella walked over to stand facing Dern. "Captain Parth suffered a wound while facing an unanticipated, mystical foe—in the guise of a butterfly. A gigantic one. He is convalescing and should recover soon."

Stan said, "He was squashed deader than hell and stuck back together like a corncob doll. That's got to drag a man down worse than a five-day bender."

Bimmit and Dern stared at Stan with pressed lips and furrowed brows.

Ella went on: "Stan is correct in the essence."

John said, "They're right. I just about puked. I bet I have nightmares."

We rowed the longboat more than a mile away from the island, which I didn't think was nearly far enough. I didn't say anything, though, since a thousand miles might not have been far enough, either.

As we drifted, I watched Ella. She seemed composed now, but I hadn't seen many things scare her so badly as the Void Walker had. She didn't even understand what it was. I didn't plan to educate her.

I sat at the tiller. "We will travel north, to warn off Dabbs's annoying visitor. And to scout."

"Why are you giving orders?" Pil said. "You aren't Parth's second-in-command or even part of the army."

Parth lay by himself in the bottom of the boat, curled up on his side.

"But I have the most experience." Actually, Pil was making a fine point. I am a lousy leader, and not much of a follower, either. She was right, but I couldn't speak up and admit it to her. That's one of the reasons I'm a poor leader.

"Experience? That's irrelevant," Pil said. "You are not part of the army."

"Neither are you. You're technically a prisoner. And Ella isn't in the army, either, but she's a better leader than everybody else in this boat and their mothers besides."

Ella pointed at each of the soldiers. "We are performing reconnaissance for the king's army, and this is a military expedition . . ." She licked her lips as she hesitated. "So, our leader for the moment must be a soldier. Who has attained the highest rank?"

Stan stared at her, his eyes growing wider and wider. "This ain't fair! I'm no officer! I goddamn hate greasy, ass-sucking officers!"

Ella closed her eyes. "Corporal Stan, you are our leader."

"Bugger that! I bust myself down to private, right now. Less than private! Apprentice shit-house-digger."

"That's not allowed by the regulations, Stan," I said. "I wish it were. I know a few dozen generals who ought to be digging latrines. Accept it, you are our leader." I clapped Stan on the shoulder. "Corporal, tell us which way to row, and I strongly suggest you say north."

Stan stared north across the water. Not a smidge of land could be seen. "Why north again?"

"We're scouting," I said. "If we ended up here, the army might too." Stan squinted one eye at me, so I hurried to cut off any objections. "It's not impossible! They won't want to turn around and retreat, so we should scout north for them. And while we're hiking north, we'll hunt for some dancing fornicator who lives on a big hill."

I didn't add that I planned to snatch the first moron I found with a brown circle and accuse him of Queen Dall's murder. I'd have to kill Parth of course, but that wouldn't be a challenge as long as he lay in the bottom of the boat like a halibut.

Stan nodded and smiled, showing his horrible teeth. "Row north. I'll steer."

"Do you know how?" I asked.

"Well . . . shit, no, I don't."

"Sit back here. I'll teach you."

With the boat manned three oars to a side, we made fine speed. I did not teach Stan the finer points of manning the tiller, nor even the blunter points. Five minutes of effort convinced me not to, unless I wanted the longboat capsized. His seamanship was so poor that I wondered how he hadn't drowned in a bathtub years ago.

Pil watched me as she rowed, her face pinched. I hoped I could figure out a way to avoid killing her before she killed me. I was the most dangerous thing in her life now, and it looked like she knew it.

We rowed north under a cloudless late afternoon sky. The breeze swung around from the east and turned warm. We all agreed that we smelled apples.

I figured we had traveled ten miles by sunset. Two more hours of rowing by starlight brought us to a forested shore. The terrain looked identical to every bit of wide-spaced forest we had ridden through since we crossed into this magical territory.

Parth still lay in the bottom of the boat and hadn't moved. John had checked on him from time to time and found him alive and awake. But he didn't answer when spoken to.

Stan and Dern pulled the boat up onto the beach. Dern was big enough that he might have done it by himself, but Stan pitched in anyway. Then we left the boat behind as we tramped away from the lake. Bimmit and John helped the captain, who could stumble along if they pointed him in the right direction and kept him from falling down.

A mile or so later, I asked, "When should we make camp, Corporal?"

"Shit, right now! Were you waiting on me to say it? Huh. I guess you were, weren't you? Let's camp, right now, pass the word. Damn it, I'd sell my mum for a slice of bacon."

"Goddamn right!" Bimmit said, starting a four-way argument over who forgot the bacon.

The soldiers were still grumbling and making sharp comments when I hit the ground. I trusted Ella to set watch and stop Stan from building a bonfire that could be seen from ten miles off, but I raised my head once before letting sleep suck me under. I saw Pil whispering with Ella. Hell, I was too tired just then to worry about killing Pil, or even her killing me. If she was young and energetic enough to try murdering me in my sleep, she was welcome to make the attempt.

I slept through the murmurs of watch being set and assignments getting doled out, but I was aware of them as a distant, unimportant part of the world. I slept through the clacking of sticks laid together and the popping of the campfire. But when a boot scuffed the dirt beside me, I rolled away from it and came up on my feet with my knife ready.

Pil stood crouched in the firelight twelve feet from me, her hands empty. She eased her long knife out of the sheath. I knew damn well she had enchanted that knife. It was sharp enough to slice through a wrist-thick branch with one cut.

"I don't want to fight. I want to talk," Pil whispered. "Can't we sit down and discuss this one time before we have to start cutting each other's throats?"

"Sure. I prefer not to kill any friends this evening if I can help it." We put away our knives and sat facing each other beyond easy reach. "You ruined my sleep to chat, Pil, so say your speech."

"I know how we can fix this. We won't have to suspect each other, and maybe you kill me or even me kill you. Don't look so doubtful. We don't have to do any of that."

I knew what she was about to say, but I held still.

"If you tell me your real name, then we'll be even." She spoke so quickly I could hardly separate her words. "We won't have to worry about one of us killing the other, because we'll each be taking the same risk!"

I leaned forward. "It's logical, Pil, and dead wrong. It won't make things better. It'll make them twice as bad."

"Why?" She raised her voice, and everybody looked.

I whispered, "Right now, I could bind you, and you're wary of me for it. You might kill me to protect yourself. I might kill you before you kill me. But if I told you my name so that you could bind me too, that wouldn't make us safe. It would make you a bigger threat to me, and you'd be very unsafe. I would kill you right away, and I hate killing my friends."

Pil stared at the ground between her crossed legs. "I guess that makes sense. We could travel to different parts of the world and never see each other again." She held up her hand before I could speak. "I know that won't work. Some god could force you to hunt me down and bind me for some asinine reason, and don't promise me you'd never do such a thing. Ella warned me four times that you can't be trusted on things like that."

That made a jagged cut, but I couldn't say Ella was mistaken. "Did she say what kind of things you can trust me on?"

Pil didn't hesitate. "She said you can be trusted to seek your own pleasure and comfort. I can expect you to lie, cheat, and sometimes steal, and to think highly of yourself to an astounding degree. You drink too much and snore. She said you are the worst enemy imaginable and crave death like nobody's business. You can be counted on to be kind to your friends if it doesn't put you out too much." She paused. "You have a hard heart, but when you love, you love forever, even when you shouldn't."

"Well . . . ." I couldn't think of anything else to say.

"Come here." I felt Pil seize my spirit as she left her own body, and she called for Fingit while pulling us toward the Gods' Realm. We failed to reach it, though.

I didn't so much feel blocked as confused. I called uselessly for Harik. It was the same experience as the last time I had tried, right down to hearing what might have been the gods answering from far-off, or they might not have. After a period of metaphysical bellowing, we returned to our bodies.

I whispered, "So, why did you do that?"

"I want to bargain with the gods to take my name out of your memory."

"That's brilliant . . . and foolish at the same time," I said. "It's an elegant solution, but one moment of carelessness might destroy me. Maybe you too."

"I'll be careful, and I'll pay the cost, if it's not too high. Otherwise, it's the knife." She drew her finger across her throat and then grinned.

I considered the plan for a moment. "It doesn't sound like it will put me out too much, and it's kind to my friend, so I'll do it. I'm not sure the gods will cooperate for a price you can bear."

Pil smiled and beat a rhythm on the ground as if it were a drum. Then she rolled to her feet and tiptoed to the other side of the camp —Stan, Dern, and Capps were sleeping there.

Ten seconds later, Ella knelt beside me. "Are you going to kill her?" she whispered.

"Not tonight. I didn't realize how little you think of me. Drink too much and snore?" I could see her blush, even in the firelight.

"She should not have repeated my words. She is good for you. She is not your daughter, nor your lover, nor even your student, really. I hope the two of you can reach terms."

"Me too." I shifted around to face her, still sitting on my butt. "She'll be a good sorcerer, if she lives."

"She is a good person. You are very, very bad for her. When you have resolved this sorcerer nonsense you are enduring together, you should send her away. Or you yourself should leave."

I didn't answer. I was surprised at how empty I felt to hear that.

Ella reached over and squeezed my arm. "I don't think little of you."

"Sitting on your behinds." Dabbs's voice came from above us. "Maundering on about your feelings, and why you won't kill one another, and who is bad for whom." The big butterfly flapped into the campfire's light. "And you tried, of all things, to chat with the gods again. I would curse you to the Void, but you just make me so tired."

The campfire died in an enormous *whump*, and sparks shot thirty feet in every direction but up.

"That could have been your heads," Dabbs grumbled. "Stop dawdling. Go deal with that vexing man. I won't warn you again."

Within three minutes, we had collected our chattels and ourselves. I led us north through the spread-out forest as fast as we could drag Parth along.

THIRTEEN

Not much has been written about the Hill People. Whenever somebody learns a little about them, the Hill People usually kill him before he can write it down. I had read one book about the Hill People, *Harps and Knives*, before I ever met a Hill Person who wasn't trying to kill me. That book described them as a singular and terrifying people. When I finally talked to a Hill Man, his behavior supported that notion.

Hill People don't see history the way most of us do. For them, what actually happened means less than how their people felt about it. For example, most people know that eighty years ago, the Hill People wiped out one-fourth of the frontier lands, slaying about five thousand people down to the last child. The Hill People remember that as "helping the land turn over to take a nap."

The Hill People cherish their own stories and myths. The "Crazy Lands" often appear in those stories and are described as places where things happen that are not normal. The Hill Man I knew described some common terrors of the Crazy Lands: the razor-beaked upside-down birds, the heroic women who copulate with you until you die, the black cows that shoot acid from their eyes, and others. It wasn't quite poetry, but it possessed a brutal charm.

As we hiked north from the lake, I discovered before midday that we were traveling through the Crazy Lands. The lands didn't become crazy all at once. I saw the sun rise. Then it rose two more times within an hour. Nobody else noticed, even when I said how pretty it was. Ella claimed that the trees were swaying together like dancers, but before I could watch them, she said they had stopped. At one point, Ella stood up taller and asked me my dogs' names. I looked down to see seven hairy dogs, each tinier than my head, all running and loping along beside me. I gazed up to think of names for them, but when I looked back down, they were gone.

I muttered, "Crazy Lands. This might be why the Hill People are wandering around looking for demons here."

"Say again?" Pil was blinking at me.

I waved it away as nothing. Then I looked over at Parth, who was standing straight and gazing around. I realized that was significant. "Parth! Are you awake? Do you remember where you were born?"

The captain stared past me. "Pelleth. Why do you ask?"

"Well . . ." I paused to consider how much detail I should give him right away, lest he be overwhelmed by recalling the experience. I decided to stay with the most basic of facts. "You were dead for a few minutes."

He met my eyes and laughed. "Preposterous. Had I been dead, I assure you I would know it."

"Bib is correct," Ella said.

"You were." Pil nodded, but her voice shook. By now, we had all stopped.

Parth glanced around at us, grinning and shaking his head.

"What is your last memory?" Ella asked.

"We . . ." Parth stared at the ground, his brow wrinkled.

The image of his screaming resurrection hit me and left my stomach shaky. "How did you get here?"

The captain stared at Pil and held his breath. At last, he said,

"That hardly matters, since I am here. I am more concerned about what we are marching toward and why."

Ella said, "North to . . . scout. And to bring a message to someone. Are you certain that you're well?"

"Who? What message?"

"Go home and don't come back," I said. "That's the message."

Parth put his hands on his hips like a peeved housewife. "Who are we searching for?"

Pil said, "A man Dabbs has a grudge against. We're warning him not to go back south because it's dangerous. Deadly." Pil set her jaw. "We almost didn't make it out alive."

I added, "Probably a rich man. He can resupply us and provide mounts."

Ella raised her eyebrows at me where Parth couldn't see.

"Well, fine." Parth put a hand up to the sunlight.

"North is this way," I said, walking past him.

Off to my left, Stan whispered, "Thank Krak's armpits and asshole, I'm glad I ain't in command anymore. Worst day of my life."

I saw the first black cow around midmorning, fifty paces to my right. She was a scrawny, near-emaciated specimen with short, downward-curving horns. She seemed not to realize that we existed. I could have pointed her out to everybody, but she didn't seem important. I told myself this was a common thing, even though I had never seen it before.

Within a few minutes, four more black cows appeared far off to my right. The next time I looked left, seven had shown up over there. Two more followed some distance behind me.

Suddenly it seemed important. "Look. Cows."

"What cows?" Parth said, glancing from side to side.

Bimmit peered ahead. "I see a bush."

"Cows." I pointed off to the right. "Those cows there." Three more edged into view on that side.

"The black cows?" Pil asked, scanning the forest to the left.

"Yes!" I pointed with both hands. "The black cows all around us."

"Fingit's hairy hammer, they're all around us!" Pil blurted.

"That's what I just said."

"Yoik!" Stan shouted. "Where did all the flipping cows come from?"

Every cow stopped and swung its head to stare at Stan. We all stopped too. I felt that if anybody twitched then, most of us would die, but that was ridiculous. They were cows.

"Keep walking," Ella murmured.

Capps snorted. "They're a bunch of damn cows. Chase 'em off."

"No, this is unusual," Parth said. "Just walk."

Capps waved his arms at one of the cows behind us and yelled, "Shoo, cow!"

Both the cows behind us tossed their heads. Four streams of black liquid shot toward Capps, and one splattered on his boot.

Parth winced and shook his head at Capps.

The cows didn't shoot any more liquid. Capps bit his hand and turned red. Then he sat on the ground and dragged off his boot, which now had a hole in the top. John helped him stand, and he limped along with John holding him up.

"That'll teach you!" John growled.

"Teach me what?"

"Don't yell at cows! I guess."

I was feeling much more clearheaded. "Everybody, let the cows alone and keep walking."

At first, that seemed a fine strategy, but its flaws appeared once fifty acid-shooting cows had surrounded us and begun gradually pressing in.

Parth examined the cow closest to him and reached out but didn't touch it. "I know this is making an obvious statement, but I want to ensure we are beginning from the same premise. If the beasts turn on us at the same time, they will burn us to ribbons."

I nodded. "I'd say that premise is accurate."

Pil said, "Do they have a leader, something like a head cow?"

"Do you mean a bull?" Ella rolled her eyes.

"I don't care which, as long as they follow it!"

"I don't see a bull." I craned my neck. "And they don't seem to be following any particular cow. I could bind one. What do you think, Pil?"

Pil shook her head. "It sounds risky."

"Pray, riskier than being wedged inside this bovine sack of destruction?" Parth appeared to be fighting a smile.

Ella said, "Let us turn about and walk the other way. They may amble past us and on to their destination."

"They may? Based on what?" Parth asked. "It's a radically intemperate suggestion."

Ella sniffed. "What would you do?"

"I shouldn't care to risk my own life so drastically. Capps?"

"Sir?"

"Turn and walk back the way we came. Don't aggravate the cows while you're about it."

"Sure, right . . ." Capps grumbled. He turned and limped toward the oncoming cows, leaving John behind. I hadn't expected the man to be capable of such obedience. Parth certainly didn't seem to care about him. Capps circled around the first cow and slipped past the second. Then he yelped and staggered to the side. "Something hit me!"

We had all stopped and turned to watch Capps. The cows lumbered on, and soon we had to walk or be knocked down and crushed by slow cows.

"Ow!" Capps yelled. "It hit me on the ass!"

Eight streams of acid fountained toward Capps, and he cursed as some hit him.

Parth raised his voice a bit. "Return to us, and hurry. And cease bellowing if you wish to live."

Capps caught us, limping fast. A nasty, fresh burn stood out on his cheek and chin.

I said, "Capps, what whacked you?"

"I don't bloody know! I didn't see it. There wasn't no cows near me. Before you ask, it felt like a plain-ass smack on the head, and didn't hear nothing, smell nothing, or taste nothing."

Pil shook her head. "Invisible. Lovely. Lovely as a rose through the eye."

Folk stories hold that all manner of beings can be invisible, especially amorous spirits that visit people in their bedrooms at night. True invisibility is rare. Most often a magical creature will hide and animate an object or person, which can seem like invisibility. Some beings, like spirits, can change form, and they may remain unnoticed while being right out in the open—just in an unexpected shape.

The subtlest means of pseudo-invisibility is convincing people not to pay attention. Some confident and persuasive magical beings can stay unseen while entirely in view. They just wordlessly convince people not to recognize what's in front of their eyes. I figured we had been briefly fooled in just that way by the cows as they arrived.

As I walked along, I began veering to my right. Within a dozen steps, I reached two cows and slipped through the gap between them.

"Bib!" Ella said, but Pil put a hand on her arm to quiet her.

I angled farther to the right and passed in front of another cow, trying to ignore the idea that acid was about to splash all over the back of my head. Instead, something I didn't see rapped me hard on the ear.

I stared straight ahead as if nothing had happened and kept walking until I saw movement from the corner of my eye. I twisted as somebody swung a short stick. Then I closed in and whacked his arm at the shoulder.

It couldn't be an invisible Hill Person since we weren't all dead. He grabbed at me with his other arm and swung the stick again. I caught his wrist and pulled it up while I pushed his locked elbow down. I dropped my weight, and the man groaned as I shoved his face into the leafy dirt. I chose not to break his elbow.

The dirt-eating fellow's friends decided not to be invisible anymore. Three more short people stood shouting at me, waving their sticks, and pointing cows at me like they were siege engines. My companions had drawn their weapons and stood back-to-back in a small circle, surrounded by grumpy cows.

"Just wait, hold on!" I shouted. "Let's talk before the breaking and burning and cutting starts."

Our foes stood four feet tall and blocky with pale skin and long, black hair. They wore stained work clothes and black boots. Two, including the one I was kneeling on, were women.

The standing woman yelled, "Let her get up! Don't hurt her, either! You'll all die, every one of you dead, so just you know that!"

I said, "Well, I don't want to die, and I don't want to kill your friend here, either. But don't fool yourself, I'm damned hard to kill. If you hurt any of us, she'll die before your cows can burn me to mush. I just might kill the rest of you too before I go down. So, herd your cows away from here, and we'll go another direction."

The short folk glanced at one another before the woman said, "I can't say you're being unfair about this—as far as you see it—but you don't see too far. We paid for you. And if we see no profit, things will go truly hard for us."

"What do you mean by saying you paid for us? Who did you pay?" I asked.

"Unimportant. Not important at all. But we paid."

The woman under my knee grunted, "You've been bought and sold and bought again three times since you came into this forest."

"The hell you say." In truth, it didn't shock me all that much. It wasn't in the top fifty strangest things I'd heard in recent years. "We're on an errand for the Gar-chap-gar, so don't be interfering with us."

"I know you are!" the woman across the way said, bouncing up and down on her toes. "We had to pay a premium for that! So, you must see that we can't just let you go free."

I hated to go to war against these cow herds, considering that most or all of us would likely die. Any survivors would be scarred and maimed, of course.

Parth said, "Perhaps we can follow along and comply. Where are you taking us?"

"We're taking you where we take the cows."

"And then?" Parth asked.

The woman glanced sideways at the two men. "And then nothing."

"Ah."

"Maybe we can trade for our freedom," I said. "Some of us are sorcerers. We can help you with weather and crops. Or create magical objects."

The woman scrunched her nose as if I'd offered to feed her a dead mouse.

"Or I can take a message to the gods for you."

"Ooh," the woman said. "Can you do that now?"

That had been a stupid offer. Dabbs had been clear about how much he hated us calling the gods. "Well, now isn't the best time."

The woman yelled, "Then why did you say it?" Most of the cows stamped the ground, and a few lowed.

Parth smiled at her. "Perhaps we can purchase our freedom."

"What with? Big words and dirty faces?"

Parth chuckled. "How amusing, no, of course not. We are traveling to visit an important, very wealthy friend of this woman." Parth nodded to Ella. "He possesses vast amounts of treasure. Immense. He shall be pleased to liberate us."

Ella's eyes grew huge for an instant before she calmed herself and nodded.

The woman spit on the ground, just missing Parth's boot. "Where is this friend?"

"To the north," Parth said. He raised his eyebrows at Ella, and she nodded hard. He made an elegant gesture. "A bit distant, but accessible."

Parth was lying without compunction, more than I tended to, but he wasn't as good at it. I said, "Listen, Cow Mistress, our friend must live farther away than this horrible place you're taking us. How about this? Take all of us to your destination but don't kill us or butcher us even a little. Two of us will go on to our friend and bring back enough wealth to double your investment."

The woman and the two men grumbled at each other. The other woman under my knee grunted.

I added, "If you agree to that, I won't kill the four of you."

The Cow Mistress jerked back. Then she conferred with her friends in a language unknown to me except for their tight-voiced fear of death. I could understand that in any language. I grasped the hilt of my sword but didn't draw it. She barked a hard word as if she were spitting out a rotten plum and then agreed to my terms.

Death threats are effective negotiating tactics in far more circumstances than one might expect.

We walked with the herd until late afternoon. Parth defended his plan against Pil's criticism that it was both reckless and stupid. I heard the soldiers and even Capps agree with her. Sadly, it was the plan we were following.

The cow herders refused to talk to us as we walked. Everybody trudged north at the pace of a disinterested cow. They must have wanted us to arrive with some fat left to flavor us.

Near sunset, I heard hoofbeats. One might think that of course I heard hoofbeats, I was in the middle of a damned cow herd. But these hoofbeats came faster, struck the ground louder, and rang on occasion with metal horseshoes. Soon, a column of riders came into view from the west, at least two dozen of them. As they trotted closer, I saw they were soldiers—well-armed, dirty, and tired-looking.

At even closer range, I could tell the column was led by a big, red-haired man on an impressive black horse. Closer than that, I saw that the red-haired man was young and didn't have his full beard yet. But he did have Parth's fine black stallion, which we had last seen on the shore when we fled across the lake.

The riders had come within rock-throwing distance before I saw that they each wore a brown circle on their arms. Finally, I could abduct one of these dopes, take him back to the king, and accuse him of murder.

The cow herders urged everybody, people and bovines, to halt. The column of soldiers waited, horses stamping, while the big young man and the lead cow herder said hello and spoke compliments they didn't mean, if their stiff postures told me anything.

Ella's breath caught. She shouted, "Karl! Lord Karl!"

The big man scanned us and then smiled as if a pretty girl had given him a mug that served endless beer. "Miss Ella!" He waved and jumped off his horse, landing with a bounce. Pushing through the cows and ignoring a sputtering cow herder, he picked up Ella in a bone-popping hug.

"What are you doing here?" they babbled over each other at the same time.

Ella said, "We have come on behalf of the king to explore this territory. We journey north and . . . are about to be butchered, I suppose."

I noticed that Ella's explanation lacked the words "scouting," "army," "murder," "treason," and "magic."

Karl smiled so hard I thought the top of his head might fall off. "Let me take you home. My father will fix things. He's fine, better than ever. Roaring. I'll find you a horse." He reached into a hard pouch and pulled out a small, supple leather bag. He tossed the bag to a cow herder, who poured some gems out into her hand, poked at them, and then nodded.

Ella said, "Wait. Bib, I'm pleased to introduce Lord Karl, the Duke of Esterhite's son. His lordship was in my charge until I came to Castle Glass."

The timeline made sense. Ella had become Prestwick's governess nine years ago. She must have left Karl behind to do it. Karl would have been eleven or twelve years old then and just about too old for a governess.

Ella gripped Karl's forearm, which was wrapped in thick muscle. "My lord, may I introduce Bib, my good friend. And this is Parth, a captain in the king's service."

Karl's lips smiled, but his eyes didn't. "Hello. Sorry we can't stay."

"If you leave now, you'll miss the party," I said.

"My lord," Ella said, "I cannot honorably desert my companions. If it is impossible for us all to accompany you, I must stay behind."

Karl clenched his teeth and reddened. Then he nodded and passed four more little bags to the cow herders, who made it clear that four wasn't anywhere near enough. He argued for a minute, called them a few raw names, and handed over two more bags. The cow herders grumbled but waved us to our freedom.

Karl said to Ella, "I don't have horses to spare for non-soldiers, except for you of course. If your friends want to go with us, they'd better pound along behind. If they have bad wind, we'll leave them."

Ella smiled and nodded at Karl, then shrugged at me.

Pil made a show of sighing.

Karl glanced at her, looked again, and smiled. "I think we have a second horse with no rider, if you want to take it."

Pil gave Karl a demure, slightly giggly thanks.

Parth stood nearby as Karl mounted his black stallion. "What a magnificent animal, my lord. Where does a man procure such a fine creature?"

"You'll never own one, so it doesn't matter, does it?" Karl didn't wait for any kind of answer. He turned his horse away from us insects and shouted to re-form the column.

Parth leaned in toward me and whispered, "When I kill him, I hope you don't voice any objections."

"You can kill him, dig him up, and kill him again. I'll bring lunch."

"That's grand. Just grand."

FOURTEEN

Karl called halt before sunset, so I only had to jog behind the trotting son of a bitch and his men for an hour. I was fit, but I feared I might find tomorrow's all-day run grueling. Capps and the soldiers had enough wind to bitch the entire time we ran, so they weren't suffering too much. Parth breathed deep, took even strides, and seemed not to care if we ran forever.

We camped beside a wide stream. It seemed that Karl's force had camped there before, since they scattered off to gather wood, fetch water, prepare food, dig the latrine, and set guard with no hesitation and hardly an order.

Our soldiers, Parth, and I joined the men in their tasks. I wanted to listen for any interesting gossip about their mission, although I heard none.

More importantly, I wanted Karl and his people to think I was as harmless as an old bunny, and that Ella just let me carry a sword so I wouldn't sulk. It would help me get one of the soldiers alone and snatch him without any furor. I would hate to leave Ella behind when Pil and I fled with our captive, but then she hadn't expected me to be on this expedition anyway.

At twilight, Ella caught my eye and I walked with her downstream. She smiled and laughed as we went, carrying on about how beautiful the day had been. Once we couldn't be easily seen or heard, she stopped talking.

"So, this is your boy, eh?" I tried not to sound harsh, but I'm sure I failed.

Ella was staring at the ground. "We shouldn't assume anything before we learn more."

"Wasn't it you who brought that brown-circle patch to Pres? Aren't these the bastards who murdered his subjects and burned their villages?"

"That is inconclusive. The murderers wore that symbol. It does not necessarily follow that all who wear the symbol are murderers." When she looked up, I saw strain around her eyes.

"That's pretty damn sketchy."

"At least you know he did not kill Queen Dall."

"Wait." I leaned toward her and whispered, "Why did you think I killed the queen?"

She whispered back, "I recognized your handwriting."

I stared. "You stole my note!"

Ella nodded.

"And painted the 'O' on the wall. In blood!"

She pulled up her sleeve and showed me a long, healing cut in the crook of her elbow.

"Gods up and down, why?"

"I wanted Pres to send us here so we can search for Desh," she said. "I did not want you sending the king north on the pretext of some false war."

"It's not false. King Ert's army was already marching, or near to it." It was technically true.

The darkness had thickened so that I could only make out Ella's face by a bit of firelight. It was still enough for me to see her swallow twice. She whispered, "Krak and his cruel children. What have I done?"

"You can't fix that from out here in the Crazy Lands."

"The what?" She narrowed her eyes.

"Never mind. Right now, you need to prepare yourself, since Karl might be a traitor."

Ella hauled back to punch me, but instead she snarled, "He is not! Don't say it—it's untrue! There are a thousand explanations."

"One believable explanation would be nice. Ella, you haven't seen him in years. I'm sure you taught him well, but what about after you left? What about his ma and pa?"

"His mother died. His father is a reptile, a horrendous man, that's true. He is the Duke of Esterhite, the king's cousin."

"Does he live on top of a big hill? With a cliff?"

She nodded. "You suspect the duke of being the fornicator?"

"He lives to the north on a big hill with a cliff, and his men wear brown circles on silver. You did say he's a nasty man, which might become tiresome. Does he dance?"

"Upon my last acquaintance with him, yes." Ella laid her hands on my shoulders and clamped down hard. "The duke may be a bad guest and a traitor, but I cannot and will not believe that of Karl. He was a rough boy but not bad. You promise me this moment that you will not harm him."

"I can't make that promise, and you know it!"

"Thank you at least for not lying about it." She gripped me even harder. "Do not harm Karl unless I give you leave, or unless you are defending someone's life. Promise it."

I wanted to say yes, especially since I would be riding away from here soon. But I couldn't quite agree. That would be another promise, another bargain, another damned thing to dig out from under. "I see that you love him, but don't let that blind you."

"He's almost my son. I cannot simply watch him die!"

I ground my teeth. "No, don't do that. I recommend against it."

Ella breathed, "Oh. I'm sorry . . ."

I waved off whatever she was about to say. I didn't need her to tell me how sorry she was that I killed my own daughter. "Fine, I promise." When she let go of my shoulders, I said, "Do you think you can trust my promise?"

"Probably not. But I am choosing to hope so." She spun to walk back to the campfire.

"Wait! I haven't had a chance to ask you about Parth. Who the hell is he?"

Ella grimaced. "He joined the king's service some months ago and is reputed to be a man of action. Pres admires him."

"Really? I think he's suspicious and creepy. I bet the man can't take a deep breath without telling a lie."

"Indeed? Pres told me once that Parth reminds him of you."

"The boy's lost his mind."

Ella didn't comment.

I said, "Does Pres rely on Parth for counsel? Maybe he has corrupted the king's temperament."

Ella's eyes widened. "Purposefully? I cannot believe that Pres could be so easily swayed to ill behavior."

"Ella, I know you tried to raise him to be a good man, but he's still a boy yet. And he may be inclined to rage and cruelty. His father was a wicked, vindictive son of a bitch. His mother was no peach, either."

"No." Ella stepped back and raised one hand between us as if I were spraying knives instead of words. "No, you're lying and attempting to confuse things the way you do. I hate that about you. Don't pout. I didn't say I hate you." She whirled and marched off toward the campfire.

I walked away from the stream in a different direction for two minutes and then angled back toward the camp. Karl's men had built up four nice fires—hot but well contained. Ella and Pil sat chatting beside one of them. Karl stood not far away with four of his men, relaxed and joking. They all laughed, and Karl roared so hard he doubled over.

I joined the ladies. "Pil," I said, "would you please consult with me over yonder for a moment?" I wanted to make a tight plan for our kidnapping.

"Not just yet," she said. "I'm enjoying the fire."

That rankled, but she wasn't my servant. I'd just have to wait.

A pot of stew hung cooking over the fire, so I stirred it like a good lackey. The three of us discussed the troop's horses, and as

Karl flopped down to sit beside Ella, I loudly admitted to not knowing the front of a horse from the back.

Karl lay his long, heavy sword beside him, stretched out his legs, and watched his big feet as he wiggled them. Then he noticed me and jerked his head. "You can go. I'll handle that." Karl had a loud, deep, brassy voice. He held his hand out for the ladle.

"Must Bib go, my lord?" Ella asked.

"He can't eat here. I don't eat with servants." He looked honestly confused, as if he had to explain why he didn't eat with rats running around on the table.

"But he's my friend, my lord. Couldn't you make a generous exception?"

Pil added, "Please?"

"I guess he could sit on the other side of the fire . . ." Karl furrowed his brow. "As long as he's quiet and takes his food some-place else to eat it."

As far as lords and such go, that was polite. I had been prepared for him to hurl firewood at me.

"Thank you, my lord, a thousand thanks!" I hopped over to the other side of the campfire.

"Well, you're hale for a grandfather, hauling your ass along behind us all afternoon. Sit for a minute. But keep stirring." Karl pointed at the pot.

While I stirred, Karl made an all-out offensive to impress Pil and overcome any resistance to his lordly charm. He complimented her beauty in between bragging about his wealth and hunting prowess. She played along while Ella acted as chaperone. Whenever Ella reined Karl in, he smiled at her with no hint of resentment. I dared to think that I might never need to kill this young man. I could leave that to Parth.

When I began ladling out the stew, one of the soldiers walked up and stood between Karl and me. He was a clean-shaven fellow in his late twenties, not large but clearly hard. He wore a sword, two knives on his belt, and a third knife in a sheath on his chest. Every-thing looked worn and broken in.

"Tadd, are we tucked in for the night?" Karl smiled at the man.

"Yes, my lord. Everything's well." Tadd spoke with a soft, flat voice.

"Watch is set? I don't want a bear climbing up my ass in the middle of the night!"

"Yes."

"Has everybody topped their water? The last goddamn thing we need is to run low on water!"

"It's done, my lord."

Karl lowered his voice. "Any problems I need to know about? Asses that need kicking?"

Tadd's eyes twinkled in the firelight, and his lips twitched up. "Not tonight, my lord."

"Wonderful! That's just goddamn fine as hell. Have somebody wake me in time to walk the camp before breakfast."

"I will, my lord. Sleep well." He glanced at Pil but kept a straight face as he strolled off toward another fire.

Karl reinforced his campaign of seduction. Ella kept a little distance between him and Pil, and I concluded that Lord Karl was just a big boy. He was strong, loud, and important but still a boy, joking with the fellows and letting his people do all the work. Maybe he wasn't a traitor at all. Or maybe his men were committing treason and he was just riding along. Or perhaps he was a traitor down to his depths, but he personally wasn't good at it, so he hired experts.

At one point, the ladies excused themselves, leaving me with Karl and my cooling bowl of stew. Karl tossed his own empty bowl toward me without looking. I could have snatched it, but I let it fall and roll.

"Careful, shithead." Karl watched Pil and Ella disappear from the firelight. He grinned at the spot where Pil had been sitting. "Damn it. Almost."

"Yes, my lord." I grabbed his bowl, glanced around, and pitched it into the darkness.

Karl pulled out a knife to trim his thumbnail. "I should give Ella a better servant than a creaky old man."

"We could use a creaky old woman." I didn't look at him, but I readied myself for a hurtling stick of firewood.

"Don't be a smartass! When Ella comes back, she'll find your tongue in the fire, you pasty idiot."

"Yes, my lord."

Maybe I didn't sound fearful enough. Karl raised his already loud voice. "Leave! Take your stew off somewhere and choke on it!"

"Right, my lord!" I jumped up and trotted away, following Ella and Pil. I caught them in the dimness, invisible to the camp.

Pil gazed off at the campfire. "Lord Karl. Of course, I always dreamed of marrying a man just like him. Now that we've found each other, I can only hope that I'm pregnant before I meet his father."

"He's a charmer," I said. "I hear the empress has two unmarried daughters, so you'll have to throw yourself on your back tonight, right away."

"Hush!" Ella turned to frown toward Karl, who was scraping dirt off his boot with the knife. "He is unrefined, yes, but he possesses good qualities."

Pil and I stared at her and waited.

"Be still!"

"We could only be more still if we were dead, Ella," Pil said.

"Fine! Follow me!" Ella sauntered back toward Karl with Pil following. I rubbed a little stew on my chin, dumped the rest, and trotted after them.

Ella and Pil reached the circle of firelight. Smiling, Karl bellowed, "Ladies!"

Pil stopped short, held up a hand, and turned her head. Karl waved at her and started talking, but she shushed him. She drew her sword just before a man cried out from somewhere by the stream.

Ella and I whipped out our swords. Pil's fine, young hearing had caught a noise that my lousy, old hearing had missed. Before I ran toward the light, something like a short, stout child made of bark charged Karl from behind, a long knife in its hand.

"Behind you!" Ella screamed.

That sounded like a good warning, so I spun around, but

nothing was behind me. I sprinted toward the firelight. Karl's attacker had dragged a cut down his forearm, but I saw the young man bend over and throw the short creature. It flew over Karl's head and into the fire. I hoped the thing might burn up if it was made of bark, but it just rolled to its feet as Karl snatched his sword.

Two more creatures appeared from the darkness behind Karl, so I swerved that direction. I heard Ella shouting for Pil to stand beside her. The two little men behind Karl veered to charge me.

They weren't that skilled. I dodged the first one's knife and thrust my blade into its chest. It stabbed at me again without making a sound or hesitating. I blocked and blocked again as the second one arrived, then I drew my knife and thrust it into the second one's throat up to the hilt. I may as well have kissed it on the neck.

Three more creatures charged out of the darkness, two toward the campfire and one toward me. I sidestepped to put my back to the fire and to get my three foes tangled up with each other. It worked marvelously, and two of them tripped.

"Slice them!" Ella yelled from behind me.

I slashed the one standing in front of me. It exploded into leaves that blew away. I cut the two on the ground with one wild swing, and they both burst. I looked around and saw four more creatures dash into the light, so I retreated to the campfire.

Ella, Pil, and Karl stood back-to-back fighting at least seven of these squatty leaf-spouters. I sliced open three of them from behind before they noticed me, giving Ella and Pil some relief. Ella killed a fourth, and I paused to watch. The creatures weren't exploding into leaves. They were bursting apart into clouds of butterflies that flapped away in all directions.

Well, that explained something. The Void Walker.

I ducked in and stood beside the campfire, growling, "Protect me."

Ella huffed, "I planned to let you die, but very well."

I pulled a single white band, which was just big enough to wrap around the creatures at our campfire. I demanded the butterflies' attention. Insects don't have much attention to spare in the first place, and these were already bound, so I felt only a tiny response.

I pulled two more bands and tossed them out. Then I showed the butterflies a sunny, flowered field far off on the other side of the stream. Of course, it was nighttime, and no such field existed anyway, but that didn't matter. Butterflies are as dim as dirt. The creatures near us fell apart into butterflies that flew away.

Karl was saying something about "greasy hell," but I ignored him and pulled another band just to figure out how big our problem was. Forty-eight more butterfly-clump creatures were bounding through the camp trying to stab soldiers. Not only was that an ill-omened number, but it was a hell of a lot of butterflies.

I was forced to pull twenty-two more bands to release all the remaining butterflies from bondage. The Void Walker could probably put them back together in a moment, but I didn't believe he would. This had been a warning to stop farting around. If he had wanted to destroy us, he probably could have sent a thousand of those creatures or made our arms and legs fly off. He might have caused the earth to gape and swallow us, if he had wanted to be theatrical about it.

Karl yanked at the brown "O" patch on his shoulder but didn't pull it free. "These things aren't worth a whore's goddamn virtue anymore!"

"What do you mean?" Ella asked.

"These are safe passage tokens, or they once were. Now they're as useless as cow flop nailed to my shoulder. Lutigan stab it up the ass!"

"What do you mean?" Pil echoed Ella, her eyes big.

Karl almost spit out some more anger, but he took a breath and calmed himself a bit. "Wearing this mark is supposed to keep us safe in these strange lands while . . . well, a beautiful girl wouldn't be interested in all that."

"So, others bear this token besides yourself?" Ella asked.

"Sure, lots of them. Hell, I'm surprised you survived this long without one!" Karl grinned at Pil. "You're lucky Ella and I were here to protect you." He sneered at me. "You're *especially* lucky, you useless twat."

"Yes, my lord." I had wondered what Karl noticed during the fight. It seemed he was too busy staying alive to observe much.

Tadd trotted up to Karl, his teeth bared as he stared at the space over his leader's head. "My lord—" Tadd cleared his throat. "My lord, we have three dead and seven wounded. Two of the wounded will probably die."

"Damn," Karl yelled. "Krak impale it with his mighty dick!" He glanced at Pil, then looked down and shrugged.

"The poor wounded men." Ella turned to me and raised her eyebrows.

I shook my head. "I can't help them." My power was limited, and I had paid a hard price for it. I had used a big parcel of it just then to save us from the Void Walker's killers, but that hadn't been for Karl's benefit, or his men's. They took their own chances when they left their warm homes to ride around waving swords. Besides, this jaunt in the Crazy Lands had forced me to use power at an uncomfortable rate.

Tadd went on. "Miss Ella, one of your men was killed and another wounded. Badly."

Pil and I ran through the camp scanning for our people. We found them close to the stream. John had been laid out with his hands over a big wound in his chest. Bimmit lay with his head on Dern's lap. Bimmit wheezed to get breath, and blood was on his lips. Dern kept trying to wipe the blood away with a dirty rag.

"Yeah, he's dying," Capps said as I knelt beside Bimmit. "Rat-gagging shame too. Owes me seven bits."

Stan shoved Capps and then kicked him in the crotch. Capps dropped to his knees, groaning curses.

Parth waited at the stream's edge, watching with no expression.

Capps had been right. Bimmit had a nasty hole in his side. He was just a few years older than Karl. I met Bimmit's eyes and said, "I'm sorry, son."

"Screw you and your miserable ass, you choke-hole!" Bimmit coughed, and I thought he might die then, but he recovered enough to wheeze some more. "I watched you pull two men back out of Harik's purse. I'd have sworn they were already dead. And you're about to let me die, you arrogant, old son of a bitch!"

I locked on his eyes. "Yes, I am. I can't save every man who gets stabbed."

Dern wiped Bimmit's mouth again.

Parth still stood impassive. Pil was frowning but touched my arm and gave it a squeeze. Stan was glaring out at the forest and cursing under his breath, but not at me.

Ella approached me with calm, serious eyes, took my hand, and led me fifty feet downstream. "I understand that you cannot save everyone. I do. But I am responsible for him."

"No, Parth is responsible for him. Possibly Stan."

"That is sophistry. The king requested that I accompany Parth. More importantly, I urged that this expedition be undertaken, and I engaged in subterfuge to ensure that it was. I am responsible for him."

"All right, his death is your damn fault," I said.

Her eyes crinkled for a moment. "Please save him if you can. Whatever the price, I will find a way to pay it."

"Shit!" Clenching both fists, I stepped in until my face was two feet from Ella's. "The things I need for payment, you can't give. But you know I'll do it anyway, just because it's you asking." I spun around toward Bimmit. "Fine. Shit!"

"I'll pay. Wait and see." She laughed, but it didn't sound like she was joking.

FIFTEEN

immit didn't thank me for healing him, and I hadn't expected him to. A person will usually be astounded to discover that a fantastical legend, like healing, is an actual thing. But within days, they stop seeing it as a legend and begin thinking of it as normal, like water from a well. Often, the number of days required is one or even less. Bimmit's ingratitude didn't hurt me, although the pain in my side burned.

Had I been Karl, whose men had been assailed by magical creatures, I would have led them all galloping away within half an hour. Karl required more time. In fact, he took more than two hours. I heard him give foolish orders that Tadd was forced to correct with tooth-cracking courtesy five minutes afterward.

It was a cloudy, moonless night. Karl commanded eight men to douse the fires right off, but nobody had saddled their horses yet or gathered up pots and utensils. The whole operation slid further into chaos from there.

Everybody finally mounted and struggled into marching order before midnight. Some of Karl's men must have seen Bimmit wounded and found his current state of health disturbing. I overheard such comments as:

"Unnatural bastard."

"Watch him. He's a wrong'un."

"Made a pact with Harik. He'll be selling our souls."

Before Karl led us off, I gathered our soldiers and whispered, "Bimmit, stay away from these northerners."

"Dead easy. I hate the cross-eyed shit-lickers, anyways," he grunted.

"Smart." I pointed at Stan and Dern. "Don't leave him by himself."

They nodded and said they wouldn't.

One of the wounded had died soon after the fight, so four of Karl's horses were left without riders. Karl refused to let any of us ride those horses or stand near them, and he said he'd prevent us from looking at them if he could. Ella complimented his nobility and generosity, made logical arguments, and finally just pouted until he gave up and allowed us to ride. But he refused to let us ride double for fear of wearing down the mounts.

I sure as hell wasn't volunteering to run. I was the oldest man there and intended to trade on that fact like it was a pouch of rubies. Nobody else dared asked Parth to pass up riding a horse, and I didn't care whether he rode, ran, or dragged himself by his tongue. I did insist that Bimmit not run at the rear lest he be quietly ambushed. Stan agreed that Dern would ride alongside Bimmit, Dern being an imposing wall of a man.

That left Stan running with Capps. As we traveled, I heard them yelling and bitching at each other with hardly a pause.

Karl and Tadd kept the pace steady until dawn. The regular open forest hadn't changed a jot since I outwitted the grass spirit and rode into the Void Walker's territory. Well, Dabbs did say that he hated untidiness.

As we rode, I chatted with the soldier next to me, a tall, gaunt fellow of middle years. I wanted to build a little false friendship so I could lure him out of the column and whack him on the head. Of course, that would need to wait until I had discussed it with Pil, but I was sowing the field for betrayal. He had nothing to say to me all night, though, and I thought he was the rudest bastard I'd met in years. Before dawn, the man ahead of me said to shut the hell up because my gaunt friend was as deaf as a rock.

Just after sunrise, we slowed to a walk. I found that perplexing, since in daylight we could ride faster and worry less about holes and drop-offs. Soon, I couldn't stand it anymore and broke ranks to join Ella.

I kept my voice low. "Do you know what in the creeping hell is going on?"

She shrugged. "Perhaps Karl is searching for a clue or a path."

From ahead of us, Karl shouted, "It's over there!"

Tadd said something so softly I couldn't make out the words.

"I tell you, the path over there!" Karl yelled louder.

"Over there" must have been to the right, because that's the direction Karl led us. I dropped back to my place in the column.

Two hours later, the column halted and I heard Karl yell, "Shit! Shit, shit, shit! Gods damn everything in sight!" The column turned and headed back the way we'd come. Karl was cursing as he passed me. He didn't show much creativity, but he made up for it with sincerity and fervor.

Not long after midday, we halted again, and this time, I heard satisfied voices from the head of the column. I rode up to join Ella and saw that a big tree's trunk had been painted red from the ground to twelve feet high. Thirty-foot-long streamers of red cloth hung from the lowest branches.

"Any ideas?" I whispered to Ella.

"I assume this represents a significant marker, perhaps indicating a direction of travel."

"A signpost, then," I said.

She blinked at me. "Yes, I said that."

Karl called the column into motion again and led us north. Five minutes later, the terrain changed in an instant. The open forest disappeared and was replaced by steep hills of bare, gray stone separated by wide, grassy valleys. A town stood far ahead to our right. A mile to our left, a river flowed fast and wide. We rode downhill on a dirt path. The closest valleys were covered in plowed fields surrounding clumps of wooden buildings.

Parth had joined Ella and me. He examined the terrain. "Is this the Duchy of Esterhite of which you were speaking?"

Ella nodded. "I have not visited this part, but I have heard it described thus."

"Hmm." I looked over my shoulder and almost halted in surprise. A wall of great, jagged hills blocked the view. They looked no more passable than an iron gate. The path ran behind us to a slope, and it disappeared a quarter mile up the hill.

To our right, somebody had painted a thirty-foot-tall wooden post red and set it into the ground.

I said, "Ella, I have never been here, but I have studied maps and possess an excellent sense of where I am. Taking into account all the riding and rowing and hiking we've done, I think we're a hundred miles or more north of where we should be."

She stared at me as our horses trotted side by side. "You could be mistaken. You have often been mistaken about things. I've watched it happen."

"Maybe." I shrugged. "Riding through a magical territory sure could cut a lot of days off the duke's travel. If he wanted to create hell and burn towns in the rest of the kingdom."

"Do not be—"

Ella's words cut off as Pil pulled my spirit out of my body and hauled me upward with hers.

"Now we can settle this name business, Bib, because I refuse to give up and accept that one of us has to kill the other. Fingit! I come to trade!"

Fingit's nasal voice drew closer. "Well . . . come on and trade, will you? I'm tired of this 'Talk to me, leave me alone, talk to me' business. So, there you are, Knife. Oh. The Murderer too? Well, I suppose that's all right."

I drew my sword, and the trading place appeared as the blade's point swept in front of me. Dusk lay on the Gods' Realm, and the marble gazebo was in shadow. The tall, shaggy forest to my left seemed to wilt as the light dimmed.

Fingit sat forward on the lowest level of the gazebo and pushed his curly red hair back from his achingly perfect face. He flexed one of his enormous hands, powerful enough to wield the unworldly tools he employed as the Smith of the Gods. "Not that I dislike you particularly, Murderer, but it would have been nice to have you announced."

"Sorry about my rudeness, Your Magnificence." I couldn't afford to aggravate Fingit, since he was the only god who tolerated me with any good humor at all. Of course, he would still be pleased to slice me into bits if he saw some advantage for himself.

"Why have you come today, Knife, bringing this grumpy hanger-on?" Fingit leaned farther forward and grinned.

The gods had named Pil "Knife" in the same way they had named me "Murderer." Pil and I had speculated whether her name held any significance. I doubted it, but the name had disconcerted her ever since it was given.

Pil stared at nothing since she had no power to see in this place. "Mighty Fingit, I want to make a tiny—and by *tiny*, I mean miniscule—alteration to Bib's memories, with his full permission."

"So that he won't kill you, eh?"

"Well, yes, you're right, that's true," Pil almost babbled. She still hadn't accustomed herself to dealing with beings who knew just about every damn thing that happened to us in the world of man. Everything that mattered, anyway. "Since you understand what I want, Fingit, please make me an offer."

"Oh, Knife, I wish it could be that neat and easy." Fingit sighed with grand effect. "The God of Death owns your friend, the Murderer. And Harik has bleated about owning him until I'm sick. Really. The rest of us gods would cut off our ears and vomit blood if Harik would shut up about it." Fingit stood in a delicate pose, dropped his voice, and over-enunciated, "'No deals with the Murderer unless I approve. All deals must go through me.' Tiresome. Great Krak and his fingers, if I cut Harik out of this deal, I'll be hearing about it for the next ten thousand years."

I nodded. "If you must—"

Fingit bellowed, "Harik! God of Death! You have ten seconds before I begin defiling your property!"

The power of Fingit's voice shook me. Although Pil was

unaware of her body, she was knocked to her knees and clambered back up by reflex.

"Bib?" Pil whispered.

"Never mind all that," I said. "Defiling is a figure of speech." I didn't feel certain about that, but we were already in through the door, with no dashing away.

I was about to ask Fingit whether he'd heard any good jokes when I saw Harik hurtling through the air. He landed on the roof of the gazebo and boomed, "Murderer! This is not pleasant, but it is perhaps fortuitous."

I didn't respond right away, since I was dumbstruck by seeing Harik fly. Or maybe he was leaping heroic distances, which would be about the same as flying. In all my many visits to trade with Harik, he had never been airborne.

Harik bounded across the roof and dropped to the ground on the other side of the gazebo. He strode into the highest level, flicking dirt off his robe, which was known to be the fourth blackest thing in all existence. That fact had been confirmed even by gods who hated him. Harik perched on a bench and arranged his robe as he stared at me. "Well?"

I stood tall. "Mighty Harik, I could say that I missed that puddle of curdled milk that you call a face. But that would be a lie, because I don't miss it at all and am just here to support Pil."

Harik said, "There remains a salty cavern where your wit once was, Murderer, so be still."

Pil said, "Is everybody finished? You remind me of my little brothers, but I can wait if you want to move on to throwing mud and poking each other with sticks."

"The Knife wants me to remove her name from the Murderer's mind," Fingit said.

"Aw . . . I was hoping to see him slaughter her," Harik said in an exaggerated whine.

Fingit shrugged. "That's not yet out of the question." He turned to Pil, even though she couldn't see him. "In exchange, I want you to kill the blonde woman."

"Ella?"

Fingit rolled his eyes. "The woman he likes, whatever her name is."

"No," Pil said. "Bib would never let me do it. He'd kill me as soon as we get back."

"Not if I take the memory of this conversation out of his head too."

"Wait!" I shouted. Pil flinched. "None of that."

Harik's eyes narrowed, but Fingit ignored me. "Once you kill her, Knife, I'll take any knowledge of your guilt out of his head as well. He'll never know."

"I do not agree to any of this shit!" I bellowed, and Pil staggered.

Fingit blinked at me. "If the Knife makes the deal, I will just do it."

Harik said, "He does not require your agreement, Murderer. You know that."

I was only half listening, because I was looking at Pil and wondering why my voice had shaken her. It shouldn't have. Suddenly I remembered similar things that had happened before. Why had I forgotten?

I glanced at the gazebo and saw Harik watching me watch Pil. Whatever I had just done, I'd better not do it anymore until I figured out a few things.

"No!" Pil snapped. "I don't agree to that deal, not at all. Here's a counteroffer. I'll throw away my sword, and my knife, and my bow —that's all the weapons I've enchanted for myself."

"Weak," Fingit said.

"Pathetic," Harik added. "You could simply enchant some more."

Fingit crossed his arms. "I stand by the offer I've already made."

Pil didn't pause before saying, "How about this? I'll be poisoned somehow. Sometime. I won't know when. It won't kill me, but I'll fall into a deep sleep for a week."

"That sounds like no fun at all. For me or for you," Fingit said.

"Two weeks?" Pil asked.

Fingit shook his head.

The idea of Fingit pulling anything out of my head didn't enthrall me, but it was better than death for Ella, or Pil, or myself. "How about—"

"Silence, Murderer!" Harik thundered. I didn't have to pretend that it shook me, and Pil fell on her butt.

Climbing back to her feet, Pil sighed. "I'll create a charm that will put Ella into a sleep for a whole month."

"No," Fingit said.

As I yawned, I said, "It would be awful if you were in that sleep with her."

Harik growled, "I will not warn you again, Murderer. I trust you remember how you were punished."

My chest ached as I recalled Harik's godly, agony-blasting thumb against my breastbone.

Pil didn't hesitate. "Both Ella and I will sleep for a month."

"Are you taking this seriously?" Fingit said. "There are a lot of things I could be doing right now. Enough with the sleeping. More dying."

I realized that no deal was to be had from these bastards other than Ella's death. Not today, at least. I coughed and kept coughing. Harik shouted and threatened, but I kept on coughing for at least five seconds. As I caught my breath, I wheezed, "Over. I'm glad that's over."

Pil raised her voice. "I'm sorry that we couldn't find a bargain to make, Mighty Fingit, but I suppose these negotiations are over."

"I regret that, Knife, I regret it quite a lot," Fingit said. "Although, if you want, you can come right back here, leaving the Murderer behind. You may find greater flexibility in your bargaining without him listening to every word."

"I won't be doing that," Pil said. She and I drifted out of the trading place, but Harik yanked us right back.

Harik said, "I find this disappointing in the extreme. Knife, you turned up your nose at some fine offers. No better offers may come around. And Murderer, you never could keep your damned mouth shut."

I smiled at the divine, butt-flopping hog. "I keep my mouth open for shouting praises and compliments for you, God of Death. I don't think such words have ever existed, though."

Fingit chuckled, and Harik glared at him.

Harik said, "If the two of you wish to remain enemies, then be enemies. I lay this curse on you, with the force of death behind it. One of you must slay the other by the fourth sunset from now. Should you both still live at that time, I shall visit damnation upon you both so foul you will wish for death."

Fingit beckoned to Harik. They both stepped to the middle level, where Fingit whispered, "Did you say, 'Visit damnation upon you both so foul'? Are you writing a play?"

During negotiations, gods whispered in that way to prevent the blind, disembodied sorcerers from hearing them. My sword let me see as the gods see, and it let me hear their whispering too. I could hardly believe they forgot I was holding it. Well, the gods were unfathomably powerful. They were not always unfathomably bright.

"I am writing a play, you illiterate thug," Harik whispered.

"Don't save me a seat. What if the Murderer kills the Knife? Lutigan is going to be pissed." Fingit glanced over and caught me looking right at him.

I held up one hand. "I didn't hear anything. I swear."

Fingit shouted, "Krak damn it with dirt and fire! Effla crush it with her horrible womanhood! Just . . . damn it!"

Harik pointed an Fingit. "Fool! Block-fisted idiot! You forgot!"

"So did you!" Fingit growled.

Harik turned to me. "My curse is upon you both! Be clear about that!"

Pil yelled, "Bib! What's happening? Should we leave?"

As I grabbed Pil's spirit and dropped, I saw Fingit roar and grab Harik in a headlock. A few seconds later, I was back on my trotting horse as if I had never left.

Ella finished her sentence. "—overimaginative. There are many explanations."

"I expect you're right about that." I nodded to her and dropped back in the column. I had a lot to think about the rest of the afternoon.

Two hours before sunset, Karl led us off the road toward the river, which was more than a mile away now. The soldiers set up camp as efficiently as they had yesterday. Pil grabbed me, and we walked half a mile upriver.

"What do we do now?" she asked.

"I say we do nothing yet. We have four sunsets to figure this out."

"Tell me your name."

I snorted. "So that you can bind me?"

Pil bit her lip. "No, I just want to know it when I die."

"Horseshit!"

She stepped back. "Protect yourself before you say it. Bind me against hurting you, then you can tell me."

"That's a stupider plan than the one Fingit was forcing on you. Hell, you're a goddamn sorcerer! Fight for yourself!"

Pil stepped away again and shook her head.

"Why are you so set on me killing you, Pil?"

"I don't know," she mumbled, looking away.

"If I threw your words in the river, they would float like crap."

She stared at me. "If I kill you, what have I got? Nobody."

I laughed at her. By her expression, she hadn't been expecting that. "Damn it to hell, Pil, you're a grown sorcerer. You don't need anybody except you. What have you got? That's the silliest thing I ever heard."

Pil bared her teeth and blew out a breath. That was good. Maybe she'd fight to stay alive if she was enraged. I didn't want her to kill me, of course, but that was a separate problem.

I was angling to find a way we could both live. It might give that farting cockroach, Harik, another hold on me, though, and that idea drained the strength out of me. I trudged back toward camp, hoping Pil wouldn't decide to kill me right this minute.

Stan and Dern ran to meet me when I reached camp.

"The rat-suck pieces of shit murdered Bimmit!" Stan yelled.

Every one of Karl's soldiers standing nearby immediately found something besides us to look at.

"You left him alone?" I asked.

"I was with him." Dern's eyes were red and his cheeks wet. "Somebody whacked me on the head. When I got up, he was gone."

I stared at the grass. "Where's the body?"

"Got no corpse," Stan said. "The choppy dicks slit his damn throat and threw him in the river. Probably. Anyways, we looked all over camp."

"Shit. You're probably right," I said. "I'll tell Ella."

I walked through camp reflecting that I should have followed my instincts, watched Bimmit die, and let Ella be infuriated with me. When I saw her across the camp, she smiled and sauntered to meet me, so she must not have been infuriated at that moment. She also didn't realize how close she had come to death at Pil's hand.

"Bib!" She grinned. "I have good news. We shall arrive at the duke's home tomorrow."

"That's just champion," I said, without much fire in my voice.

Ella lay her hand on my shoulder. "What's amiss?" I saw her other hand go to her sword's hilt.

"We're not about to be assaulted, at least not yet. I have bad news about Bimmit, though."

When I told Ella about Bimmit, she bellowed, "Krak damn your mothers and their whore sisters, you murdering, slithering, fornicating serpents of pus and woe! Damn it twenty times, and damn you, you cowards!"

It brought the camp's meal to a complete halt.

Right after dinner, I found a not-too-rocky spot and lay down for the night. I expected to enjoy the best sleep I'd had in days.

Earlier, I had pushed Pil to kidnap a soldier tonight and carry him west, just the two of us. She had refused. She said that so long as we were cursed to kill one another, she would prefer not to be alone with me. And no, having a helpless captive along wouldn't make things better. In the end, my counter arguments proved weak.

I considered grabbing a soldier on my own and leaving Pil behind. But as long as she and I were linked by Harik's curse, he would be peeved if I rode off someplace where I couldn't kill her, or her me. When a god gets peeved, that's just a promise of the pain to come.

Maybe I should go ahead and kill her. That would be the smart thing. I began planning the murder and broke out in a sweat. I blamed it on fatigue and a clouded mind, so I lay down to sleep instead of plotting Pil's execution.

Once I put murder aside for the night, my mind gnawed at the fact that my voice had shaken Pil when we were in the Home of the Gods. I had never read or heard of such an occurrence. I didn't know what it meant or how dangerous it was, and I had nobody to ask.

Maybe it hadn't happened at all and I had imagined it. Or one of the gods had made me think I had done it in order to break my concentration. Harik had looked as if he was noticing, but it was hard to tell. I had once caught his attention drifting during a negotiation, and he said he'd been imagining me dead. Unembarrassed, he explained that he liked to imagine all sorts of beings dead as kind of a hobby.

That's what I was dealing with. I sighed, rolled over, and fell asleep.

The screaming woke me after just an hour or two. I rolled to my feet and ran across the camp with my sword, eager to kill somebody.

Parth was sitting on the ground, propped up by Capps, gazing around with glassy eyes.

"I didn't see a damn thing," Capps said. "He just popped out with all that squawking. Hey!" He shook Parth.

"Stop that! Desist!" Parth clambered up off the ground.

"What's wrong?" Pil had walked up behind me, and Ella not far behind her. "Is it a bad dream? My father had a remedy—"

"What dream? There was nothing!" Parth scrubbed sweat off his forehead. "Go! Go away!" He snarled like he'd kill every one of us with his teeth.

I shrugged and walked back to my sleeping spot, where I dropped right back into sleep. Parth screamed me awake again a few hours later, and I found Capps taking care of him. When Parth screamed again before dawn, I didn't even sit up.

SIXTEEN

I have grown accustomed to being the most deceitful person in the room, no matter where that room exists. That's one reason I have lived to become a mature individual and an outright ancient sorcerer. So, it disturbs me whenever I suspect that somebody's behavior might be more devious than mine.

On the day after Bimmit's murder, before we set out riding, Karl wandered off to yell at his soldiers about pointless things. That allowed me to share breakfast with Pil and Ella. Pil smiled at me and said good morning as if she hadn't shared her fears with me yesterday and I hadn't stomped them into a mudhole. She made a joke and then asked me to pass the bread. Pil belched like a ten-pound bullfrog, shrugged, and grinned at both of us. She asked me whether I wanted her to sharpen my knife, because she could put a razor edge on a blade in minutes.

I became convinced that Pil had lain awake all night planning how to kill me today. The first step would be convincing me everything was normal. However, she was so normal my hairs were standing up.

Pil lagged behind when we formed up for the day's travel, chatting with Capps, who was less pleasant than a spoon in the eye. I pulled out of line and pretended to straighten my horse's reins until at last she passed me with a grin and a wave.

I resolved to keep her in sight at all times.

Throughout the sunny, sweaty day of riding, the rocky hills grew taller and the shallow valleys wider. Karl pushed on without a break for the horses or for us. I kept to my own thoughts and ignored the soldier beside me, a different one from yesterday's deaf man. This one kept going on about his three sweethearts.

Midafternoon, we approached a hill standing three hundred feet high from the valley floor. A wooden keep squatted up there behind a stockade wall, while a loose city of wooden buildings spread across the valleys and flowed partway up the hillside slope.

We pushed our mounts uphill on the dirt road, which soon switched back and forth as the slope steepened. We passed three defensive trenches, clumps of armed men tramping each way, and two ox carts hauling stone blocks up to the top.

Half of the stockade wall had been knocked down, which was no great loss since it had seen too many years of sun and weather. Near the wooden keep, about fifty workmen scrambled around laying a stone foundation for a building much larger than the current stronghold.

Karl led us to his father's plain, three-story wooden keep. Four guards stood by the tall main doors, which looked too dilapidated to ever close again, never mind bar. A single torch lit the entryway, and we walked from bright sunlight into musky shadow within ten steps. Karl pointed at Capps and the soldiers. "Wait here at the entry."

Parth whispered to me, "This is a terrible idea. You kill this oaf while I surprise the guards with a thorough stabbing."

I shook my head. Parth hesitated and then sighed.

A broad, tall room beyond the entryway was nearly as dim. Karl held up a hand and glanced back at us, whispering, "The Audience Chamber of Awe."

The walnut-paneled space would have been lovely with five times as many lanterns and thirty fewer years of neglect. Threadbare, faded rugs covered most of the wooden floor. The ceiling soared to twenty feet, supported by an intricately engineered system of rafters. I didn't need magic to sense that dozens of pigeons felt those rafters had been built for them. The thick, well-scattered white spatters on every rug showed it.

Four uniformed guards stood to attention at the far end of the room. It struck me that today I had seen far fewer uniformed soldiers than I had men with the grisly look of mercenaries. A tall platform supporting a heavy wooden chair stood behind the guards.

A burly, heavy-browed man seated on the chair bent down and spoke to a slight young fellow wearing a faded robe that was too long for him. I assumed that this thick-necked, brown-bearded fellow on the chair was the duke. He wore a bright red silk doublet, appeared well-fed, and looked displeased, so that was evidence of royalty. He semi-whispered, "I wonder if this little rat's dick has any money with him."

The "little rat's dick" in question was an upright, hefty fellow standing twenty feet in front of the duke, wearing expensive clothes and a marvelous yellow cloak. He raised his hand in an unctuous gesture and wheezed, "My Lord Durch—"

The duke flung his goblet at the man's feet. It splashed the fellow's trousers and bounced, ringing away toward a shadowed wall.

The wheezy man gave a bow so tiny it was near invisible. "I beg your pardon, Your Grace. I regret to say that you are five months in arrears on your loan. My masters require that the loan be paid current before any additional loans may be considered. At the very least, they require a payment on the interest at this time." The man bowed again.

"Preposterous!" Durch grimaced and shifted in his chair, then shifted again. A pretty girl in a peasant dress trotted to the platform with his goblet, which glittered with gems in the lantern light. She poured it full and handed it to the duke without looking up from the floor.

The duke smiled at the well-dressed man and said, "I see. Yes, I see then. Cheese?"

The girl rushed to grab a tray.

"Thank you, no," the man said.

Durch leaned back and drank from his goblet. "Have you sent word to your fine masters that I have received you?"

"I shall do so shortly."

The duke lurched forward like a springing panther and bellowed, "Explain to them why you won't eat my damned cheese!"

I admired the banker's self-control. He didn't so much as twitch. I examined Durch's face to assess just how insane he was, but he had cocked his head and was appraising the banker with a dispassionate eye. He might not be an actual crazy man.

The banker bowed again but didn't say anything.

Durch winced, belched, and sat back in his chair. "I have deigned to speak to you. You're no more than a common tradesman when you get down to it, you know. Fine. I'll get more treasure within two months, and that's when I'll pay your damned masters. Increase the rate of interest if you want. Now leave me alone and don't come back before two months have passed."

The banking gentleman inclined his head. "I, Edwan, will convey that message, Your Grace. My masters will be disappointed. I will say that they would never consider the idea of force, nor even of threats. Yet Your Grace may find credit difficult to secure from any lenders in the Empire—any lenders at all." Edwan spun in grand style, and he didn't stop to ask Durch's permission. He swirled his yellow cloak, which looked damned impressive.

Durch nodded toward a darkened corner, and a squat soldier with long arms trotted out to escort the fast-moving banker. Long Arms offered Edwan a small bow and then grabbed him with great economy of movement. He held Edwan out with one hand and punched the man in the base of the skull with admirable efficiency. The banker pooled to the floor like a coil of rope.

Long Arms gazed at Durch.

The duke winced at the ceiling for a few seconds. "Oh, lock his whining ass away. I may want to yell at him later."

Long Arms nodded and beckoned to two soldiers, who rushed to remove the unconscious man.

"Well done, Arm of Fury," Durch added. He yawned and drank from his goblet. "Well, that should buy us a month or so. What's next, Grand Adjuster of the Schedule?"

Beside the duke's platform, the small, robed man opened his mouth, hesitated, and fiddled with the cuff of his embroidered lavender robe. He gazed up at the warped rafters and the shitting pigeons for a few seconds. Durch cleared his throat. The Grand Adjuster started, almost smiled, and looked around the room with glassy eyes until he spotted Karl. "Your Grace, it's your son! Lord Karl has returned!"

Karl motioned for us to stay as he strode across the stained rugs. He bowed to his father.

"To hell with your courtesy!" the duke snapped, holding out one hand. "Give!"

Karl fished in his pouch and pulled out a cloth sack, which he handed up to his father.

Durch snatched a pewter plate from a small table beside him and tossed the bones of at least two chickens off it. He peered into the sack for a moment and then emptied a sizable pile of gems onto the probably greasy plate.

Karl said, "If I had been just one hour earlier, you could have paid that bastard and been done with him."

"Shit on that! I am done with him. I'm as done with him as I will ever get." Durch kept examining the gemstones. "When the damned bankers ask about him, I'll say the pissant never got here."

Karl said, "Well . . . that man, being such a soggy piece of bread, didn't come here alone. Won't his friends run and tell?"

Durch winked. "They never got here, either. Arm of Fury's sending somebody to kill them." He grinned at his son. "Unless you want to do it?"

Karl shook his head.

"Huh. Keep your own hands clean. Not bad thinking." Durch pointed at his son. "Remember! Never pay unless you must! And when you must, pay as little as possible! Right?"

Karl nodded.

"If those bloodsuckers in the Empire get their money, they won't care that I stuck their little boy Edwan in a cage for a few months. Or maybe they'll never need to know about it."

"Yes, Father. Um, look who I found!" Karl beckoned to us.

Karl sure wasn't beckoning to me. I danced a bit to stay behind Ella and not let Pil get behind me.

"Governess?" Durch said. "I thought you went to work for the king. I don't have any babies whose asses need wiping. What the hell are you doing here? I didn't mean that quite as rough as it sounded."

Ella curtsied and smiled. "I serve the young king, Your Grace. I accompanied a small group to explore the remarkable land to your south. It is quite astounding. Have you seen it?"

Durch stared at the floor for a few moments. Then he released a five-second fart spanning two octaves. He muttered, "Going to behead my goddamn cook." After a sigh, he said, "I've never been there. Couldn't possibly be less interested in the damn place. Karl tells me it's a flopping cesspool. But you must have investigated there enough by now because you've come here."

Ella said, "We have completed—"

Durch held up a hand. "Why does the boy king even care about that land, anyway? He's never once hauled his ermine-coated ass around the hills to visit Esterhite! What's he so busy doing? Why is he sending his slutty fake mother into the wilds for him?"

Karl shifted but stayed quiet.

Ella lowered her voice. "Unknown interlopers burn his lands and slay his subjects. Unknown that is, apart from their symbol."

Durch lowered his voice to match. "That must be a brutal kick in the nuts. What does he plan to do about it?"

"He intends to destroy his enemies without quarter or compunction."

"That sounds like hard work for a young lad. Make sure he's in bed at a reasonable hour." The duke grinned. "I'll bet you can think of ways to convince him."

Karl spoke up at last. "Father, this is Ella's companion, Pil."

Karl tried to stand tall next to Ella while slipping a protective arm around Pil's shoulders. He failed at both and almost lost his balance.

Durch looked away from his son. "Huh. You can visit us a while and not be lonely then, Governess. You'll stay. It's settled, by Krak's ass! Hah! You can tell my girls fairy stories like you once did." Durch pointed at Parth and me. "Who the hell are these people? Karl? Why are they standing before the Seat of Might? Why are they in my presence?"

"The pale one is Parth, one of the king's officers."

Durch raised an eyebrow. "Welcome. I'll have somebody find you a bottle and a whore."

Parth inclined his head. "Thank you, Your Grace, but a sound horse would be even more welcome. I'm partial to black."

"And this man is Bib, Ella's old servant," Karl said.

"Why the sword? Does he cut her meat with it?"

"Sentiment, Your Grace." Ella's face was red, but her voice sounded steady. "I cannot bear to take it from him."

I gave the hideous old goblin an enormous smile. "I'm not right in the head, Your Grace, not right, but I sew and polish boots like a whirlwind."

Durch waited. When nobody else spoke, he said, "What do you want from me? Nobody comes out here to the elbow of the world without wanting something."

Ella cleared her throat. "While I welcome Your Grace's hospitality with profound gratitude, we cannot stay. Pressing matters demand that we return—"

"Shut yourself, woman," Durch grumbled.

While Ella hissed, I kept my real goal in mind: I wanted Pres to listen to me when I recommended foolish military exploits. That meant bringing him a person to accuse of murder, a traitor. I squinted at Durch, sitting on his fat ass ten feet above the ground, as traitorous as they come.

If I hauled Durch back to Glass, I'd be doing an actual good thing, which I hadn't expected. Pil might like that. She might hesitate to kill me if we were doing something good. Ella really liked doing good things, so if I did this, she might forgive me a little more.

And if I brought Durch to the king, that would lift my promise to the Void Walker debt too.

I decided to do one good thing for a whole bunch of selfish reasons. I would capture Durch and take him to the king for judgment. I would be as righteous as hell.

Durch expected to have us in cages or dead within the hour, I could guess that. Maybe within minutes. Staying out of a cell was my first challenge.

The duke cleared his throat. "Governess, I understand that you don't want to stay here. It's a goddamn shame. You know that I can't trust you any more than a snake in my boot. My daughters would have liked seeing you and showing you their kittens, that sort of thing. Karl! Don't tell your sisters that she was here!"

Even in the dimness, I saw that Karl had turned pale.

Durch went on. "You must know a lot about the king and his plans, governess. You're going to tell me every single bloody-fingered detail. Before I chop off his head, I want to know the color of his underclothes and which way his dick bends."

Ella glowered.

Durch snorted. "I know you think you can handle torture, that you're a tough bitch, and maybe you are. So, I'll keep your friends here alive and torture them for you." He squeezed his fist a few times as if he were holding a hammer. "Maybe I'll start by burying the old man in red-hot coals. Then I'll cut a few things off the girl before I get creative. Be thinking about how much torture you'd like to see."

Karl said, "Father, we don't have to torture the women, do we? We'll torture the others, of course."

"Don't talk like a ranting fool!" Durch shouted. "Nobody respects a ranting fool! These women's allegiance is to the king, not to you." He drank from his goblet again.

Being imprisoned was not the end of things. I knew that for damn certain. But I would find my next steps more challenging if Durch had me caged. I blurted out, "Your Grace, I see that you're hiring mercenaries. Let me serve you!"

Half a breath later, Parth raised his hand. "Me too."

Ella stared at us both.

"You can still torture the girl," I said.

Pil cleared her throat. It sounded a lot like her holding back a laugh.

Durch sneered at me. "Maybe we could sharpen our swords on you. A flippy old fart like you might be good for hauling sacks of apples and bread."

I stepped forward. "I'll kill any three of your men. Just point them out. Or I'll thrash two, if you want me to let them live."

Durch glared at me with his mouth twisted, as if he couldn't believe what I'd just said.

"Your Grace!" I hurried to add.

The duke flung his goblet at me. It would have hit my shoulder, but I snatched it out of the air with my left hand. The feat was easier than it looked. All I had to do was reach straight out to grab it. Durch's expression told me it had looked as impressive as hell.

"He's the old servant, eh?" the duke said to Karl. "Who's the young one then—Krak's bastard son? Damn my gut!" Durch leaned forward and shook his head. "No, I won't hire you!" he bellowed like an old cow.

I held out the goblet to the peasant girl who came running for it. "Your Grace, I know a little bit about healing. Roots and such. I'd be pleased to treat your indigestion later on, if I'm not dead."

"Agh! Shove your roots up your ass! You'd love to poison me, wouldn't you?"

I had no intention of poisoning the man. I wanted to see him executed. "The offer stands, Your Grace, in case the pain gets bad and you change your mind. You can always kill me afterward."

I saw him wince and waver on a decision. Then he shouted, "Arm of Fury! Disarm them. Hell, strip them and lock them away!"

Preparing to stab Arm of Fury in the heart, I turned and then stopped. He had come back with three dozen armed soldiers crowding into the room. I spun back to the duke, thinking I might take him hostage, but he had disappeared. Maybe the platform had a trap door. His four guards had leveled their spears at us, and eight crossbowmen had popped up on a gallery ten feet off the ground.

"I'm sorry, Ella," Karl said. "At least you're still alive, by the gods! Father will change his mind about this torture shit. Probably. If you tell him everything you know, that will end things."

My array of tactical options was paltry. The room was full to choking with wood and cloth, but my magical power wasn't boundless. I would have to rot a lot of wooden weapons to help us. The lanterns hung on wooden pegs, so I could knock them to the floor. Maybe we could sneak out in the dimness and confusion. Or maybe we could be trapped in a burning wooden room with three dozen people between us and the door.

I glanced at my allies and saw that we had all arrived at similar conclusions. We held up our hands.

Arm of Fury himself took our weapons. His aggressive title didn't match his calm eyes or deliberate way of moving. He said nothing but didn't employ a speck more force than he had to.

His men used plenty of force shoving Parth and me into a side chamber and stripping off our clothes. They punched and kicked us a few more times than was strictly required to get our clothes off. They did not bind our hands or feet, though. Parth accepted the indignities with a shrug.

The cursing, laughing guards hustled us along a hallway, around a corner, and down a long set of creaking wooden stairs. The steps led to a dank passage smelling of wet soil and rust, lit by one torch at the far end. A guard unlocked a cage, and two more shoved me inside. Others pulled Parth farther down the hallway. He grinned at me as they dragged him past.

I held still until it sounded as if all the soldiers had climbed back up the stairs. While waiting, I examined the outline of a body in the back corner of my cell. I thought it might be breathing. When the hallway fell quiet, I said, "Maybe this is fun for you, friend, but I'm already bored as hell. We could throw dice, but I'm lacking money. And clothes."

The body rolled over and struggled to push itself up to sit against the wall. It whispered, "Come here."

I examined the outline of what appeared to be a man missing one leg. Scooting over, I knelt beside him. "Desh?"

Desh the sorcerer held up both arms to show that his hands had been cut off. I squinted at his face and saw empty sockets instead of eyes. Something was wrong with his mouth too. "Desh, can you hear me?"

Desh leaned forward and slurred, "About goddamn time."

SEVENTEEN

When I met Desh, he was a balding young man with big, round cheeks and bright eyes that were full of love. That love was for his boyish idea of magic and the beautiful things it made possible. Those eyes were ruined now, and his ideas about magic had been ruined too. The last time I saw him, he admitted that he didn't think magic was beautiful anymore.

That was inevitable but also a shame, since he was probably the most powerful sorcerer in the world. Or he would have been if he had a finger left. I don't mean that he could smash mountains or make fish sing. Desh was a Binder, like Pil. He could create any magical weapon, or hat, or spoon, or other doodad that he was clever enough to devise. He was pretty damn clever too.

That's not what made him so formidable, though. Some gods had mentioned Desh to me recently. If the gods had told me the truth, which was always a dubious proposition, Desh no longer needed to trade to get magical power. He had made a bargain that must have been so canny it made every god weep, and now he received power without doing a thing. I didn't know how much or how often, but the mere fact of it had smashed my ideas about trading with the gods.

Now Desh was crippled. If I suspected he was a threat to me, this would have been a wonderful time to kill him. But I didn't see any threat there—just an old companion in a little difficulty.

Desh said, "Can you heal me before you go? I'd owe you a favor."

"Desh, I'm not taking six steps out of here without you. And screw your favor to the masthead. That's not me being nice, either —it's self-preservation. If Limnad found out I left you here, she'd be picking her teeth with slivers of my thighbone."

The young man smiled, and I saw broken stumps of teeth. "Good. I have power to spare."

I hesitated. "Well . . . I do need a favor, I guess. When we kidnap that bucket of rat guts, Durch, I intend to take him back to Glass alive. So please don't kill him for doing this to you."

Desh snorted. "He didn't do it. Do you think that wobbling ass could have put me here? I'm insulted."

I waited a few seconds. "Don't tease me with it! Whoever wrecked you might want to wreck me too. Who did it?"

"Sorcerers. At least two, but I only saw one of them, dressed all in red like a mystical radish. They trapped me in my cloak and disintegrated my sword and knife."

I held my breath. If the radish-mage wasn't Dimore, it was his twin brother. It raised so many questions I could hardly hold them all straight in my head. The most profound was how Dimore and his allies could have trapped Desh in his own magical cloak. Nobody could use magic on an enchanted object except the one who enchanted it. That was a fundamental law. Somebody had tossed that law out with the fish guts.

Now wasn't the time to discuss magical mechanics, though. I said, "I won't insult you by asking if you're sure about all that."

"Good. I won't have to take vengeance by peeing on you." Desh grinned, showing that all his front teeth, top and bottom, had been broken off.

I said, "We're leaving here soon, so let's think hard about a healing strategy. I don't want to heal you so well that I cripple myself."

"Should I come back?" Parth said from the hallway outside my cell. I whipped around to find him with one hand on a cell bar, standing naked and thankfully shadowed in a strategic manner. His smile did catch the light. "I'm prepared to escape now, unless you can present me with a sound alternative."

I nodded toward the man. "Desh, this is Parth, a fellow who seems to be handy with locks. Parth, this is Desh. Even crippled, he's a better man than you and me put together. Leaving him behind is a bad idea."

"Hm." Parth looked around. "I hardly think I'll just sit in that cell."

Desh said, "You could join us, but it's already crowded in here."

Cautious footsteps sounded from the top of the stairs. Parth scampered back down the hallway toward his cell. In a few seconds, Karl appeared in front of me. He stood well back from the bars.

"Would you like to mock us?" I said. "I'm sensitive about my scrawny butt. I don't know about this fellow." I nodded at Desh. "I'd probably go with 'pathetic blind cripple' and improvise from there."

"That's not too damn funny," Karl whispered, even though nobody else was nearby. "Is this a time to be joking around? I'm here to offer you your damned life, if you want it."

"Hell yes I want it! What's the price?"

"I need some advice." Karl looked down.

"Fantastic! I've got an ocean full of that. What flavor?"

Karl leaned toward us, his shoulders sagging. "I thought Pil was warming to me, but she's mad at me now. Since she's Ella's friend, and you're Ella's servant, I thought you might know something about . . . something I could say. What does she like?"

"Is that all? Easy." I nudged Desh, who nodded for me to go on. I held up a finger to start counting. "First, Pil likes not to be tortured. Second, she also likes her friends not to be tortured. Let's see, she likes sunflowers and sharp knives. And she likes pie, but everybody likes pie. Mainly it's torture, though. You won't go wrong by not torturing her."

Karl grimaced. "I don't blame you for not wanting to help me. You're in a terrible spot, just so damn bad. But if you hand over some real, helpful advice, and if it works, I'll smuggle you out of here. Not him, of course," he said, pointing at Desh. "Not the creepy bastard down on the end, either."

Parth laughed from his cell down the way.

I nudged Desh's shoulder. "Sir, do you have a snip of romantic wisdom for our host?"

Desh slurred, "When she's talking to you, don't get caught thinking about something else." He muttered to me, "Drives Limnad crazy."

"See, that's some advice based on painful experience," I said. "You can't purchase that with gold."

Karl sighed, and his face sagged. I knew that expression well. It was the face of somebody foolishly in love. Well, Karl and his father planned to torture us, so to hell with him.

"Anything else?" I asked.

Parth called out, "I could educate you on the foundations of love poetry, if you can devote a few hours."

Karl stepped forward and kicked the bars of my cell. Before I could grab him, he stomped away and up the stairs.

"Let's get to work," Desh said. "He may be back in a minute with an ax."

I pursed my lips in thought. Our escape would involve fighting for sure, so I needed at least one good hand. "How satisfied will you be with a left hand and a left eye?"

"That's fine, Bib. Really, charming. I'm ready."

I whipped around as the light grew brighter. It was just Parth outside our cell with the torch.

"Thanks, Parth, that's handy," I said.

"What? Oh, fine." Parth faced the stairs. "I suspect I can smash two skulls with this torch before it disintegrates."

Restoring Desh's left hand took me ten minutes or so. A hot wire of pain cinched my own wrist and gradually dug in all the way through the bone as I worked. Replacing Desh's eye wasn't nearly as pleasant. When I finished, it felt like vibrating icicles were jabbing through my eye into my brain.

"Thank you, Bib," Desh said, as if I had just bought him an ale.

I hated to see him so aloof, but sorcery changes a person. Desh went on. "I need something more. Please."

"Sorry," I panted. "Can't make your willy any longer. As it is, it'll scare the horses." I wiped my cheek. My left eye was leaking like a waterfall.

"Not that. I felt little tree roots in this dirt wall. If there's a big root close by, can you bring the end of it out here?"

"Why? Never mind, how can I comprehend the subtle mind of Desh the sorcerer? That was sarcasm."

"Yes, I understood that. Will you do it?"

"Lutigan piss fire upon it, do whatever he wants, as long as you do it quickly!" Parth snapped, still watching the stairs.

I pulled a white band and explored four feet of earth behind the wall. "There's a big one about a foot in. As big around as my wrist."

"That's perfect."

I shook my head. "It'll take five minutes. Maybe more."

"Krak!" Parth spat. "No more than that! Otherwise, I shall return to my cell and allow them to kill you."

"I promise it will be worth it," Desh said.

I was already pulling a yellow band. I created in the tree the sensation that nourishing water lay just on our side of the wall. Three more bands helped the root writhe and twist in the earth. I couldn't make roots grow fast, but I could make them move with irresistible force. Within a few minutes, the root dug and stretched its way through the soil until a spot the length of my finger appeared in the wall.

"Perfect!" Desh knelt over the root. I hadn't noticed him drag a cut down his forearm with one of his new fingernails, but now he rubbed his blood on the root. He started scraping at it with his thumbnail.

"What now?" Parth scowled and kicked at the dirt floor.

"He's scratching a dirty poem on the wall," I said. "If you have a favorite, he can do that one too."

Parth chuckled. "I will read his once you've been killed."

Desh pushed himself up to stand on his one leg, dug his fingers through the now-loose soil around the root, and grabbed it. Then he pulled it out of the wall. And he kept pulling. He stopped when he had dragged a twelve-foot length of thick root out of the dirt.

Parth held the torch closer to the bars. "I expected it to be longer."

"Hah! Unlock the door, will you?" I said.

The root seemed mighty flexible, like a cable or a thick rope. Desh held it three feet from one end and let that end drag the ground. Those three feet stiffened as rigid as a cane, and he took a couple of halting steps in the cell using it.

"Good enough," he said. He looped the rest of the root up and around his shoulders. The remainder dangled in front of him.

Parth swung open the door. "Now that I see what you have created, I want one too."

Desh ignored that. "I believe the family lives on the third floor of this keep. Are you determined to take Durch captive?"

"Oh, yes," Parth said. "He's a traitor."

I followed along. "And we can't leave without Ella and Pil."

"Ella is here?" Desh asked.

I nodded at Desh while Parth said, "When do you believe the torturing will commence?"

I considered that for a moment. "Durch doesn't seem like a monument to patience. I'm surprised we haven't already been dragged out and tied to something spiky."

"So, we go now rather than waiting for dark," Desh said. "We'll lure some guards down here, take their weapons and clothes, and . . . shit, what then?"

I held up a hand. "The main problems are the guards in the Awful Chamber, the crossbowmen on the gallery, and Big Fury. Maybe Karl. And maybe reinforcements from outside the keep."

"Perhaps the duke also has dogs that would devour our flesh," Parth said.

I grinned at Desh. "Do you want to enchant the entire keep so that it crushes our enemies and leaves us alive?"

Damned if he didn't appear to think about it. "That's inefficient. Bib, the magical attack has to be yours. I mean, this whole place is made of wood."

"All right," I said. "First, I'll collapse Durch's platform so he can't escape. When everybody looks at that, I'll rot the gallery off the wall and drop something heavy on Big Fury. Parth and I will kill the men guarding Durch, and Desh will secure him. Then I will run upstairs for Ella and Pil while you two defend the stairs until I come back down."

Parth nodded slowly. "That's stupid."

"I'm open to improvements," I said.

"The two of you could die covering my escape with Durch." Parth smiled as if he'd just offered me a slice of cake.

Desh sighed.

"No thanks. It's this or getting tortured to death," I said.

Parth and Desh hid in the first cell while I crept up the stairs. I opened the door to find two guards sitting at a table. One was eating stew.

"Oh, sorry!" I said before running back down the stairs, my bare brown ass flashing.

Parth tripped the first one as he chased me down the cell block. I dropped down and broke the man's neck. Parth had smashed the second guard against the wall, punched him a few times, and let him slide to the floor.

I broke that man's neck too. I owed Harik lives.

Neither Parth nor Desh seemed concerned about the murder. Instead, we were all concerned that there had been only two guards and one of us would still be naked. Since my first job was to stand in the back and rot wood, Desh and Parth got the clothes. Desh didn't need a sword, though, so I took the second one.

We rushed into the next room. It held plenty of weapons, but it was empty of both people and clothing. All three of us agreed that the Awful Chamber lay behind the next door. Things hadn't gone perfectly so far. Reality had not matched my plan in every way, but it had been close.

From that point on, reality dand my plan matched a lot less. Not only did they not match, but they had never met and hadn't even heard of each other. They didn't live in the same kingdom. One was a fish and the other was a jar full of buttons.

Parth opened the door with care. A tubby guard was in the act of reaching for the door from the other side. The guard's eyes sprang open, and he bellowed, "Balls! What the hell is this?" His voice echoed off the other end of the chamber.

The room fell silent. Then the guard gagged as Parth stabbed him through the chest.

I poked my head out and noticed two things. Durch was not planted on his Mighty Seat to my left. He might have been standing in a big clump of people in the middle of the room, but I wasn't certain. Also, four of the crossbowmen on the gallery to my right were staring at us. Two raised their weapons.

The wooden gallery stood ten feet off the floor and was supported by four angled beams. I pulled eight blue bands and whipped them out to the top of each beam, rotting the wood five hundred years' worth in five seconds. The gallery collapsed, and all eight crossbowmen tumbled to the floor. Two had already fired, one missing Desh's head and the other striking where Parth's chest would have been if he hadn't dropped as quickly as a cat.

Collapsing the Mighty Seat would serve no purpose if Durch wasn't sitting on it, so I tossed that part of the plan into the harbor. Desh shoved his way past me as Parth bounced to his feet. Six guards with spears were charging us from Durch's platform. Parth and I were supposed to deal with them.

Desh reached the guards first and swung the flexible end of the root one-handed, like a whip. The man on the end blocked the root with his sword, but Desh's weapon swept it aside. I heard the man's arm bone crack over the rising voices in the room. The root smashed the man's shoulder too and knocked him flying. The root's end kept going and snapped against another guard's neck with a boom that shook dust from the rafters. That guard's head didn't pop off, but it lay at a crazy angle when he hit the ground.

Everybody went silent again in the echo of the boom. Parth and I charged the remaining four guards. One overreached, and I chopped his spear shaft before coming back to mangle his wrist. Parth yanked another man's spear out of his hands before thrusting into his belly. Both of our victims staggered back.

Parth shouted, "Go find Durch!" He engaged the two remaining guards as I ran toward the middle of the room.

Three more men charged toward us from around the Mighty Seat. Desh swung at them, striking one squarely. The man's chest split partway open, and the other two guards flung themselves backward.

I scanned the middle of the room. A well-dressed young couple in matching green stood with four bodyguards dressed in lighter green. The couple stared at Desh with open mouths. The man had wrapped one arm around the woman's shoulders.

I saw Durch beyond them, fleeing toward the main door with half a dozen guards. Three more of his men fought a rear action against two of the bodyguards in light green. The last damn thing I wanted was to chase Durch all over the countryside.

The complex system of beams holding up the ceiling looked marvelously efficient. It supported the ceiling's great weight using the smallest possible amount of materials. It was as solid as a boulder, so long as all the pieces fit together. When I rotted the center spans of the rafters closest to the door, those rafters, the ceiling above them, and a good part of the third floor collapsed.

It crushed three guards and blocked the door. Still forty feet from the door, Durch yelled curses at the crumbling ceiling.

A crossbow bolt whizzed past my shoulder from behind. I rolled to my right and heard another pass above me. Four crossbowmen stood in the wreckage of the gallery, all reloading. I couldn't spare the time to run over and kill them since Durch's guards were right behind me. Instead, I spun four blue bands, regretting the use of power more and more, and whipped them out to rot the wood under the crosspiece of each weapon. Two crossbows flew apart right away, whacking their owners in the face and chest.

Spinning the other way, I saw that the folks in green were having a shitty day. The woman was down with a crossbow bolt in her shoulder, the man had drawn his sword, and only two vof their bodyguards had survived to fight six of Durch's men.

I glanced around the room. No Karl and no Big Fury. However, at least six more guards carrying swords were rushing down the stairs. Maybe they had been quartered on the second floor, or more likely, they'd been up there throwing dice. Parth ran to meet them, and Desh stumped along behind, leaving me alone.

We were having a shitty day too.

I turned to go after Durch, which meant helping the people in green. One of their bodyguards cried out and fell. I rushed forward to aid the man in green and his last bodyguard, who were attacking Durch's men with considerable ferocity.

Behind me, Desh's weapon threw off an astounding boom—twice as loud as the previous ones—and I heard people cry out. I cut down one guard who was panting. Hell, I was panting too. Ten years earlier, I could have done this all day. Another guard lunged, sure to kill me, only to find I had left that opening so I could draw him in and cut his throat. The man in green wounded a guard but then walked right into the next guard's attack. He fell, blood spraying from his neck.

A guard to my left nearly chopped off my head with a desperate swing. My watering eye never saw him, but I heard him grunt and blocked by reflex. After our blades clanged like bells, I disengaged and thrust through his chest, twice. He fell backward, leaving nobody between Durch and me.

I glanced toward the stairs to assess that situation. Desh was lying on his back shaking his head. The root was nowhere in sight. Parth stood at the bottom of the stairs facing three guards, but Ella stabbed one of them from behind. She and Pil must have run down behind the guards, killing the men as they came.

Durch roared at me like a cross between a bear and a mule, his face near purple. "Filth! Goddamn commoner! Not fit to touch my chamber pot!" He pointed behind him. "That was the only way out. You're trapped! You're dead, you groaning lizard's tit!"

Before I could answer, something knocked me off my feet. I didn't feel any pain, but I couldn't move my right leg. After blinking hard several times, I craned my head around to see a crossbow bolt protruding from the back of my leg. From the way my thigh bent in the middle, the bolt had broken the bone.

Durch appeared above me, and he drew an expensive knife. He spat on my face and knelt to drive the blade into my chest.

I laughed, and the duke hesitated, squinting at me, so I tossed a blue band around the man's knife. The polished mahogany handle crumbled away, and the knife flopped out of Durch's grip.

"Shit!" Durch fumbled to grab the knife by the tang.

I had already pulled another band and was surging it beneath Durch, my left palm against the floor. The wood under him cracked and then rotted. He fell one foot, hit the subfloor, and lost his balance. He stumbled toward me, so I reached over and poked him in the eye with my thumb. It wasn't hard enough to blind him, but it made him howl and grab his face.

As Durch hooted and cursed, Ella knelt beside me. She laid her hand on my forehead and bit her lip as she examined my wound. "I wanted to be the one to hit him."

"You still can. Wait, you mean you weren't rushing over here to save my life? That hurts." I broke out in a cold sweat and took a deep breath.

"Fie on him. Poke him in the other eye if you like. But hurry, I suspect we are trapped."

EIGHTEEN

There weren't many people I trusted enough to let them yank a big shaft of wood and metal out of me. Pil might have been planning to kill me, and Desh had only one hand, so they were poor choices. Parth had proven to be a good ally in a fight, so maybe I was doing him an injustice by not asking for his help. He didn't appear to be such a smooth, unsettling bastard now that he shrieked himself awake at night. I couldn't dredge up the courage to trust him, though.

I looked around for Ella. She had dragged Durch off to the side wall, where she and Desh were now speaking harshly to one another. I couldn't hear all their words, but Ella threw one hand up and yelled "Brass mule!" at the ceiling. I might have tried harder to understand them, but I didn't care about much besides my leg.

"Ella!" I shouted. "Will you pull this out of me?"

"Of course!" she called out. She snapped a couple more words at Desh as she trotted over to me. Desh toddled along behind.

"Hurry!" Desh snapped as he tested an appalling bruise that covered the side of his face. "Your barrier won't hold."

I said to Ella, "Give me something to bite down on."

"Durch's ear, perhaps?" Ella chuckled.

I thought about laughing, but the pain was creeping up my leg and into my back. Then somebody dragged my spirit out of me and whisked it upward. I didn't sense Pil or Desh on the journey with me, so I had been called by some god.

"Murderer," Harik purred like a big cat. "You are as careless as an infant. You allowed the crossbowmen to live when you could have dedicated their deaths to me."

"Mighty Harik, the only thing I ever dedicated to you was a ripe fart."

"You subsequently failed to destroy all their weapons, turned your back on them, and paused to consider the battle around you. Standing entirely motionless while you did it. Were you inviting death?"

"I would never invite something so intimately connected with you. Death, poetry, unnatural acts with the beasts of the sea, none of it." Harik's question about inviting death was a ridiculous stratagem to knock me off balance.

I mentally drew my sword so I could see here in the Gods' Realm, or I tried to. In the world of man, my sword lay in one of Durch's storerooms instead of touching my naked and bleeding self. I couldn't draw it here if I didn't possess it back home.

"No sword?" Harik spread the question out like oil. "Another example of your carelessness. Will you dribble food down your shirt next? Saddle a cow standing beside your horse?"

"You called for me, you wasp-necked bottle of piss! Choke it out so I can say no and go home."

"Very well, choke on this. Murderer, your laxity extends even to the husbanding of your power. You must realize how perilously little you have remaining."

I knew how much power I had. I knew down to the thousandth of a square, which was the unit in which power was measured. I had just burned half a square in the battle against Durch's men. Healing Desh and summoning the root had cost me more than half a square, and I expected that repairing my leg would require another one-tenth.

I admitted to myself that I had been worrying about my expenditures of power. When Pil and I ran away from Castle Glass, I had been carrying eight and one-third squares. That was quite a lot for a sorcerer to have all at one time. Now, as I spoke to Harik, I had about two and one-half squares remaining. That was normally a respectable amount, but times had been as normal as a duck with three wings.

Harik was right about my power. Whenever he was right, my only hope was to scream as loudly as possible about how wrong he was. "It astounds me, Your Magnificence, how little you understand sorcery, and sorcerers, and many other things worth understanding. As soon as you finish sharing your lies and suppositions, I will return to my world and travel straight back to Castle Glass. No magic required. I bet I won't draw my weapon. I may nap part of the way."

I could hear Harik smiling when he answered. "I thought you would become more devious with age, but those were pale and ineffectual lies. Perhaps sorcerers were not meant to live so long."

I gave him a bright laugh. "Both man and god have tried to wipe me out, but I'm still here drinking and philandering."

Harik paused for ten seconds. He was probably speaking to other gods who were present, but I couldn't hear it. He said, "You still owe me lives."

"I'm killing people like they were guppies."

"You must open the way for the gods."

"Right, I carry that sword all the hell over the place to accomplish that."

"And . . . pay attention, you must start the war, fight in the front lines, and lose."

I didn't know where Harik was headed with all this. In such cases, a good general strategy was to be annoying. "Damn it to Effla's tits and toes, that's why I'm traveling straight back to Castle Glass! Keep up! Maybe gods aren't supposed to be immortal."

"You may not understand this," Harik said, "but you cannot accomplish your tasks with only 2.504 squares."

I shouldn't have been surprised that the immortal toad knew my power as well as I did.

Harik said, "I offer you a bargain. You will be awarded four squares in exchange for killing the Knife. Don't put on that disgusted face! Killing her is to your advantage. And in any event, one of you must die within a few days!"

"No."

"Just no? Not even a counteroffer?" Harik didn't sound surprised.

"No. Are we going to haggle forever over this? I'm done."

After a pause, Harik spoke as if he had just sat me down for a lecture. "Listen to me, Murderer. You may believe that you will forever after nobly resist all temptation to bargain for power. You will fail. You will reach some crisis that may only be resolved using magical power that you do not possess. Do you recall how that feels?"

I remembered that feeling as if it had happened ten seconds ago. I had made a deal out of love and grief, and because of it, I now ruined lives wherever I went. "How many more do I have to kill before my debt is paid?"

Harik laughed. "Pathetic. You are not allowed to know the number. Your ignorance is central to the bargain. I will offer you an alternative, however. Kill the fair, black-haired man traveling with you. I will pay you three squares."

Damn it, I already halfway wanted to kill Parth. This was probably a bad bargain, but not a terrible one. I paused, wishing I could feel myself take a breath.

There's one advantage to being an old sorcerer. I knew that this is how the gods snare us and drag us in. They offer something that doesn't seem so bad, and maybe it's not. But often enough, it's bad in ways we don't realize until it's too late. So the gods offer to help with another deal, and more deals after that, and at last the gods have helped so much there is no way back.

I said, "No, I won't take it."

Harik shot right back, "Kill that finely repulsive duke sometime on your return journey. Two squares."

"No," I said just as fast. "I'm tired of trading, you crusty pool of dribble and slime."

"Interesting," Harik said slowly. "Murderer, leave my presence and consider this with great care: How much will you pay to have no power?"

Harik flung me back into my world at brutal speed. My body spasmed. I yelled, slammed my fist on the floor, and shouted obscenities.

Ella knelt down close to my face. "Is it that bad? You screamed two words I have never before heard you say."

"Just pull it out."

Ella removed the bolt and straightened my leg, then I spent several minutes healing the damage. It still pained me afterward, but compared to my wrist and eye, it felt like a brisk massage from a clever healing woman who won't charge too much.

By the time I was on my feet, I heard the angry men outside slamming something big against the barricade I had dropped from the ceiling. Pil and the last living bodyguard trotted up with their arms full of bloody guard shirts and tunics.

"Disguises," she said.

Peering around the collapsed Seat of Might, I saw that somebody had bound Durch's hands and looped a rope around his neck. Parth held the rope and snarled at the duke before slapping him so hard he fell to his knees.

"Don't kill him! I need him!" I shouted. "I mean, we need him." I started to run to them, but Ella grabbed my arm.

She held out my clothes and my sword. "I shall begin charging you each time I recover your sword." She said it with a straight face, but her eyes crinkled.

I almost kissed her but ran toward Durch and Parth instead. Parth kicked the duke, who fell sideways.

"Leave us something the king can torture to death," I yelled. "At least let me put on my damn clothes before you decide to kill him."

"I would happily leave you to wear a shrub about your loins. Unless this puddle of filth reveals where Capps and your men are imprisoned, I will behead him one shallow cut at a time."

I glanced at Durch's eyes, which contained a grain of hope. "Oh, go ahead, then. Kick him a time or two for me."

Durch jerked his head and cursed me as I walked away.

Desh slapped my shoulder. The bodyguard in green was now supporting him. Desh said, "The only way out is that door you blocked."

"Well, Lutigan stab it in the eye!" I reached for my trousers, but the barricade rattled as some boards tumbled off the pile.

"There's a fast way out, but kind of ticklish," Desh said. "Here." He half hopped to the wall opposite the main door and outlined a spot half as big as a regular doorway.

At the other end of the keep, the top fourth of the barricade slid off and clattered to the floor.

"We'll make a back door! Rot the wall right here!" Desh said. "Drop some more ceiling at the main door to keep them busy, then we'll scoot out."

Even though Desh knew materials and craftsmanship as well as any man alive, I had to ask, "Is the whole wall going to fall on us?"

"No. Probably not."

The soldiers poked a big hole in my barricade from the other side, and I saw a face through it. I spun eight more bands and dropped another section of ceiling to block it, regretting the power. The screams and cursing of Durch's men made me feel a little better about it, though.

Everybody crowded behind me, including Parth, who was shoving the bloody duke in front of him. Still naked, I lay both hands against the wall and rotted the small section.

Ella kicked the wall out and said, "Go!" She scrambled through first with her sword drawn as I began dragging on my clothes and a guard tunic. Pil followed and then the rest. I crawled through last with my nudity finally covered. The shouts and slamming faded now that we stood on the other side of the keep.

No guards or soldiers were running around on this side. It surprised me to find the cliff's edge less than thirty feet away. The keep really was sitting at the highest point on the hill.

Parth had tossed the duke's rope to Ella and was sprinting to the right along the keep wall. I followed and saw five posts near the cliff's edge, each as tall as a man. Three of them supported hefty wooden arms sticking out over the cliff, and a tight, barred cage hung from each arm. Stan, Capps, and Dern sat cramped in the cages, dangling over three hundred feet of nothing.

We swung them back in. Stan and Capps yelled thanks at us until we told them to shut the hell up. Dern clung to the bars with his eyes shut, and trembled.

I grabbed Durch's rope away from Ella and then marched left toward the river. Nobody was going to accidentally fling the duke off the cliff if I could prevent it.

Ten minutes of traveling downhill disguised as innocent, wholesome guards took us to a rough slope. We scrambled down it, and I hustled Durch along without much care for his flappy skin. His dignity suffered, but he lived. Then the river lay a quarter mile ahead and two hundred feet below us.

During the scramble downhill, Parth caught up and put himself on the other side of Durch from me. I pulled the duke away to block Parth from him.

Parth grinned at me. "I do not intend to kill him. He is a traitor and must be judged." He rubbed at a stain on the sleeve of his crappy guard's uniform.

"You probably miss your pretty blue shirt, huh?" I said.

"It doesn't matter," Parth said in a way that meant it mattered a lot.

When we reached the river, Ella said, "Castle Glass lies west, eight days ride, but the river is perilous. We must cross at the bridge." She pointed south, closer to the city, and I saw a long, wooden trestle bridge.

I stood on tiptoe to examine the situation. "This shouldn't overly tax us."

Ella said, "Bib, did you plan your escape at the keep?"

"Partly."

"Mostly," Desh said.

"I should say entirely, or near so." Parth grinned.

Ella patted my shoulder. "Let me do the planning."

I thought that mighty unfair, but before I could say so, about four dozen soldiers and mercenaries ran out of the city toward the bridge. I recognized both Karl and Big Fury. We all crouched to hide.

Durch's men ran around for a few minutes before half of the force posted themselves on the far end of the bridge, leaving the other half on the near end. I wasn't sure what they intended to accomplish since we weren't on the bridge to be trapped between them.

Pil said, "We're going to have to think of a different plan, not that we even had a plan to start with, but I guess we all thought we'd cross the bridge. Did anybody *not* think that we'd cross the bridge?"

I shrugged, and nobody answered. "I suppose we can go north along this river. Or we can journey south, back through Dabbs's land."

Parth growled, grabbed me by the nasty guard's tunic, and shoved me. I rolled once and came up on my feet, staying low. Parth blinked a few times. "That was rude. And abrupt. I apologize for that behavior."

"Never mind, I didn't want to go that way anyhow." I did not take offense to Parth's assault. He had appeared horrified for a moment, although he'd composed himself quickly. "Does anybody know how far other bridges may be?"

The young bodyguard in green I had been ignoring spoke up in a deep, tremulous storyteller's voice. "I know. The closest bridge is twenty-two miles south."

"Young man, what is your name?" Ella asked.

"Jack. I suppose I'd be dead if not for you, so I'm in this with you neck-deep."

"What about bridges to the north, neck-deep Jack?" I said.

"The closest I know of is over fifty miles. But we have a ford in County Pister, just thirty miles north." His face sagged. "If the county's still a place, now that the count and countess are dead."

I sighed. I couldn't help it. It had been a long goddamn day. I had left camp that morning convinced that Pil planned to kill me before dark. Then I had endured hard riding, extended combat, imprisonment, a serious wound, defying a god, and engineering an escape that was later mocked by my ex-lover. "Shit," I whispered.

Durch laughed at me through the gag Parth had cinched around his head. I refrained from punching the duke's squat nose.

Hoofbeats caught my attention. Two dozen horsemen rode out of the city to the bridge and joined the closer group of soldiers. Then Karl led the whole mess of them across the bridge to form one big group. He yelled at the men for a couple of minutes, although I couldn't make out the words. Big Fury spoke more quietly for half that time. Then the whole damn bunch marched and rode away west on the other side of the river from us.

"Well," Desh said. "I wouldn't have predicted that."

Pil said, "It seems like bad tactics to me, just assuming we went that way because that's the road back to the king."

"They appear to lack subtlety," Ella said.

"Or it is a trap, and they are dripping with subtlety," added Parth.

"All right," I said. "Assume that they're clever boys. They made a gigantic show of hustling across the river. If we've already crossed, they would run us down. If we saw their performance from this side, we'd stay on this side. Who would want to wander around over there with Karl's army of killers?"

Stan said, "So we stay on this side and . . . hide? Or charge off to Piss Country?"

"County Pister," Jack said.

"Shut the hell up! You don't get a say," Stan snapped.

I said, "No. The problem is, I bet they left big gangs of mercenaries on this side to hunt us. So, we cross the bridge, hide, and make Karl think we never crossed."

I explained the plan. Nobody liked it, and I didn't think much of it, either, but necessity drove us to it.

After dark, we crept close to the bridge. No soldiers guarded it, which was an invitation to cross the damned thing. It was just what Karl wanted us to do. So, we needed to convince Karl that we were too smart for his pitiful trap.

We ran across the deserted bridge. Everybody but me climbed the closest hill, which overlooked the river. I couldn't quite make myself let go of Durch's rope. If Parth chose to kill the duke, neither Ella nor anybody else up there could stop him.

"I understand that you mistrust me," Parth said with a strained expression. "After all, I accused you of treason and murder. I promised a mystical being I would kill you. None of that sounds good. But we have stood together in battle, and we have faced deadly cows. You can believe me when I say I will not kill this crapulous baboon." Then the bastard turned his head a fraction and smiled at me.

I handed him the rope.

Desh had advised me on where to rot the trestles using the least power possible. When everyone was atop the hill, I slapped my palm against the end of the bridge. I rotted the wood at those critical spots, burning two-tenths of a square. The swift current did the rest, tearing most of the bridge free with a grinding crash before dragging it along downriver.

Once I had climbed up to join the others, Ella clapped my shoulder. "Beautifully done!"

"Yes," Pil said. "They'll be sure we stayed on the other side and wanted to trap them over here. They'll jump around like mad crickets trying to get back across the river."

"I hope so," I said. "Let's hike through these hills and stay off the road. We'd be wise to gain some distance from that bridge. I bet they heard its destruction in County Pister." I grinned at Parth and Durch. "Your Grace, I'm pleased to see you still alive, since it's not yet time for you to be dead."

We hadn't hiked half an hour when Ella raised her voice to Desh. "I would expect such words from him, but not you!"

They had been trudging along thirty feet to our right, with Ella supporting Desh. He was still trying to get by on one leg and a bent-tipped sword for a crutch. It had proven laborious.

I had noticed muttering from them for several minutes. Now Desh answered Ella, but in a soft voice.

Ella answered right back, loud enough for us all to hear. "You may not invoke the gods! I dare you to do so and not blush with shame!"

Now Desh raised his voice. "I didn't promise. I said a lot of things, but I didn't promise."

"Hey," I said to them. "The duke's men may be on the other side of that hill if you want to trot over and ask them which one of you is right."

They both stopped and quieted down.

I walked over to them. "Do you want to explain it?"

"No." Ella frowned. Desh shook his head.

"Then I guess you're stuck with me to judge you," I said. "Desh, be damn sure you really didn't promise whatever it was. I can give testimony that breaking a promise to Ella is a serious offense."

Desh nodded.

Ella looked as if I'd punched her. After a couple of seconds, she recovered enough to lean toward Desh and whisper, "I have more to say on this subject! Think about how you'll answer."

NINETEEN

Sorcerers often have little in common with one another, apart from doing magic and being devious. I know that those are significant commonalities, but what I mean is there are all kinds of sorcerers who behave in all kinds of ways. Many are near hermits and use magic mainly for learning. Others don't give a damn about why the world is the way it is, as long as the world has plenty to eat, drink, and frolic with. I admit that the latter description tends to apply to me.

Some sorcerers spend their short lives serving others, maybe their neighbors or maybe kings. Others are vile, cheating, murdering ass-rats who love only themselves.

Since we sorcerers perform unnatural feats that are beyond common men, most of us are pompous, touchy bastards. For some, touchiness arises only when their patience is pulled thin, but it's always just under the surface.

I wasn't the cruelest sorcerer who ever lived, but I might have been the most arrogant. Therefore, I wondered whether the gods had tossed Pil and Desh into my path as a joke, since they were two of the least haughty sorcerers I had ever known. And if the gods had indeed put us together, I wondered why.

My curiosity about that was sharpened when Desh nearly murdered Ella.

We camped atop a hill before midnight, and we built no fire. A fire might have been spotted from thirty miles away. Also, we hadn't seen a single stick of wood since we entered the hills.

So, it surprised me to see Desh pull a solid, foot-and-a half-long board out of his shirt. He spotted me watching him, and he waved the board. "I knew I'd need it. You knocked it off Durch's wall. That gives it a little power." He unfastened his belt, and I realized he'd been wearing two of them.

"That belt belonged to a guard?" I asked.

"Yes." He examined the leather.

"Hm. A dead one?" I asked out of professional curiosity.

"He was dead when I was done. I need a favor now. Restore my other hand. It will benefit us all, I promise."

"You don't have to promise, I believe you," I said. "Sit down." Ten minutes later, I had brought Desh's right hand back into existence with skin as soft and pink as a baby's. "Let me fix your teeth as well."

Desh shook his head. "Save the power. Nice teeth won't save our lives."

"What about your other eye?"

Desh hesitated. "Not yet. Help me walk."

I supported Desh as he stumped over to Pil and held out a hand. "May I borrow your knife?"

Pil stared at him, and I thought she'd refuse, but at last, she passed it over. "It's very, very sharp."

I knew that to be true. She had enchanted it to be as sharp as glass.

We walked past Ella to the duke, who sat on the rocky ground with his arms around his knees. Without slowing down, Desh sliced Durch's upper arm deep enough for blood to flow at once. Durch yelped and tried to scramble away, but Desh grabbed his hair and held him, with my help. He coated each side of the blade in Durch's blood.

Desh smiled as he held up the blade for me to see. "Wet with the blood of my enemy. Help me over there." He pointed the knife toward a place away from the others.

Desh settled on the ground, surrounded by the board, belt, and bloody knife. I turned to leave him. He didn't need me around to watch him enchant things. Only Desh and the gods knew what sort of powers he'd craft into his new leg, if it *was* a new leg. I might not have been subtle enough to predict his intentions.

Ella passed me, headed for Desh.

"Wait!" I said.

She did not wait. She stood over Desh, whispering with verve and even shaking her finger.

Desh whispered an answer without looking up.

Ella whispered some more.

Desh answered in a louder whisper and raised a hand for her to stop. He still didn't look away from the board in his other hand.

Ella snarled, "Look at me!"

Desh swung the board and knocked Ella's feet out from under her. She fell on her butt and tried to roll away from him, but he was already atop her with a quickness I hadn't expected from a one-legged man. He pushed the glass-sharp knife against her neck.

I drew my sword, but I didn't do anything for fear of the sharp knife cutting Ella's throat.

Desh said in a soft, even voice, "Listen to me, Ella. Are you listening?"

Ella gave a tiny nod.

"Your idea is a bad idea. You can build a school, but I won't have a thing to do with it. From now on, think twice before you harangue a sorcerer. Think, because I don't want you to be terrified of me. Do you understand?"

"Yes," Ella whispered.

"Good. Because if Limnad senses any threat from you, she'll put your bones in one river and your flesh in another, and I won't be able to stop her."

Desh rolled off Ella and sat on the ground again, holding the knife up to examine it in the bright starlight.

I helped Ella stand and led her away from Desh. She was wiping blood off her throat from the shallow cut he had made, and she trembled, probably more angry than scared.

"Were you going to let him kill me?" she said, her voice tight.

"No, of course not."

She let out a big breath. "Good."

"I'd have had to kill Desh first thing so he wouldn't keep stabbing you to death while I was healing you. Then when Limnad found out about it, she'd kill you and me both. We would all be dead."

After a pause, Ella said, "Perhaps the best thing is for me to stay away from him."

"You don't have to do that! Just be nice. Treat him like you would an affable bear who wandered over to drink and play cards. A bear that could tear your head off in an instant if it wanted."

"Is that how you expect people to treat you?"

"Yes. Almost everybody. A few people have permission to be mean to me."

I expected her to laugh. No, I expected her to say something mean to me, to prove she could. Instead, she started sobbing silently, her shoulders moving up and down. She raised her hands to wipe her cheeks. When I reached out to hug her, she pushed my hands away.

After Ella caught her breath, she whispered, "I did not intend to do that. It's just that . . ."

I leaned toward her and lowered my voice. "Just what is it? Maybe I can help."

She shook her head. "I have created nothing. My children died before they lived. The boys I raised, Pres and Karl, are becoming hard, cruel men. I failed as a sellsword, and I refused to be Manon's mother. She might be alive still if I hadn't said no. This sorcery school seemed needed. Possible." She shrugged.

I put a hand on her shoulder. "You have years in front of you." That was probably true. I prepared to add a bunch of lies to spare her feelings, but they wouldn't quite come out of my mouth. Instead, I said, "Not everybody in this world was put here to create something."

Ella took a moment and then walked off to an empty spot where she lay on the hard ground.

Over the past two years, several people had asked me why I loved Ella. She was a challenging woman to know, let alone love. I told most of them to go to hell, and I beat the shit out of a couple who didn't ask politely. When Desh asked, I explained it a little. Among other things, I loved her courage. She was brave enough to love me despite all the recklessness and uncertainty that came along with that. At least she had been for a while.

A few hours before sunrise, Parth woke us all by screaming so loudly I thought he'd ruin his voice forever. He had stopped by the time I scrambled over to him. Capps was shaking his arm hard, and Parth was panting. Then he sat straight up.

"Desist shaking me, you oaf!" Parth said to Capps.

I said, "Parth, have you ever talked in your sleep?"

"I am not aware that I have."

"Have you ever shrieked like your heart's being pulled out in your sleep?"

Parth stared, and I thought he might say yes. "Certainly not."

"All right. I'm willing to say I was mistaken. But if I think I hear such a thing again, I'll tell you about it."

I walked back to my sleeping spot without waiting for him to respond.

Desh created a wooden leg overnight. Sunrise found him walking and then running around the hilltop as readily as a man with two real legs.

"I don't believe it." Dern watched Desh run. "It's unnatural."

"You shut that crap off right now!" Stan said. "He's a sorcerer and can be as unnatural as he likes."

Dern shook his head.

Stan smacked Dern on the arm. "Lord Bib saved poor Bimmit's life. You didn't say balls about that being unnatural."

Capps snickered. "Lord Bib."

Stan turned to Capps. "Climb up my ass!"

Dern said, "Wasn't any bits of Bimmit cut all the way off. It's got to be worse if something's cut off."

"The two of you are dumber than chickens! Wait until you're dying, and a sorcerer won't save you because you spoke bad about him. Or her! You wait." Stan stomped away to congratulate Desh on his new leg.

We trooped down the hillside and through valleys until midday, always moving west. However, if we wanted to return to the king before the leaves fell, we'd have to travel the road. I believed it to be one hill north of us, or two at most.

"Let's climb up this one and scout," I said. "I'd rather travel by road, if nobody on it wants to kill us."

"Oof!" said somebody behind me.

I turned to see Limnad, the blue river spirit, hugging Desh so tightly she might have been trying to force the two of them into one skin. He embraced her as if he wouldn't mind.

"People on the road want to kill you, Bib," Limnad mumbled without pulling her face away from Desh's neck. "But people everywhere want to kill you, so you shouldn't just be afraid of the road."

"I'll watch out. Are any of these people close?" I asked.

Limnad lifted her head to blink at me.

I looked down. "Close" meant something different to a spirit than it did to us, and I had no conception of what. Limnad had tried to explain it once, but all I gathered was that her cousin, that bitch from the Mo-pi River, was far too close. "I'm sorry, Limnad." I smiled at her. "Does it seem as if any of them can reach me within a day?"

"No. Not unless I pick one up and bring him here. Do you want me to do that?"

I considered it for a moment. Limnad could kidnap Karl for me. But she would risk being wounded. Also, we had Durch already and didn't need two pains in the ass. "No, thank you."

Limnad released Desh, but she kept one hand on his arm. She lifted her nose at Ella. "I see that the Bitter Chasm in Which Virtue and Manhood Go to Perish has not tricked you into a horrible death yet."

Ella paled but didn't answer.

"Ooh, the harlot is terrified of me!" Limnad rushed to Ella and circled her like water flowing around a stone. "I like this." Limnad halted nose to nose with Ella, who trembled in place. "Desh, you did this for me!" She returned to Desh so fast I hardly saw her move, embraced him again, and kissed his lips. And she continued to kiss him.

Stan, Capps, and Dern had been ogling Limnad without shame, since she appeared in the form of a beautiful woman who was also naked. They seemed to appreciate the first ten seconds of Limnad's kiss. Then they began glancing away and shuffling their boots. At twenty seconds, they all found less unsettling things to examine. Dern even turned his back.

Pil whispered to me, "This is taking too long. We need to keep walking!"

I glanced at Ella, who was leaning against a rock, sweating. "Well, Pil, would you like to tell Limnad to hurry it up?"

Pil shook her head.

"Yes, I value my life too," I said.

Most of a minute later, Limnad stepped back, smiled at Desh, and said, "The water is warming."

Desh pressed his lips tight. "Not yet. I want to stay."

Limnad flowed backward and seemed to grow a foot taller. Her voice was normally bright, even giggly. It came out dead flat now. "I searched for you. Why do you want to stay?"

Desh nodded toward me. "I owe it to Bib."

Before I could answer, Limnad spoke up: "I would never hurt Bib. But I could tear off the heads of everyone else here, jam their hands into their ears for fins, and make them into fish. Would that change your mind?"

Parth backed away.

"Please don't do that, Limnad," I said. "Desh doesn't owe me a damn thing."

"Maybe I don't formally." Desh shrugged. "But I feel I should go with you."

Limnad grabbed Desh's head, one hand on each side of his face. "I can't go with you. Men build stone against stone all down this road, and in their squatty towns, and even the places they pee."

That would make sense. These hills were bare of trees but rich in quarries. Every house and barn would be built of stone.

"I can only reach you a few places. Don't stay here with Bib and his pets." She kissed him again, but not as long.

Desh said, "I am staying."

Limnad shrieked loud enough to hurt my ears. She pointed and me and snarled, "Your fault!" Then she disappeared while a ten-second deluge soaked us all.

"Desh," I said, "I'm tickled that you're going with us, although the reason puzzles me."

The sorcerer stared at me.

I realized I was on the edge of an impolite question about Desh and the gods. "Well, you're here, and Limnad didn't bury me so that only my toes poke out," I said. "That may be my greatest victory in this whole endeavor."

We climbed the next hill and evaluated the area. The late spring day had become cloudy and might rain later, but the air was clear enough to see that no big gangs of murdering soldiers were visible within fifteen miles. A large town lay a couple of hours west of us. We headed that way, hoping to beg or steal horses and supplies.

Desh and Parth were chosen by everyone who wasn't me to scout the town. Nor was I allowed to volunteer for the actual scouting. Ella joked about getting lost in taverns, and Desh described sword fights that would slaughter half the town. They spoke kindly while telling me I couldn't be trusted, and in fact, I was unable to contrive a good argument for myself.

I couldn't hold back on giving advice, though. "Try not to offer services in exchange for the mounts. I'm anxious to get back to the king. Of course, we all are, except him." I pointed at Durch. "Thievery may be your most logical path to acquire what we need."

Desh said, "I'll consider your words." He reached into a big pouch that had been hanging from the guard's belt he had stolen, and he pulled out Durch's goblet decorated with gems. "I might offer this in trade."

Durch groaned through his gag.

"You greedy ass-sucker!" Jack said. "I poked in every damn

corner and every pile of bird shit looking for that!"

We all stared at Jack, who had been a quiet fellow to that point.

"Is it possible you accompanied us merely to acquire it?" Parth purred. "To ascertain who has it, slay them in the night, and flee a wealthy man? It seems possible to me."

Jack backed up but ran into Ella. "No! I never thought that. We're allies! Go sell it! I don't mind! We're friends."

"That's awful sweet," Capps said. "Come here with us and you can say how much you love us all."

Dern grabbed Jack and stalked away from the road, shoving the struggling man ahead of him. Stan and Capps followed, while Jack explained how innocent he was in a higher and higher voice. Parth shrugged, then he and Desh hiked across the road toward town. A light rain started falling.

Pil pulled up the hood of her cloak, which she had enchanted to repel water. I glanced back and forth between her and Ella as the three of us stood in a triangle.

"So," I said, "does anybody want to hear the story of Effla and the sea monster?"

"No!" Ella barked almost before I'd finished saying the words.

"That's right, I've told you before."

Pil said, "Ella, I need to speak with Bib about sorcerer matters, such as spells, and evil spirits, and binding, and all those sorts of things. Do you mind if we leave you for just a few minutes to do that? It won't take long."

Ella frowned. "Preserve your secrecy, if you wish. I have learned that knowing less about sorcery leads to greater happiness."

Pil gave an anxious smile. "Thank you." She led me down the road where our conversation wouldn't be overheard.

"What's the matter, Pil? Is there some crisis about to kill us all?" I smiled, but she didn't.

"Bib, please tell me your real name."

"I'm sorry, I won't do that. It wouldn't solve anything."

Pil bit her lip and said slowly, "It might. You can't know for certain."

"I have a pretty damn good idea."

"All right." Pil straightened her shoulders. "We have only a few days before one of us dies, or one of us has to kill the other, I mean. How many more days is it—do you remember?" Her words came faster and faster.

I said, "Two. That's just short of eternity when dealing with gods."

"Harik is not going to relent, and before you ask how I know, I'll tell you that I talked to him and Lutigan about it. They have some game or contest going on about us killing each other, and they are not going to give up and let the other win. They. Are. Not."

"You trust them?" I thought about how young she was and managed not to smile.

"Not in the least, not the least bit. I'd trust a hungry wolf more than I trust them to tell me the truth, but you know what I *do* trust? I trust their arrogance, stubbornness, pettiness, and disregard for us as living creatures. I trust that."

"And those are their good qualities. I can't condemn you for holding that view."

Pil stepped back. "I'll ask you again. Bib, please tell me your name, right here and now."

I let my mouth drop open. "No. I can't believe you're pushing this."

"I won't kill you," she said with no expression.

"I don't want to kill you, either."

"But you will if you have to." She was breathing fast, but her voice didn't tremble.

I shook my head but didn't say anything.

Pil must have already been holding it under her cloak. She jammed her glass-sharp knife into her own heart. Her eyes and mouth jerked open as her whole body spasmed. She swayed and dropped, but I caught her before she hit the ground.

"Goddamn! Pil, damn it to your mother and her womb!" I laid her back on the wet dirt. The wooden knife handle stuck up out of her chest. She had driven the blade all the way in, and blood was already soaking her shirt.

"You killed her?" Ella yelled as she scuffed to a stop. It was raining harder.

"No!" I snapped. "She did this to herself." I had already pulled a green band to explore the damage, and it was bad. I figured I might save her if I said to hell with caution.

I ripped the shirt and slipped the knife out, hoping I wasn't cutting her up even worse. Blood blossomed out of the wound. I pulled two bands to stop the bleeding, then another band, and then two more before her heart was whole again. Maybe two minutes had gone by. A stone had appeared in my heart, and it grew to a little spiked ball before settling as a hot coal.

Pil woke up while I was healing the damage to the flesh between her heart and skin. "Thank you," she whispered.

"Eat a bug," I said, still working. "Eat shit. Eat a shitty bug."

When I finished, I sat back on my heels and shallowly breathed around the pain in my chest. "I don't even want to look at you. I sure as hell won't introduce myself."

Pil sat up without wincing. I had done good work. "Please do tell me your name. That's the only way out."

"What in the sandy-assed hell does that mean?" I examined her face, but it didn't give anything away.

"I'll do it again. Until you tell me your name or let me die. Because I won't kill you."

I looked around for Pil's knife, but it wasn't in the dirt where I'd left it. Her hands were empty. The rain was mixing with the blood on the ground under her. Neither Ella nor the men had the knife.

"See?" Stan said in what he might have thought was a whisper. "Dead. Alive. Dead. Alive. They can do this all day."

"Where's your knife?" I said in a hard voice.

Pil looked down and shook her head. "Please tell me your name. I know that trust is a bad thing . . ." She shrugged.

I had only known Pil a few months, but she had never seemed insane. She'd always been dependable and trustworthy, as far as trust between sorcerers goes. When sorcerers aren't crazy, but they act crazy, the gods are normally engaged in some secretive, revolting shenanigans.

Pil met my eyes and whispered, "Bib, tell me, or kill me now."

I jerked my head back and shouted "You greasy vipers!" at the sky. I winced and, with less force, called out, "Bite it with your sister's teeth! And I mean you, Harik and Lutigan!" I stood and helped Pil up. Her knife was in her hand. Maybe it had been there all along but charmed invisible. I shook my head and kept quiet about that minor puzzlement.

Pil and I trudged another hundred feet away. She held her blood-slick shirt closed with one hand.

I knew I should let Pil kill herself, but the thought of her lying dead on this muddy road made me feel hopeless. "Never have I said this name to another person, and I don't intend to say it out loud now." I leaned toward her. "Look close, and I'll pass it to you."

Almost touching noses, Pil and I stared far into the wells of each other's eyes, to a place that every sorcerer has in common. Deep down, I spotted tiny figures moving inside her eyes, with many shapes, and often different numbers of arms and legs. I gazed at them for a few seconds before they all stopped at the same instant and looked back at me. Pil was seeing the same kind of thing within my eyes.

In my mind, I whispered, "Asa. My name is Asa."

"Thank you," Pil whispered back. "Now Harik can remove his curse that one of us kill the other. He promised, but only if you told me your name within the hour."

"Humph. Well, let's end this before my eyes fall out from all the bad decisions I've been making."

In that moment, I saw it. I blinked hard and stared again before I pulled away from Pil so fast I tripped and fell on my ass. She asked me if I was all right, and when I didn't answer, she knelt down and shook my arm.

I noticed all of that with a tiny part of my mind. The rest was thundering in shock. The figures in Pil's eyes were the same as the glowing figures on Dabbs's wings and legs.

The Void Walker had said he was in Pil's head. I didn't think he meant it literally.

And Dabbs had said that he wasn't in my head. Who the hell was?

TWENTY

urch spat in our small campfire. "That little bucktooth
bastard is probably looking for us a thousand damn miles
from here. Yes, I said bastard! I don't think he's even my
son. He's no smarter than a toad." He spat again and laid his chin
on his knees. He rolled his eyes and resembled a disgruntled bulldog
with a beard.

"You've said the same thing every time we stopped to sleep or
make water for the past four days." I said it without much interest.
For four days, my mind had been folding itself around the fact that
the Void Walker was physically inside Pil's head. I hadn't hit upon
any productive way to think about it. I had discovered the most
destructive way to think about it, though.

Who was in *my* head?

Parth said, "Durch, one might think that you are speaking the
exact opposite of the truth about your son's proximity. Perhaps you
wish us to relax and thus be shocked when he overtakes us."

Durch shook his head. "No, he's just an idiot."

"Shut your gaping maw about it then!" Capps yelled. "Unless
you get a revelation and have some new ideas to go on about, crimp
your mouth shut!"

Everybody else nodded, and Jack kicked dirt at the man. The firelight showed the faded bruises on Jack's face, and he had displayed ill temper since Stan, Capps, and Dern had pummeled him into line.

After days of hard riding, we all were ready to gut somebody over a vexing word or a sideways look. We had been resting just enough not to over-tire the horses, which meant a few short breaks in the day and several hours to eat and sleep at night. I believed that Karl was right behind us, wearing out horses to save his father.

I expected that tomorrow we'd finally pass the range of high hills that blocked Esterhite from the rest of the kingdom, and we'd reach Castle Glass three days later. One of us might well slay another out of pique before then. I hoped it wouldn't be anybody I considered important.

Pil kept her distance from me during those days. She probably thought I was mad at her, and she was right. Ella tended to sit near Pil and chat with her at night, I suppose to teach Pil how to be properly mad at me in return.

Parth continued to wake us up screaming at night. Usually, he did it once, but on the third night, he woke us four times. I spoke to him about it, but he seemed mystified in a prickly way. I concluded that maybe he was unaware of these episodes. Or, if he was aware, then he was desperate to pretend he wasn't.

Desh kept busy tinkering with things. He enchanted the lousy guard's sword. Since he didn't have a forge and the base item was poor in quality, the enchantment wouldn't last long. The sword might shatter in a fight, just like Desh's mighty root weapon had done. Desh confided that the root had almost bashed his head flat when it broke. After he finished with the sword, he fiddled each night with bits of wood, the end of his belt, strips of cloth, and even grass.

Parth and I didn't drink and sing songs together, but we did become cordial. For the moment, we had nothing to fight over. We each cursed Durch in ways that challenged the other's creativity. On occasion, we discussed the world beyond Glass. I found that he was well traveled, and his thoughts were surprisingly subtle.

After Capps yelled at Durch a little more, Stan grew tired of listening to the duke's bullshit and gagged him again. Desh and Pil stood first watch, and the rest of us slept until Parth's first howls. I shivered at hearing him.

We rounded the last hill in the range the next day at midmorning and rode straight for Castle Glass to the southwest. The weather had been cool and damp since Desh bought the horses, with heavy storms at times. Now the clouds crackled and drenched us with such fury I couldn't have been wetter had I been lying underwater. I glared at Pil in her water-shedding cloak.

We slowed our horses to little more than a walk and suffered the storms until late afternoon. Then the rain ceased, the clouds thinned, and the breeze blew the sky clear in less than fifteen minutes. I halted so I could appreciate the clear sky, the crisp air, and the army we had found camped in front of us.

"Red and gold banner," I said, squinting. "At least we don't have to sweet-talk our way through some foreign army."

"Perhaps Pres is here," Pil said.

"No, he's not," said Parth. Pil tilted her head, so he added, "That green banner is General Pobla's standard. He must be returning home."

Ella pointed at two riders galloping toward us. "We shall have an escort to meet with the general."

Parth murmured, "Might we instead receive an escort to meet with syphilis?"

"What?" Pil asked.

Parth shook his head and grinned. "My only wish is that we were more presentable. Behold the mud." He pointed at his own nasty, trail-stained clothes.

The riders arrived, and one recognized Captain Parth. The other soldier greeted Stan by name, ogled Pil, and winked at Stan when most of us were looking at the army. They guided us into camp with no ceremony but no hostility, either. We dismounted in front of a big, green tent, and Ella led us in. I elbowed Parth aside to grab Durch and bring him into the tent.

General Pobla had served four generations of kings. He sat at a large, carved wooden table that must have been a pain in the ass for his aides to haul around. Below his bald scalp, the general possessed such mythic wrinkles that the flesh seemed to melt off his face. His shoulders lay square, though, and if his stomach bulged a little, his hands looked like they could crack rocks.

Eight soldiers attended Pobla: a junior officer, an aide, and six men standing around until it was time to kill people. He might have been frowning under the wrinkles, and his eyes narrowed to slits. "Captain, report!"

Parth greeted his superior with a well-oiled nod. "Sir, the Duke of Esterhite has betrayed us. He confessed. We have retrieved him to suffer the king's judgment."

Pobla examined Durch before he stood up and bowed. "Your Grace, if that's true, then you're an ungrateful, fornicating hog, and I'll pull your guts out myself. But it may not be true at all. Consider the source." He sniffed toward Parth. "Until Your Grace has been judged by the king—and nobody besides the king—you will receive your rightful honors and comforts."

The general waved to the aide without looking. "Unbind the duke. Then, a bath, decent clothes, a hot meal, and a cot."

As his gag was pulled off, Durch snarled, "These are the traitors, not me! Base, groaning bags of worm shit! They wrecked my home and killed my retainers. My son will testify to it. He should get here soon, maybe tonight!" He sneered at Parth. "The king won't take your piddling word over mine, you foreigner! I'll see you hanged. Crushed by stones!"

"Your Grace, please," Pobla said, with a gentle wave toward the tent flap.

The aide sawed through the duke's bonds and led him out of the tent. Durch tried to stomp Ella's foot on the way out, but she dodged out of his way.

"Now we have to catch him all over again," Desh whispered to me.

I shook my head. "Where can he go that's better than this?"

"Captain!" Pobla barked. "Explain yourself!"

Parth's brows lowered, but he kept quiet. I approved. Any response to such a command could be used to trap him.

"Answer me!" Pobla shouted.

Parth slowly nodded with a reflective smile. "My sister's murder at the hands of a bald man disturbed me particularly. It led me, as a boy, to consider—"

"Quiet!" Pobla breathed. "You imbecile. You brought the bandits in the west to justice, correct?"

"I killed most of them, yes," Parth said.

"Then why are they robbing, burning, and raping the western towns again? Eh? Did they rise from the grave to plunder a second time?"

"Unlikely, sir. When I departed, I left them thoroughly slaughtered. In my professional opinion, other people, still living, have chosen to take up banditry."

"Shut your yawning crack, smart-ass!" Pobla had gone red, especially his bald skull. "I think you're an accomplice. The bandits paid you off, you reported them wiped out, you left for rewards and glory, and they skittered back out of their holes to burn and thieve once more! Didn't they? Didn't you? Eh?"

"He hates the shit out of you," I whispered to Parth.

Parth sighed but didn't look at me.

Pobla said, "Parth, your bandits are forcing this army to return home with our goddamn objectives in the east unmet!"

I asked, "The king called you back?"

Pobla darkened. "After he returned from treating with that mud lump Ert."

"So, he's no longer chasing after the duke's brown-circle boys . . . and the war with Eastgate is over?" I asked.

"From what I hear, the conflict with Ert never started. Never should have been an idea in anybody's head." Pobla slapped his table and glowered at me. "It sounds as if some pathetic, gray-haired stick of a man arranged the whole thing."

I'd have a hell of a time now convincing Pres to go to war with Ert, no matter how many traitors I brought him. I started puzzling over options.

Parth spoke up. "I understand your orders, sir, but would it not be wise to send for confirmation from the king before abandoning the field?"

"I am abandoning nothing!"

"Of course, sir, but as you stated, the objectives remain unmet. Perhaps some miscommunication occurred."

"Clearly you do not understand my orders, you frilly thug," Pobla snarled.

"You might at least leave a sizable force here to provide strategic options should you need to return quickly," Parth said.

Pobla stared at Parth for several seconds. "Captain, do you love traitors?"

"I do not, sir."

"Do you eat the same food and roll in the same filth as traitors?"

"If so, it was mere coincidence." Parth dipped his head.

Pobla stabbed at me with his finger and yelled, "Then why is he walking around un-beheaded? Why isn't that traitor chained? Why hasn't that man, who murdered your queen, had the resounding shit thrashed out of him yet?"

I began to think that walking into this tent had been a mistake.

"I promise I shall kill him, sir," Parth said, "when His Majesty confirms that he wishes the man's existence to be obliterated. Without confirming it . . . well, obliteration is quite challenging to recover from. I assure the general that is true."

"Smart-ass. Go ahead, kill him now! I speak for the king!"

Parth gave Pobla a wide smile. "Yes sir. What means of execution is to be employed? Disemboweling?"

"That is customary for traitors." Pobla sat back down.

I glanced back at Ella. She nodded and moved her hand closer to her sword. Desh saw us and did the same.

Parth took a breath and paused for a moment with his hands poised, as if he were about to play the piano. "I wish to make no misstep in so serious a matter. Does the general order this traitor disemboweled?"

Pobla leaned forward with his elbows on the table. "Yes, I order it, damn you to Krak's drowsy crotch!"

I took a breath and relaxed as much as I could without falling down. I'd kill Parth first, then the two guards closest to him.

Parth nodded. "Very well, sir. I will be pleased to carry out the sentence in His Majesty's presence." He smiled as if he'd just handed Pobla a diamond and a magic sword.

"What?"

"By the king's law, disembowelment may only be carried out with a member of the royal family attending." Parth bowed deeply. He mouthed a filthy word while he was down there, but I think only I saw it.

"Bullshit! Cut off his head, then!"

"But you have pronounced sentence, sir." Parth shook his head. "Only the king may alter a sentence that results in death."

Pobla clenched his teeth and turned red. Then he turned maroon. At last, he pointed at me. "Men, disarm him! Bind him and throw him in the most repugnant mudhole you can find."

I glanced at Parth.

He whispered, "If you expect any more help from me, go ahead and die."

Ella murmured from behind me, "I will accompany you and ensure the safety of your person. Hand me your weapon."

I drew my sword. The soldiers froze. Parth skipped away like water on a hot skillet and stopped with his sword pointed at my throat. I handed the sword to Ella.

"I shall transport his weapons to the king, General." Ella fixed an eye on the old man, and he physically wavered. He had to know that Ella was like a mother to Pres.

"Fine," Pobla grunted. He waved one hand. "I don't want to look at this filth anymore."

Ella smiled at me. "My fee to care for your sword is one gold coin this time. Next time, it will be ten."

Pobla had trained and disciplined his soldiers well. Three of them took me on an inspection of the camp, evaluating various muddy depressions and pools for repugnancy. I thought they might be joking, but when they selected an awful-looking hole, I realized that they were not just screwing with the brown-skinned fellow. They were following their orders in detail.

A fourth soldier had been trailing us with a mallet. I couldn't resist making whimsical comments about what he planned to do with it, but nobody laughed.

"I see that General Pobla disapproves of his soldiers laughing." I glanced at the nasty pool of mud. "You boys are as tight as stone statues."

"Were you trying to be funny?" asked the man with the mallet. "Sorry. I'll pay attention next time and try to pick out the funny bit." Then he reached into a big satchel to pull out manacles, a chain, and a long iron stake.

Five minutes later, I was manacled and bound to the stake in the middle of the muddy hole by a five-foot-long chain. No matter which way I stretched, I couldn't get entirely out of that damned water.

TWENTY-ONE

I had been sitting for two minutes with muddy water wicking up my trousers and into my ass when Ella arrived.

"This is unconscionable!" she said. "I should haul Pobla out here by his ear and make him drink this!"

"I appreciate your passion over my welfare, but I can slip out anytime I choose."

"Very well. By sorcery, I assume, but I shan't ask for details."

Desh, Pil, and Stan walked up behind Ella, and Pil handed me a soft towel. "Clean your hands."

"Hah! This mud wallow will get them dirty again in ten seconds."

Stan unfolded another towel to show a whole chicken, roasted and still steaming. "We were goddamn brilliant! Went over to the cook fires, and I played at getting touchy-grabby with Master Pil." Stan had called Pil by her proper title, Master. Now he nodded at Pil, who smiled like a girl up to no good. "Then she chases my ass all over, swinging a stick of firewood and cursing me worse than my first wife ever thought of."

"He ran through the middle of a fire," Pil said, patting the soldier on the arm.

"And while all of that horseshit from hell was blowing up . . ." Stan stopped to giggle. "Master Desh walked in the back and stole Pobla's supper, his fancy tablecloth, and every other flipping thing that wasn't on fire or nailed to a table!"

I wiped my hands clean. "Thank you, that's kindly taken." I held the chicken in one hand and started pulling off strips. "Do you have enough?"

Before anybody answered, my spirit was swept out of me in a rush. I had never been summoned with that much intensity before. I came to rest in the gods' trading place before nausea even touched me.

"Squatting in mud. Debased and dependent on others even for sustenance," Harik said. "Will you next sing and jape for coins? Befoul the water with your own repellent human waste?"

"It's meditative. Come sit next to me, Mighty Harik! Although I doubt you're capable of learning or of thinking about anything but yourself. I will share my chicken, though."

"It's beneath me even to hear you offer such a thing. I bring you here to trade, Murderer."

"I am uninterested." I dropped away toward my world, but Harik pulled me back. So, it was going to be a contentious visit.

"Do you wish to draw your sword and look upon me? Oh, you're unable." I heard a hint of Harik sighing, as if he were settling on a bench. "You should not have given up the sword. You should have instead killed your enemies and dedicated their deaths to me."

"You sure do want me to dedicate things to you lately. You never talked that way before, Mighty Harik. Why now? Sorry, why now, you scrofulous, oozing toad?"

"I shall make the first offer. That should please you. Protect that foolish duke's life for the next week in exchange for one square."

I stopped to wonder what that was about.

"Murderer! Do not gawk. I have made a magnificent offer."

"It is magnificently absurd, and I'd be a magnificently stupid ass to take it." If the king decided to execute Durch, I'd be forced to defend him. "Even *you* are not so dumb as to make such an offer. What do you really want?"

"Aha! Thank you for asking! I want you to kill that floppy little king. You make the first offer."

I laughed. "No, I won't get involved with that."

"How better to cripple his kingdom and assure its defeat?" I could picture Harik using his hands to explain it to me. "Really, if you spurn this deal, I must question whether you even care to try."

"Your Magnificence, I spurn the shit out of it."

After a long pause, Harik's voice dropped. "Murderer. Offer me a deal to kill one or the other. The king or the duke. Do not defy me."

I didn't answer. Instead, I fell away from the trading place, and Harik didn't hold me there. Within moments, my ass was in the muddy water again.

"We have enough," Desh said.

Pil pointed to a cloth sack over her shoulder.

"I fear we are attracting notice," Ella muttered.

I glanced around and saw two small groups of soldiers watching us. "You go find some warm spot with beer and bouncy music. This is plenty for me."

"No, one of us is staying with you every minute," Pil said. "I know you can break free whenever you want, but that doesn't mean you won't get hurt doing it, so you stay in those manacles. We'll protect you and have your sword ready, and when you finally see the king, I expect you to make Pobla look like an ass."

"Before you thrash him," Ella said.

"Or kill him," Desh added.

"Well . . . I had planned to wait until midnight, rise up like Lutigan, and destroy half this camp," I said. "I'll put that off until tomorrow night and try this for now."

By sunrise, I was shivering so hard I couldn't make a fist, but at least I hadn't been alone through the night.

For the next two days, I walked in the middle of the army, manacled and chained. It was not much of a hardship compared to some I've experienced. Ella and the others worked hard to keep me fed, watered, and as comfortable as practical. More than that, my life didn't seem to be in danger. I returned to Castle Glass as a surly prisoner.

Although the iron manacles had scraped most of the skin off my wrists, I was not allowed in the king's presence without wearing them. They were symbolic, since Pres understood that I could kill him if I wished, bound or not. I would probably not survive, but he would definitely be dead.

The king met us in his library, which I felt was a good sign. We had gathered there on the day I arrived at the castle, back when Pres had no notion yet of pulverizing my hands and feet. The room was more crowded this time. The first time, Ella, Pil, Parth, and Queen Dall had joined Pres and me. This time, Desh, Pobla, and Durch attended too, along with Sir Linkan, who must have been pardoned. Four soldiers, a servant, and a fair-skinned young man I didn't know made the room cramped. Another general and a junior officer stood behind the king, their eyes flitting around the room.

Dimore the red sorcerer was nowhere in sight. I had described him to Desh, who was now anxious to meet the man and kill him.

It was a tense, crowded room. The only thing that made the place bearable was the king's wine, which was tasty, plentiful, and poured for all. Although manacled, I held the cup and clinked as I drank.

While everybody was collecting themselves, Pres walked over to me, took my free hand in both of his, and examined it. "I know it doesn't mean anything, but I think I was kind of crazy."

"Oh, no, it always means something when a king is crazy. It means something bad for everybody else."

He nodded. "I shouldn't have done it, Bib. I'm sorry. I'm glad you were able to fix it."

I wanted to hate the boy. I had even considered killing him once I got free, but I realized those had been grudging daydreams. "Pres, I had intended to be mad at you forever, but it's too much work. If you don't mind, I'll be mad at you until after supper and then knock off."

Pres smiled and started to step back, but this time, I caught his hand. "Your Majesty, I venture that I might ask a favor of you."

Pres gave me a tired smile. "Of course."

"It's a big favor. Just an avalanche of a favor, and you won't want to do it. But it will be better than the alternatives. Promise me you'll listen with an open mind."

He grunted and said, "I'll listen. Maybe not tonight."

"Time is important in doings such as these," I said. "Is that cryptic enough? I'm trying to talk like a sorcerer."

"Not as good as Desh." The king stepped to the front of the room.

Maybe I could convince Pres to cooperate in losing his war if I could make it painless enough. I had a significant reservoir of grievance and guilt to draw from in order to convince the boy.

Pres pointed at Durch and raised an eyebrow at Pobla. "General, what is this?"

"Your Majesty, I have brought back the damned traitorous sorcerer who was abetted by Captain Parth. That warrants some investigation, my liege. And there are some vague accusations they made of His Grace, the Duke of Esterhite, that, if you permit me, should be put to rest."

The king chewed his cheek for a moment. "On any other day, that would have all my attention. On any other day, I would have sharp words for Bib about dicking around and starting wars on my behalf. Not today, however." Pres turned toward the young man standing next to him. "Hal."

Hal stepped forward. "Three days ago, an army from the Kingdom of Bredgarde invaded us from the west. They appear to be taking and occupying every city and large town as they go, likely in order to secure their rear area and supply lines. The scout who brought us this news believes that they will arrive here in three days, or possibly four."

Everybody except Desh and me started talking at once.

After several seconds of chaos, Pres shouted, "Quiet!" The room grew still. "If that's a sign of our discipline, we'll be wiped out down to the last baby. Control yourselves. General Pobla, you picked a fine moment to return. With our full army in the field, we'll hack King Staggs and his thugs apart and send the parts home to their wives."

I appreciated the king's fighting spirit, but I needed one detail. "How many men is this Staggs asshole bringing?" Everybody stared at me. "It seems like an important question. If we don't know, how can we build enough wagons to haul their legs and heads and such back home?"

Hal raised his eyebrows at the king, who nodded. "The scout says over two thousand. Maybe as many as twenty-five hundred."

I started to rub my hands together before I remembered the manacles. "How many in your army, Your Majesty?"

"That's not important," Pres snapped. "Enough."

"So, not as many as Staggs has?" I said.

Parth cut in. "The bandits we suppressed last winter may have been supported by Bredgarde. Perhaps they were even Bredgarde soldiers in disguise." He smiled at Pobla. "That explains why our bandit difficulties have returned."

"Maybe," the king said, while Pobla grunted.

"Your Majesty," I said, "maybe you'd like to add a few more ruthless sorcerers to your fighting force? And where is Dimore, by the way?"

"Who?" Pres asked.

"Dimore. Sorcerer. Round like a melon, red like an apple, or at least his clothes are."

Pil nodded.

Almost everybody looked confused, including Parth.

"I don't know who you might be referring to," Hal said to me, "but if you're offering your magical services—"

"No!" Pobla shouted.

Durch bellowed, "They're traitors! You execute people like that. You don't give them jobs!"

Pres waved them down. "Bib, I need proof I can trust you. Because if I can't trust you, can I trust Desh and Pil? Or Ella? We'll settle this now so it won't distract us from the war." He swept his gaze over us, his young face hard. I wondered who he'd pay the most attention to. At last, he sat back against his desk and said, "Pil, what do I need to know?"

I found that surprising. Other people in the room found it shocking, outrageous, or hallucinatory, according to the looks on their faces.

Pil's eyes widened, but then she smiled. "The duke plans treason and has been attacking your towns in the east, Your Majesty. His men wear the brown-circle symbol."

"Lying bitch!" Durch hurled his wine cup at Pil, striking her on the chin and leaving a cut. It splashed wine on her and Desh.

Parth bounded to Durch, seized his arm, and twisted it behind his back.

"Take your greasy, foreign hands off me!" Durch shouted.

Pres pointed at Durch. "Be still! Quiet! Don't twitch, Your Grace!" he whispered to Hal, who clenched his teeth and nodded. "I apologize, Pil, for the duke's horrible behavior. In my own home. It's awful and beneath my house's dignity."

Pil smiled again, rubbing her chin. "Please don't concern yourself. It's only wine, not acid or something. We saw cows that . . . although, well, perhaps we should talk about it another time."

Pres smiled at her and then glanced around. "Does anybody agree with Pil's accusation?"

"Me!" I shook my manacles.

"And me," Ella said.

I glanced over. Parth was nodding, and Desh had raised his hand.

The king stood up straight and glowered at Durch with loathing. "Pil, did he murder my mother?"

Pil didn't hesitate. "No."

"What?" Pres blurted.

I started figuring out whether I could kill all the guards with just a pair of manacles. Probably not.

"He's a horrible traitor and murderer, Your Majesty," Pil said, "but your mother's death isn't one you can condemn him for."

"How do you know that?" Pres took one step toward Pil and collapsed. He didn't try to break his fall. He dropped as if every muscle had been cut at once.

"Pres!" Ella cried out.

Hal leaped to kneel over the king, but he collapsed in the same way. He smacked into the floor face-first.

I heard something clatter behind me. The servant had crumpled and lay still against a bookcase, his tray on the floor. More bodies hit the floor from the direction of the king.

Desh caught my eye. "Don't drink—" His eyes glazed, and he flopped onto the rug like a basket of fish.

I pulled a green band to investigate why people were being stricken. That was a fortunate move since the world disappeared in the next second. My band told me I was dying fast. It was a magical poison, which startled me, but it was easy to reverse if I acted in time.

Although it's an imprecise description, I gelded the poison in my body.

I didn't need to open my eyes to see. They were already open, and I just started seeing through them again. My ears worked too. I heard somebody far away shouting for help. Ella lay beside me. Pobla was down, along with the other general and his aide. Durch stood glancing around him, his eyes huge. Pil was kneeling on her hands and knees by the door. Anybody else would have been out of my view.

Just enough time remained for me to save one other person. I pulled another band and grabbed Ella's ankle. Within three seconds, I felt her foot move.

Curing Ella forced pain into my body, as if I had poured lye into my veins. I pulled another green band and sent it over to Pil, who was sick as hell but not dying. Desh was already sitting up on his own. Durch still stood in the middle of the room like a penguin that's been poleaxed. Parth had left the room—I realized the voice shouting for help had sounded like him.

My exploratory green band told me everybody else was dead: Pres, Pobla, Linkan, Hal, and the other general with his aide. I hadn't seen the servant and the guards drink, but they lay dead too. They must have nipped a taste before we arrived.

I struggled to get an arm under me and then pushed my way up to sit against a side table. Desh was kneeling over Pil.

Two guards rushed into the room, and one dove to the king's side, knocking Durch out of the way. After some seconds, the guard gazed around the room and swallowed. "His Majesty is dead."

Ella made a sound like getting kicked in the gut. I reached and grabbed her hand to squeeze it.

Durch looked down at Prestwick's body and pursed his lips. "Well. I guess that makes me king."

TWENTY-TWO

I have no objection to killing kings. Some say regicide is the foulest of all crimes, but I say when a man starts collecting taxes and chopping off heads, he's daring everybody in creation to come kill him. If he didn't want to get killed, he should have been a baker.

The same is true for sorcerers, of course.

In the king's study, with the memory of poison pounding in my veins, I required most of a minute to reach my feet. If Desh hadn't helped me, I'd have taken twice as long. I did not stride over to Durch and stab him in the heart first thing. Maybe that was a mistake.

Pil sat on the floor against a bookcase, panting with her head back. Her color was good, so I didn't feel great concern for her health.

The two guards grabbed Durch's arms, and he bellowed like an aggravated mule. "Let me go! I'm the goddamn king now, and I'll have you tortured to death! Your wives and babies too!"

The younger guard raised his eyebrows at his grizzled companion. The older fellow paused before saying, "Your Majesty, I just want to keep you safe . . ." He glanced around. "We can defend you better over behind that big-ass desk. There may be assassins."

"Oh. Damn, that's good thinking," Durch rumbled.

The gray-haired soldier guided Durch toward the desk with one hand touching the duke's arm and the other hand on his sword. On the way, the young guard lagged a bit so he could give his friend a big-eyed, silent whistle behind Durch's back. Ella had raised Pres like he was her son. Now she crawled to his body and lay beside it, holding him tight. In death, he looked like a boy again, all the hardness and cruelty drained away.

I knelt beside Ella and touched her shoulder, but she shrugged me off. I knew the grief on her face. It was so great a thing that all she could do was stand under it and let it crush her. "I'm sorry. I'm here," I whispered.

The shouting had drawn seven guards, three servants, an officer, and two clerks, which made for a crowded room. Most of them accomplished nothing except getting in each other's way. The officer tripped over Hal's body and fell on his ass. Durch had seated himself behind the desk and was examining everything on it.

I motioned Desh over to a corner. "You seem fine."

Desh smacked his lips. "My mouth tastes like copper. I'm good apart from that." He held up an acorn. "It's for poison. Disease too. I had time to shove one into my mouth. Pil wasn't as quick. She had one in her hand, which saved her life but barely."

I raised my eyebrows, not wanting to ask the question out loud.

Desh smiled. "I taught Pil how to make them. She's clever. It's nice to see a sorcerer with some morals. That's not intended as an insult to you."

I nodded, but then my stomach fell. "Pil is a moral young person now, but what will she be when the gods get done with her?" The gods loved to turn sorcerers into the opposite of what they were to start with. I hadn't always been a murderer.

Desh's face sagged for a moment as he watched Pil. Then he handed me the acorn. "Take this one for yourself. It only works once, and only for sorcerers."

"Thanks." I opened my pouch to drop it in, but my fingers

touched the copper cup I had found on the Void Walker's island. I didn't remember putting it in there.

Desh's eyes widened when I raised the cup. "Pretty."

A slip of waxed parchment lay under the cup. "Shit," I said when I looked at it. An image of the cup was drawn on it, signed with the letter D. "Dimore, I guess."

Desh snarled, the most emotion I had seen from him in days.

I said, "Dimore told me to travel east to help the king, and I found this cup there. Do you think drinking from it might raise Pres from the dead?"

Desh rubbed his jaw. "You know Harik better than I do. Does that sound like something he'd allow? I'm skeptical. Instead, it might raise Pres as a monster that would destroy everyone who ever hurt his feelings."

With my finger, I traced the tree engraved on the cup. "I can't tell a damn thing about this, but if we're going to try helping Pres, we should do it now while he's fresh. Although . . . this cup is your area of knowledge, Desh. Besides, if Dimore is the one who cut off your hands, it's linked to you." I handed him the cup.

He took the cup, as if giving it to him was the only logical decision.

I looked around. "Do you see any water in here?"

Desh frowned. "Would you trust it not to be poisoned? We don't know who in the name of Madimal's webby feet poisoned us all. I nominate Dimore since he wasn't here."

I grabbed a servant's arm, my manacles clanking. "Hurry, bring me some water! Run!" The man's mouth fell slack, but he sprinted away when I scowled at him. I pointed at Durch. "That bellowing squashed turd says he's king now. Desh, he may be the poisoner. He's crude and brutal and stupid to boot, but he's sly."

Desh held out a hand. "Hold up those manacles."

I held out the manacles like a toddler waiting to have his muddy hands washed.

Desh ran his fingertips over the locks. "What about Parth? Could he be the killer?"

"No, he ran for help."

"Where is he now?" Desh asked.

I glanced around the room but didn't see the captain. "Huh. Half the castle is in this room now. Why hasn't he come back?" I felt a sudden creeping urge to find the man.

Pil was on her feet and shuffling toward us, one hand on the wall. Ella had sat up and pulled Pres's shoulders into her lap. Her head drooped over him with her blonde braid dangling.

The servant charged back into the room, water slopping out of a mug as he shoved it at me.

Desh had been fiddling with one of the locks using what looked like a sliver of wood. I held back a sarcastic comment. The manacle fell open.

"Now I have you," Desh muttered. Five seconds later, Desh picked the other manacle open.

"Desh, what do you think?" I nodded at the cup.

"It's enchanted for certain, but I don't know what it does yet."

Pil said, "What are you two talking about?"

"Doing something stupid." I sighed. "If it really can bring him back, doing it now is his best chance. If it can't bring him back . . . well, we're not going to hurt him."

I marched back to Ella, pushing two guards out of the way, and I knelt down. I whispered to her, "Darling, we have one thing to try. It probably won't help him, but there's a small chance."

Ella stared up at me with red eyes, wet cheeks, and snot on her lip. "Here! I'm moving!" She tried to scoot over, stand up, and not drop Pres all at the same time.

"Stay there!" I reached back to Desh for the little cup and filled it with water. "Here. Trickle it into his mouth."

"What the hell is this crowd all about?" Durch yelled. I heard him shove back the desk chair.

Ella cradled Pres's head with one arm and tipped the cup with her other hand.

Durch yelled, "Guards! Stop whatever shit is going on there!"

Most of the guards hesitated when I pulled my knife and said, "Don't do it, boys." The older guard stepped back and pulled his young friend with him. Another guard reached for Ella, though, and the man next to him drew his sword. I whipped a deep cut across the first one's arm, and he yanked it back with a curse.

The second guard stepped toward me with his sword high. I yelled, "Stop!" and raised my hand. He didn't stop. In fact, three other guards reached for their swords.

I could envision a fight in which my friends and I killed all the guards, and the officer, and Durch too as long as my sword was out. But some of us would be injured as well, or even killed. Hell, Ella was just about defenseless. It seemed a poor trade. The guard swung at my head from a nice, wide stance. I stepped inside his swing and kneed him as hard as I could in the groin.

In most instances, I dislike the tactic of kicking a man's crotch, but not for reasons of mercy. My foot is not my most adroit weapon, and the groin is often a deceptively difficult target. The kick is likely to connect with the upper thigh to little effect, especially since men cherish that area and tend to move rapidly when it is under attack.

In this case, my groin kick was a strategic move. It sounded like I had smashed a sack of corn with a club. Every man in the room twitched in reflexive sympathy. The guard's raw groans, interrupted by his vomiting, slowed the men further, which was a bonus.

I nodded toward the groaning guard. "I didn't kill him. We're all friends here," I called out, smiling around at everybody. "It was just one of those sad misunderstandings." Those were unblushing lies, but nobody drew a weapon or closed in on us.

Durch pushed between two guards and stared down at Pres and Ella. "I don't care what all this butt-bleeding uproar is about! Stifle it right now!" He bared his teeth.

Ella had dropped the empty little cup, and it rolled onto Pres's chest. Water lay on his lips and cheek, but he was still pale and dead. Ella gazed up at me, her eyes wide, but I had to shake my head. Her face went blank.

Desh knelt down and whispered to me, "Bib, we should leave."

Durch was scrutinizing Pres and Ella, working his jaw as if chewing a tough piece of meat. Whatever idea he came up with when he stopped chewing wouldn't be good for us.

I pitched the cup to Desh. "Ella, let me help you." I lifted her by the arms until she was standing, then I guided her toward the door.

"I didn't give you permission to leave!" Durch barked.

"You're not king yet, you slimy blowhole," I said.

At the doorway, Ella wheeled and screamed, "No!"

I had been waiting for it and held her by the waist and one arm, ready to pull her into the hallway. "It's not safe. We have to leave."

"No!" she bellowed again, reaching toward Pres's body. She drew a huge breath and swung her elbow back into my nose.

I almost let go when my broken nose blinded me. "Desh, help me!"

"I'm trying! Ow! Damn it!"

Ella stopped flailing, so Desh must have grabbed her free arm. She still writhed, threw herself, and kicked my shin once. The whole time, she kept shouting "No!" as if she were leaving half of herself on that floor.

Pil guided me as I dragged Ella back through the door and into the hallway. Desh held Ella's arm and pushed from the front.

As Desh left the room, I called to him, "Slam the door behind you! Pil, grab Ella for me!"

I heard the door slam. As Desh and Pil struggled with Ella, I ran my hand along the wall until I touched the door. I pushed a white band into it and warped the wood against the doorframe for just a moment before somebody tried to pull the door free.

"That door will never open again," I said, grabbing one of Ella's arms. "They'll have to break it down."

Fifty feet down the passageway, Ella stopped struggling. Instead, she walked whichever way we guided her, silent, with her head down. Ten minutes later, we reached the gate leading out of the castle courtyard. My vision had cleared, but I was a bloody mess.

"What about our horses? I bet Durch's men will follow us, and they'll be riding horses, won't they? We'll need those horses." Pil was babbling a little. Her eyes were tense, her forehead creased.

"Our horses are at the stables." Desh pointed down the hill.

Pil nodded. "Right. That's right. We need a horse for Bib too. I'll run ahead."

"Wait!" I said, but she was already loping toward the main part of town.

"Maybe I should catch her," Desh said.

Before I could answer, Pil stopped short, staring down the hill. I looked past her and saw dozens of people hurrying in different directions. At least five bodies lay on the dirt with people standing or kneeling around them.

I left Ella with Desh and sprinted down the road, past Pil, to the first person on the ground. He was an older man, beefy with thick, gray hair. He writhed and groaned with his eyes closed, not answering the frantic questions from the woman leaning over him.

Scanning, I counted eight more people laid out like this man, and that was only on the upslope side of town. There could have been dozens of them across the whole city.

"I can't help these people," I said as Pil arrived beside me.

She stared at me but didn't say anything.

"I don't have enough power. And I'm sure to need the power I have for something else, maybe to save your damn life!"

Pil ground her teeth. "How many can you heal?"

"Hell, I don't know! None!" I pulled away from her, not realizing until then she'd been holding my arm. "Even if I could, which ones would I save? I'm not smart enough to decide which people should live."

"You act like you're smart enough to decide which people should die! I don't see how this is any different." Pil glared at me, hard and maybe a little disgusted.

That shocked me for a few seconds. Saving these people wouldn't help me achieve my goals. Every bit of power I spent here was one I might need to be done with the gods, to tell them to eat gravel.

But healing these people was the kind of thing I once would have done, before Harik helped me turn myself into a murderer. When the God of Death told me that I would never escape the gods, he had probably known that I'd end up in this spot.

I pushed the whimpering peasant woman aside and bent over the man, pulling a green band. He had been poisoned, but thank

Krak's ears and elbows it wasn't a magical poison. It was deadly enough but diluted. I stripped the poison out of his veins, and a slight burn spread throughout my body.

I ran to the next victim. He was a little boy, already dead and turning blue. I sprinted on to a young woman, trying not to think that I might have saved that boy if I had bypassed the first man.

As I knelt over the woman, I yelled to Pil, "Find a child who's alive and call me there when I'm ready!" Adults, being larger, would have a better chance to survive without help. That was my theory, at least. I healed the woman and stood, my veins burning hotter. Pil was waving at me from thirty paces away, and I ran to her.

I wasn't sure how many people I healed. Pil found several more children still alive, and I healed them in turn. Desh helped me walk from one to the next when my body started blackening and peeling from the inside. It felt that way, at least. That might have been an overly theatrical image, or maybe it wasn't.

I helped at least three adults after we ran out of children. Desh and Ella dragged me to the last two, each supporting an arm. When I had finished, my body was nothing but a sack of lava. I passed out with one and one-half squares of power left.

TWENTY-THREE

omebody was dragging torches back and forth inside my body, which was a great improvement. Even before I opened my eyes, I knew I was on horseback but sitting in front of somebody else who had the reins. I forced my crusty eyes open. It was late afternoon, and we were riding west around a short, wooded hill. Desh sat the horse in front of me.

"Are you awake?" Ella said from over my shoulder, her voice tight. I realized that our bodies were bound together with ropes, and she was holding me with one arm. It must have been uncomfortable as hell.

"Yes," I croaked. I tried again and just squeaked.

"He's awake," Ella called out, drawing rein. "Here." She fiddled with something on her saddle and then handed me a jug of water. "I apologize for the bruises you must have on your behind. Pil and I dropped you in the attempt to seat you upon the horse."

I waved that away with one hand while I held the jug to my lips with the other. After a long pull, I had to gasp since I still couldn't breathe through my broken nose.

Desh rode back to us. "How do you feel?"

"Manly," I lied. "Ready to jump a five-rail fence. How many did we save?"

"Fourteen," Desh said.

"Wonderful. Were they grateful?" I winked at Pil, who had ridden up on my other side.

She smiled. "Some of them were happy—the ones you saved and their families of course. The families of those who died . . . well, at least we stole horses and escaped before they overran us. In their grief."

"We brought another horse for you," Ella said. She began cutting the ropes that bound us. I slid to the ground and looked straight up into Capps's face. "Toad lover from hell."

Capps grunted. "Thanks for saving my ass from death. You didn't have to do that."

I closed my mouth for a moment, then said, "I didn't know I had. And I probably wouldn't have if I'd known."

"Doesn't change things."

"He was the last one you healed," Pil said.

"Why didn't you throw him in through the tavern door and ride away?" I asked.

"Parth is the poisoner," Desh said. "He was planning all along to kill Pres and anybody else he could. He left Capps to die. That kind of thing weakens the bonds of loyalty."

Pil added, "Capps has been telling us a lot about Parth, and I think you should hear it too."

"I suppose I should." I mounted the horse, a mare with poor hindquarters. "Where are we going?"

"Away from death at the hands of the townspeople and Durch's minions," Ella said, her face pulled as tight as a bowstring.

I said, "I approve, of course, but it would be nice to have a more definite goal in mind. Getting close enough to stab Parth in the heart is a good choice, in my opinion. Let's find a place to camp and make a real plan."

We rode another hour before finding a thicket of trees tight enough to shield a campfire's light. With Pil on watch, the rest of us settled down to a meal of tough bread, dried beef, and watery beer.

I said, "All right, you thug. Reveal Captain Parth's history, hopes, and dreams."

Capps rubbed at his nose. "He's not a captain, not really. I've served him five years, and he's never followed any calling but one. He's a master of making bad things happen."

Ella said, "That makes no sense."

"That's what I told him! I said bad things for some is good things for others, so it can't be all bad. Parth told me that's what makes it art." Capps tore off a heroic chunk of bread with his teeth.

I squinted at Capps. "That sounds like bullshit. Why would he do such a thing?"

"It's hard to explain." After we stared at him a bit, Capps said, "Well, he's awful good at killing people, and making them kill each other, and tearing shit up. Stealing things, of course. People pay him to do it, and we all like doing stuff we're good at."

I said, "Who is he? Is he really from Pelleth, or is that a frilly lie?"

"He is," Capps said. "I think so. Said his given name was Gurni Hopper, but he changed it when he decided to admit he was a bad man. Said nobody was going to void their bowels when they heard Gurni Hopper was coming to town to kill them."

Ella shook her head and looked away.

Desh said, "What do you mean he decided to admit he was bad?"

"Just what I said. Told me he was born bad. Baby Gurni felt no more for his ma than if she was a milk pail. So bad that his folks booted him onto the street when he was a boy and had a big party after." Capps held up one hand. "I swear it. Parth doesn't get drunk much, but when he does, he's a talker. Not saying he's all bad. He likes animals. Real fond of pigs. Doesn't give a flip about money, so he gives it to whomever wants it. Of course, he says most folks who get money will do themselves harm, so it's a bad act. I don't know— that requires more hard thinking than I care to give it."

I paused to digest that. I guess everybody else did too.

"Don't believe me?" Capps leaned toward the fire. "Here's how Parth himself said it, in between rounds of vomiting. Young Parth made a fortune by murder and thieving, which he thought was right nice. With all that gold, he could do ten times more bad things. But in six months, all he had left was his sword, his clothes, three silver coins, and a wooden carving of a duck."

I put my hands on my hips. "Come on . . ."

Capps broke in. "I ain't done. He wasn't sure how he lost that fortune, so he figured he was just bad with money. He went on to do well starting wars and such, and of course killing folks and taking their things, so with his second fortune, he hired a famous man of business. That fellow simply did not understand a damn thing about being bad. Soon, Parth was dumping his body into the harbor. A year later, all Parth had was his sword, his clothes, three gold coins, and a wooden carving of a duck."

"Have you ever seen this duck carving?" Desh asked.

"I have. It's a crappy little thing. The point is, Parth said he realized he wasn't bad with money. He just doesn't like using money to do bad things. He likes his badness hands-on."

Desh shook his head. "No. I don't believe it."

Capps sighed. "Here's what Parth told me about Durch. He said doing bad, wicked things should be like playing pretty music on a spinet, all artistic-like. But Durch does bad things like he's slamming the keys with a skillet in one hand and a live fish in the other."

"You can't expect us to believe all that," I said.

Capps shrugged. "It's the truth, whether you believe it or not. Parth can't help being bad. But he said if a man's got to be bad, he may as well create something beautiful while he's at it. Poisoning all those people back there was just one note in whatever song he's playing. I hate that I got caught up in the bad part of it, though."

Desh eased his knife out of the sheath. "What is Parth's next note?"

Capps leaned away from Desh. "You got to promise you won't kill me if I say. And you'll set me loose."

From Capps's other side, I said, "I won't kill you unless you make me. But I won't set you free until I'm sure you're not lying."

Ella stood and stared down at Capps. "Where is he?"

"Parth has a camp," Capps said. "An outpost, like. He may go there. Or not."

"Where?" Ella snapped.

"Why? Go someplace else and forget him. Somebody will kill him someday for being a wicked asshole."

Ella unsheathed her sword in a slow, easy motion.

"Damn it." Capps hung his head. "Half a day west of here, south of the main road a piece. It's an old, bitty farm with fallow fields. You can find it easy."

It chafed me that Parth was out there breathing someplace, but his death wasn't my only concern. Durch would be king now, and I'd be tickled to see the farting hog get killed losing the war. That simplified my work considerably. My best move now was to find King Staggs and tell him every little thing I knew that might help him overrun Glass and put Durch's head on a spike.

But right now, Ella wanted to slay Parth, as sure as cows dangle. She wouldn't turn aside for anything so trivial as a war. When she found him, the quick, slippery bastard would kill her for sure unless she had allies. I couldn't leave her alone to face him.

Of course, after we killed Parth, Ella might not want Glass to lose the war. It had been her home for years, and she loved Karl. That was fine. At least Ella would still be alive to ride back to Glass, or journey to the Empire and become an elephant handler, or whatever she wanted.

"I'm going with Ella to kill Parth, if she'll let me," I said. "Capps, you'll lead us there. If I see that you've been truthful, you'll go free. If not, I'll put you and Parth in the same grave."

Capps groaned.

"You're right, I was lying. I won't stop to bury either of you bastards."

Ella turned to Desh. "Well?"

Desh nodded. "I'll come. Parth is too dangerous to have him flitting around free."

"Me too," Pil called from off in the thicket.

"Very well. We shall depart before sunup," Ella said.

"Sure. At least Parth won't screech us awake all night." I lay on the stubbly ground and rolled over a couple of times to avoid a few of the bigger roots. Desh was sitting up by the fire, cutting a long piece of leather. "I hope you're making something to keep you alert, Desh. You sleep less than any creature I've ever seen."

"I just have a little more to do. Don't worry, I'll make something nice for you."

For some reason, I slept hard. It was still dark when Pil kicked my boot and startled me awake. I waved a hand in front of my face and mumbled, "Why . . . I expect you could have stabbed me a dozen times and rolled a rock over me before I wiggled. That's disconcerting."

Pil said, "When sorcerers reach a certain age, we start to make allowances." She squeezed my arm, but the comment stung.

Sunup found us riding northwest, following Capps as he searched across the wooded hills for the East Tuck Road. I expected Staggs's army to march right up that road, since it was the most direct route from Bredgarde to Glass. Capps explained that the army was more than two days away still, based on what Staggs's spies at Castle Glass had told Parth.

I tallied the days since Harik had laid the deadline for war on me, and I came up with fifteen. I had six more sunrises to see that Glass lost this war. My palms sweated for ten minutes.

We traveled easier once we reached the road, and late in the morning, Capps halted beside a twisted nightmare of a dead tree. "Parth is south a mile or so, unless he's someplace else," Capps said.

"He had better be here!" Ella shouted. She looked around, her face reddening.

"We can all holler as loud as you like." Capps spat on the road. "That won't make him be here if he's someplace else. Do you want to find out? If you don't, there's a tavern just down the road in Tobbler."

We walked our horses well off the road and tied them in a stand of trees. From there, we followed Capps at a careful pace until we reached a big fallow field around an old farm, just as he described. As I hid in the tree line, I saw a small wooden farmhouse past the closest field, with its door open and its thatch roof fallen in. A bigger wooden barn stood nearby with a roof of wooden slats and three horses tied up in front.

Two men stood on opposite sides of the field, watching the area. They were armed but not in uniform.

We withdrew a hundred feet, and Pil strung her bow. Desh held a sling made of the leather he had been cutting the night before.

Ella pointed at Pil and Desh as she whispered, "Kill the sentries. Then provide cover as Bib and I sneak to the farmhouse. We shall rush in and kill Parth."

"What if he's not alone?" Pil asked.

"Then we kill everyone," Ella said.

"What if men show up from elsewhere?"

"Shoot them! That is what providing cover means."

Desh and Pil had enchanted their weapons, so I never doubted that the first part of Ella's plan would succeed. One sentry tumbled sideways when a stone smashed into his head. A moment later, the other man stiffened when an arrow appeared in his throat. He turned around twice and then ran five steps toward the farmhouse before falling forward and lying still.

I followed Ella at a fast stalking pace toward the farmhouse, our swords drawn. We were still fifty feet away from the farmhouse door when Desh shouted, "Drop!"

I collapsed to the ground and heard two arrows, or maybe quarrels, whip past above me. Ella dropped too, but not before she shouted, "Gods pound it!"

"Are you hurt?" I yelled at her. I could see blood on her left sleeve.

"Hell yes, I'm hurt, you idiot! Come on!"

We scrambled up at the same time, ran three steps toward the farmhouse door, and scuffed to a halt when armed men began running out of it. Somebody at the barn cried out, and I glanced that way as I retreated. Five crossbowmen stood in front of the barn door, three busy reloading and two busy falling to the ground.

There might have been five more crossbowmen someplace, or ten, or fifty. If so, the safest place would be next to the enemy. I roared and charged the men closing with us from the farmhouse.

The first one's eyes widened as he faltered. I thrust into his belly and then shoved him into the man behind him.

The second man struggled to push past his dying friend. I rushed on and sliced that man's throat with a neat cut. Then I stepped back to avoid getting caught as the two of them flailed and fell. Four more men were approaching from behind them. One of those was Parth, grinning like it was a holiday. Ella stood beside me, ready to attack.

"Look to the left!" Pil yelled.

Four more armed men were sprinting toward us from the trees out beyond the field. It was a good ambush. Parth and his five hooligans attacked from the right while four more men attacked from the left. Both groups could stay clear of the crossbowmen while they shot bolts into all our tender parts. If we had tried to run, we'd almost certainly have gotten killed. Getting killed still wasn't out of the question.

Two men from the farmhouse assaulted Ella at the same time. Another one tried to scramble toward me past his two dying comrades. I crippled his leg as he came. He collapsed, adding to the human barricade in front of me. I heard a cry from my left and glanced. Two of the four attackers out there were tumbling to the grass, one with an arrow in his side.

Parth laughed at me but didn't try to push through the dying men. "Come, Bib! I promise to make it endless and agonizing! Most dangerous man in the world, indeed!"

If I charged the scurrying weasel, he might well kill me. He was faster than I had ever been, even when I was young. Instead of attacking Parth, I turned and sliced the arm of one of Ella's two attackers. She landed a horrific cut to the side of her other attacker's head.

I sprinted around Ella to close with Parth, but I ran straight into the two remaining men from the left. I fenced with them for a few seconds before I realized that Ella was pushing toward Parth. "Pil, kill these assholes!" I shouted, pointing with my free hand at the men I was facing. I retreated three steps and then ignored them, turning toward Ella and Parth instead.

Ella was already down but not dead. Lying on her back, she blocked two thrusts from Parth in two seconds. Before I could rush toward them, a rod of fire shot through my hip and butt from one side to the other. My legs gave way, and I dropped to my knees. I might have taken pride in the quality and inventiveness of my cursing if I could have remembered it afterward.

Ella parried another thrust from Parth but cried out when the blade pierced her shoulder instead of her chest. If I was going to be killed by some ass-stabbing mercenary, it wouldn't happen before I did something for Ella. I pulled two blue bands and rotted the base of the wooden farmhouse wall just beside Parth. A six-foot-wide section of boards fell out onto Parth. He cursed, pushed the boards off himself, and stepped back.

Nobody killed me in the next two seconds. I looked past Parth and saw two crossbowmen loaded and aiming, one at me and one toward Desh and Pil. I dropped to my knees and howled when pain ripped through my butt cheeks. I fell forward onto the dirt, cursing, but nothing zipped through the air above me.

When I looked up, all the crossbowmen were down. Parth had fled and was mounting one of the horses. He kicked it into a gallop and rode out of sight around the barn, leading both the other mounts.

I pushed up to my knees again and saw Ella stand, bleeding from her arm, shoulder, and thigh. Her face paled when she saw me, and she limped over fast.

"Don't stand up," she said, even though I wasn't trying to do any such thing. She held my face in both hands. "Look at me. Keep looking at me."

"All right, you grabbed my interest. How bad is it?" I was a little scared, but mostly I felt curious, like wondering how many puppies would be in a litter.

Behind me, Pil began laughing. She didn't stop, either. Ella glared at her.

"What the hell is it?" I said, and my voice was whiny enough to embarrass me. "Tell me."

"Your ass has been impaled, Bib," Desh said.

I wrestled Ella's hands away and craned my head to look behind me on both sides. One of the mercenaries had thrust his sword all the way through both of my butt cheeks from side to side. He must have died at that instant, or at least been disabled, because the sword was still stuck in my bottom, supported as if my backside were a sword rack. I said, "I'll be damned," and fell straight forward onto the grass, just turning my head so I wouldn't land on my broken nose.

I didn't pass out, but I did sweat, shiver, and pant while I listened to Desh and Ella argue over what to do about my butt.

"Parth got away," I mumbled at one point.

Pil patted my shoulder. "He did. You'll have to kill him another time. Do you want to do it with the sword they left in your ass?" She giggled, took a breath, and laughed out loud until she walked away.

"Where's Capps?" I asked. "He led us into this ambush."

"The scummy bastard ran when the fighting started," Desh said. "We should have tied him to something. Bib, can you heal yourself right away after we remove this sword? I'm afraid we'll hurt you in some way that will need repair immediately."

"Why not?" I said, a little light-headed. "Just get it out."

Desh had a steady hand, and he removed the blade without much extra damage to my back parts. I did go ahead and heal the wound, although the pain left behind would make the saddle mighty uncomfortable for a while. I also healed Ella's wounds in her leg and shoulder. The arm wound given her by the crossbow bolt was minor, so I left it alone.

"What now?" Pil said.

Ella finished wiping down her sword. "We locate Parth once again, and this time, we kill him."

"Good," Pil said. "Can you track him?"

Ella scowled.

"He's one of King Staggs's men," I said, "so he'll probably meet up with Staggs and the army soon. If we find the army, we'll find Parth before long."

"Why?" Ella said. "Why should you wish to encounter the Bredgarde army? They are the enemy."

I said, "There might be useful intelligence." I didn't say that it would be me giving useful intelligence to them. "I think it's our best chance to find Parth."

Desh narrowed his eyes at me but didn't say anything.

"Well, since we can't track him . . ." Pil wrinkled her nose as she watched Ella.

"Fine, I agree. For now," Ella said.

As we hiked back to our horses, Desh held out the sword he had removed from my backside. "Do you want it? Souvenir?"

"Hell no! Throw it away!"

He laughed. "That's a wasteful attitude. I'll hold it for you." He shoved it in his belt next to his own sword.

TWENTY-FOUR

"I don't want to push too hard in places that aren't appropriate," Pil said, "because, well, of course you have your own way of working as a sorcerer and everything, but you are being a mean, selfish asshole."

"Push a little harder, Pil. You're being vague."

Pil had led me aside on the pretext of needing some private "sorcerer talk." We now rode a hundred paces behind the others. Desh had snorted at Pil's explanation but hadn't commented.

"Tell Ella about your part in the war," Pil said. "She thinks you're on her side, and you're letting her think that."

"I am on her side," I said. "I'm on the side of her not getting killed. If she catches Parth, he'll gut her. Since I plan to protect her from that, why not bring her along to the place I already intend to go? Parth is as likely to be with Staggs as anyplace else."

"That's logical, and it's also a bunch of crap. You want her with you, and you want to fulfill your debt, and what she wants can get ground up with the corn. You think you're saving her, but really, you're using her. It's beneath you, or at least it would be normally."

I stared around at the late afternoon sky, as pure blue as Ella's eyes. "You just don't understand. If I tell Ella about betraying Durch, she'll tell me to hang myself and go hunt Parth on her own. Then she'll die."

"You don't know that."

I raised an eyebrow. "Which one of us knows more about death?"

"You know I'm right." Pil wasn't backing down.

Hell, maybe she was right. I didn't intend to bet Ella's life on it.

We had ridden past the town of Tobbler and then five more villages since the ambush, wary each time of Parth and another attack. We met nothing more ferocious than some bored, yapping dogs and a young woman who wanted to sell us cloth bags.

The city of Darcross stood about halfway between Glass and the border. There the main road met the Northern Passage, a miserable, winding track with a name that was grandiose and unimaginative at the same time. Ella intended to push east straight through the city and ride all night.

We spotted smoke well before we made out the city itself. I dreaded what we would find when we got there. In these forested lands, people built everything out of wood, from mansions to privies, and they must have lived in terror of fire.

The familiar stretching and nausea hit me, and then some god dragged my spirit up and into the Gods' Realm.

"This is an awful time to chat, Mighty Harik," I said. "I was about to trim a carbuncle, and my enjoyment will be diminished if I have to talk to you first." I drew my sword and then stopped breathing.

Krak, Father of the Gods, had seated himself in the middle of the marble gazebo, clad in his robe that was known to be the whitest thing in existence. The slanting sunlight caused most of his face to glow with knowledge, and it shadowed the rest with suffering, or maybe annoyance. His wavy silver hair and virile beard topped a body popping with far more muscles than any other god could brag about. Rumor said Krak's cocky eldest son had once dared to manifest a physique challenging his father's. Krak had banished his child to the Void and ordered his name forgotten, which didn't work so well with immortal beings possessing eternal memories. Even motionless, Krak radiated power, as if the entire realm might tilt when he raised his hand.

Two other gods sat on the level below Krak.

At his father's right hand sat Weldt, the God of Commerce. Like most gods, his body and face were ideally beautiful, although his chin seemed a bit large and his hands somewhat small. His black, cropped hair and pale skin set off his gray robe, which might have been created from an iron bar beaten thin and folded into a robe shape. He looked grumpy.

Weldt's wife, Effla, the Goddess of Love, sat at Krak's left hand. She lounged on the bench with languorous ease, one hand resting on a massive beast beside her. It appeared to be a cat, although it could just as well have been a puny tiger. Her blonde, prettily disarrayed hair eased its way like lava down her cheek, neck, and shoulder. Her mahogany skin gleamed like liquid sex. Effla's deep-cut gown ran all the shades of red from whisper pink at the hem through throbbing maroon at her shoulders, and a five-strand necklace of rubies lay on her breast. She looked bored.

Krak stared at me. I stared back. Effla and Weldt fidgeted and sighed, glancing at me once in a while.

I didn't want to speak first, but if something didn't happen soon, I thought I might conflagrate under Krak's gaze. "Father Krak, it seems like you're busy, so I'll just go."

"Don't move!" Krak shouted. My head vibrated from the center out to my hair. "Do not dare leave." Then he stared some more.

The urge to look away grew in me, greater than any desire to drink or urge to pee I had ever experienced. I resisted until Krak squeezed his fist, making a sound like a stone slab cracking. I rushed to examine the brown dirt at my feet.

Effla said, "Dear Murderer, I desire to share some thoughts about magic with you."

My head flew up, and I met her eyes. In an instant, I wanted her more than I had ever wanted any woman. She didn't stupefy me the way Sakaj did when I looked at her. I felt keen of mind and aware. I was aware that I craved Effla and would soon carry her off behind the gazebo, where I would make love to her until I died. She said two or three more things before I realized she was still talking.

She was saying, "Listen to me now. I am sharing something precious with you. You have been wasting your power rather than cherishing it. Why save meaningless creatures who will never care about you? Who in fact despise you?"

She stopped talking and seemed to be waiting, so I concentrated on not saying something embarrassing. "I know you're right, Mighty Effla, but it seemed like the smart thing to do at the time."

She smiled, and I started sweating. "The smart thing?"

I wiped my forehead. "Maybe not smart, but the *thing* to do."

"That is your soft, old self speaking. Embrace your new self, Murderer, for you now stand face-to-face with risks that may drain you. You must be single-minded. Already you have depleted most of your power, and your greatest challenges lie ahead."

My mouth was open to agree with her, ask her to command me, and beg her to get on with the ravishing. Instead, I said, "Why do you care?"

"What?"

"Why do you care what happens to me? That's a mighty ungodly attitude as I understand it." My desire for her floated away on the comforting breeze of the Gods' Realm. I rested the point of my sword on the dirt and pushed the hilt toward her.

Effla smiled at me again and leaned forward, showing a disturbing amount of cleavage. "I do care. You may soon know how much I care. But first, allow me to help you with your magic problem."

I smiled back at her. "What magic problem, Mighty Effla? I think you're trying to lead me around by the metaphorical dick. Maybe the literal one. I need to know more."

Krak cleared his throat with the power of a log being split.

Weldt spoke up: "Let's not waddle around, Murderer. You need the power we have. You're low, you know it, we know it, so don't try to lie. You spent power like a drunkard with five gold coins and a broken heart. You're facing death, and maybe some awfully nasty bits before death. So, make me an offer."

"I'm not interested in a deal." I pointed my sword at the god. "In fact, Mighty Weldt, I'd like to know what in the ass-chapped hell you did to King Pres of Glass."

Weldt scowled at his wife and then at me. "What are you talking about?"

"How did you corrupt the king? Forget I said that. Why did you do it? Why did you even care?"

Weldt grinned. "This is pathetic. Just the most asinine, impotent negotiation ploy I've seen in a century. Make an offer, you gnat!"

"Well, if we're going to talk about impotence . . ." I glanced at Effla. Their marriage wasn't described as happy.

Weldt sat taller. "You filth. Do you think you can manipulate me with such a sad taunt?"

"What taunt?" I said. "You were the one who mentioned impotence."

Effla snickered.

Weldt hissed at his wife and then turned back to me. "Let's return to the immediate matter. You're a wastrel. I have power. Make me an offer, or die in agony."

"Why did you bend the king's mind to cruelty?"

"I did no such thing! Stop talking about it!"

"A sorcerer accused you, and I'd take a sorcerer's word over yours, Mighty Weldt. I'd take a floppy dandelion's word over yours."

Effla giggled.

Weldt glared at her. "Shut up, you moist heifer!"

Effla leaned back and stretched. "I would if you had anything to shut me up with."

Weldt surged to his feet. "You rutting bitch! Just be quiet!"

"Enough," Krak said in a flat voice. Weldt sat down and looked away toward the pink forest of jagged trees. Effla kissed her cat on the head.

"Father Krak," I said, "this is an interesting gang you brought to talk magic with me. Where's Fressa? I'd have expected the Goddess of Magic to be in on this."

"She's busy." Krak stood with his fists at his sides, and his arms tensed as if he were about to lift something heavy, like the entire gazebo. "I'm beginning to think you're too damn much trouble to fart around with, Murderer. And trust me, you don't want me to think that. Deal with me for the power you'll need."

"I might, Father Krak, if I could figure out what the hell this happy clown and juggler show is all about."

"You dare question me?" Krak's voice dropped so low my teeth shook.

"Not at all! I'm just making observations. Effla and Weldt are powerful gods, but it's obvious they don't want to be here any more than they want to be with each other. That's why they performed poorly today." I thought about winking at Weldt, but that might have been too much insult.

Krak said, "Deal now, Murderer, or you will grieve over this opportunity when you are forced to return to me."

The saddest part was that I *did* need power. I'd have to make another damn deal to get any, and I'd face some other grueling task to perform, or maybe have to give up one of the few things I still loved. Now was the time to make that deal, but I would rather not do it with Krak, who was the cruelest of all the gods.

I suspected my insults had already poisoned Weldt's and Effla's minds against me for today. I already owed Harik too much, Lutigan hated me too viciously, and Sakaj was too damn crazy. Harik owned me, but if Krak sanctioned a deal, then Harik would go sit and sulk someplace.

"How are Fingit and Gorlana these days?" I asked.

"Uninterested in you," Krak growled.

Maybe Fressa wasn't as busy as Krak said. Magic was her domain, and I had heard from other sorcerers that she could be a soft touch at times. "Father Krak, I agree to enter negotiations, but only with Fressa. This is her area, after all."

"Impossible," Krak said.

That was an odd choice of words. "I know that everything is possible for the omnipotent Father of the Gods."

"I will not allow it," Krak grated.

I wasn't listening to Krak, though. When I said Krak could do anything, Weldt had swallowed. "I'm concerned. Is Fressa unable to join us?" On a whim, I added, "Is Fressa well?"

"Of course she's well!" Krak bellowed, knocking me on my butt. "How could she not be well? She's a god!"

Still sitting, I said, "Meaning that Fressa is unwell."

Krak snarled at me, but Effla's skin paled from nut-brown to tan.

I stood. "I hope it's not serious."

No reaction from the gods.

"So, it is serious."

Krak shouted, "This is an idiotic conversation, and you are an idiot! All of the gods are well!"

His voice staggered me. I whispered, "Is Fressa dead?"

The gods' lack of reaction said everything. I yelled, "Do you mean Fressa is dead?"

Effla took a breath and examined me.

Krak flung me back into my body with such might that I was knocked off my horse. I bruised my shoulder on the hard road.

By the time I stood, Pil and Desh had ridden over to me. Desh said, "Harik?"

Pil shook her head. "No, I bet it was Lutigan."

"Nope. Krak."

Pil made a face.

I lowered my voice. "I think Fressa is dead." The idea was too big for me to keep inside. I had to talk about it.

After a few seconds, Desh said, "What's the joke?"

"I really think she's dead. Krak didn't say as much, but Weldt and Effla gave it away."

"Gods are immortal," Pil said. "They don't die."

"This one did. I don't know any details, but my instincts say it's true."

"If it's so, which I don't stipulate, how could it have happened?" Desh asked. "Did Krak crush her out of existence?"

I shook my head. "I don't think any of the other gods could have slain her. They all despise each other. If murder was possible, they'd have wiped one another out eons ago."

"Is she the only one?" Pil put her hand over her mouth and pulled it right back down. "Could it happen to other gods? I mean, have other gods been dying too? Could Fingit die tomorrow?"

I raised both hands. "None of those is the important question. The important question is if gods can be killed, can a man kill one?"

"Or a woman?" Ella had caught my horse and ridden back to us. "I have grievances against some of them."

"I doubt it, but we're speculating uselessly," Desh said. "I want to carefully consider the idea before talking about it anymore." He turned his horse and rode toward the smoke-capped city. I mounted, and we all followed him.

The sight of Darcross grew grimmer as we rode near. Black smoke hung above it in the still air, and sunset drenched the whole place in orange light. I saw flames above the steep roofs in two places.

"Let's ride around," Desh said.

Ella shook her head. "We should aid these people."

"How?" I asked.

She stared at me, waiting.

"No," I said. "Even if I were inclined to soak that whole city with a downpour, it would take ten sorcerers to draw a storm big enough."

Ella said, "You have three."

"Pil and Desh are the wrong flavor for this work."

She clamped her jaw and kicked her horse into a gallop but not straight toward the city. I relaxed a bit when I saw that she was angling to skirt the place.

A few seconds later, her horse neighed and stumbled to the ground, throwing Ella over its head. She made a somersault and landed on her feet, then stared around with huge eyes as if she couldn't believe that had happened.

An arrow stood out of her struggling mount's neck.

"Get down!" Pil shouted, and Ella dropped.

I peered toward the city and saw Parth standing with his horse between us and the closest buildings. He held his bow aside, and the son of a bitch smiled as he waved at us.

"It's another damned ambush!" Pil yelled. "We're so stupid we deserve to be killed."

I didn't bother commenting. Parth hadn't fired until we were far into his range. We could run away and present him with fine targets that were motionless from his point of view. We could ride left or right, which made for a trickier shot, but it would put us in his field of fire for a hell of a long time.

Or we could charge the bastard and take his head if we survived the run.

I had made my decision by the time I reached Ella. She grabbed my arm and swung herself up behind me. I didn't consult with the others. I kicked my horse and drew my sword. If I lived another fifteen seconds, I'd be close enough to rot his bow.

Parth drew and fired at me. I spun a blue band and rotted the shaft free of the head, which bobbled in the air and dropped off to the side. He was backing away, and he fired again. I just had time to rot the arrow before it reached me. I jerked to the left, and the loose arrowhead smacked into my right shoulder. That arm went numb, and I dropped my sword.

I hoped I'd be quick enough to deal with the next arrow, because Parth sure as sheep shanks wouldn't miss. But instead of firing, he jumped on his horse and galloped into the smoky city. I drew rein before I reached the first building. Chasing Parth into the city really would be a trap.

I heard screams from the closest building, a broad, two-story affair vomiting smoke from an upstairs window. Ella leaped off my horse, stumbled, and then sprinted toward the building's door. I drew my knife with my off hand and rode after her, just in case Parth was hiding around the corner.

The door had been nailed shut from the outside. Crying, coughing, and howling came from the inside. "Come help!" Ella screamed at me. By then, Pil had dismounted and was running to join her.

I knew how much power I had left. I had too damn little to be tearing apart buildings and fighting fires. Desh sat his horse beside me, saying nothing. Pil and Ella had drawn their blades and were hacking at the boards blocking the wooden doorway.

I closed my eyes and tried to shut out the screams. I focused on how I needed to pay my debts to the gods, and on not betraying everybody I cared about if I failed. I admit to spending a few seconds imagining the look on Parth's face when I killed him. I would need power to accomplish any of those things.

A sharp rap on my knee opened my eyes.

Pil had whacked me with the handle of her knife, but she didn't seem excited. "Why are you sitting there?"

I started to complain that I couldn't help, but instead I reached into my pouch for the copper cup. I held it high and shouted, "Maybe it puts out fires!"

Desh looked intrigued.

I jumped to the ground, grabbed a water pouch off my saddle, and poured the cup full. Running to the smoking, crackling building, I threw the water on it and watched nothing happen.

"Shit!" I shoved the cup back into my pouch.

Ella grabbed my shoulder. "Save these people!"

"I can't. But I can kill the shit out of Parth and avenge them."

Ella's face stretched as if she were in physical pain. "We'll kill him some other day! These people would rather be alive than avenged!"

"I don't have enough power." It sounded weak even to me.

"Oh." Pil glanced back at the building. "Well, your sorcery business is your business of course."

I sighed and lifted my spirit up toward the Gods' Realm. Pil grabbed on for the ride as I called Harik. I had hoped that the God of Death would answer me, but when I drew my sword, Krak glowered down at me.

Krak lifted his chin a fraction. "Speak."

Pil stood to my left, but I ignored her. I smiled. "Father Krak, I apologize for anything I said earlier than might have seemed rude." I waited.

"Keep going."

"Your Magnificence wisely foresaw that I might wish to trade for power soon, and that has indeed come to pass." I didn't dare ask Krak to make the first offer. "I humbly request six squares in exchange for losing the Knife's real name from my memory."

Krak raised his left hand. My sword tore itself out of my grip. Everything but the sense of sound vanished.

A few seconds later, Pil breathed, "Goddamn . . ."

Krak said, "That's yours now." He threw me back into my body hard enough to rattle me, but I didn't fall.

Pil looked at me through the smoke, her eyes as big as plums.

I grinned at her and held out the Blade of Obdurate Mercy. "The sword in the trading place is just a manifestation. Here's the real thing, all for you." Pil accepted the weapon and smiled like I'd given her a flying kitten. "I'm sorry," I told her. I didn't feel a bit bad, though. I felt like jumping around and giving presents. Krak had just lifted one of my debts to the gods.

On the other hand, Krak had refused to trade with me. With so little power, I had no hope of accomplishing my tasks. I was sure to fail.

That idea sat on me for a couple of seconds, and in a strange way, it was a relief.

It also meant I didn't need to save power anymore.

I ran to the blocked door and pressed my palm against the barrier. I rotted just the wood around the nails, using far less power than I had expected. I helped Ella and Pil pull the door open, and ten or twelve sooty men and women ran out coughing.

"There are more," Ella said, pointing down the street.

"Parth has been as busy as a nasty beaver," I said. We ran to another, smaller building that was blocked shut, and people inside were shouting. Within thirty seconds, I had freed the nails. Desh helped us open it up.

We ran to the next one.

In all, we opened twenty buildings that were ablaze to various degrees, and we set nearly two hundred people free. After that, we found more blocked buildings, but none with people in them who could still scream. I thought it peculiar that we didn't find a single child locked up. We found them all in the town square, terrified and crowded around the well.

I had power remaining but not much. I didn't brood about it. I had often said that sorcery isn't all about magic, or even mostly about magic. Of course, I had known when I said those things that I was full of shit.

TWENTY-FIVE

Desh disappeared just after the Darcross survivors brought us supper.

After we cared for our horses by firelight, the townsfolk offered us a small, unburned house for the night. They brought us mutton, bread, turnips, and beer. I heard Desh say something about rain tomorrow. When I looked around a minute later, he was gone.

I didn't care. I was busy drinking beer and sulking. I ignored the food and made a good number of rude, sarcastic comments. Then I walked out into the street and shouted for more beer. I kept shouting until a teenage boy trudged over with a full pitcher. His gaze was dull and his face slack. He plodded away at the same pace, as if there was no place worth going.

Back inside, I left the pitcher on the table and curled up in a corner to sleep. I tossed about on the packed dirt floor for half an hour and then scrambled outside to puke for a few minutes.

"Victory feast for the hero, huh?" Pil said when I walked back in the house.

I ignored her and flopped down in my corner to sleep.

Something poked my chest, and I opened my eyes to daylight. Ella was pressing the point of her sword against my breastbone.

"You may use my weapon," she said. "I would not wish to see you slain by any vagabond or angry boy." She gave me a hand up and passed me the sword.

"What about Pil's sword?" I asked, squeezing my eyelids tight against the hammering baboons in my head.

Ella smiled. "She gave it to me."

"It's enchanted."

"I know. I think she likes me better than she likes you. Come saddle your horse." Ella winked at me and strode outside with the bravado of a woman carrying a magic sword.

Ella's old sword was sharp and well-balanced, but it fit poorly in my scabbard. "Damn it, damn it, damn it," I muttered as I shuffled outside.

Pil and Ella had saddled their mounts and stood watching as I dragged myself through the task. I didn't care if they had to wait. Desh was still missing anyway. I didn't care about him, either.

"This sort of behavior is why he's so difficult to live with." Ella said it so loudly I couldn't even pretend I hadn't heard it.

I lay my forehead against my horse's neck and sighed.

From behind me, Desh said, "If you don't firm up, Parth will carve you into parts and fry you. If you want to save time, I can cut your throat now."

"Sure, right now I'm embarrassing all my prissy sorcery teachers." I stood tall, swayed a little, and straightened my horse's saddle blanket.

"I'll do that," Desh said, pushing his way between me and my horse. "Here." He handed me the sword that had bisected my buttocks.

"All right." I stepped back, resting the blade on my shoulder, and took two deep breaths.

"You're welcome." Desh didn't look away from his task. "I expect you to vanquish your enemies with it. As long as it lasts."

Holding the blade away from me, I examined it. "Thank you,

Desh. I assume you enchanted it. If I'm wrong about that, I'll blush and say I'm sorry."

Desh waited to speak until he had cinched the saddle. "That sword likes blood to flow. You can kill people if you want, of course. But if you wound someone badly and let them live, the sword will invigorate you a bit. So long as their heart still beats, I mean."

I squinted at the sword. "I don't understand."

"If you disable your enemies instead of killing them, you can fight all day. Heck, you can fight until you die of thirst. I thought that would be handy for a sorcerer of significant years."

"I can't what?" I shouted. "I can't kill them?"

Desh grinned at me. "Sure, you can kill them. Slay all you want. Depopulate nations. But the sword will only help you if you leave your enemy's heart beating."

I became aware that my mouth was hanging open. "Limnad put you up to this, right?"

"It was my idea. You're welcome."

For a moment, I thought this might be a drunken dream. "But . . . look, it hardly even has an edge! It won't be worth a damn for cutting!"

"That's true, it's a weakness." Desh held out his hand.

"You can have it back. I appreciate the sentiment, though."

Desh twisted and thrust the sword at a six-inch-thick wooden fence post. The blade drove through the post and eight inches out the other side with a sound like dropping an iron ingot on a wooden floor. "I can't remember how many times you've told me that the point is a better weapon than the edge, Bib." He tossed the sword back, and I caught it by the grip.

"I see. Thank you, Desh, truly. It will require—"

"I know, fine." Desh waved one hand. "Maybe it'll make you a better person, although I doubt it very much. I put more power into it than anything else I've made. Make me happy I did it."

"I'd like to promise I will, but I'd be lying. I promise to try." I scrutinized the blade, which looked unexceptional in every respect.

"Oh, it has a name, by the way."

"You didn't! I hate that shit!"

Desh laughed. "I enchanted it, so I get to decide if it has a name. I didn't call it Bloodlicker, or the Sword of Resounding Coagulation, or anything like that. I made it simple. Ass-Hanger."

I blinked. "It's like goddamn poetry," I said without expression.

The flat, gray clouds began sprinkling. Desh raised his eyebrows and looked up.

We mounted our horses and rode west along the road.

Ella grumped, "Parth must be twenty miles away now."

"Or he's waiting for us behind that bush," I said, pointing.

Over the next hour, the rain freshened and then started pelting us. I rode in front with Ella, while Desh and Pil rode behind. I heard them talking back there but couldn't make out what they said.

Midmorning, I spotted five horsemen on the road riding toward us, over a mile away. Unless they had mighty sharp eyes, they hadn't seen us yet. I pointed at them and drew rein. "Five riders."

"Parth?" Ella asked.

I examined the men. "I don't think so. Parth sits his horse in his own way, like a cat up on a rock. Smooth."

"If they're scouts for King Staggs, we should go around," Desh said.

I shrugged. "What if Parth and Staggs are swapping lies over a drink right now?"

"I'd still rather not be forced to kill his men, or get killed, or captured. Ride around," he said.

Ella led us off the road to the right. Within a minute, I saw more horsemen through the trees. We wheeled and cut back across the road, but even more riders were picking their way through the woods on that side.

By then, the horsemen on the road were hailing us.

"Do we run?" Pil said. "Talk? I don't want to fight—there may be a hundred of them."

"They're the enemy," Ella grated.

"We don't have to tell them that, do we?" I said. "If we don't proclaim it, they'll never know."

The veins stood out on Ella's neck, but she didn't answer me.

I said, "We can be polite, pay our respects to the king, ask about our old friend, Parth, and leave with friendly sentiments. You can cut off the king's head later this week, after you're done with Parth."

Ella hissed out a sigh. "Very well!"

I guided my horse toward the soldiers, who wore green tabards. At least they'd be easy to tell apart from the men of Glass wearing red and yellow. I drew rein fifty feet from the horsemen, and they did the same.

I called out, "Good morning, General! I am Carwell, the greatest actor in the east, and these are my actor friends. We have no grievance against any soldiers or armies. We just want to ride on to entertain the folk of Bredgarde. Maybe you fellows would like a performance while we're here?"

A tall, wide-shouldered man answered, "It's lieutenant, not general, but I figure you knew that, didn't you?" His broad forehead tapered to a thin jaw with a significant overbite. His eyes flicked over us, stopping often to peer hard at one thing or another.

The man crossed his arms. "Would you believe that my nephew is an actor? His mother wants to cut her damn throat in shame, but have I watched him? Maybe I have. Was I embarrassed? Maybe not, or not much. Do you sincerely, in the gut of your heart, expect me to believe you are actors?"

I gestured expansively. "I can perform a soliloquy of my own composing right here from horseback, Lieutenant."

The man grabbed a sapphire pendant dangling from his neck. "Who are you really?"

I opened my mouth to tell him the truth almost before thinking about it. I rubbed my lips to prevent any facts from coming out. I had seen truth-telling charms before. They didn't sap a person's intention to lie, or even their commitment to a lie. Such charms made people answer fast, before they had a chance to think, and the truth tended to come out. Or whatever they really believed came out.

Once the charmed person blurted out the truth two or three times, they usually accepted that matters were out of their control and resigned themselves to being forthcoming. I was fortunate enough to know what was happening.

After a pause, I said, "Carwell, the greatest actor in the world!"

The lieutenant must have suspected something because he shot back, "Who are you?"

I swallowed to cut off my unthinking answer. "Carwell, the finest actor in the world, and the most magnificent orator too."

"Why are you here?"

Swallow. "The people of Glass don't appreciate art or artists, and they wanted me to pay my bill at the tavern. I am riding west hoping to find a more enlightened audience."

"Who are these people with you?"

Swallow. I pointed at Ella, Pil, and then Desh. "This is Swan, my leading lady. The girl is Dona, who plays the young lass in love. He is Bagber, the villain, brute, and juggler."

"Do you plan to harm King Staggs or the Kingdom of Bredgarde?"

Swallow. "Certainly not! I can't think of anything that would be worse for us. I doubt we're capable of hurting anybody. These weapons that we carry are props from our shows, and we display them to frighten bandits." I nearly smiled getting that last lie out, since every one of us was carrying an enchanted sword.

The lieutenant strained to purse his lips despite the overbite, and he stared at each of us. We must have appeared passably innocent because he let go of the pendant. "You can go, but I can't allow you to trot through the middle of the army by yourselves. I'll detail an escort."

"Thank you, sir. Are you sure you don't want to experience my soliloquy?"

Pil leaned toward the lieutenant. "No, no. No. Please don't."

"We'll be here for an hour if he does," Desh added.

"I have other duties," the lieutenant said. He called out to a dozen riders off to our right, and four of them cantered over. "Ben, ride with these actors back through the lines and past the baggage train, then set them off toward home. Don't let them cause trouble, and see that trouble doesn't come to them."

The youngest of the four yelled "Yes sir!" and snapped a salute.

"Relax," the lieutenant said. "Save that fighting spirit for the battle, or your heart will explode before you take a single head."

The three other riders smiled in an unpleasant manner at Ben's back until the lieutenant glared their smiles away.

Ben met my eyes, his face tight. "Come on! And keep up! I don't intend to miss the battle."

Ben led on, setting a hard pace. His three men rode behind us, calling out insults that I could hear, but not loud enough to reach Ben. Their curses were brutal but didn't show much imagination.

After twenty minutes, the lieutenant and his scouts had disappeared far behind us. We hadn't met anybody on the road. Two of the soldiers—big men who were alike enough to be brothers—galloped up to pace Ben. One shouted, "It's time to break and rest the horses, right, Corporal?"

"No!" Ben yelled. "Push on!"

The soldiers slowed their horses to a walk, blocking the road. I could have ridden around, but then I'd have three nasty armed men behind me instead of one. I slowed my horse too. Desh and the others did the same.

Ben turned, and as he rode back, one of the big soldiers shouted, "You're the smartest man in the whole goddamn army, Corporal. Calling a halt here is genius. The king himself is no smarter."

"I didn't tell you to stop!" Ben yelled, a little whiny.

The soldiers drew rein. "You must have, because we're stopped," one of the big men said. His left front tooth was broken off.

His partner added, "Look at those beautiful shade trees yonder. Corporal, thanks for stopping where we have beautiful shade trees." Both of them trotted their horses off the road.

The soldier behind us, short and skinny, said, "Go on, you actors, you get to rest too. Follow on. Goddamn actors."

All of us rode off into the trees with Ben following, calling out for everybody to stop. Once out of sight of the road, Skinny sighed. "Dismount. You'll need to sit on the ground to rest. Sitting a horse is no rest at all."

I swung to the ground but held my horse's reins in case the bastards wanted to run off with our mounts. Ella and the others did the same.

"All right. All right," Ben said, staring at the sky. "Ten minutes rest, but that's all."

"We don't need no more flippin' actors back home," said Broke Tooth. He dismounted, and his big friend did the same. "Damn actors are worse than beggars. Worse than lepers."

"Worse than rats," Skinny said, still mounted. "So, we'll take your horses as a service to the Kingdom of Bredgarde, hoping that you never arrive. Reins." He held out his hand.

"No! Wait!" Ben sputtered.

Broke Tooth snickered. "We won't need to ride to hell and gone looking for the baggage train while dragging along some filthy actors. We won't end up late for the fighting."

Ben opened his mouth and paused, narrowing his eyes.

I held my horse's reins as I eased back to a spot where I could see all four men.

"Damn it, don't behave that way," Skinny said to me, drawing his sword. Broke Tooth and his friend drew their weapons too.

Big Friend laughed, a sound that turned my stomach. "And just so you don't bribe your way there, give over all your valuables and weapons and such."

"I'm not sure that's necessary," Ben said.

"Wait!" I held up both hands. "Maybe we can buy our freedom. We have something worth more than everything else we own."

"Bullshit!" Broken Tooth said.

"It is! Let me show you." I reached into my pouch and eased the cup out with syrupy slowness.

Broke Tooth frowned. "What is that? It's not even silver."

I tossed the cup to Broke Tooth. While everybody watched him, I drew my sword as I stepped toward Skinny. I thrust up through his belly and into his heart. He gurgled and fell backward off the horse. I spun to Big Friend, who was squinting at me as if I'd been joking when I killed his comrade. I slashed the side of his neck—not as deeply as I'd expected, but he would die within a minute.

Broke Tooth raised his sword to slice my skull in half. I lunged and thrust into his chest with enough force to pierce his heart. But with my new sword, that was too much force. The blade passed through his body and protruded a foot beyond, dragging my arm with it. I rushed to recover and jumped back as Broke Tooth shuddered and collapsed.

Big Friend lay on the bloody grass trying to talk, but he made no sense. Ella had rushed to grab the bridle of Ben's horse, but with unexpected alertness, he wheeled his mount and kicked it into a gallop, escaping her by inches.

Desh unwound his sling from his waist, but Ben had ridden around some trees and out of sight before Desh could reach for a stone to hurl. "That looks like trouble. Bib, you shouldn't have said we were actors. Next time, make us tax collectors or executioners, somebody with a better reputation."

"Damn it, Desh! What the hell kind of sword did you give me? The thing nearly pulled me off my feet!"

Desh wrinkled his brow. "It definitely shouldn't do that. I bet the sword's fine—it's a wielder problem. You'll get used to it."

Pil knelt over Big Friend, who grew still a few seconds later. "The sword's probably working perfectly. I'm not sure that Bib knows what 'leaving their heart beating' means."

I didn't comment. Once I had drawn the sword, I'd had no notion of leaving anybody alive.

Ella reached and squeezed my bloody hand, which surprised me. "We should avoid the road," she said. "We must engage in stealth and trickery to find Parth now."

"Certainly," Desh said. Pil and I nodded.

Pil stared at a far-off clump of trees. "Horses."

I heard them a moment later. A man galloped his horse around the trees and pointed. "There they are!" shouted a voice I recognized as Ben's.

More riders kept appearing from behind the trees, like pulling a snake out of a hole. Before Ben had closed half the distance to us, he was being followed by at least fifty men on horseback.

Pil muttered, "Does anybody care to run? How about fight? Cry?"

"My nag won't last twenty miles in a determined pursuit," I said. I lay my sword on the grass and didn't feel much regret letting go of it. "I guess one good thing will come from this shitty situation. I bet Ben will make sergeant."

TWENTY-SIX

I had aggravated the lieutenant, whose name turned out to be Andris. He had evidently been mighty proud of his truth charm and resented that I had overcome it. He disapproved of my lies so much he ordered a bored soldier to punch me in the face and stomach for a while. Such experiences always hurt like hell, but knowing I had survived the same treatment in the past allowed me a fatalistic resolve.

Andris no longer believed me to be an actor, especially after he examined my sword-handling callouses. I gave a wonderful performance during the beating, though, screaming like my face was being torn off my skull and pretending to sag against the rope that bound me to a tree. All that fake agony may have made my abuser overconfident. He put less muscle into his work as we progressed.

While this was happening, I could see other soldiers beating Desh, Ella, and Pil, even when the rain fell hard. Desh took the pounding as if it were a task to be handled, like chopping wood. Ella shouted, threatened, and spit blood. Pil shrieked louder than me and thrashed too, glaring at everybody with raw hatred that I assumed was for show.

I had rotted my rope so that a sharp yank would break it. I had not done the same for my friends, partly because I wanted to preserve power. Why waste magic on ropes when I could cut them once I escaped? But mainly I didn't want them causing trouble by escaping before I arranged to meet with King Staggs.

Right from the start, I told Andris who I really was before he even asked. Everybody followed that lead and volunteered their identities. Desh, Pil, and I all admitted to being sorcerers. Andris glowered back and forth from one to another of us while clutching his truth charm. Then he declared he didn't believe us and commanded his men to start the beatings.

Andris walked from tree to tree, shaking water out of his eyes. At each tree, he stopped his thug long enough to question one of us. I guess our stories didn't change, because he altered course and demanded to know why we were riding west on the road.

I spit bloody rainwater and gasped out the truth. "I'm bringing secrets to King Staggs to help him win the war!"

Andris leaned in and muttered into my ear, "That's a damn, blazing lie." He stepped back and frowned at the charm in his hand before letting go of it. "Why are you here?" he yelled at me.

"I'm still here to help Staggs win!" I yelled back.

Andris growled as he kicked the ground, slipped on the wet grass, and nearly fell. He stalked over to Ella and asked her the same question.

Ella must have heard me tell the lieutenant what she thought was an obviously impossible lie about betraying Glass, so she came out with a corker too. "My mother is dying in Sappler, and I'm rushing to see her before she passes."

Andris grunted and told the soldier to resume thrashing Ella. He stomped over to Desh, careful of his footing.

Before Andris even asked the question, Desh followed my lead by telling a big lie. "We're after a treasure in these woods. It's guarded by two trolls, but they are sickly ones. Do you want to come with us? We'll share."

Andris kicked Desh in the crotch, and Desh shouted three curses before groaning. The lieutenant trudged over to Pil and sighed. "Young woman, what are you people doing traveling west?"

Pil smiled, her teeth coated with blood. "We're opening a brothel. I hear your mother is looking for work."

Andris slapped Pil with the back of his hand. Then he punched her twice, once on the ear. Pil went limp and dangled from the rope. I couldn't tell whether she was faking.

"Let's stop all this for a while and let you think about it," Andris said. "Don't worry, if these men tire their arms out, I have a regiment of brutes to replace them." Leaving two men to watch us, the lieutenant and our tormentors marched off to join several other soldiers.

Ella, Desh, and Pil all had puffy, bruised faces and split lips. I figured I must look the same. During the beatings, as the afternoon lengthened, more troops had been passing by on the road and through the woods too. In fact, hundreds had passed, maybe over a thousand.

Andris and his bullies swaggered back to us, not five minutes after they left. "That's enough of a breather," he said. "Do you want to tell me the truth? If you don't, I'll have one of you beaten to death." He tapped his chin with a finger and gazed at each of us in turn before pointing at Pil, who still looked unconscious. "Her, with the nasty mouth."

"If you take me to the damn king, you won't have to kill any of us!" I said. "Hell, your men's hands must be too swollen now to hold a sword. I guess the king won't like that much."

A handsome soldier on a tall chestnut stallion trotted up behind Andris, flanked by a dozen more horsemen. "What the good goddamn do you think you're doing, Lieutenant? Why aren't you scouting the bloody road? Have you lost your mind?"

Andris spun around and stiffened. "Sir, I am questioning these spies."

"Huh. That's some vigorous questioning, I'd say."

"Yes sir." Andris stood taller, which I wouldn't have thought possible.

The mounted officer wiped rainwater off his face and sighed. "Well, carry on then." He guided his horse around and trotted it back toward the road, followed by his men.

Desh muttered, "Well, shit."

I had planned on being taken to the king because I was a sorcerer and had secrets to sell. Now I decided to give up that idea. I marked the spot where Andris had lain our weapons under a tree. Everybody would have to be cut free before we grabbed our blades and ran north, away from the road. It would require disabling four or maybe five men, which sounded crazy, but I could employ both surprise and magic.

"I wish we'd gone north," I moaned loud enough for everybody to hear.

Before I did anything else, Pil's rope fell to the ground. She lunged toward the soldier who had beaten her and jammed her knife into his chest. She must have been holding the weapon, invisible, the whole time. The solder coughed and pitched backward.

Andris and all his men stared at Pil. A few shouted.

I yanked my rope apart, and Desh's rope came loose at the same time. I don't know what Desh did after that because I was busy kicking the soldier in front of me in the knee. I probably didn't break it, but he squealed and fell anyway.

When I glanced around, I saw Pil cutting Ella free. Desh was sprinting toward me, his tormentor rolling on the ground behind him. As I ran toward the weapons, I pulled two white bands and whipped them into the sky.

All the soldiers were rushing toward us by then. They disappeared when, in an instant, the rain became a blinding deluge. I didn't have much power and didn't want to use all of it, so the fierce rainstorm only existed in a circle thirty paces across.

Although I couldn't see, I put my hand right on my sword's grip as perfectly as if I'd been staring at it. Then I fumbled over grabbing the rest of our weapons. I found my knife but no other knives. The swords were bigger, so I located them by flailing around a little. I also touched Pil's bow, but not her quiver of arrows.

The rain would only endure a couple of minutes, so I turned to get my bearings. I slipped and smacked my palm right onto Pil's quiver when I caught myself. A soldier trotted past me in the rain, cursing Andris's mother and his own too. Then I ran north, away from the center of Staggs's army, with my arms full of swords, a bow, and a quiver.

When I broke free of the hard rain, I saw Ella and Pil through the trees, sprinting ahead of me. Desh was angling off northwest. Not everybody had a good bump of direction, and I knew Desh's to be measly. Yet I couldn't wave at him with my arms full of swords and such, and I didn't dare yell or whistle, lest I give us away.

Pil saw Desh and said something to Ella. They both angled to reach him, so I did the same. I slowed to glance over my shoulder and saw enough trees to block the soldiers' view of us.

The deluge behind us ended as if a bucket had been emptied. Pil and Ella joined Desh, and they all slowed to let me catch up.

I held Pil's sword out to her, but she slapped me in the face, hard, before she took it. "Arrogant, self-centered bastard."

Ella and Desh snatched their swords from me. Ella said, "Now she knows you."

Pil had hit me right on one of my worst bruises. I stood with my mouth open. "Um . . . well, you could have killed me just then with your invisible knife, but you didn't. I don't guess you hate me as much as you could." I handed her the quiver and bow. "If we stand here insulting each other, they'll catch us."

Pil spun and jogged north, not speaking or waiting for us. Desh followed, and Ella fell in beside me.

Ella said, "She would not despise your actions so much except that she cares about you."

I shook my head. "That just confuses the hell out of me."

"That is unfortunate. I believe her understanding is perfectly clear, and it has nothing to do with romance."

"Hell, I would never have thought it did."

"Stop!" a man shouted from ahead of us. Ella and I had lagged while talking, and I couldn't see Pil or Desh past a little stand of trees. More voices joined in—so many I couldn't make out the words.

Ella hissed and crept toward the voices, staying behind trees as much as possible. I followed her. We reached the edge of a thicket beside a clearing that was a hundred paces across.

At least fifty soldiers occupied it. Some stood guard, while others went about camping tasks such as trench digging and unloading pack horses. Several men were escorting Pil and Desh toward the middle of the clearing at spear point.

Ella whispered, "Do you see Parth?"

"No," I whispered back. "Nor Capps. I don't see a monstrous black horse, either."

"What sort of magic can you employ to aid us?"

"I can steal your nose."

"What?" Her eyes widened.

"Nothing. I have none to offer," I said.

"Then it will be a challenge to rescue them."

Three soldiers were raising a green standard in the middle of the clearing. It hung limp in the rain, so I saw no detail. "That can't be a general, can it?" I murmured. "I don't see a tent, or wine bottles, or a mistress."

Ella frowned at me. "I doubt that all of this is commanded by a corporal. Pil and Desh are being presented to someone."

Maybe a general would be easier to convince than Lieutenant Andris had been. As a rule, the higher an officer's rank, the easier he is to manipulate through flattery and his unwillingness to admit he doesn't know everything. "We'll talk our way out."

"No!" she said through clenched teeth.

"Hell, when Parth wanted to kill me, you asked me to trust you with my life. You said you'd talk our way out of it."

Ella grimaced. "That ended poorly."

"Yes, it did. Come on." I walked out from behind the tree with my hands high.

Whispering, Ella called me a couple of salty names.

"Hello, boys!" I called out. "I'm here to chat with your boss. I bring gifts and gossip about your enemy!"

The rain stopped as the closest men ran out to me, their spears and swords held ready. A scarred young man asked a gray-haired soldier, "Want to take the sword?"

Gray Hair shrugged. "He said not to take the last ones."

I wanted to make a smart comment, but I bit it back. I looked around for Ella and jerked when I saw she wasn't with me.

"If he won't protect his self, we got to do it," the scarred soldier said. He jabbed his spear in my direction while Gray Hair held out his hand for my sword and knife.

I passed them over. "Shit," I muttered. "I wish Ella was here to hold my sword."

"Hush!" Gray Hair said like he was talking to a loud dog. He and four other men led me into the camp.

A tall fellow flanked by two taller soldiers stood on the muddy grass twenty feet from Pil and Desh. Their swords lay on the ground close to the tall man's feet, and Gray Hair tossed my sword and knife there as well. Another soldier knelt off to the side, trying to turn a damp mess of sticks into a campfire.

The tall man topped me by almost a head. He had wide, flat shoulders, a broad face, and a cavernous mouth that was busy laughing when I arrived. He gave me a tooth-filled smile, the kind a fox gives a mouse. He said in a room-filling voice, "Young Desh, this poor man has been battered worse than you. Who is he?"

Desh smiled. "This is Bib, a sorcerer, sir. Bib, this is General Barton, who commands all the Bredgarde armies for King Staggs."

I squinted at the general. He made a comic show of squinting back at me.

Giving this man secrets about Glass should be every bit as useful as telling them to the king. "Hello, General. You look to have a cracking good army here. I expect you'll plow the army of Glass like they were loose dirt. I'd favor a chance to help you with that, though."

I saw Desh's eyes flick back to me. He might be suspecting that I really did intend to betray Glass and help Staggs.

The general snorted. "That's kind. You're a civilized fellow, I suppose. Your manners are better than my sister's." He drummed on his leg with his fingers for an uncomfortable length of time. Then he yelled, "It's generous, I'd say, if you're sincere and know anything at all about things. I might be happy having a sorcerer on my side too, so there's that." He winked at me. "How can I know you're really a sorcerer, Bib? Show me something magical so I know what I'm buying."

I shrugged. "General, sorcerers learn not to be wasteful of magical power. You never know when you might need to make a villain combust or conjure water in the desert. Power is not to be squandered. I will answer all questions you care to ask me, though."

"No!" Barton shouted. Then in a quieter voice, he said, "Oh, no. I shouldn't consider this demonstration to be a waste. Not if I were you."

I'd be damned if I spent the little power I had left to satisfy some drooling jack pole of a soldier's curiosity. "I could make your rings disappear, but we both know that's not sorcery. I could start that fire and save your man there from cursing and apoplexy, and I'm happy to do it, but that's not sorcery, either. Sorcery . . . well, that tree over there doesn't bend to prove it's a tree, and sorcery doesn't, either."

Barton chuckled. "That is such bullshit."

"Yes sir, it is. I'm still not spending power to make bugs dance or rain fall up."

"So, I have a sorcerer who's shy of sorcery." He looked at the sky and shouted, "How can I trust such a man?" He turned to a rough chest behind him and picked up a short, heavy sword. "No, I don't see how you help me even a bit. I'd better kill you."

The men beside him raised their swords. So did eight men behind us.

"Wait!" I said. "Let me appeal to King Staggs! He may want to hear me out, or at least kill me himself. You, his loyal man, wouldn't cheat him out of that fun, would you? Let me lay my case in front of him."

The general smiled, showing every tooth. "You are a persistent little squat, Bib who-may-be-a-sorcerer. Sit in my mud here and tell me all about it. Then I'll decide whether to interrupt the king."

TWENTY-SEVEN

The general sat tall on a little three-legged camp stool while water wicked up through the crotch of my trousers. He had propped his sword against his thigh and rested his hands on his knees. I sat unarmed and cross-legged on the rain-soaked grass, gazing up at him from twenty feet away. Dozens of his soldiers surrounded us, some glaring with disgust. Pil and Desh sat on each side of me. They were fine sorcerers but not all that physically intimidating.

General Barton's physical and moral superiority over me was staggering. That shit was unacceptable.

I smiled. "We'll be sitting in the dark in fifteen minutes, General, if your man can't make some fire." I pointed with my chin at the soldier kneeling over the sticks. He struck the flint harder and faster, his head down as if he couldn't hear me. "I offered to start a blaze for you, and I meant it." Turning a spark into fire would be a grueling task in all this wetness, but I had been taught by a woman who could make wood burn with a hard look.

The general coughed. "Go ahead. Ceril, feed my horse some carrots."

Ceril, who clearly wished he could sink into the earth, saluted and trotted toward the horses. While everybody else watched the young soldier, Desh nudged my leg and slipped me a rough wooden box the size of two fingers.

"I believe you've chosen well, General," I said, crossing to the moist pile of sticks. It looked worse than I expected. "I was hoping to warm up my old butt later, so a fire would be comforting."

"Are you mystical enough to talk and start fires at the same time?" Barton asked. "I want to know what you came to tell the king."

I slipped the box's snug lid open. It may as well have been airtight. A dry wad of tinder lay inside. "I expect I am, sir." I lay the tinder against the sticks and struck a spark. The tinder, which Desh had no doubt enchanted, caught the first spark, and I leaned down to blow on it. Within five seconds, the sticks became a popping little blaze. I stood and said, "No need to do both at the same time, General. I'm done with that."

As I sat down between Pil and Desh, the general put his elbow on a knee and propped his chin on one fleshy hand. "Maybe I should ask you to make some things disappear after all. Give them some wine," he said, and a servant stepped out of the shadows carrying a tray loaded with a bottle and glasses.

"King Prestwick has been murdered," I said.

"I heard that yesterday. Tell me a new thing."

"Durch, the Duke of Esterhite, is setting himself up as king."

The general sat up like a dog that had seen a squirrel. "That's new by the gods!" he yelled. "I don't know the man. What's he like?"

I paused to think. "Have you ever had a mean dog that killed chickens and bit all the other dogs?"

Barton nodded.

"Durch is like that, except he's a coward and only smart enough to kill chickens."

The general smiled. "This is good news!" When he laughed, his mouth opened so wide I could almost see down his throat.

"Oh, there's more," I said. "Both of the king's senior generals are dead, which means Durch will probably command the army himself. Or maybe his son will, a crude boy who's as dumb as a stump."

I paused for the general to say something, but he just watched me, his eyebrows up. After several seconds, he murmured, "I thought if I stayed quiet, you'd tell me that his whole army has been stricken blind or has the runs."

"No, but the king's sorcerer seems to have run away."

Barton pounded his knee with one fist and burst out, "If you keep the good news coming, the king may give you his daughter's hand!"

"Then I wish I had more. I expect you know that a foolish man commanding an army might do any ridiculous thing—maneuvers you couldn't imagine and wouldn't be ready for."

The general stuck out his big chin and growled. "Amateurs. They're the ones who will kill you."

"Now, something bitter," I said. "I don't know this to be true, but Durch's son may have brought his army from Esterhite along. He has a core of soldiers and a fair array of mercenaries. I estimate at least five hundred men."

Desh whispered to me, "Bib, why are you saying all this?"

I don't know whether Barton heard Desh, but he jumped to his feet and bellowed, "Why are you telling me all this? Are you a traitor? I hate traitors worse than I hate hornets!"

I whispered back to Desh, "I made a bargain." He gave a tiny nod. I told the general, "I'm not Durch's man, so I'm not betraying him." Of course, I likely would have told Barton the same things even if Pres was still king. I couldn't count that as anything but betrayal. "I do want something, though."

The general gave a wide smile, his eyes bright. "Certainly you do. You are of course entitled to some reward."

"There's a man employed by your king to perform certain services. His name is Parth, and I want him." One of the soldiers beside the king shifted his weight but then held still. I went on: "The king doesn't even have to deliver him to me. If you tell me where Parth is, I'll go to him."

The general sat back down and stretched out one leg. "I don't suppose you want to buy this man a drink and rub his feet, eh?" He laughed, showing me the back of his throat again.

"No, I intend to kill him all to hell," I said.

"I know about this Parth. A pale, little man. What has he done now?"

I said, "The murder of innocents."

"And betrayal," Pil cut in.

Desh said, "Regicide."

"Bearing false witness." Pil glanced at me with a tiny shrug.

I said, "Consorting with unnatural beings and promising to work their will."

Pil squinted at me.

"Grass spirit," I whispered. I met the general's eyes and raised my forefinger. "Plus, arrogance that led to most of his men getting slaughtered." I turned to Desh. "I don't know why I ever said a civil word to the man."

"Do you know why he screams at night?" Barton asked it with a flat voice and a blank expression.

Pil and Desh stayed quiet. If the general was just asking from curiosity, why would he try to control his face? He wouldn't. So, he cared about Parth, at least a little, and he gave it away. Or did he act that way on purpose to make us think he cared when he'd be just as happy for Parth to be eaten by pigs? Maybe Barton was testing us somehow.

As I eased the little cup out of my pouch, I thought hard about the next words to come out of my mouth. "I believe the behavior began during his journey in the east. I never heard him speak about the reason."

Barton nodded. "Chilling, isn't it? I wish never to hear anything like it again." He clapped his hands and spoke out, "But your question is about finding Parth so you can 'kill him all to hell.' I promise you're not the first. I wish not to disappoint you, Sorcerer Bib, but I don't know where the scoundrel is just now. Off someplace doing ill, I suppose."

Without looking down, I had been pouring the little cup with wine from my glass. I didn't know what the crappy little thing was good for, but I predicted we'd need some kind of help in a minute. "That's regrettable, sir. Might you at least aim us in a direction?"

"That I can do!" he yelled, smiling. He stood up and stretched his back. "This damned stool will kill me yet. It's worse than sitting a cranky mule. Direction? You know, I think you might be among the few who can slay Parth, which says well for you. But I can't just allow you to kill the boy."

Barton raised his sword and nodded.

I threw the wine from the copper cup at Barton's face. Nobody moved. Barton blinked at me with wine dripping off his nose. The damned cup had to be good for something, but this wasn't it.

"That's wasn't helpful," Pil said.

Desh flung a handful of sand and dust straight up into the air. Instead of coming down, it seemed to keep spreading wider. Everybody hesitated. After the wine incident, I didn't dare do anything.

Every campfire in the clearing was doused in a whoosh of sparks and smoke. Although a half moon dangled over the horizon, the world near us looked as black as Harik's eyebrows. I scrambled around the dead campfire in front of me. I found that the wood hadn't quite cooled when my left hand strayed into it.

The burn didn't feel severe. I kept low as I rushed toward the spot where I thought our weapons lay. By then, we existed in a hell of shouting, boots squishing in mud, and bodies hitting the ground.

My left shoulder banged into somebody who was also half crawling toward the weapons. I assumed it was Pil, so I edged away to give her room. Somebody ran into my other side and tripped over me. I heard Pil grunt as the man fell on her. I paused, but the man gurgled. Pil said, "Don't stop, Bib!"

I arrived at the spot where the soldiers had dumped our weapons. When I reached out, my hand went right to the hilt of my sword. I made a wish for Desh to get his own blacksmith shop and a puppy. At the same time, I rolled away, leaving my knife. A sword blade thunked into the ground just behind me.

Still rolling, I called, "Watch out, Pil!" I hoped that helped her. It sure as shit didn't help me. I kept rolling as somebody ran after me, just missing every time he whacked the ground with his weapon.

At last, I rolled into somebody else, who tripped. He fell into my pursuer, and they both cursed as they squished around trying to stay upright.

I crawled away from those two, my body coated in mud, and I clambered to my feet. My eyes had adjusted enough that I saw outlines of people if they weren't too far away. I scanned to get my bearings. East was obvious since the moon had just risen. I would never find Pil and Desh in this dim pandemonium, so I trusted in their own abilities to escape. Turning to run north, I was almost beheaded by a big man with a shield, probably one of the general's guards.

Ducking the blow, I cut at the guard's legs, but he dropped his shield to block. He tried to overpower me with the shield, but I rolled off. He was a fine fighter. I stepped back and slipped just a bit, and he moved forward with care. He covered his body with the shield and set me up for a cut if I tried to slash his legs. So, I didn't slash low. I feinted the slash and thrust hard at his shield, trusting that Desh's Ass Sword would punch through.

The sword performed well. It thrust through the shield and the man's body until the hilt banged against the wood. It kept going, and the hilt drove the shield against his chest. He staggered back a step, dragging my arm along. I almost fell on my face.

I recovered in a hurry, skittering back ten feet. The big man swayed and fell to the side, limp. Another man was standing just behind him, shivering. He turned his head, and the moonlight picked out his profile. Then General Barton collapsed to his knees, raised his sword, and fell forward into the mud.

I cursed. That had not helped me ensure that King Staggs would win the war. Barton had appeared a clever man. His soldiers had seemed to like him. Staggs would miss such a general. Just as bad, now that my friends and I had killed the general, nobody in Staggs's army would trust any of the information I had given him.

Our entire journey west had been pointless.

I couldn't stand around whimpering and cursing the world in the middle of the dead general's camp. Keeping low, I ran to the edge of the clearing where Barton's men kept the horses. I didn't have time to select the best mount. I unhobbled the closest horse and jumped on its back. My crotch was so caked with mud I almost slipped off the other side, but I hung on to its mane. I could ride bareback about as well as I did with a saddle, so I kicked the gelding and cantered north, away from the center of the camp.

Over the yelling behind me, somebody howled, "The king is dead! They killed the king!"

Like being slapped in the face, I realized that Barton was a falsehood. King Staggs had pretended to be Barton when talking to spies and miscreants like us, and I had just killed him.

And Staggs had called Parth "my boy." Did that mean he was the king's son? Or was he a sneaky fixer who the king liked?

I urged my horse into a gallop.

The familiar pulling sensation carried me to the Gods' Realm, where I was deprived of all senses but sound.

Harik's voice came from nothingness. "I believe you are obliged to ensure that your friend's kingdom loses the war. Correct?"

"That is so, Mighty Harik." I almost dropped back out of the Gods' Realm. I couldn't think of any good thing that might happen in the next few minutes. But if I fled, Harik would just retrieve me like a fishhook.

Harik went on: "I would say that murdering your enemy's king is the very definition of winning the war. Does that not seem correct?"

"That could be the case, from a certain point of view," I said. "But since Staggs's spy killed Prestwick and I then killed Staggs, I propose that the war is currently tied."

"You cannot expect me to accept such a ludicrous assertion." Harik didn't sound angry or even annoyed. He sounded like he was enjoying this.

"I believe it is logical and correct, Your Magnificence." I didn't really believe any such thing. My argument was quibbling of the worst sort, and I wouldn't have tolerated it for a minute. "It's the only sensible way to consider this."

"Even if your position had merit, just four sunrises remain before your dead friend's country must definitively lose the war.

Should that not happen, you will fail and provoke suffering for yourself and the shabby beings to which you ridiculously attach yourself. In fact, be ready. Practice how you will abase yourself and beseech their forgiveness. I stand ready to offer criticism."

I waited several seconds and then ignored everything he said after "lose the war." "So, you agree that the war is currently all even. Wonderful! Is there anything else?"

"We do not agree with you," Harik said, his voice oily. "But we won't reach so far as to say that we disagree."

"You and Lutigan are fighting about it, eh?"

"Not at all!" Harik snapped. "Since you have left the situation less than definitive, we will reconsider the penalties you shall suffer if you fail. First, you will betray the Knife at a time of Lutigan's choosing. Second, the blonde woman will come to hate you in an absolute and murderous fashion."

My heart sped up. I became *aware* of my heart speeding up. I could feel my heart. As far as I knew, no sorcerer in history had perceived anything but sound in the Gods' Realm, except for me. And I had only done it with the sword that granted such a power. The fact that I could hear my heart astounded me so much that I almost missed the next thing Harik said.

"You will suffer one of these two punishments now since you have performed in such a mediocre fashion," Harik said.

"That's . . ." I couldn't complain that it wasn't fair, or right, or logical. As far as the gods were concerned, men deserved none of those things. "Which one?"

"We're not going to tell you. You may experience it for yourself." When I didn't answer, Harik said, "Be mirthful! If you finish your task by the fourth sunrise, you may yet avoid the other punishment."

"If I'm successful, will you rescind them both?" I thought I could hear whispering, but I couldn't make out the words.

After a few seconds, Harik said, "Relieve you of both punishments? Why would we ever do that?"

Harik tossed me like a ball back into the world of man. I drifted into my body, which sat on the galloping horse, and my seat didn't even shift.

272

I clung to the horse's neck as he ran. I didn't want to think about what to do next. The lack of hope dragged at me, but I reached into myself and dug a little out. I wasn't sure what ridiculous thing I could do to prevail. But if such a ridiculous thing existed, I felt sure I'd have to do it back at Castle Glass.

TWENTY-EIGHT

In my time, sorcerers who lived much past twenty often became eccentric or even went insane. Standing helpless before omnipotent beings while they yell and threaten you with oblivion was stressful. Knowing that your carelessness may lead to that oblivion or to incalculable suffering did not help. Years of that could unbalance anybody.

The gods could convince sorcerers to trade away memories or feelings, or even give a sorcerer appalling knowledge of something he'd be better off not knowing. This could change sorcerers in unpredictable and even profound ways. I almost always refused such deals when possible.

Sometimes sorcerers agreed to do things that might be unpleasant, or even horrible. I once agreed to kill people until Harik told me I had killed enough. When trading with gods, I tried to limit myself to bargains of this sort, since I figured they would change a sorcerer less than those other types of deals. After twenty years, I came to realize I had been wrong about that, but by then, it was too late.

The gods could take somebody away from a sorcerer, usually a person they loved, just by reaching down and changing the way that person felt or thought. The person would never realize they had been changed. I found those to be the most awful arrangements, because they harmed people who were blameless and should have been left alone to drink too much or play with their children.

When bargaining with gods, there were no good deals of course, only bad deals and deals that were less bad. I had told Desh that the day we met, but I hoped he had gone on to prove me wrong. He had made some kind of outrageous deal, but maybe he'd paid an even more outrageous price.

Occasionally, gods would make something happen to a sorcerer as punishment instead of a bargain. Harik had just punished me, either by making Ella hate me or by requiring me to betray Pil. The gods loved that sort of theatrical, quasi-mysterious bullshit. Sometimes they hurt sorcerers for what seemed like no reason at all. Whenever sorcerers asked why, the gods said they could do whatever they wanted because they were gods, and that was that.

I'm not complaining, because I knew how this worked and made my own decisions. But if all of that isn't enough to make a person crazy, I don't know what is.

A mile north of Staggs's camp, I found a modest rise and looked back. I had some notion of watching for Pil and Desh in case they needed help, but the idea showed itself to be ridiculous. Even with a half-moon, I could hardly pick out human shapes. I also had no call to think that either of them would travel north as I had.

I turned east and urged my horse into a canter. Sunup still lay hours away, and throughout the night, Staggs's enraged men would search every tree, hill, and hole within miles. Also, when sunrise came, it would leave me just three more dawns to meet Harik's arbitrary, pain-in-the-ass deadline for losing the war. So, I abandoned Desh and Pil to make their own escapes.

If I pushed my horse, I could be halfway to Castle Glass while it was still dark. Castle Glass. Why hadn't Pres changed that pretentious, ridiculous name when his father died? The nasty man was dead. To hell with the old brute. Too late now. Durch would probably call it Durchland.

I shook my head as I realized I had come close to dozing off on horseback.

I rode into a range of higher hills, and first light showed me a big town ahead to the right. I might even have called it a small city. I also saw thirty horsemen approaching from the direction of the castle. They wore no uniforms.

My horse had been traveling all night and was a bit of a nag to start with, so fleeing seemed a poor tactic. I expected these men could run me down if they wanted. Instead, I might ride up to them and act friendly. Maybe they didn't care about me at all and would wave me along. Without uniforms, they could be bandits, which might not be awful since I looked like a mud-caked wild man too poor to own a saddle.

Or maybe they were Durch's mercenaries. Even if I knew nothing else, I knew that Durch didn't like me.

I took a third option, which was to gallop for the little city and hope to get lost in it. As soon as I cut toward the city, the horsemen swung to chase me. I leaned over the gelding's neck and encouraged him to run. He showed more heart than I would have expected, and I reached the edge of the city half a minute ahead of the riders.

Toward the end of the chase, I had identified the lead rider as Arm of Fury, Durch's calm killer and flunky. I didn't see Karl. Maybe Durch was keeping his son home and safe.

The streets were narrow and crooked, and they grew more crooked as I rode deeper into town. I slipped off the sweating, blowing horse at a cross street and slapped his rump to send him on down the main road. The cross street proved even tighter and dimmer. When I heard Big Fury's horses gallop past, I pushed open the door of a tall and faded wooden building beside me.

A woman and five children were stumping around the small room, putting away mats and cooking breakfast over the fire in the middle of the floor. The woman screamed. A second later, the children all screamed. I imagined what they saw: a panting, skinny figure covered in dried mud with wide eyes and a sword on his belt. I held up my hands and smiled, but that just made them scream louder.

I had burst in on these people with the notion that I might climb up through this structure to the roof. From there, I could observe Big Fury's men and remain somewhat hidden, but now I heard shouts in the street. That plan had gone all to hell.

Rushing back outside, I smacked into a man carrying melons, bowling him to the ground. Some melons smashed and the rest rolled everywhere. I paused long enough for the woman to run out behind me and hit me on the shoulder with a stick of firewood. A teenager across the street hurled a melon at me, and it smashed against my thigh not far from my groin.

I ran away from the main road, passing two tidy townspeople who yelled for me to stop. A third called me a demon as she made a sign to ward against evil.

Hoofbeats sounded from the street behind me, so I turned right at the next lane, then left at the one after that. Mercenaries were shouting to each other from different parts of the little city. Then some townspeople began screaming. The hoofbeats sounded closer behind me.

I skidded and turned down a narrow lane, too narrow for a horse to pass through. I intended to climb a building further on if I could find one with suitable handholds. The lane stopped at a dead end, with no doors or handholds in sight. I turned back but spotted horses at the entrance to the lane.

Pressing my body against a side wall, I watched two armed men stalking down the lane toward me, single file since the space was so narrow. Before they saw me, I jumped out and thrust into the first one's chest. His friend pushed past him, so I stabbed the friend through the belly. He yelled and staggered back.

As I rushed forward to escape the lane, three more men came trotting down it toward me. I stabbed the first one in the throat. The other two scrambled back to the street where they could stand side by side, backed by two more men.

Big Fury appeared behind his fighters and called out, "Is that you, Sorcerer Bib?"

"No, it's your mother. I'm busy having carnal relations with a rat and a raccoon, so go away."

The man chuckled. "You can't get out, and anyway, we don't want to kill you. We'll take you to the castle, safe as can be."

I laughed. "Where Durch will immediately kill me."

"Maybe not." He shrugged. "I know you're not a servant, but he still thinks you are and won't hear otherwise. So come out. I imagine you're a foul man, but few are all bad. You might like kids. Maybe dogs too."

I nodded. "Sure, dogs, cats, alligators, I love them all. Come down here so we can talk about it."

"Uh-huh. The idea I'm pushing across to you is you ought to give yourself over if you like kids. We grabbed a few and will cut them up if you don't. Maybe kill a couple. All right, not maybe, we *definitely* will slay a few, but you can stop all that."

I lowered my sword to stare at him. "These are Durch's own subjects!"

"Yes, that's true," Big Fury said. When I didn't speak, he waved to somebody up the street. Someplace farther along, a child screamed. "Just take a thumb for now," Big Fury yelled in that direction.

I did not enjoy many tactical advantages. I could employ almost no magic, and I sure as hell couldn't surprise my enemies. Superior morale lay with Big Fury's men, since they outnumbered me by a shocking margin. I did possess the advantage of terrain. They could only come at me single file in that skinny lane, and I could kill a wagonload of them before they overwhelmed me or brought up some crossbows. Hell, they might stone me to death.

Anyway, defending myself in that alley wouldn't help a single damn one of those kids.

I lifted my spirit and called for Harik, who answered my nauseated self after what seemed like a long delay, if time could have any real meaning for me there. I doubted it could.

"What are you begging for now, Murderer? Complete your current tasks before bothering me. I'm rehearsing."

I couldn't resist. "You mean you're not a perfect being? You have to practice? Everybody I meet for the rest of my life will find that fascinating."

Harik threw me away like a boy chucking a stone at his brother. I staggered a little when I reached my body. Then I lifted my spirit right back up, and Harik answered almost at once.

I rushed to say, "I apologize, Your Magnificence, that was mean."

"You apologize? You must indeed be desperate." I thought I heard him yawn. "How much power do you want?"

"I don't want power. I want you to save those children in this city, the ones being terrorized."

Harik laughed, a drawn-out, guttural thing, not like his normally smooth self. "No."

I didn't know why I felt surprised, but I did. "Just no?"

"Correct. If you want them preserved, do it yourself. I can't bother with such meaningless nonsense."

I took a few seconds to consider how I might attack Big Fury and his men with various magical stratagems. I would need more power for any of them.

And that was it, then—I would always find myself in this spot eventually, needing power to survive. Unless I sat in a darkened room by the sea and never set a toe out, the gods would own me until I died. I had been foolish to believe things could be some other way.

"All right, you pus-green nightmare of bile. I want six squares. Please make the first offer."

"Certainly. You must save every child, then select three of them and murder their families."

"I appreciate your tough negotiating stance, Mighty Harik," I said, wishing I could shudder. "I'll take Big Fury prisoner and give him to Limnad the next time I see her. Five squares."

"Oh, you anticipate seeing her again? That's almost interesting. As interesting as you ever manage to be."

I forgot about the negotiation for a moment. "Why wouldn't I see her again?"

"Pretend I said nothing." I imagined Harik flipping the sleeve of his black robe and sitting down. "In truth, I am interested in only one thing: extending your open-ended debt. You must take a further unknown number of lives for me."

I blinked. "Does that mean I'm close to being done with the ones I owe you now?" I realized I was blinking when I shouldn't be able to.

"Nothing like that at all. I merely wish you to accept the impossibility of retiring all your debts." Harik's tone became harder. "There is no relief, so stop lying to yourself."

I didn't hesitate. "I'll kill Durch for three squares."

"Bah. You already want to kill him."

"For four squares, I'll kill Durch, Karl, and all the adults in their family. I'll wipe out the entire royal line, except for the kids." I regretted the offer the moment I said it. They weren't just Durch's nasty relatives. They were Prestwick's family too. But it was too late to unsay it.

"That's tempting." Harik sounded interested. "But no."

I imagined Harik standing up and stepping toward me.

"I will only offer to extend your current debt."

My breath caught. I really was seeing Harik step toward me. In an instant, the entire trading place became visible under silky moonlight. With what might have been the greatest act of self-control in my life, I held still.

Harik went on in a soft voice: "To make the deal more palatable, I will offer the six squares you originally requested."

I had seen Harik dozens of times over the years and heard him many dozens more. He had never understood that sometimes his face gave away his intentions. I saw this time that he intended not to surrender his point. Expanding my debt was the only offer he would consider.

"Then we cannot come to terms, Mighty Harik, you nondescript wad clinging to a mule's ass. Farewell." I lowered myself back toward the world of man, wondering what to do next.

<h1 style="text-align:center">TWENTY-NINE</h1>

I returned to the narrow alley after insulting Harik. As usual, no time had passed while I had been fiddling around in the Gods' Realm.

Big Fury and his nasty crew still blocked me from escaping the lane. If I stood and fought, I'd be killed in the end. But I would wipe out some of the bastards before they brought me down, and they'd have no reason to hurt any kids once the fight started.

Or, I could surrender to Big Fury and possibly be killed later. But maybe not. I could escape on the way to Castle Glass. In fact, my odds of escape were good, and Big Fury had promised to let the kids alone if I surrendered.

Although it tasted like I was chewing dirt, I decided to surrender. I sure had surrendered or been captured a lot these past weeks, though.

Before I spoke, Big Fury snapped, "Get that out of sight!" A man flinched, bleated that he was sorry, and scampered down the street carrying an ax. It wasn't a fighting ax. It was the sort executioners use, designed to whack off the heads of people in disfavor. It would be an efficient tool for hewing off a sorcerer's hands.

To hell with surrender. And if I wasn't giving up, to hell with waiting.

I ran toward the men blocking the lane. The two in front were experienced mercenaries and must have witnessed a lot of crazy, hellish things, but they stood there and watched me charge them. They might not have believed I was doing it. I had sometimes seen men react that way.

I thrust into the handsome one's chest before he moved. The one with droopy eyes jerked and then slashed at me. I dodged and opened his throat before he recovered.

Everybody behind those men started shouting as if they realized all at once I was coming to kill them. I shouted back, and a horse sidestepped, knocking Big Fury aside. The two mercenaries in front of him both thrust at me. I twisted and parried, piercing one's throat, but the other man's sword scraped deep across my left shoulder. I knocked that man's sword aside, took the low line, and stabbed him in the groin.

He shrieked, dropped to his knees, and collapsed onto his side like cut wheat, unmoving. The men closest to us reacted. One slashed at me, two banged into each other trying to shift position, and a fourth flinched away. Behind them, Big Fury was drawing his sword while loping down the street to my right, toward the children and an unknown number of his men.

My shoulder wound was stinging, but I blocked the fellow slashing at me. I left him holding his sliced belly together, his mouth and eyes wide. Then I lunged and stabbed the next man in the chest, using too much force. My blade went all the way through him, and before I could recover, his chubby friend stabbed me on the kneecap. My leg tried to collapse, and the two remaining men pressed me, one high and the other low.

I stumbled and grappled with the chubby one. His friend hesitated, not caring to thrust all the way through his comrade to kill me. I made a hard but awkward cut at the friend and sliced his sword arm. As he dropped his blade and staggered away, a wash of energy went through me from the Ass Sword. My leg felt stronger, so I threw the chubby fellow down and rolled all the way over him.

I came to my feet and spun. I could have easily murdered the chubby man, but instead I slashed him across the face and scalp. He howled and grabbed his face with both hands. Another wave of energy perked me up.

Three more men closed on me from the direction Big Fury had run. They worked together with care and confidence. I darted in, slashed one's throat, and disabled the other two with deep cuts to the legs. One of them stumbled to crash through a wooden door. The other flopped onto the dirt, and more energy ran through me. I had suffered a bad slice on my left wrist, but I felt as refreshed as if I were waking up after a nap.

Three more men shuffled and feinted toward me, but two hesitated and let their friend attack first. I cut his shoulder and slashed him hard across the chest. When he spun away yelping, I felt heartier than I had in years. Not stronger, or even faster. I just didn't feel tired, or hurt, or even beaten up by time.

I fenced the two men who let their friend go first. They backed away without even trying to strike me. I left them both dying on the ground at the cost of my left earlobe.

Now Big Fury led four other men toward me, filling the street. He didn't screw around talking or threatening, which I respected. His men pushed to surround me while he attacked. After the first pass, I respected his swordsmanship too. He was one of the best fighters I had faced in a long time.

I retreated four steps, hoping to draw them in, but only one of his men went for it. I nipped in, as fast as I had ever been, and pierced him deep in the thigh. He stumbled and backed away before his leg collapsed. I didn't notice any more energy, though. Maybe this was as good as I was going to feel.

Big Fury's glacial confidence focused my attention. I knocked his sword aside, and he parried. I riposted, he dodged, and one of his men almost hacked off my sword hand before I jumped back.

His men didn't come after me confidently, maybe because of all the bodies lying in the street behind me, but Fury was holding them together like they were stones in his house. I searched for an opening. It came when an arrow punched into Big Fury's neck and out the other side. He staggered, and the men with him shied off, searching for the bowman while trying not to look away from me. I killed two of them. The third turned and ran.

A few more men charged me from far down the street. When an arrow brought down the one in front, the rest skidded and ran too.

I glanced up and saw Pil on a rooftop. I waved, but she didn't wave back. Instead, she watched the mercenaries retreat.

I pretended to run after the mercenaries, but the survivors mounted in a rush and galloped away. I searched for the children instead. Past a bend in the street, I found two women and a man weeping, gathered around a little girl whose throat had been cut.

"Flaming piss-bucket sons of bitches! Goddamn you!" I shouted at nothing I could see.

"Are you talking about yourself?" Pil called down to me from a rooftop.

"What?"

She grimaced. "Maybe you should be." She disappeared back past the edge of the roof.

I checked the little girl in case the wound wasn't as bad as it looked. It was. Her family scowled like I was a vulture.

I spun back toward the men I had wounded, the ones who couldn't run. Some were on the ground and some were limping or staggering away. I stabbed the closest one in the heart, and I felt weaker.

"Curse you to live in Fingit's nasty drawers, Desh Younger!" I shouted. I put my hands on my hips and surveyed the wounded men I couldn't kill unless I wanted to flop on the ground like a carp.

I waved my hand toward the bleeding men, as pompous as Harik himself. "I grant you all your lives! They're a gift from me, so get on out of here. Wait, you with the nose, go back and pick up your friend! He's not dead! What kind of man are you?"

"Bib!" Pil beckoned from a street corner, and I trotted to her. "Do you feel good about sparing those men? Do you feel moral and worthy and clean and handsome?" She glared at me, her sarcasm harsh enough to slay a team of mules.

I tried to answer truthfully. "Not so much, really. In fact, disappointment has bitten me hard over this."

"Then why didn't you kill all the wounded? That sounds like something Bib would do, doesn't it?"

I sighed and held up the Ass sword. "Desh put a curse on this damned blade . . . not a curse, exactly. It's too much to explain here in the street."

She pursed her lips. "That's fine, I'll ask you a different question. Have you realized yet that you and Parth are brothers? No, I don't mean that you fell out of the same woman, but if you were to consider the idea honestly, you'd realize that you're almost exactly like him."

"That's all flap and bull!" I laughed at her. "He's a cold, evil dog, fit only for killing."

"Why do you say that?"

"He poisoned all those people back at the castle, that's why."

Pil nodded. "He killed all those people with poison. You've killed a whole lot more with a sword, and don't say his victims were innocent, because from what I can tell, more than a few of your victims didn't strictly deserve to die."

"Well, he lied to us all the way . . ." I hesitated.

Pil raised her eyebrows at me, and I looked down, embarrassed. She said, "Right! Does he lie more than you?" Pil grabbed my shirt sleeve just below the bad scrape on my shoulder. "You've lied to Ella about your intentions ever since we arrived in Glass. If I counted up the lies I've heard from you, I'd be queasy for a month."

She was less than half my age, but I felt like an unruly child. "I'm sorry, Pil—"

"Be quiet, I'm not done. Parth ran away and left Capps to die, and even though Capps turned out to be a lying turd who led us into a trap, it was still a bad thing. You left Desh and me in King Staggs's camp. You haven't even asked whether Desh is alive."

My heart sped up. "Is he?"

"Yes, but I'm not done. Ask yourself what you want. No, don't even bother because I'm going to tell you. You want Glass to lose the war, and you know what Parth wants? He wants the same thing. You should be allies!"

I pulled away from her. "We're different! He damn near burned a city down with the people in it!"

Pil sneered. "That's right, he ran into that city and sacrificed its people to cover his escape, but he didn't kill the children, did he? You did the same thing in this city—you ran in and put all these people in danger to save yourself. You managed to get a child killed doing it, though, so good for you."

I slumped and crossed my arms, the Ass sword dangling from my hand. My cuts had begun to sting. "I need a drink."

"Bib, I'm not saying these things because I hate you. I love you more than anybody since my first teacher, the one before Dixon."

"You had a teacher before Dixon?"

"Shut up!" she shouted. "I love you more than my own family, even though you're the most aggravating person I've ever met. You have many bad qualities, and you lie to everyone on the face of the earth, but I have never known you to lie to yourself. And I can't stand watching you do it now."

Pil walked up and gave me a brief hug before stepping back.

I sighed. Pil was more right than wrong. "I guess I've become a little crazy over all this." I wanted to promise her I'd do better, but it seemed like too much trouble. Instead, I wanted to lie down on the dirt and sleep.

Distant shouting echoed from toward the edge of the city, and it sounded like more than just a few wounded men. Suddenly sleep seemed stupid. I didn't know what was happening out there, but it might be a chance to do better if I was bold. If nothing else, it would be a chance to escape Pil's ass-chewing.

I smiled and patted Pil's shoulder. Then I ran to the only horse nearby and mounted.

"Wait!" Pil yelled.

Smiling at her, I kicked my horse. I galloped down the street toward the edge of the city. Pil kept yelling from behind me.

I charged past the wounded mercenaries, almost running a couple down. A small battle was being fought a quarter mile outside the city. It appeared that Big Fury's retreating mercenaries had run into a large troop of King Staggs's horsemen. I slowed my mount, not knowing any reason why I should get involved. In fact, I was nearly certain that I should turn and ride away. Horses stamped, snorted, and shoved while men hacked at each other. Ten or twelve bodies lay on the ground, along with two horses, while twenty more horses ran free. Men on each side were still struggling to kill one another, or at least survive.

I spotted Parth in the middle of that boiling nightmare. He sat on his straining horse two hundred paces away from me, fighting one of Big Fury's men and not looking my direction. The mount I had grabbed wasn't the fastest beast I had seen today, or the sturdiest, but she weighed five times as much as me. I charged Parth.

One of the soldiers saw me coming and rode out to intercept me. I left him with a wrist sliced halfway in two. A bit of energy rushed into me as the soldier cursed, and I galloped on without losing stride. That man's curses caught a mercenary's attention. He peered at me for a second before stiffening. He wheeled his horse and galloped away from the fight.

Through his own dumbass luck, a soldier backed his horse right into my path as I reached the battle. My horse slowed, swerved, and bashed into his horse so that their sides shoved together. I thrust at the shocked soldier, but his horse bolted and carried him away from my sword.

Parth pulled his horse around in a tight circle and spotted me. He bared his teeth as we closed, and he whipped a brutal cut at my head, too swift for most people to follow. I ducked toward him, letting it whish over my head as I thrust at his side. He knocked my sword away in a block that was so fast I almost didn't believe it.

I circled Parth's blade to stab him in the armpit, but he was already urging his horse to sidestep out of my reach. I might have commanded my horse to briskly pursue him, if Krak had come down to give her intelligence and to stop time so I could train her for a month. I urged her straight ahead, ducking a cut from Parth. My dim horse carried me fifty paces at a gallop before we wheeled. Then I charged at Parth, who was riding to meet me.

Maybe I should have killed Parth's horse, but I couldn't embrace the idea. My scruples on the matter were unfortunate, since on the next pass, Parth sliced my horse's neck. She lurched and fell sideways. I rolled off and came up on my feet as if I were twenty years old, right before another soldier ran his horse's shoulder into me. I tumbled and lost my sword, but I rolled to my feet again.

The soldier who had bashed me raised his sword to chop my head in two. He froze and sucked air when an arrow showed up in the middle of his chest. His horse walked onward with a calm, even stride while he swayed in the saddle.

Spotting my sword, I rolled again and snatched it. I heard hoofbeats behind me and jumped to the left, away from Parth's sword arm. I ducked and dodged as the hoofbeats arrived, and something slammed the left side of my head. When my vision cleared, I saw Parth a good distance away, turning to take another run at me.

Blood was running down my left shoulder like a waterfall, and I reached up to my neck. My throat wasn't cut. However, my ear had gone to join my earlobe someplace, along with a good piece of the scalp and skin from the left side of my head. That wouldn't kill me, though. The way this fight was going, Parth sure as hell would.

I spotted Pil a hundred paces away, trotting toward us with her bow and leading a horse that was not fully cooperative. I pointed at Parth and bellowed, "Shoot him! Shoot him!" Instead, Pil shot somebody behind me—I supposed a soldier who was about to plunge a sword into my back, or kick me in the head, or kill his horse so it would fall and crush me. In any event, she didn't kill Parth.

I had only a sliver of magical power left, but there would be no need to save it if Parth cut me into chunks the size of my thumb. I used it all on a yellow band to convince Parth's mare that a wolf was on her back, clawing and eating her alive.

The mare did not accept that proposition right away. Parth galloped toward me. I sprinted to the side to gain a few seconds.

Parth's horse snorted and screamed. I looked back and saw the mare bucking and rearing while Parth clung to her mane and spoke what looked like soothing words. It didn't help him. A few seconds later, she launched Parth through the air. He hit the ground hard on his shoulder and head. After a couple of seconds, he struggled to get his arms under him, but he collapsed. I didn't know where his sword had flown off to.

The mare still thought Parth was a wolf, and she looked inclined to batter him to death with her hooves. I almost allowed her to kill him for me, but this was a man I wanted to dispatch myself. I let the mare go free, and she ran away.

A soldier sprinted to put himself between Parth and me. He thrust for my heart, but I disarmed him and then cut him deep at the knee. He fell on his butt, screaming, and more energy seeped into me.

I walked on toward Parth, who was again trying to clamber to his hands and knees. When I was three paces away, something grabbed me by the neck as if I were a scruffed puppy.

Pil said, "Asa, I bind you."

I struggled, but my neck held me in place. "Stop it!" I yelled. "Let me go!"

"Asa, I bind you." When Pil said those words, both of my wrists halted as if nailed to a wall. I couldn't see the bands of magical power wrapped around them, but I knew they were there. That's what happened when a sorcerer bound somebody.

Pil was still fifty feet away from me, and she hadn't been shouting those words. They had been in my head. "Asa, I bind you." Both my ankles locked into place.

"Let me go, Pil, or I'll carve my name on your liver!" I shouted. "At least let me kill him!"

Parth had climbed up and was watching this as he swayed on his feet, a deep furrow between his eyebrows. When I mentioned killing him, he glanced around for a moment. By the smile on his face, I assumed he spotted his sword. He ran out of my sight away from Pil.

Pil said, "Bib, I command you not to kill Parth and to get the hell away from here." The band disappeared from my left ankle, and I could move again. When Pil bound me, I had been trapped, motionless. Upon getting my first command, I was set loose so I could carry out her will. After carrying out the fifth command, I'd be free to do what I wanted. What I wanted was to break Pil's arms and legs before I threw her in the river.

I sprinted away from Parth and his few remaining soldiers, who seemed to have killed or chased off all the mercenaries. That sent me running right toward Pil and her horse.

THIRTY

When I reached Pil, her unstrung bow was on her back and she was holding the horse's reins in her right hand. With her left, she rubbed at her eyes, which looked as big as my fists. "Take the horse and go."

"To hell with you! I refuse to mount this animal!" I shouted as I sheathed my sword and shoved my foot in the stirrup.

Pil had bound me, so I couldn't harm her. She had commanded me to run and save myself, so I couldn't disobey. I swung up into the saddle. "Choke on your lying tongue, you sow!" I didn't have to be nice to her.

"Go on," she said, leaning to look past the horse at Parth's soldiers as they brought him a mount.

Stories were full of sorcerers who dared to bind spirit creatures. The foolish sorcerers were always slaughtered by whatever being they tried to control. I wasn't a spirit, but even for a regular person, there were many ways to obey a command.

When Pil handed me the reins, I grabbed her wrist and hauled her up onto the horse in front of me.

"Stop!" She twisted and struggled, almost losing the bow off her back.

I pushed the beast into a canter and then a gallop. "Stop? Is that a command?"

When a bound creature is commanded, one of the bands on its neck, wrists, or ankles dissolves. After the fifth command is obeyed, the bound creature is free to do whatever it wants. Usually, it wants to kill the sorcerer.

Pil had already given me one command.

I bent my head close to hers. "Do you command me to stop?"

She glanced back over my shoulder. "No, don't stop."

"Yes ma'am." I reined in my horse to a mere walk.

"Go! Ride!" Pil shouted.

"I am going and riding. You said to get the hell away from here. You didn't say how fast."

"I command you to ride away from here fast!"

The weight disappeared from my other ankle. That was the second command. I kicked the horse, which galloped east for ten seconds before I pulled us into a gentle curve to the right. Pil had never bound anything and didn't know what an ass-whipping it could be if she gave ambiguous commands.

Soon, we were heading south. Pil elbowed me in the ribs, but I shifted away from the worst of it. "Where are you going?"

"Unbind me, and I'll tell you."

"I told you to ride away from here!"

"No, you told me to ride away from there." I pointed at the spot where she'd given the command. "I am obeying like a good, gullible, bound sorcerer who is going to be free someday. We're not going back there. We're riding away from there in an ever-expanding circle." By that time, we were headed west. I glanced back and saw Parth with four men, all mounted and chasing us around the curve.

"You raw bastard!" Pil yelled.

"Unbind me. Maybe I'll forgive you."

"I command you to ride east back to Castle Glass as fast as you can, keeping your horse healthy and both of us safe."

When Pil gave the third command, the weight drifted away from my left wrist. I pulled my mount's head over to gallop east. "Why did you do it? Bitch."

"Why did you try to kill Parth?" she snapped.

"What? That's a stupid thing to ask. I'm killing him because he's a cruel sack of turds who needs to die."

Pil stared at the horse's neck. I almost didn't hear her say, "I bound you because I owed Parth a life. I couldn't let you kill him."

I let that sit in my mind for a few seconds. She had indeed promised the Void Walker she would give Parth his life. "That's a reason, sure, but I don't forgive you. Unbind me. Maybe I won't kill you today."

She shook her head. "I can't."

I now understood why that was true. If she unbound me, I would kill Parth or make a magnificent attempt. Even if I let Pil live, she'd face whatever punishment the Void Walker chose for her. She and I had discussed Void Walkers on the journey west, so she knew about them now. She was right to fear an unhappy Void Walker more than she feared death.

After fifteen minutes, I shouted to Pil, "We have to slow down. Otherwise, this poor horse's heart will burst." We had the misfortune of riding the least robust mount in the whole chase.

"You go! I'll stop them!" Pil yelled as she threw herself to the side. I grabbed her arm and pulled her back up.

"That was stupid. Dumb as a dog on a fence."

Pil spoke up over the sound of our horse blowing. "I could command you to disable Parth but not kill him."

"Even dumber than a dog on a fence. I'll have to hold back, and he'll kill me. He's a dangerous man." I turned the horse to run up a short hill.

"Do you have a plan to escape?" she asked, bouncing as the horse broke stride.

"No, I just want to have a good view when he murders us." I kicked the horse, which strained and leaned into the climb.

At the lip of the hilltop, I drew rein and pushed Pil off the beast. She smacked into the ground and lost her bow while I swung down. Parth and his men were urging their struggling horses up the hill. "Grab your bow and shoot some!" I shouted.

Pil scrambled to pick up her bow but hesitated. "I can't. I might accidentally kill Parth."

I grabbed the bow and an arrow from her, but I couldn't point it down the hill. Every time I tried to aim, my arms lowered the bow no matter what I wanted.

"Damn it to Fingit's hairy belly, Pil! Either set me free or command me to disable the toothy son of a bitch. It's better than singing songs while he cuts me up and his horse prances on what's left."

"I command you to disable Parth but not kill him!" Pil said as Parth's horse topped the hill right in front of us.

The weight on my right wrist dissolved, leaving just my neck bound.

I ducked and swung at Parth's leg as he passed, but I hit his boot and the Ass sword wasn't sharp enough to cut through it. He thrust at my face, and I leaned back out of the way before thrusting at his hip. He blocked and reined his horse around to bash me. I leaped away.

One of the soldiers rode toward me, trying to pin me between him and Parth. I stepped inside the man's swing, grabbed his wrist as he rode by, and dragged him out of the saddle. As he fell, I used both hands to throw him under Parth's horse.

That produced some gratifying results. The horse stomped the man's arm before backing up. Parth sawed on the reins. The soldier tried to roll out from under the horse but instead got tangled in the rear hooves, where he was stomped again.

I snatched my sword off the ground as Parth's horse reared, and I gave the horse a mighty whack on the rump with the flat of my blade. The horse came down, gathered itself, and jumped like a deer. It threw Parth away from me before galloping straight across the hillside.

Parth came to his feet prepared, his face as blank as if he'd just woken up. I spotted Pil farther away, lying on the ground next to a soldier, with two more men standing over her. She wasn't moving, but I knew she wasn't dead because I was still bound.

One of the standing soldiers, a small man, knelt beside his

wounded friend. The other, a bald fellow with no helmet, ran toward me.

Parth and I made four passes against each other. Although he was faster than me, he didn't have as many years of precise, ruthless butchery with a blade. I could have killed him by the third pass, but Pil's command forced me to hold back. I merely pierced his shoulder, which didn't disable him, but it did send me a nice wave of energy. He gave me four small wounds, which must have made him feel that he was winning. Strictly speaking, he was.

The bald soldier arrived and lunged at me while my blade was engaged with Parth's. I dodged and whipped out a tight cut, slicing the man's throat. I didn't quite parry Parth's next thrust, and he stabbed me through the fleshy part of my armpit. I slashed him across his right thigh as he recovered, but he was moving back and just got a bad scratch.

Parth must have decided I was overmatched, because he smiled as he threw several quick attacks at me. I jumped back and then retreated four steps, blocking him by inches. I backed away again and sidestepped, hoping Parth would open himself up to a thrust that would disable but not kill him.

Something slammed into the back of my head, and I staggered. In the next instant, I cursed myself for leaving the horse-stomped man alive. The bastard hit me again, and things went black.

Piercing pain between my legs woke me. I struggled, but something had pinned me facedown on the dirt. The first thing I saw was Pil thirty feet away, gagged and bound to a tree. Blood had run down her forehead and face. Small leather sacks had been pulled over her hands and tied at the wrist. She looked pale despite the blood, and she was crying.

Parth grabbed my hair and twisted my head around to face him as he squatted beside me. "I hoped that would wake you." He grinned for a second before wrinkling his brow over his sunken, red eyes. His jaw was as tight as if he'd been hanging from a cliff by his teeth. "That's grand. I'll try not to kill you. I have some experience, and you must admit you deserve what you get. You killed the king."

I raised myself to call for Harik, but he ignored me. I called on every other god except Lutigan, who hated me, and Krak, who despised everybody. None of them would listen.

Back in the world of man, I said, "Not to make apologies, but killing Staggs didn't help my cause any. It was unintentional."

"I consider that a fine apology. You're an honorable gentleman, eh?"

"Not even my mother thinks that. Was Staggs really your daddy?" I was sweating and started to shiver.

Parth tightened his grip on my hair and shook my head like a bell. "He has been for the past three years."

I nodded but couldn't think of anything else to say.

"Don't die," Parth said. "I do not intend to kill you. Garitt, bring something to keep this assassin warm."

My mind wandered until somebody threw a blanket over me. At that point, I realized I was naked. I saw that my hands were pressed tight against the ground with rope and stakes.

"Better?" Parth asked. "Since you have committed regicide, I cannot simply execute you. We must honor the king."

"Right, it's bad that the king's been killed, and I'm the wickedest son of a bitch ever to kick a baby. Hurry it up." I gasped for air. That ignorant speech had used up all my wind.

"You don't lack for bravado. At least so far." Parth smiled and let go of my hair. My cheek smacked onto the ground. "By the way, I appreciate the gift." He leaned down to show he was holding the Blade of Obdurate Mercy, which the gods had taken from me and given to Pil.

"It's cursed," I grunted.

"I hardly think you would carry a cursed sword."

"Of course it's cursed. Look what happened to me." I chuckled, or I intended to. I might have just croaked a little.

"My father would have found your company amusing, if you hadn't killed him."

I peered at Parth. He looked nothing like Staggs, but I supposed he really could be the king's adopted son. That didn't change things much at this point.

Parth smiled, but his sagging eyes didn't. "My father decreed impalement to be the punishment for regicide, so this reeks of propriety." He nodded at somebody behind me.

Once the agony ripped through my fundament, it became my whole existence—present, future, and past. As each moment happened, I understood what was being done, and the anguish of that knowledge was as bad as the pain. I saw each second approaching to bring more torment. I grieved for myself as I was destroyed, even though I couldn't live through this, and it wouldn't matter what was left.

Screaming didn't change a damn thing, but I did it, and I kept doing it.

"Shh," Parth said. "Don't thrash. You may hurt yourself. You may hurt yourself worse, I mean. I hate to do a shoddy job, and I was unable to locate the perfect sapling for this."

At some point, I gave up screaming for a few moments in favor of moans and panting. Pil was still tied to the tree and had begun sobbing.

"The key is to follow your spine." Parth sounded like he was explaining how to bake a peach pie. "That avoids piercing important organs and puncturing large veins."

The pain spiked in the middle of my back. I passed out before I could scream.

Even before I opened my eyes, agony charged up and down my back. Somebody slapped my cheek.

"Wake up!" Parth said. Another slap.

I opened my eyes, trying not to scream or even breathe. I realized I was being held up by my arms.

Parth stepped back and scrutinized me as if I were a sculpture. "I have witnessed men survive two days of this, if they possessed great will to live. I hope you possess such will. I wish to return after the battle and observe you for my father's sake. Look at me. Stand up." He motioned to the men holding me, and they released me.

I wobbled on my feet but stood as firm as possible when agony pushed up toward my neck. The stake moved a bit. It must have been set into a hole in the ground.

"I advise you not to sit," Parth said. He beckoned, and a soldier brought him a horse. "You may be a sorcerer, but you cannot simply make that stake disappear. I heard you say as much to Pil when she had been shot with an arrow. Something about rotten wood in the wound killing her for certain."

Parth glanced at Pil, who was now mounted in front of a soldier, still gagged and tied. She stared at me, her face drawn. I heard in my head, "Asa, I unbind you."

"About damn time, you ungrateful viper!" I yelled, and then I screamed for a while as the pain ricocheted around inside me.

Parth grinned down from his horse. "That was entertaining. I wish I could stay, but now that I am king, my time is no longer my own." He pushed his horse into a canter, followed by over a dozen men.

Some blunt part of me observed that he must have found rein-forcements. I cursed that blunt part for wasting time on useless things. I cursed the rest of my parts while I was at it.

I raised my spirit to call on Harik, Fingit, Gorlana, and every other god, even Fressa, who I suspected was dead. If there was ever a time for a god to be listening, this was it. But none of them answered me.

I mumbled, "I guess I shouldn't have called Harik a repugnant, weeping slime hole in a crappy secondhand robe."

THIRTY-ONE

Ella once told me I should have killed myself instead of murdering people for Harik. She said it would have been the proper thing to do, and nobody knew what's proper better than Ella.

I could have told her that I had seen too much, and I had witnessed despair in the morning become victory in the afternoon. Sometimes it was the other way around. Regardless, things always changed, and they could change into something better.

Such philosophies should be reexamined when a man is naked, impaled, agonized, and slowly bleeding to death.

It surprised me to feel a kind of relief over the situation. I would rather not have been impaled and dying, of course. But for some time, I had been hoping for a better existence than slaughter and gods slapping me around like I was a cranky chicken.

That had been foolish, and deep down, I had known it. Harik, that oozing toad of a god, had mocked me for thinking I could get away. So long as I lived, he would own me. When I died, he would claim me.

No wonder thinking about gods and debts had been exhausting me lately.

I let those ideas sit with me as I shivered, groaned, screamed, and cursed. The pain came in waves that rode on a tide that raised them as time passed. I knew enough about healing to imagine what was happening to my body, but I said to hell with it. Such thoughts couldn't help me.

My legs tired out and began shaking. I found that I could rest them a bit by leaning back against the stake, if I didn't mind some exceptional agony. By sunset, I had asked myself dozens of times why I didn't collapse and let the stake push the rest of the way through me. I did not have a good answer to that. I just didn't do it.

Once it was full dark, a god snatched my spirit and pulled me upward. When the pain disappeared and the nausea hit, I started crying.

"I bring you before me a final time, Murderer, that you may enjoy my presence ere the end," Harik said.

I turned away from Harik. I didn't want to risk warning him that I could see, and tears on my face might make him suspicious.

It was dark in the Gods' Realm. A field of drooping flowers stretched downhill to the horizon, lit by millions of fireflies. "Mighty Harik, I have never more than tolerated your presence. Sometimes, I suffered it. Sometimes, I imagined you were a chair or a wet towel. And who the hell says 'ere' anyway?"

"You should be nicer to me, Murderer. Your life is being driven out of your body. You cannot last long."

I wondered why Harik had brought me. To gloat? To endure another insult or two? Or did he want to deal?

"If there's not a deal on the table, I have more pleasant things to do back home," I said. Trusting that my cheeks had dried, I bumbled through turning partway around and stared as if sightless. From there, I could see Harik without looking straight at him.

The gazebo was full.

Krak sat in the middle, surrounded by his brood. Harik, Lutigan, and Fingit sat with him. On the lower tier sat Effla, along with Sakaj, Goddess of the Unknowable, Trutch, Goddess of Life, and Gorlana, Goddess of Mercy.

On the top tier sat Weldt with two goddesses I didn't recognize on either side of him. From her black hair and ale-brown robe, I figured one was Casserak, Goddess of Health. That would make the blonde in the leaf-green gown Chira, Goddess of Forests.

I didn't see a goddess wearing Fressa's prismatic armor. The God of Deep Waters, Madimal, also seemed to be missing.

Standing on the top tier in the back were Lutigan's three sons, Paal, Gondix, and Zagurith. They had threatened to kill me once, and I supposed the idea of my being dead tickled them.

"Don't you want to beg for your life?" Harik asked me.

Krak smiled.

Sakaj whispered, "Don't bait him!"

"Throw him away and let him die," Lutigan whispered. I considered that statement proof that the gods didn't know I could hear them. I supposed it could have been a clever ploy, but the gods didn't embrace cleverness. When one is omnipotent, subtlety just wastes everybody's time.

"I don't want to beg, Your Magnificence, but I'm not above discussing the situation." I edged around, unsteady, to almost face the gazebo.

Trutch, Harik's wife, scowled and whispered, "Now you've got him talking! We were done with him! I hate you so much!"

Krak raised his fist and whispered, "We agreed to this."

Everybody froze and stopped talking.

Krak went on: "Harik is sacrificing for the common good. He is allowed to torment the Murderer one last time."

Harik smirked.

"Yes, Father," Lutigan whispered.

"We have engineered this moment with great care," Sakaj whispered, glaring at Harik, "so I don't want you shattering everything, you eternal horse's ass!"

Krak frowned at her and relaxed his right fist so that a single ray of the impossibly searing light of the sun escaped. Sakaj stared at her feet. It felt like I'd been hit in the forehead with a hammer, but I managed not to react.

Harik stood and smiled down at me. "Hmm. Why don't we discuss you making an offer?"

"Well, I only need a square. In exchange, I won't bathe for a month."

"That's laughable," Harik said. "You already haven't bathed for three weeks."

"What do you propose instead?" I asked.

Half a dozen gods hissed or whispered, "No!" Three of them rose to their feet. Effla lowered her eyelids and whispered, "Harik, I will crush your manhood like a biscuit."

Harik waved them away. "Oh, I have no counteroffer, Murderer. Your sad plea doesn't merit one. Is it the best you can do?"

I couldn't tell what in the name of my Aunt Delphi was happening. Harik seemed to be playing with his toy—me—before I was thrown out. The other gods appeared unaccountably anxious to see me dead. I wouldn't have thought some of them knew who I was. "I suppose I can do better, Mighty Harik. For three squares, I will kill the next fifty people I see." If Harik was going to deal at all, he wouldn't turn that down.

Harik's arms dropped, and he leaned forward to stare at me.

"Don't you do it," Krak whispered. "I will take you to the Dark Lands and pull off your head like a cork."

Fingit raised his head. "The Knife is calling for me, begging to trade, and she sounds desperate. Or perhaps terrified or flustered. It's difficult to tell with her," he whispered. "What do you want to do?"

"By the hairy sacks of the Void!" Weldt whispered. "Why don't we just crush the Murderer out of existence and be done with him?"

A few of the gods nodded. Krak and the rest glared at Weldt as if he'd suggested they lick poison out of a dragon's nostril.

"We agreed about this," Krak whispered. "Best not to do it ourselves."

I wanted to scream, *Do what? Not do what yourselves? And if not yourselves, then who?* I stayed quiet, though.

Weldt looked away and sighed.

"Bring the Knife," Krak whispered.

Pil materialized to my right. Since Parth had her sword, she couldn't see in this place. "Mighty Fingit, I come to trade."

"Pil?" I said as if I hadn't known she was there.

"Bib? You're alive!"

"Not for much longer, you nasty sack of weasels! Really, Pil, I'm dying because you betrayed the shit out of me!"

"I'm sorry," she whispered. "I wish I could make it different."

"You're not the one with a tree up your ass, so cheer the hell up."

"I couldn't imagine more appropriate final words for you, Murderer," Harik said. He tossed me away with a tenderness I had never felt from him before. I eased back into my dying body.

Another wave of agony surged through me. When I was done screaming, I stood trembling and trying not to pant. Breathing hurt like hell.

Magical power flowed into me. I received five squares from somewhere, or someone, for some reason. In a single moment, my hopelessness washed away. In the next moment, I wondered how I could use that power to survive, and I had not one idea. Hopelessness started looking mighty good again.

At the very least, I could stop the bleeding. I pulled a green band and, in a couple of minutes, took care of that.

Parth had been right about my not being able to rot the stake. It would leave bits of awful dead wood behind and kill me soon. But so long as the stake was set in the ground, I was stymied.

I pulled a band of power, trying to move only my fingers. If I wasn't cautious, the stake could still tear up my insides or even kill me. I used the power to rot the stake almost all the way through right above the ground. A tiny bend would break it free. I eased to the side, slipped, and staggered when the stake came free. That was awfully unpleasant. I hated it even more when I tripped and fell on my side.

My vision clouded while I screamed, but I stayed awake. It was fortunate, since that adventure had torn me up inside and I was bleeding a fair amount. I pulled some more green bands, panting and cursing Parth while I stopped the blood from flowing.

Then I giggled. At least nobody was around to laugh at my bumbling escape attempt. With the next breath my mouth went slack as I realized that giving a shit about such things now meant I was close to panic and probably death. I blinked hard a few times, trying to focus.

Now I had a puzzle. Possibly, I could locate a bear and call it, but I doubted it could seize the stake in its teeth and remove it without killing me. The fact that I even considered the notion told me I was almost delirious. The sapling was fresh, but I couldn't figure out how to root it to the ground so I could try to pull myself free.

After some period of dazed staring into the darkness, I asked myself how much I really wanted to live. From listening to the gods, it was clear my future would be bound up with them. I would always be in their debt and always thrashed by their brutal whims. But now, I had unexpected questions. Why did the gods want something done to me? To be honest, they had a cartload of reasons. The real question was what could the repugnant, goat-hopping, privates-flapping gods not want to do themselves?

I raised my knees, clamped my heels onto the lower part of the stake, and straighten my legs to pull out as much of the stake as I could. That amount was none, because the stake was bloody and slick. My heels just slipped off.

Maybe that was better. I would need to heal myself the whole time I was removing the stake. Only Krak knew how badly I'd tear myself up in the effort.

Still unable to think of anything else, after an uncertain time of groaning and yelling, I pulled a blue band and rotted two notches on the sides of the stake. I placed one heel in each notch, pushed, and drew out two fingerbreadths of the stake before I started shrieking. That had been a bad idea.

I panted, sweated, and shivered in the cool night air as my sweat dried. I squeezed my eyes shut and even banged the side of my head on the dirt to call up a better idea. There was no better idea. The best idea was a bad idea.

Gripping the stake with my heels again, I pulled a green band to have handy for healing. I strained and howled but kept pushing until

I straightened my legs. The stake had cut one of my lungs on the way, and I coughed up blood until I could heal the damage.

I rotted two more notches in the stake, pulled another green band, and pushed with my legs again. I screamed and passed out before I had straightened them all the way.

When I woke up, I had been out just a few seconds, but that was long enough to lose the power I had readied. I pulled another green band and stopped some bleeding. Two new notches made room for my heels. I pulled power to heal myself and pushed until the most jolting pain of the day plunged into my back. My hips and legs went numb.

I yelled and beat one hand against the ground until I found the damage to my spine. A delicate ten minutes later, I had repaired it and my legs worked again.

My heels searched for the notches, but this time, I kept missing. I realized that my body had been pushed too far and was giving up. After two deep breaths, I managed to find the notches and straightened my legs. The stake tore something big in my belly, and I had forgotten to call up any power before this push. I pulled a band in a hurry and rushed through patching the wound.

After I pulled another healing band, I rotted two more notches, slipped my heels into them, and pushed with a slow, even strain. My vision faded, but before my legs straightened all the way, the stake came free.

I stopped all the bleeding and mended the worst damage, lying on the ground and breathing until my heart calmed. When I felt sure I wouldn't expire without warning, I fell asleep on my side.

I woke in the dark when somebody tried to tie me up. I started to roll away, but my wounded insides stopped me in a hurry. I grunted and fell back down. Then I realized that nobody was tying me up. Maybe that had been a dream. Somebody had lain a blanket over me, though.

"It's not a competition, Bib," said a shape that sounded like Desh. "You didn't have to get run through with a tree just because I got dismembered and blinded."

I breathed, "Well, it was an experience I'd never had, so what the hell."

Desh knelt and put a hand on my forehead. "Don't expect to find me burned up or crushed under boulders next time. I yield. You don't feel feverish."

I nodded and realized he probably couldn't see it. The night had grown cloudy, and I felt it might rain soon. "Have you seen Ella or Pil?"

"I've seen them both. Ella ran across Karl and a patrol. He took her back to his father for safekeeping. He probably wants advice on romance too. Pil is stalking Parth. Apparently, she wants to avenge you."

"Shit! Where is she?"

"Somewhere behind Parth's army. I couldn't talk her out of it, so I gave her my sword and my sling."

"Mighty nice of you. You're a hell of a man."

"You know better than that. She had just killed three soldiers to escape." He hesitated. "She did a thorough job."

"If you're in a giving mood, do you want to give me your clothes?" I smiled so he'd hear it in my voice.

"No, but I can find some for you. Don't leave this behind, though. You'll need it at the battle." He handed me the Ass sword. "I found it on the ground. Magical objects should be ugly so that nobody will want to take them."

"Huh. When do you expect the battle to be joined? And where?"

"No later than tomorrow. Maybe this afternoon," Desh said. "It looks like the field of battle will be in the Harrows."

The Harrows was a small set of hills west of Castle Glass. They were mostly uncultivated because they contained not a damn thing of value and the soil would hardly grow weeds. "This afternoon? Shit! I'll have to rush. Desh, would you tarry a minute while I finish healing myself?"

"Oh, I won't leave you here. Ella's already mad enough at me."

I spent most of an hour putting my insides neatly back together and my outsides too. Desh had scrounged me a uniform from one of Parth's dead soldiers. "Did you find me a horse?" I asked.

Desh shook his head.

I sighed, stood up, and almost fell down again. The pain from healing myself took my breath away for a moment. I squeaked, "I apologize, Desh, but I'm going to walk slower than a one-legged chicken. You don't have to wait on me, you know."

The sky was growing lighter in the east, and against it, I saw Desh wave. "Don't worry. But I have a favor to ask before we leave. Fix my teeth and my other eye. I'll provide the power."

"Sure, no favor necessary."

Desh handed me a small wooden bottle the size of my palm, sealed with thick wax. He had given me one like it before, filled with magical power. "I created this the first chance I got, which was last night. In case you've forgotten, break loose the stopper and inhale from the bottle. That way, you get all the magic goodness."

I opened the bottle and sniffed it. Magical power washed into me, ready to use however I wanted.

"Desh, this is too much! It's a whole square. I only need about one-twentieth for this!"

"Do something dramatic with the rest." Desh chuckled. It was uncommon for him to laugh.

I spent fifteen minutes fixing Desh's teeth and eye. By the time I finished, my own eye was throbbing and weeping so much that I hardly felt my teeth.

"Thank you, Bib. Are you ready to go?"

"Sure, but keep watch for a horse. If I have to walk all the way, I won't get there until harvest."

Desh turned away and whispered.

Limnad walked out from behind a tree. "Bib! You're not dead!"

"It takes more than a tree up my bottom to kill me."

The spirit glanced at the stake as if it were a caterpillar beneath her notice. "Don't be foolish. When I saw you last, in your heart, you were preparing for death."

"What? I was not!"

Limnad cocked her head and lowered her brows like a child

who's being told a fib. "I know spirits. Yours was nearly done. What happened? Did someone kill your brother in a blood feud? Did you fall in love?"

I opened my mouth and closed it again.

Limnad said, "Oh. Her."

Desh stepped in. "Limnad, we need to reach the Harrows quickly."

"The Harrows? Do you mean the Hills of Unnatural Waning and Death?"

"It's a poetic name," Desh said to me. "Means nothing."

Limnad giggled. She grabbed me in one arm and Desh in the other as if we were jugs of wine. "Hold tight, Bib. If you throw up, I'm going to write a song about it and sing it to everyone you know."

THIRTY-TWO

Desh was probably the world's foremost expert on spirits, since he had been Limnad's lover for more than a year and all his body parts were still connected. I possessed a reasonable understanding of the subject, or I thought I did. The next few hours with her and Desh revealed that I knew less about spirits than I did about whatever rocks lay at the bottom of the ocean.

Limnad carried Desh and me twenty miles in forty seconds. Each time she lifted her foot to take a step, the world whizzed by at an almost incomprehensible speed until her foot touched the ground. Then the world halted in a totally new place. When she took the next step, the world went crazy again.

"You don't need to hold on so tight," Limnad grumbled at me.

After the first few steps, I had to shut my eyes, or I really might have puked. With my eyes closed, it felt as if she must have been walking at no more than a snappy pace.

I forced myself to open my eyes again, and the jarring, jumbled world was easier to take. Limnad always stepped beside a tree, or a big rock, or some other concealed place. In the past, whenever I had called for her, she had appeared from behind a tree or some cover almost immediately. I had figured it was some kind of spirit magic. Now I knew what kind.

Limnad halted beside a small, shaded river.

"Fun, right?" Desh looked at me with a straight face.

I began taking shallow breaths when Limnad dropped me, since my insides were still grinding from healing myself. I paced in a small circle, trying not to stumble too much.

Desh ambled into the river, which was too shallow to cover his head. After standing still for a moment, he sank straight down.

I glanced around. I was alone. Feeling awkward, I decided I may as well follow him. If I dunked myself and he was hiding someplace laughing at me, that wouldn't be the worst thing that had happened recently.

Wading to the spot where I had last seen Desh, I took a breath and let my legs collapse. I fell straight through the river bottom into a large, air-filled chamber that looked to have been hollowed out from stone. The low ceiling was as clear as glass, revealing water above us. Dim light wafted down through it.

"Welcome to our winter home," Desh said, kicking a bolt of silk off a scuffed, splintery, uneven wooden chair. "Sit." I didn't see another chair, and Desh sat on the stone floor. I eased down to sit on the awful thing and found I had never sat on a more comfortable piece of furniture.

The room held a small bed, two cupboards, a big worktable, three bookcases packed with books, and stacks of wood, cloth, and leather. I also saw a lot of tools lying around, including a couple I couldn't identify.

"How do you get the books down here?" I asked.

"Drain the river."

I nodded once. "Sure. That's what I would have done."

"Well, Limnad stops it for a few minutes," he said. "We'll abandon this place soon. Bib, forgive me, but what the hell is going on?"

I debated how much to tell him.

"If you say what you know, I'll do the same. Fair trade."

"All right, Desh. I owe debts to Lutigan and Harik."

Desh frowned but didn't say anything.

"I started this war for Lutigan. For Harik, I must make sure Glass loses."

"That's awkward."

I nodded. "And I have to fight fifty feet ahead of the front line."

"Whose front line?"

I paused. "He didn't specify. Maybe that's a loophole."

"I wouldn't count on it, but maybe," Desh said. "What else?"

"This will sound insane, but recently, I started seeing in the Gods' Realm, even without that stupid sword."

Desh stared at me.

"It happened gradually."

Desh took a breath. "I hate to say this, but are you being strictly truthful with me?"

I nodded.

"I had to ask."

"I know," I said, still nodding. "But that's not the strange part."

"What?" Desh leaned back. "Cough it up. What's the strange part?"

I said it fast because it sounded ridiculous. "The gods want me dead, but they don't want to kill me themselves. They want somebody else to do it. I don't know who. Or why."

Desh rubbed his forehead. "Do you know what that means?"

I shook my head.

"I don't either. I have no idea."

"I don't expect you to know. But that's what the hell is going on." I leaned back to ease my insides a bit.

Desh nodded. "My turn. You probably know that I got an open-ended debt from She-Who-Must-Not-Be-Named. I won't go into the details of the deal. They're not important. The significant thing is how I got the deal."

I grinned. "Yes, I have been curious about that."

"While bargaining, she implied that she needed a certain severity of consequences from me in order to close a deal. It was almost as if she needed it so she could do something."

"Right!" I cut in. "I heard the same kind of thing from Harik. Like he needed a specific amount of . . . I don't know, something to make things happen."

Desh nodded slowly. "Maybe so. I pushed the point as far as I could. She got mean, which I expected, but then she became flustered. And then she got desperate."

"Hell, that can't be right. She-Who-Must-Not-Be-Named doesn't get desperate or flustered."

"She did then. So desperate that when I demanded an open-ended debt, she gave it to me." Desh leaned forward. "I get power every day with no bargaining, until she has provided the total amount of her obligation—an amount that only I know."

"Or until you die," I said.

Desh smiled for a moment. "Of course."

I watched his eyes, but I didn't ask the next question.

"What did I pay?" Desh absently crossed his arms as if he were cold. "I cannot know happiness."

"Goddamn it, Desh," I whispered. "That's bold."

He shrugged. "It's not forever. Only for twenty years."

"Bah! What are you whining about, then?" Actually, as a sorcerer, it was damn unlikely he'd live twenty more years. It might be rude of me to say such a thing, though.

Desh furrowed his brow. "We have a lot of facts, but I don't know what they mean."

"As much as I'd like to solve it right now, we don't have time today," I said. "And if we get killed today, we won't need to worry about it."

Limnad rushed into the room through the ceiling and leaned against Desh. "You are not allowed to die today!" She turned to me. "Bib, you may not get him killed today. Promise me you won't!"

"Bib can't make that promise. I'm going to battle, and he can't stand in front of me."

"Battle?" The spirit plopped like a raindrop to sit on the floor. "You don't need to walk around in a battle, or ride, or butt-scoot, or whatever people do. You gave Bib a sword. Let him butt-scoot to battle."

"I promised to help the Kingdom of Glass," Desh said.

"The king got poisoned! That promise is no good!" she shouted loud enough to hurt my ears.

Desh said, "The sorcerer who blinded me may be there."

Limnad shot up like a geyser. Her skin turned deep blue, and she growled, "The Radish will be there?"

"Maybe. I need to—"

Limnad yelled, "We need to go kill him! We need to kill him right now!"

"Wait!" Desh held up both hands.

"I will pull off his fingers and then his arms!" she howled, circling the room. "I will shove his arms in his butt and his fingers into his belly so that he looks like a pathetic cow!"

"I'd never tell you what to do, Limnad," Desh said, "but you know that a battle is dangerous. If you die, I'll be sad."

Limnad halted nose to nose with Desh, her face hard. "Then I will not die."

Desh walked to a stained cupboard. "How do you feel, Bib?"

"Recently impaled." Actually, my pains were fading faster than I expected.

"I'm sorry, but you'd better prepare. I think we're leaving for the battle soon." Desh glanced at Limnad, who was standing where he left her, now an even darker blue. Her hair was floating above her shoulders as she muttered to herself.

Desh tossed some plain, gray clothes to me. "Better than those awful, bloody things you're wearing."

I changed clothes, and when I looked up, Desh was holding a round, wooden shield out to me. "Fifty feet ahead of the front line? You'll need this more than I will."

I took the shield, which was warped, splintered, and a bit oblong instead of round.

Desh had wrapped a sling around his waist and hefted a heavy-looking, rusty war hammer. He also grabbed a burlap sack. "Ready?" Without waiting, he stood in the middle of the room and jumped straight up through the ceiling. Limnad sprang through in a different direction.

I followed Desh and came up in the river, with my head well above water. My mind jerked. I had spent an hour with Desh, but four hours had passed here, making it just past noon. The pain from healing my own wounds had disappeared. My pains from helping Desh had faded quite a bit, although my right eye was still leaking and blurry.

Wading ashore, I found Desh pulling pieces of scuffed, water-stained leather armor out of his bag. Limnad flitted like a surly dragonfly while Desh fastened on his armor. Then she grabbed us both and hell-walked south to what I supposed would be the battle.

When Limnad stopped, I saw the shallow hills of the Harrows less than a mile away. The army of Glass occupied a hillside and part of the valley beneath it. The Bredgarde army covered the other side of the valley and the hill above it. We stood at one end of the valley, able to see the entire battlefield.

I estimated twenty-five hundred men in Parth's army and even more in Durch's. Both forces were deploying for battle, but neither had attacked yet. The formations hadn't settled, and I saw small groups of men scrambling into place on both sides.

As I examined the field, Desh was saying, "Limnad, I need your help with the Radish."

"You need me to kill him!"

"Yes. But he's a dangerous sorcerer. Please hide where you can see everything. Watch for the Radish and don't get caught up fighting. When you see him, rush in, destroy him before he knows you're there, and retreat."

"Oh, yes," Limnad said. "I'll kill him. I'll protect you from him, today and forever." Limnad seemed to vanish.

"Glad I'm not Dimore, the Radish Sorcerer," I said.

"I hope she's careful. She gets emotional. Have you decided which side to fight for?"

"I don't see any advantage in fighting for Parth, and besides, he's a torturing son of a bitch."

Desh nodded and hefted his hammer. "I'll join Durch's right wing. That will give me a better view of things, and it will be easier to run if I need to." He grinned. I had taught him that running is always a valid tactic.

"You're welcome to fight up front with me." I drew the Ass sword. "Think of the glory. They'll build statues of us."

Desh shook his head and walked away toward Durch's army. He called over his shoulder, "Be careful. You're not well yet."

I trudged off at an angle from him, headed toward the center of the battlefield. I began pulling white bands and flinging them up into the gloomy clouds. I should have a small but nasty thunderstorm by the time I reached the battle.

My plan was simple, almost mindless. I would stand in front of Durch's lines, as Lutigan required. When the battle started, I would call a lightning bolt and blast King Durch into shreds of nasty, badmannered meat. Glass would lose, which would satisfy Harik. Then I'd retreat back through the lines as the leaderless army of Glass fell apart.

What about Parth? There would be another day to deal with Parth.

My only problem was that I'd be attacked by dozens of Parth's soldiers when the battle started, before I killed Durch and retreated. I had a tactical advantage in magic, but I could use another. Surprise would be useful but unlikely.

I would settle for uncertainty and a little intimidation.

I approached the battlefield from the end, right between the two front lines. Leaning my sword over my shoulder and letting my shield arm dangle, I trudged straight down the middle of the valley with all the urgency of going to wash my clothes. I watched the ground ahead of me and never glanced to either side.

The lines were more than three hundred paces long. When I had walked fifty paces, the soldiers on both sides were growing quiet. By the time I was one hundred paces in, the only sounds I heard were my own footsteps. I imagined ten thousand eyes watching me cross the next fifty paces in near silence.

In the middle of the battlefield, I turned, located Parth standing on the hillside, and pointed my sword at him. Even though he stood halfway up the hillside, I could see his mouth and eyes pop open.

Then I spun around to take my place in front of Durch's army. I walked four steps, spotted Durch, and paused. Ella was standing beside him, held by two soldiers. Any lightning I threw at the debauched old vulture would destroy her too.

Battle horns sounded from the Bredgarde army behind me. I glanced back to see hundreds of men yell and march toward me.

THIRTY-THREE

I could have fled toward Durch's lines, but I stood fast. That sure as hell wasn't due to courage. I had performed some theater earlier to convince the enemy that I was a casual, fearless slayer of men. A murderer who would laugh when I sent their heads back to their mothers. I wouldn't be satisfied stabbing them in the heart. I would stab them in the belly too, because one mortal wound wasn't painful enough.

One or two bits of that might have been true.

I chose not to throw away that advantage. Instead, I faced the shouting Bredgarde soldiers with my sword still lying across my shoulder. I also pulled three white bands and tossed them into the sky to freshen the thunderclouds.

Horns sounded behind me. Durch's men shouted and cheered. I heard them charge, their footfalls a disorganized mess. When I glanced back, I saw them entering the field as a mob, while Parth's men trotted toward me in sharp formations of a hundred men each.

The men of Glass, led by that ignorant butt-waffle King Durch, were about to be butchered.

I heard sprinting footsteps behind me, and Stan planted himself on my right. He shook his sword at the Bredgarde soldiers and shouted, "Run faster, you squinty bastards, I'm getting bored!"

"Hurry back to the lines, Stan!"

"Balls to that. I don't leave my friends to get cut up by themselves. When those farts get close, we'll fight back-to-back." Stan spit on the moist, black dirt.

Parth's closest formation came within a hundred feet of us, and I called a stroke of lightning down on them. It flung dirt in all directions, and thirty men fell. The rest of the formation staggered and dragged to a halt.

Stan pushed his helmet back and chewed his lip. "I like that better. Do some more of that."

I threw lightning onto the formations to each side of the first one. Then I hit the one behind it. About three hundred of the original four hundred men were still standing, and they fell back in a well-ordered retreat. Stan laughed and showed them his ass.

I held myself back from chasing them, but it was a struggle. I had just tasted a hundred soldiers' deaths, each as firm and sweet as a peach.

Staring at the ground, I muttered, "No, this is a waste of time and power."

"What?" Stan yelled.

I shook my head at him. We wouldn't defeat Durch by slaying his enemies for him. Soldiers from the army of Glass began racing past me toward the retreating Bredgarde troops, and I glanced back toward Durch. Ella still stood right beside the king.

A drastic change of strategy was required.

I spun another band and brought down lightning halfway between Durch and me. It left a dozen men on the ground.

"Hey! The damn enemy is over here on this side!" Stan shouted.

I twisted and saw another formation of Parth's troops closing at a fast trot. They speared and swept aside Durch's disorganized men. I brought up my shield in case arrows reached me before the troops did.

Hundreds of men were about to die in this battle, maybe thousands, but it wasn't my doing. Staggs would have invaded Glass even if I had never come to engineer a war. But while I was here, I might as well take as many lives for Harik as I could.

An arrow whizzed in front of me and plunged into Stan's chest. He staggered and fell on his back, dropping his sword.

I called lightning onto the closest formation of soldiers, and the entire group shuddered to a stop. Then I knelt beside Stan, who was taking shallow breaths. If I took time to heal him, I would be overrun.

Seeing Stan about to die reminded me why I hated wars. Skill meant less than luck when trying to survive amid hundreds of swinging weapons. And I preferred to choose who I killed. I held my judgment in such matters to be superior to that of any king or general. In fact, of the thousands of men on that battlefield, I figured only a few dozen were brutes who really needed to be murdered. I'd be pleased to drink with any of the rest, if they were buying.

I despised myself for letting this slaughter happen. Admitting that was like putting down a big weight. I could do something about it. Best not to let Harik catch me thinking that way, though.

I called down more lightning on Durch's troops. My power reserves had grown meager, but I strengthened the storm with some white bands anyway.

Lifting myself toward the Gods' Realm, I called, "Harik, I've come to trade!"

It was snowing in the Gods' Realm. Enormous flakes fell from a solid gray sky, so round and even it might have been a bowl turned over me. With no breeze at all, the lazy flakes dropped straight down.

Within seconds, my bones ached from the cold. Snow lay deep on almost everything. Snow-heavy branches in the forest to my left splintered and crashed.

"Murderer, you wish to trade?" Harik yawned. "This is tiresome. I assumed I would never see your living form again."

Krak sat in the middle of the gazebo, his face a storm of fury and petulance. Harik stood on the bottom to his right, and Lutigan sat fuming at Krak's left hand. Fingit sat on the top level next to Sakaj, She-Who-Must-Not-Be-Named. Fingit sagged, staring at his feet. Sakaj shifted on the bench and glared at everybody.

"I must thank you, Mighty Harik, for saving my life." I tried not to look directly at any of them.

"What are you mumbling about?"

"At the moment of my greatest need, the thought of Your Magnificence gave me the strength to fight."

"I find that unlikely," Harik said. "And if it is true, then I find it sad and repulsive."

"Well, the five squares helped too," I said.

Harik whispered to Krak, "What should I tell him about that?"

Krak surged to his feet with the power of a breaching whale, but he whispered, "Why did you bring him here if you don't already know what you plan to say? Idiot!"

Harik glanced at Lutigan and Sakaj, but they were busy examining other parts of the gazebo.

Fingit whispered, "Tell him the truth."

Harik rolled his eyes. "Yes, amusing, little brother. You're a wit. Now go play with your imps."

Fingit smiled. "When has any sorcerer known the truth and failed to harm himself with it?"

"That's right, they do, don't they?" Lutigan whispered.

Krak shrugged.

I called out, "Oh, Mighty Lutigan, overripe scat of the lowest worms in creation, are you still there?"

"I was pausing to savor the memory of your suffering," Harik said, "despite the shard of disappointment I experienced when you survived. I assuredly did not help you. The Knife granted you that gift of power."

"Ah. I hate to sound ungrateful, but why did Your Magnificences allow that?"

Harik went on. "It was terribly careless of Fingit. His wits have been abandoning him. Perhaps he is not entirely immortal."

I thought Fingit might bitch at Harik about that, or even hit him, but the Smith of the Gods stared at his feet again and sighed.

Krak whipped around and punched Fingit on the arm. Fingit grabbed his bicep and screamed silently while his eyes rolled up.

I said, "That's mighty interesting. What did she pay for that power?"

"Ask her yourself! If you ever see her alive again," Harik said.

"I will, and I'll pass on your respects. However, my immediate interest is ten squares. I yield to you the honor of making the first offer."

"Really?" Harik drawled.

"Oh, yes."

Sakaj whispered, "Harik, send him away. He may die in battle, and we have to make plans in case he doesn't."

Fingit whispered, "You could send him back, of course. But does anybody care to bet that he'll die in battle? I'll wager two winged horses and a cottage on Mount Humility that he walks away from this nightmare."

Lutigan whispered, "Harik, see what the walking goiter wants from you. Find out what he'll part with. Maybe he'll get reckless and destroy himself."

Krak nodded.

Harik said, "Very well, Murderer. I offer two squares if you kill that awful duke, the blonde woman you like, the Knife, and the Nub."

By the Nub, he meant Desh.

Both Fingit and Lutigan jumped up to whisper a river of curses that had been perfected over millennia. Harik held up one hand to quiet them and whispered, "Patience! I will not have him slay your toys."

Krak whispered, "Shut your whining faces. You can find new playthings if it comes to that."

Since Harik thought I couldn't feel my body, he'd believe that anything I did was giving away my emotions. I widened my eyes. "Damn, what an insult to your brothers! It's like peeing in their ambrosia. I thought you must have been kidding about how contemptible you find them, but I guess not."

Fingit and Lutigan whispered a few more horrible curses at

Harik. Lutigan made a strangling noise, and Krak glared at him. Sakaj chuckled silently.

"So," I went on, "for eight squares, I'll kill Durch. I'll kill Parth and his servant on their way home too. And . . . I'll give you knowledge you don't already have."

"Hah!" Harik said. "It is not possible for you to know something I don't know."

"And yet I do." I was betting the gods knew nothing about the Void Walker, since Dabbs had declared his land a god-free territory. If I was wrong, my deal would fall apart and the gods might punish me. But they preferred not to destroy me using their own godly hands. They had said so.

All the other gods turned to Krak. After a few seconds, he whispered, "He's full of crap. The little wad of meat thinks he can trick us! I should burn him into a grease spot now."

Sakaj whispered, "We should wait. After all, we're immortal." She smiled, making me glad I wasn't looking straight at her to be mesmerized with desire. "His life will end in an eyeblink all on its own."

Krak nodded. "Harik, just do what you'd normally do, except smarter."

"Yes, Father," Harik whispered.

"Say hello to the other gods for me," I called out, "whichever ones are here. I hope Gorlana's here—I haven't spoken to her in eons."

"Do not concern yourself about anything other than your own pathetic life," Harik said. "You cannot know anything of which I am ignorant, so that is a useless ploy. I offer three squares to extend your open-ended debt by an unknown number of lives."

"That's more entertaining than a drunken archbishop," I said. "For seven squares, you can add ten more killings to my debt."

"Ridiculous! You are not allowed to know the number of deaths you owe."

"I won't. An unknown number plus ten is still an unknown number."

Harik pointed his massive chin at me. "You are attempting to be clever. Stop it! You're never more ridiculous than when you try to act clever. However, I find your mathematical proof acceptable. I offer four squares for an additional four hundred deaths."

"Twenty deaths for six squares."

Harik folded his arms. "Murderer, your schemes are transparent beyond reason. Childish even for a man. You need this power to devastate the battlefield and so save yourself." He paused, and I blinked a few times for his benefit. "In doing so, you will slay hundreds of men. I shall not accept a meager twenty deaths. Three hundred lives for four squares."

"Six squares for fifty killings," I shot back.

"You dare push me on this? Very well. Two hundred lives for just two squares." Harik stood radiating power. Snow had touched everything in sight except his black robe.

"You're right, Mighty Harik. Five squares are enough to kill a double armful of men. Seventy-five deaths for five squares."

"Well . . . no. Instead, I offer five squares for one hundred and fifty deaths. You must also kill the nasty duke's son." Harik smiled, like tormenting me was better than a concert.

I blinked, and this time it wasn't for effect. "This is how you do it then," I breathed. "Ella will hate me when I kill her boy. He's the only child she has left."

Krak was nodding, and Lutigan for once didn't look as if he'd swallowed three porcupines. Harik pointed at me. "That is my last offer, Murderer. It is my only offer."

I pictured the battlefield seething with enraged, screaming soldiers, and I saw Karl dead at my feet, curled up like a baby. I stopped picturing things before I came to Ella.

"I agree," I whispered.

Harik heaved me back into my body, and I stumbled to one knee. My right eye throbbed.

One of Parth's formations was pushing its way through a clump of Durch's soldiers. I grabbed Stan by the wrist and dragged him at an angle back toward Durch's lines. As I pulled Stan, I tossed one white band after another, each into a different part of the sky. I burned power as if I could never run out.

Pausing in a less crazy spot, I knelt over Stan. A minute later, I had stopped the worst of his bleeding, but he wasn't likely to live. I threw ten more bands into the air as fast as I could, pulling in clouds from every direction.

One of Parth's formations reached me, broken and disorganized but still pushing ahead. Two of the soldiers attacked me, then another, and then a fourth. I sliced one's throat, but a man replaced him right away. I retreated three steps and half severed a soldier's hand when he came after me too fast. Energy flowed into me, and my eye eased.

Over the next minute, I killed another man and disabled two more. By then, I felt pert and quick. I circled, stringing out the soldiers so that I faced no more than two at a time. I hurled more bands when I could, dragging in storm clouds from miles around. They were thick and ferocious enough for me to call down lightning a dozen bolts at a time, and I had the power to do it.

At last, the straining, clashing thunderheads covered the entire battlefield. I tossed one more band. Intense, pounding rain slammed the entire valley, as thick as if it were poured out of a bucket. I couldn't see more than twenty feet. Three men had been fighting me when the rain hit, but soon they stumbled away, staring at the mud-slick ground.

I rushed to Stan and hauled him back away from Parth's army. Then I flung more white bands into the sky in a constant stream, dragging in clouds and water from farther and farther away. I kept the rain hammering for five minutes. Runoff was churning through the valley up to my knees, and I staggered toward higher ground, keeping Stan's mouth above water.

Burning power at an appalling rate, I kept shoving the storm into greater violence. I said, "Limnad, I need you."

Limnad stepped out of the wall of rain with an enormous smile, bouncing like an otter. "Yes, Bib?"

"Limnad, there are a few things I need done. Would you help me? And ask Desh to help too?"

"This is the best magic I have ever witnessed, Bib. I will help, even if it means traveling a thousand miles."

I calculated that she could make such a journey in about thirty-three minutes, so the offer wasn't as magnificent as it sounded. I described my request.

I let the storm beat down for a minute and examined Stan again. Whenever the rain flagged, I pulled in more clouds. I removed the arrow from Stan's chest and did a sloppy but adequate job of keeping him alive in between bouts of freshening the downpour.

Ten minutes into the storm, I allowed it to begin slackening. Soon, it had faded to a drizzle. The storm clouds had emptied themselves. Great pools of water covered most of the valley floor, and the rest shone with black, sticky mud.

Most of the soldiers had retreated to their own lines and up the hills, although some had fled the wrong way. I didn't spot any massacre of prisoners, though. Everybody crept around without much obvious purpose, as shocked as if they'd been beaten in an alley.

At the rear of Parth's army, nowhere near Parth himself, a white flag was whipping back and forth. I knew that Limnad was concealed up there waving that white standard. I turned to see an identical white flag behind the Glass army, not anywhere close to Durch. That would be Desh waving the white flag on Durch's ignorant behalf.

I had stopped the battle. Now it was time to lose the war.

THIRTY-FOUR

After I had drowned the battlefield like it was a mouse in a waterfall, Durch and Parth used shouts and hand signs to agree they would chat. Maybe each feared that the other had created the deluge and hoped to carry out a quick assassination. Or perhaps they suspected sorcery and intended to put all sorcerers to death so they could get back to regular, dry warfare.

Each king sent an emissary to meet in the valley between the armies. The men slogged and strained through the dirty pools, slowing with every step as more pounds of mud clung to their boots. Parth's man fell on his butt and slid ten feet down the valley before he halted his journey with his hands. He recovered, and two minutes later, he offered to clasp hands as a sign of good faith, sticking out a dripping gauntlet of black mud. Durch's man stared at it, turned, and struggled back toward the hill.

The emissaries agreed that the parley would happen a hundred paces uphill from their armies. That appeared to be the closest solid footing.

King Parth and eight guards had already arrived to parley when I walked up. I made a point of swaggering. Parth stared at me, shaking his head, and then said a few hot words to the soldier next to him. I gave Parth my sweetest smile and then ignored him.

Pil arrived next, trotting toward us from farther up the valley. She ran and hugged me, whispering, "I take responsibility." When she released me, her eyes were as calm and frank as if we were meeting to build a fence together. "I belong to Lutigan now."

"We can figure a way to get you free from him."

Pil shook her head. "I don't mind." She touched my belly, such an odd gesture that I didn't speak before she strode off thirty paces to stand.

I reached to my belly and found her knife's hilt sticking out of my belt. I knew the knife was hers because it was invisible.

Karl marched up next with four soldiers. He glanced at Pil and then me before glowering at Parth, sixty paces away. Parth grinned and pointed at Karl, who turned red.

King Durch appeared just seconds later, along with eight soldiers. Two of those men shoved Ella along with her hands tied. Durch stopped thirty paces behind his son. Even from so far away, I heard the king belch like a dyspeptic hog.

Durch pointed at Parth and bellowed, "I can't believe I had you in a goddamn cell and didn't kill you right there. I'm going to start killing every waxy-looking bastard who presents himself."

"You wished for this truce," Parth yelled. "Speak, if you have anything worth hearing."

Karl shouted, "I'll shove my sword in one of your ears and out the other!" He was so loud that his soldiers back in the main army began cheering.

Parth ignored him. "Durch, do you know anything about that damned rain? Was it him?" Parth pointed at me.

Even from so far away, I saw Durch's brow crease. "What do you mean? That shit pile is a servant."

Parth bit his upper lip. "Durch, you should surrender now! You're too stupid to be a king!"

"This parley is over!" Durch screamed.

"No, it's not!" I shouted. I had been pulling storm clouds

together again for five minutes. Now I flipped a band into the sky. Lightning arced between the clouds, and thunder cracked so loudly my ears hurt.

Durch glanced at the sky. Then he shouted to his son, "Turn around! We're leaving! No, that way!"

I squeezed some more thunder out of the clouds.

Behind me, Parth laughed.

Durch yelled, "It's nothing, keep going!"

I picked out a spot two hundred feet in front of Durch and called down a stroke of lightning.

Durch and his men jerked, and a couple staggered. Durch pointed at me and yelled at Parth, "You mean him?"

Parth laughed again. "Go ahead and ask him to bring you a chamber pot!"

I shouted, "This parley is not over! In the name of the gods, I demand that this war be settled here!" My stomach clenched when I invoked the gods, but I managed to say the words without gagging. "You'll do it with ritual combat and then take the rest of your soldiers home alive!"

After a few seconds, Durch bellowed, "You can't make me do that!"

I coaxed out a nasty thunderclap.

Durch glanced around at the clouds. "Burn in hell, you wagging twat!"

A lightning bolt slammed into the ground just ninety feet from Durch. Two of his men were knocked off their feet, but they crawled back up.

I shouted, "We'll settle this by ritual combat, won't we?"

Parth yelled, "I agree to entertain the idea, but I must know who Durch's champion will be!"

I yelled, "I volunteer to be King Durch's champion!"

"Straight to blood-soaked hell with that!" Durch yelled. "If I agree to this asinine bullshit fight, I'll pick my own champion! Beck, go down there and cut off this Bredgarde whiner's head."

A solider I had never met stepped away from Durch, drawing his sword. He was a tall, wide-shouldered man who paced along as easily as a hunting animal. When Beck approached me, I drew my sword and pointed for him to go back to Durch. Instead, he lunged at me fast, a move that I'm sure had killed a lot of his foes. I countered and cut him deep across the bicep of his sword arm. Energy seeped into me as Beck turned around toward Durch, holding his arm.

I shouted, "Your champion hurt himself on the way here. I volunteer to replace him!"

"Damn your dick five times!" Durch screamed. He slapped another soldier on the arm. I realized he had surrounded himself with the best fighters in his army. "Haddell, you go."

Haddell stepped away from Durch. I knew the man from a year before when I had spent afternoons sparring with him and his friends, beating two or three of them at a time. He shook his head and said some quiet words.

Durch growled something I couldn't make out.

Haddell said, "But I've taken a vow, Your Majesty!"

"What the goat-grubbing hell kind of vow, you turd?"

"I . . ." Haddell glanced around. "I took a vow not to say!"

Durch pulled out a dagger. Haddell backed away, and none of the other men tried to stop him. Their loyalty to Durch seemed a flimsy thing. Durch pointed at another man. "You!"

"I've taken a vow too, Your Majesty."

A third man nodded and spoke out, "Yes, vow! Very religious—lose my damn soul if I break it! Bad for you too, Your Majesty!"

Durch grabbed that man's arm and stabbed him in the stomach. The soldier screamed and collapsed to his knees, holding the wound.

I shouted, "I still volunteer, Your Majesty!"

Durch stepped past one of the men holding Ella, grabbed her from behind, and pressed his dagger to her neck. "If you lose, I will kick her severed head over there to join you!"

I examined Ella's face.

She shrugged and rolled her eyes.

"That sounds mighty fair!" I yelled.

I turned to stare at Parth. Only an idiot king would fight as his own champion. However, Parth had already fought me and knew he could beat me. What he *didn't* know was that Pil had commanded me not to kill him. I could kill him all I wanted now.

I raised my eyebrows twice to goad the man.

Parth tapped his fingers on the hilt of his sword. "You undoubtedly are a hard man to kill. The hardest I have ever known."

Nodding, I said, "A hell of a lot harder to kill than your father. He collapsed like rotten celery."

Parth ground his teeth but answered in an even voice, "I suspect that six inches of steel in your heart would accomplish it. Or in your brain."

"Why not both?" I said. "If you think you can manage it."

Durch shouted, "Raise your voices! I can't hear you from over here. It's rude!"

I waved at Durch without looking at him.

Parth said, "Bib, are many of your foes taken in by such obvious insults? My passions aren't so easy to manipulate. You have been facing a poor quality of enemy."

"You're not facing me at all," I said. "You're standing there thinking about which of your men you'll let me kill."

"A weak tactic," Parth said, but his fist was clenched.

I said, "The road home will be glum for you, Parth. You'll have lost the war, and your men will be talking behind your back about what a coward you are."

Parth snarled at me. Then he took a breath and said, "Very well. Jape, you shall be my champion." He pointed at a strong-looking man of average height with dark brown hair and sunken cheeks. He was missing his two smallest fingers on his left hand.

Of course, if Parth lost, he would ignore the outcome and resume the battle another day. For that matter, Durch would do the same if he lost. One finds a lot more honorable kings in stories than in actual kingdoms.

I pointed at Jape and shouted back at Durch, "This is the one? I was hoping for somebody taller, but . . ." I shrugged.

Jape drew a beautiful sword, just a masterpiece, and he held a knife in his off hand. He faced me with Parth forty feet behind him.

Karl and his men stood some distance behind me. Durch, his men, and Ella stood even farther away behind Karl. Pil stood away to my left.

"Begin!" Parth shouted.

"Yes, begin!" Durch yelled.

Jape edged toward my off hand to set up an attack.

I dropped my sword and backed away with my hands up. "I yield. The war is over, and Glass lost."

Jape hesitated before turning to Parth, who was looking at me from under raised eyebrows.

"No!" Durch shrieked. "No, goddamn it, no! It's cheating—he's a traitorous shit, no! This will not stand! It won't, even if I have to kick every man in Bredgarde right in the balls! I do not agree to this!"

Durch, whose face had gone crimson, stopped to take a breath. Then he fell straight forward onto the ground, as stiff as an elm tree. A squatty soldier I had never seen stood behind Durch holding a bloody hammer. Three other soldiers grabbed the man as he thrust the weapon high in the air. It resembled Desh's hammer.

Ella kicked one of her captors in the shin. He bent over, and she smashed her shoulder into the other one hard enough to knock him tumbling. Still bound, she twisted free and sprinted away toward Pil.

I snatched my sword off the ground and hamstrung Jape as he stood bemused. More energy washed into me. Parth was standing just half a dozen steps away. I could fall back to Pil and Ella and so escape. Fleeing would be wise. Nobody had liked me before the battle, and they'd like me even less now.

Running away from Parth had never been a serious option, though. I bared my teeth and ran toward him.

Parth's soldiers charged to protect their king. I had expected that, so I jerked to a stop and backpedaled. All seven tried to attack me at once, even though there wasn't room around me for such an onslaught. I killed the first one to reach me and thrust into another's throat while he was tangled with his friends. I retreated again.

"Faster!" Ella shouted, now in my view. Pil was sawing at Ella's bonds with her sword. Somewhere behind me, Karl was yelling for his father, genuine anguish in his voice.

The next one of Parth's soldiers attacked me in a highly skilled manner. I traded thrusts and parries with him for two seconds before I had to retreat again. He was too smart to rush after me, but I sliced one of his friends deep at the knee. He fell, and more energy seeped into me. I felt as sound and agile as I had been twenty years before.

The ground shook hard enough to knock me down, and Dimore the sorcerer appeared off to my right, as round and rosy as ever. Every other person I could see was on the ground too. As I jumped up, Dimore knelt and slapped the ground with his palm.

Clumps of muddy dirt started flying up from the earth as fast as if they were falling out of the sky. They weren't so thick that I couldn't see, but they distracted me, especially when one hurled itself up between my legs. I gasped, leaned over, and was knocked off my feet when somebody slammed into my side.

I slid on my belly and saw that Ella had pushed me down just before Karl split my head in two from behind. He must have struck her left arm instead of my skull, and her arm looked to be half severed above the elbow. Karl twisted and thrust his big sword at me. I was in a poor spot, but with luck, I might have rolled up and killed him anyway, or at least I might have escaped.

I won't ever know, because Ella, holding somebody else's sword in her right hand, thrust through Karl's side and into his heart. From the look on her face, she might as well have killed herself too.

Jumping to my feet, I saw Karl's guards retreating. Pil was fighting one of Parth's soldiers, and two more soldiers were rushing at me. A fourth man swung at Dimore, but the sword blade dissolved into dust. As the soldier stared at his hilt, Dimore grabbed him by the forehead and shoved him to the ground, where he didn't move.

Limnad appeared behind Dimore, moving almost too fast for me to follow. An instant later, Dimore was pressing his palm against her chest. Her body stiffened and began blowing away as if it were sand in a high wind. Within a couple of breaths, she was gone.

Parth's two soldiers had reached me with Parth just behind them. I dodged the soldiers' thrusts, but Parth's blade scraped my ribs. These men would likely expect me to retreat, so instead, I pressed them with attacks that bordered on reckless. I stabbed one in the heart and threw myself away from Parth's swing. Then Pil came in from the other side and sliced the remaining soldier's neck.

Parth slashed at Pil, but she leaped away, then with crazy speed, he spun back and blocked my thrust. I followed with a slash that almost cut his throat. He retreated and came right back to thrust at my chest, but he almost impaled his face on my blade instead.

When Parth retreated again, he had the look I had often seen people get when they realized they couldn't beat me. He hesitated. I thrust and then slashed to set him up for the kill, but he was fast enough to block.

The Ass sword shattered. Pieces hurtled, and one spun me halfway to the right. I saw it poking out of my shoulder, so I pulled it free.

I was panting. When the sword broke, it leeched out all the energy it had given me.

Parth must have fallen when the sword sundered but was on his feet again. Sadly, he didn't have a big piece of my sword sticking out of his forehead.

I called out to Pil, but all I could produce was a cough. On the second try, I said, "Throw me a sword!"

Pil gaped at me, pale and breathing hard.

"Throw me a damn sword!"

She tossed her sword, and I twisted to catch it. Something on the side of my neck stung, and I reached up to slap it. One of the slivers of my sword was sticking out of my neck. It must not have cut anything important since I wasn't bleeding to death. It was damned awkward, though.

Parth approached me with care, and I didn't rush to attack. My arms and legs felt like they weighed fifty pounds each. After two passes, I hadn't touched him. He peered hard at me before the next pass. I parried his attack, got lucky, and slashed his forehead above the right eyebrow. Blood flowed like a waterfall into the eye.

I pressed Parth on his blind right side, and he stumbled back. When I thrust for his heart, he parried, circled, and stabbed me in the stomach all the way through my body. Such a deep thrust is a mistake, normally. In this case, he severed my spine. I collapsed onto my back with the lower parts of my body useless. I even lost my sword.

"Damn you to Lutigan's sweaty pits!" I groaned.

With enough time, I could have healed all that, even my spine. Since Parth was walking toward me, I had about three seconds.

"I thought I was done." Parth spat on the ground between us. "You are indeed a hard man to kill."

As he said those ridiculous words, I drew Pil's invisible knife. If Parth came close enough, I could cut his leg or even his ankle tendon. And then do what? Flop over and smother him with my belly?

Parth did not step close enough for me to cut his feet.

"You're a careful son of a bitch," I grumped. "I intended to bite off one of your toes."

"I prefer that you not touch me and do something sorcerous." He grinned and leaned forward, using both hands to reach out and lay the point of his sword against my chest. I could stretch to cut his wrist if I wanted, but then he'd just take away the knife and slay me one-handed.

If life was so damn hopeless, this would have been the ideal time to close my eyes and let it end.

Damn Parth anyway. I didn't intend to die without him.

Parth leaned farther, smiling at me. As he pushed the sword down, I used Pil's knife to knock the blade to my left. Simultaneously, I rolled left as much as half a body would allow. Instead of transfixing my heart, his blade passed beneath my chest muscle, scraping along my ribs.

I grabbed the sword blade with my left hand and yanked it toward me as far as I could, which wasn't far. It sliced my hand, but I pulled it just enough to drive the point of Parth's blade out through my side.

Parth had been leaning over to keep his feet away from me. He sure as hell didn't expect me to seize his ass from beyond the grave. He stumbled forward just enough for me to stretch my right arm, slash with Pil's glass-sharp knife, and slice his throat. Parth's blood splashed over me, and I smiled as he staggered backward before collapsing.

THIRTY-FIVE

I tasted blood. I hardly had time to wonder why before somebody walloped me across the right cheek.

"Bib, wake up!"

Wallop across the left cheek.

"Wake up!" Pil shouted.

I opened my eyes but didn't speak in time to avoid another whack on the right cheek with Pil's palm. "I'm up!" I gasped, protecting my face with my hands. I croaked, "Stop! Where's Dimore?" I tried to sit up but failed.

Pil sat back on her heels. "He's gone, so don't worry about him —worry about yourself if you want to live. Some things are cut up or bleeding inside you, so think about looking inward or whatever it is you do to figure that out. You probably want to do it before you fall asleep again."

"What about Ella's arm?" I asked.

"If you don't think Ella and her arm can sit down and wait . . ." Pil glanced off to the right. "Well, she's already sitting, but if you die, then you won't help her arm too much, will you?"

I nodded and pulled a green band to explore. I probably would have bled to death had Pil not beaten me awake. I guided her through easing the sword fragment out of my neck, and I dealt with that in case the steel had grazed an artery. It was a damn wonder Pil hadn't killed me by slapping me.

Then I healed most of the damage in my midsection. I left the spine alone. I was already losing my concentration and didn't want to bumble around.

"Bring Ella." I smiled to show I felt fine. I'm sure it showed the exact opposite, but Pil stood and tramped away.

Pil guided Ella to sit beside me. I expected that Ella might be grieving for Karl and probably feeling guilty too. She was, in a way. I knew how grief can make a person want to sleep forever. It's the only way to escape a thing so enormous. But Ella's face wasn't exhausted, or withdrawn, or closed off. It just existed, without life, like something that never had been alive.

I said nice things and patted her hand while I healed her, not talking about Karl at all. She didn't answer. I wouldn't have said that her arm and I were unimportant to her. I imagined that nothing was important or unimportant, either. There wasn't enough meaning in her world for questions of importance.

A minute later, I fell asleep.

It was nighttime when I awoke, and I saw Desh's face in firelight as he sat beside me. I breathed deep a couple of times. "Was that your hammer I saw bashing Durch on the head?"

Desh nodded. "And me swinging it. I feel bad for Durch's men. They caught me and locked my villainous self up with three chains. The next time they looked, I had disappeared like a bad smell."

I nodded. "Did you recover the hammer?"

Desh grinned for a moment. "No. It doesn't matter. I'll make another if I need one. I'm sorry about Ass Hanger. I thought it would be more durable."

"You twiddling bastard! You almost got me killed!"

"I believe the sword was under great strain because its enchantment was so incompatible with your nature. I sure learned a lesson there, eh?"

"I did not volunteer to contribute my blood to your understanding of magic!" I tried to sit up again, failed, and realized I was lying under two blankets.

Desh said, "I appreciate it, nonetheless, Bib. Maybe I'll run across a way to make it up to you."

I snorted. "What happened to the armies? Did I miss the big battle?"

"Pil ran them off."

"What?"

"She chased the armies away. While I was chained up for killing Durch and you were lying here dying, she faced down the generals on both sides." He grinned, then said, "As Stan told it, Pil pointed out that the kings and princes of both countries were dead, and she described the agony they had experienced when hurled into the grave. She added that kings weren't the only ones who could die before the sun went down, either. Also, nobody could predict what the new kings would want. A war could be the last thing they'd want, and they might be in the mood to torture generals. Then Pil tortured one of the generals to death and brought him back to life to make her point."

I raised my eyebrows.

"Stan explained it just that way," Desh said.

I chuckled.

"After that, she promised if they weren't off the battlefield by morning, they would be destroyed by flood, lightning, hailstones, and a plague of wolves."

I laughed hard. "I wish I had seen it!" I giggled once and then let silence stretch for a bit. "I'm sorry about Limnad."

Desh sat up straight. "Why? Did something happen to her?"

"I . . . Dimore killed her."

Desh whipped his head around left and right.

Limnad stepped out of the darkness but didn't say anything.

I stared at the spirit. "I must have not seen what I thought I saw."

Desh stood and walked to Limnad, who was blinking at the sky. "Limnad, is this true? Did Dimore kill you?"

"No! That's silly." She sniffed. "Not unless you have a terribly liberal interpretation of death."

Desh said, "I see. Kind of. I'm glad you're alive. What did Dimore do?"

Limnad walked circles around Desh, almost as if she were dancing. "He invited me to his home. It was an invitation I was powerless to refuse. Then I couldn't leave until he said so. A fussy person might say that in his home I was technically dead. But he let me go and gave me a present." She stared at Desh and then me. "You should only go places where he isn't. He's not a good person at all."

I said, "Thank you, Limnad, that's the smartest advice I've heard in years."

"Why didn't you tell me?" Desh's voice was tense.

Limnad arched an eyebrow. "Do you tell me everything?"

Desh sighed and glanced at me. "Excuse us." He and Limnad walked away into the darkness.

I spent most of an hour repairing my spine, moving with deliberation since I felt a bit shaky. I walked around for a few minutes, lay back down, and slept until morning.

Pil brought Stan to see me after breakfast. He was recovering from his wound and had been too sorely hurt, even with my battlefield healing, to travel back with the army. Pil had found beer, so Stan and I enjoyed a few reminiscences. We even drank to some of our dead friends, and he wiped his eye in a manly way.

I didn't thank him for running out to join me before the battle. In his world, it was the kind of thing comrades did without question or thanks, and everybody else in creation could go choke on a bone.

As I was fumbling in my pouch for a few coins to give Stan, I touched the little copper cup.

"What the hell's that piddly bit?" Stan asked.

I tossed him the cup.

"Tree of Morning," Stan said, holding it up to the light and squinting at it.

"Huh?"

"Tree of Morning. From my goddamn homeland! Sepple! We got all kinds of important trees that the grammas love to yammer about. Tree of Morning, Tree of Salt, Tree of Sun and Moon, Tree of Sheep, Tree of Butter, Tree of Midnight, Tree of Knives . . . I could keep talking, but I'd rather keep drinking."

"Wait," I said, "are they good luck or something?"

"Not if you got the goddamn Tree of Knives! Right?" Stan drank out of the beer jug.

"No, really."

Stan sighed. "I don't believe in this shit. Don't tell my gramma I said that. They ain't lucky, they . . . well, the folks as believe in them draw or paint a certain tree for a certain thing, or maybe carve it on something. In Sepple, they got goddamn trees painted everyplace. You can't sit or pee without hitting one."

I stayed quiet.

"Hell, all right. Like maybe you'd draw a Tree of Salt over your stove for better-tasting food. Or if you hate some crusty bastard, you could carve the Tree of Knives on the underside of his bed. In that bed, he'd be limp as a stocking." Stan looked away. "Not that I'd do such a thing. I don't believe in that shit."

"So, it's like a hex?"

Stan snorted. "Never say that to the folks where I come from. Hexes are foul things made with virgin's blood and baby guts. Trees are . . . not foul, I guess. It sounds stupid when I say it out loud."

I pointed at the cup he had dropped onto the grass. "What about the Tree of Morning? What's it for?"

Stan glared at me. "Do you want me to go ask my gramma?"

"No, whatever you can tell me is fine."

Stan shook his head and scratched behind his ear. "Um, it's sort of about getting a good, flaming start on things, or starting up again after you quit. My ma carved it into my pa's chair and made him sit in it when he came home drunk. Sometimes she made him sleep in the damned uncomfortable thing all night." He glanced sideways at the cup. "It's all that kind of thing. But I don't believe in that shit."

"Thanks, Stan, that explains every damn thing about it, I guess."

He nodded, broke wind, and handed me the jug.

Dimore had said go east and find something to help the king, and I guessed the cup was it. Prestwick's heart had been twisted, and Parth had probably done it. Maybe it was part of a campaign to confuse and kill the people of Glass before Staggs invaded. Or maybe he was an asshole.

Things might have ended differently if we'd asked Pres to drink out of the cup ten minutes sooner, before all the poisoning. I shoved the little thing back into my pouch.

At noon, we mounted for the two-day journey back to Castle Glass: Desh, Pil, Ella, Stan, and me. Within an hour, we spotted a figure standing on the road ahead of us, not moving. As we neared, I saw it was Capps.

The man appeared to have shrunk, but I supposed it was just him all bent and slumped now. He watched us from under his eyelids with his face turned down, and there was hardly a spot on him that wasn't dirty. He looked to be unarmed.

I called out, "I'm not inclined to be merciful to you, son. You betrayed us into an ambush and spied on us too."

"Don't want no mercy."

"What do you want, then?" Desh asked.

"Something to do. I don't care what."

I said, "Hell, I wouldn't trust you to feed pigs! You told us all those lies about Parth's life, but he was the Prince of Bredgarde the whole time."

"Those wasn't lies," Capps said. "Some wasn't. A few."

Pil looked at Capps like he was nothing but a branch lying on the road. "Admit it, you led us into a trap at the farmhouse, didn't you?"

Capps looked at his boots. "Sure. That was the plan."

"Did you let Parth poison you so we'd think you deserted him?" Desh asked. "That's a harsh master."

Glaring up at Desh, Capps said, "Of course he didn't poison me!" He paused. "Poisoned myself."

"Why?" I had asked a weak question, but I was busy imagining Parth explain to Capps how him drinking poison was part of the plan.

Capps's face relaxed. "He told me what to do."

"I guess he did, you fool!" Pil pointed at Capps. "If he said to eat fire, would you do that too, or maybe cut off your mother's head?

Capps frowned and stared at the road again. I scrutinized him as Desh and Pil discussed what to do with the man.

His answer seemed simple—"He told me what to do." But I didn't think it was. Capps acted like Parth was his personal god. Maybe he really did think that. So, what would he do now?

Pil dismounted. "Bib, we can't take him with us, and we can't leave the treacherous snake behind us." She drew her knife.

Capps backed away.

It wasn't like Pil to just murder somebody. On the other hand, she hadn't seemed herself the past couple of days. Part of me was jealous that she'd get to take this life instead of me, and another part didn't want to see her kill so easily.

"Pil, wait!" I said.

She hesitated and gazed up at me, as if surprised that I'd care what she did to Capps.

I could murder the man, and that was my preference. But I'd appear a raving hypocrite if I stopped Pil and then killed Capps myself. Why would I have stopped her at all?

Dismounting, I pulled a water sack off my saddle. "I have a solution." I walked to Capps with the little cup and the sack. "Capps, when you drink from this, it will be like a fresh start, a new morning."

Capps eyed the cup as I filled it. "Bullshit!"

"It will. Which one of us is the sorcerer here?" I was probably telling him a stinging great lie, but I didn't expect it to do anything so severe as kill him. I held out the cup.

Capps took the cup, peered into it with one eye, and then tossed the water down his throat.

"You ought to feel it about now," I said, taking the cup. "No matter which way you walk from here, it's all new. Whatever was eating on your ass, you can leave it behind." I stowed the cup and turned my back on him to remount.

Capps was standing straighter. "I don't believe you." He said it as if he could be convinced but didn't want to show it.

"The hell you don't. You look five times the man you did when I rode up." That was a lie, but not a horrible one. Maybe he looked twice the man.

Desh rode up beside Capps. "I want the duck."

Capps looked at the dirt and shrugged. "What duck?"

"Parth's wooden carving of a duck. Give it to me."

"I don't got it."

Desh stared at Capps for a good while until the man reached into his shirt and pulled out a worn piece of wood the size of two fingers.

"It's all I've got that was his." Capps looked like he might cry, but he passed it over when Desh held out his hand.

Desh dropped the carving into a pouch as he rode on past Capps. The rest of us followed.

I said, "Goodbye, Capps. Go make your mark."

Five minutes later, Pil rode up and gave me an unreadable stare. "You should have let me kill him."

"Well, you didn't need my permission to do it, but I appreciate your accommodating me."

Pil said, "Why didn't you kill him, then? You're going to feel funny when he shows up one night to cut your throat and rob you."

"Maybe. Doubt not the power of the magic cup, though."

I myself doubted the cup had any more power than the turd Desh's horse had just dropped onto the road. It didn't concern me too much, though. I spent more time wondering what Pil had traded away to the gods for the five squares she sent me.

Dimore, the mystical Radish himself, appeared in front of my horse. He reached up to touch my mount's nose, and the rest of the world, along with everybody in it, faded out of my sight. I was left alone with Dimore, my trembling horse, and a flat, purple landscape.

The sky resembled blue and orange sand that had been swirled together, spinning without much purpose. A great, spreading tree with silver leaves stood a short walk away. I examined the thing and realized it was in truth a long walk away and stood far taller than any tree I had seen—at least three hundred feet. I gazed around at the world of purple flatness, empty except for the tree and us.

This was like nothing I had ever seen when trading in the Home of the Gods.

Dimore turned his back to me and stumped away, rubbing his hair. "You can get down if you want." He sighed.

I reached for a yellow band, but nothing happened. I kicked my horse's ribs, but he didn't even lean. I slid to the ground and drew my sword, but I hesitated to kill Dimore just yet. After all, he had brought Limnad back after killing her, so that spoke well for him. Also, I didn't know where I was, and I had less of an idea of how to get home.

I lifted my spirit to call on the gods, but my spirit remained in my body.

Dimore turned and scowled at me as if I had just wiped mud on the wall. "Stop that. I have business with you, and I'll keep you here until I get an answer I like."

The sorcerer's pissed-off tone seemed too familiar, so I took a chance. "All right, Void Walker, what is this business?"

Dimore raised his eyes toward the nauseating sky. "At last! You are dimmer than the spot between Krak's butt cheeks."

"You don't want to be a butterfly today?"

"It doesn't matter. I can crush you just as well in this form. Or eviscerate you. Or freeze you so cold I can shatter you with my fist. Or eat you alive as if I were a tiger."

I held up a hand. "That's enough."

"No, it's not. I can do those things to all your friends at the same time I do you. And their horses for that matter. I can turn everybody in the kingdom to dandelion fluff or burn them alive from the inside over a period of weeks. So, don't screw with me."

I tried to calm my breathing. "I won't."

"I haven't even begun to talk about the things I can do with insects. You couldn't imagine." Dimore scratched under his left arm and then smiled like a little boy. "This is kind of fun."

"Your business has every bit of my attention." I tried to smile and failed.

"Good!" Dimore clapped his hands. "I want you to kill somebody."

"Really? Just to make things clear, there's a high probability I'll say yes." I tried not to wipe my sweaty palms on my trousers.

"Will you? I hope so. A few months ago, I'd have not doubted it." Dimore flicked a finger toward the ground. Two chairs and a table made of white sandstone rose out of the purple dirt. A crystal decanter and two crystal glasses sat on the table. He seated himself with a profound sigh and waved me toward the other seat. "Beverage? Of course you'll drink a beverage, what am I saying?" The decanter filled with what looked like red wine, and he poured. "Do you know why you're here?"

"To kill somebody for you?"

Dimore drank off his entire glass of wine. "I can't say you're wrong. But more immediately, you are here because you just showed that moronic troglodyte some kindness."

"Capps? I can go back and undo that." I left my glass alone.

"I wish you could." Dimore leaned back and stretched his arms. "But no. Before that, I could have counted on you to commit this murder unprompted. Now you may hesitate, and for reasons you may not expect."

"I see. No, actually, I don't."

"You will kill who I say when I say so. One single killing is all I need." He raised an eyebrow at me.

I almost laughed. When I realized that I had nearly guffawed in a Void Walker's face, my throat closed. I shook my head. "It hurts me to refuse you, but I have to," I said. "Unless you tell me who you want dead, I can't agree."

Dimore frowned. "That's impossible. I suppose I must destroy all the people who have ever given you a friendly look."

"Wait! Can I specify people who I most certainly will not kill?" I smiled and cursed the fact that I knew next to nothing about this being.

"No, you can't do that, either. I am not one of your waggledy-baggle gods who plays at making bargains."

"Not even Pil? You are in her head after all."

"No, and we'll talk about that another time." He rapped on the table. "If I bang on this too-scratchy sandstone twice more, a swath of people across two continents will be destroyed by an infestation of worms in their guts. Dogs and horses too. And you of course."

"Is there any—"

Dimore rapped on the table again and gave me a slow blink.

What if he told me to kill Ella, or Pil, or Desh? What if he told me to kill a child? Hell, a baby? Could the Void Walker throw around as much destruction as he promised? If the stories were true, he could. If I said no, thousands might die instead of just the one he wanted me to kill.

I mentally laughed at myself for thinking that way. Agreements made today could change tomorrow. The chances of changing this one seemed low, but it was possible.

Ella's image slipped into my mind. There was a way to avoid being forced to kill, and she had recommended it once. I could either whine about this problem or kick it in the balls. If this rancid, bobbling clump of goose shit in a gold box pushed me to it, I'd kill myself. I made the silent promise right then.

"I agree." I smiled at the Void Walker, and I meant it.

"That's fine. Drink to signify your compliance."

I drank.

Dimore tossed off another glassful and wiped his mouth with two fingers. "By the Void, that was exhausting. You're a pain in the ass."

"I have been told that more than once." My heart was thumping, and I was sweating like a cold wine bottle. "May I leave this unsightly place?"

"Before you do . . . oh, this is tiresome. You have stumbled upon the nature of a sorcerer's eyes. Don't deny it."

I grinned and shook my head. "I won't."

"Few figure it out. I mean, it happens infrequently. You didn't deduce it, of course, you just stumbled onto it, but even so, you may not be the idiot that the gods describe."

My eyebrows shot up. "You talk to the gods?"

"Hush, that's not the point. Maybe I do, maybe I don't." Dimore sighed so deeply it was almost a yawn. "Three other Void Walkers besides me inhabit Pil's head. Not her mind. Her head—physically, I mean. We don't control her. If we did, things would be awfully different, I can tell you that!"

"I see." I waited, ready to leave as soon as I could. I realized I didn't want to know the answer to the next question.

"Aren't you going to ask the next question?"

I hung my head. "Who is in me?"

"Nobody embarrassing. Maybe you can meet them someday." Dimore leaned back. "Now, one more thing before I'm done with you. Next time you journey, go northeast."

"That's all? Northeast?"

"Do you want a beacon to follow? An invitation to a masked ball?" He shook his head.

I found myself scratching my ear and stopped. "Is that a command, or advice?"

"It's advice. I advise you to travel northeast, because every other direction will be packed with unpleasantness and destruction. And . . . stop being optimistic. It doesn't suit you. It's inappropriate, considering your likely future." Dimore waved.

My world faded back into view. I was still riding. Dimore's interview seemed to have happened between one step and the next.

Pil said, "This will be trouble for sure. You really should have let me kill him."

I didn't have any words just then, so I smiled at her. I thought of her real name, but nothing came. The Void Walker had just called her Pil. I didn't know how or when it had happened, but somebody had removed Pil's real name from my mind.

THIRTY-SIX

We camped for the night when we were still a day's ride from Castle Glass. Ella lay on her side under a tree and stared at nothing. I covered her with a blanket, brought her food and wine that she ignored, and sat with her. I didn't talk or try to make her talk, either.

After everybody had eaten, Desh said, "I wonder who will be king now?"

I said, "I don't know a splinter's worth about nobles in the kingdom. I hope it's somebody who will change that damned ignorant name to something besides Glass."

Pil said, "Parbucket. The Kingdom of Parbucket."

"Krak's knobs, why?" Desh said.

Pil pressed her lips together. "It's a perfectly good name; in fact, any one of you should be happy to be named Parbucket."

"I like it," Stan said.

Pil pointed at Stan. "Thank you! It's a fine name. I named my dog Parbucket and called him Bucky when I wanted him to come."

I shrugged. "If it's a dog's name, I like it too. Not that anybody will listen to us."

After a few seconds, Desh said, "Who's going to be king,

though? Stan, you'll be a subject of the new king, so who do you think it will be?"

"Hell no, picking kings is too much work for me," Stan said.

"The Earl of Standriver," Ella said, without sitting up or looking at us. "He's next."

"What's he like?" Pil asked.

Ella didn't answer for several seconds. "Old." She closed her eyes.

Desh turned to Stan. "Where is Standriver?"

"Thirty miles south." Stan dug some gristle out of his teeth.

"I'll fetch him." Desh leaned back against the tree he was sitting under. "I'd rather nothing happened to him on the way to the castle."

"I'll come. Maybe he'll give us presents." Pil smirked.

Leaning over our campfire, I built it up for the night. Desh looked upon me with pity and built it twice as big with half the effort. Stan took first watch.

"I thought this was safe territory. Civilized," Pil said.

"It is. The bandits here say hello before they stab you in the gut." Stan coughed and spat.

I sat for a bit next to Ella, who seemed to be asleep. Then I lay down close by.

The rain came in before dawn, so we mounted and trotted off in the darkness. Pil and Desh rode south. The rest of us followed the road, not that we really risked getting lost. The drops fell all day but never hard. It was a fresh, early summer rain.

Ella never spoke. Stan and I sang songs, and he taught me all the ones that his friend Ralt had made up.

We reached the City of Glass before the watery sunset came, and we urged our mounts up the winding trail toward the castle. The guards slapped Stan on the back, insulted him, and promised to buy him drinks. He wandered off to the barracks.

When I asked a castle guard who was in charge around there, he led me to General Harmeth. The general had quartered himself in a small, tidy room near the barracks.

Harmeth served wine, spilling some, and he smiled a quick apology. "Welcome back. The army tromped back here in good order, and thank Gorlana five times we brought most of our men home." He glanced toward the hallway. "Is Master Pil with you?"

"No," I said, "she is bringing the new king here in glory, scattering flowers all the way."

Harmeth took a deep breath and smiled. "I'm sorry she's not here! She's . . ."

"Terrifying?"

He nodded and then stopped himself. "Maybe formidable would be a good word. You say the king is coming? I guess you mean Callan, right?"

"If Callan is the Earl of Standriver, then yes. If he's somebody else, then I'll be murdering Callan before supper tomorrow."

Harmeth stopped smiling. "Yes, Callan is the Earl of Standriver. Same person." He cleared his throat. "Again, welcome back, and it's a fine thing that you're alive. I wish we had spare rooms for you, but the castle is choked with visitors and other people."

I knew damn well he must have empty rooms. A half dozen castle dwellers had been wiped out in the past couple of weeks, so this pissant simply didn't want us around. "Oh, we'll find rooms in the city. We'll be close enough to hear any nastiness and run right up here." I winked at Ella, who had been staring at the floor this whole time.

I paid for a room at the Kickskillet Inn, and we took residence. We owned almost nothing, so moving in was a sad little affair. I hurried down the hill to buy new clothes and food. Ella ate a little, which I considered a good sign.

After ordering a bath, I washed Ella and put her in clean clothes, then did the same for myself. There wasn't a single amorous moment involved. She slept in the bed while I made a pallet on the floor for myself. I thought she might have bad dreams or even scream like Parth, but she barely wiggled.

Ella slept most of the next two days, but we talked now and then about nothing I could remember later. Mostly, I talked and she listened. The next day, I got her up to walk around the city, and she went wherever I pointed her.

Desh and Pil returned that afternoon while Ella and I were out walking, and they brought the new king. The horrible fellow looked ancient. I hoped he had living children or grandchildren to take the throne when he pitched over dead. They waved as they rode past, and we waved back. Pil and Desh came to visit that night. We said hello, and I sent them away.

Ella spoke more and slept less in the next days. While walking one morning, she stopped dead in the road. "I wasn't nice to you, and I'm sorry. When you killed Manon, I mean."

"None of that matters now." I smiled, although whenever I thought about how I killed my daughter, it sure as hell mattered every time.

"I didn't know it was like this. I treated you like a naughty boy who had broken a vase." She opened her mouth to say more but shook her head and walked on.

Ella slept uneasily for the next week, sometimes calling out, sometimes crying in her sleep. I slept on the bed with her, with no frisky antics. We talked all day about every meaningless topic we could think of.

During that time, Desh came down to invite us to the coronation. I said no. He came back with the earl's urgent enjoinder that we attend. I told him to tell the earl to suck on a wagon hitch. I supposed they went ahead and crowned the bastard, but they did it without us.

Whenever we walked in the town, Ella looked wan and strained. In our room, she might weep for what seemed like no reason. I considered that an encouraging development.

Pil came to borrow me one evening, and the three of us laughed about her taking me away to have "sorcerer talk." Ella smiled and waved us out.

"I'm leaving soon," Pil said.

"Hell, I'm shocked you didn't leave weeks ago."

"I told you I belong to Lutigan now, and since he and Harik hate each other, I may be asked to kill you someday."

"That's the jolly life of a sorcerer," I said. "It'll be easier now that I don't know your real name anymore."

She cocked her head, likely trying to decide whether to trust me. "I don't know yours, either."

"That's one less reason to kill each other. But you would kill me if you needed to, wouldn't you?"

"Of course."

I smiled. "Good girl. And I don't mean that as an insult, Master Pil."

She grinned. "I have a gift for you, and I think you'll like it better than whatever crappy present Desh gives you." She flipped open a satchel and handed me a blue woolen cloak. "Stay dry."

"Thank you, Pil, that's kindly done." I held up the garment, sure it would shed water like a duck. Further, it was light and would fold into a trim little parcel. "Did you know Desh gave me one of these the day we met?"

"No, he never mentioned it at all." She gave a tight smile. "Not even once, especially not during those three hours when he described every little thing that happened the morning he met you." She rolled her eyes. "Hell, him giving you the cloak was the danged high point!"

I laughed at that. "I came within a sliver of killing him. Pil, I have a favor to ask. Do you recall the night I made those trees sway and creak when people walked under them? You asked me how I did it."

She lowered her brow but nodded. "And you told me. I owe you a favor because of that."

"I'm asking for that favor now. Tell me what you paid for the five squares you sent me when I was impaled. Tell me how you came to belong to Lutigan."

"Those are two separate things. You only get one."

I smiled my most affable smile. "If you answer both, I'll owe you a favor."

Pil shook her head. "Just one."

"All right. What did you pay for the five squares?"

She glanced down. "I sold my memories of my first teacher, the one before Dixon. Now that I've done it . . . I know I had a teacher, but I don't remember a thing about him . . . or her."

I waited for her to say more. She might say a lot. Giving up memories of people, especially important people, could change a sorcerer in unexpected ways. Desh had sold his memories of his mother, and from what I could tell, he never believed the same things or dealt with people the same way again.

Sometimes giving up memories of a person didn't change a damned thing, and the sorcerer went traipsing along the same as before. It was unpredictable.

Pil went on: "It's a funny thing. I did it because I loved you, and I couldn't stand for you to suffer and die. Now that it's done, I know that I loved you once, but I can't remember why or how it felt. I didn't expect that. Is this what it is to be a sorcerer?"

I cleared my throat. "Hell no. This is just something that happens once in a while. Sorcery is about acting tough, being sneaky, and waving your hands around a lot."

I was hoping she'd laugh, but she didn't. "Thank you, Pil. You sacrificed a lot for me, and I owe you a debt."

"No, you don't. It doesn't feel like I sacrificed anything." She showed no awareness that tears were running down her face.

It was almost inevitable that the damned gods would do something like this to Pil, but it still hurt to watch. "Well, tuck my debt away. You might want it sometime. Now, I have a request, which isn't a favor. Really, it's an invitation. Stay through tomorrow. I want all of us to have dinner together."

Pil shrugged. "All right, it's not as if I have to race out and save a burning city or something."

The next night, I paid the innkeeper to set up a big spread in our room and hire a servant to bring us food and wine. Pil, Desh, Stan, Dern, Ella, and I sat around laughing as we massacred three legs of mutton and eleven bottles of wine. Ella smiled right along with the rest of us and drank more than a bottle by herself.

Late in the evening, I said, "So, everybody listen to me for a minute."

"No!" Desh snapped, standing up.

I peered up at Desh. "Did I offend you? If I didn't, I can take another run at it."

"No, no! I have a gift for you!" he said, his face red. He waited five seconds and then roared, "I have a gift for you!"

"It won't be as good as mine," Pil whispered.

The door banged and swung open. A teenage boy trotted in carrying a long bundle. He passed the bundle to Desh, who nodded and handed him a coin.

Desh shoved plates and mutton bones aside and lay the bundle on the table in front of me. Then he presented it using both hands as if he were a charlatan hawking a fake love potion.

I unwrapped the bundle, which contained the magnificent sword that had belonged to Parth's champion, Jape. The weapon was beautiful without being frilly. The embellishments weren't just pretty. Each made the sword deadlier.

I feared that the long blade and wide crosspiece would give the sword poor balance, but it rested ideally in my hand when I lifted it. "Desh, the words thank you seem as dull as ash when talking about this gift."

Desh smiled, held up a finger, and paused.

Pil whispered, "He gets pedantic when he's drunk."

Desh frowned at her but said, "Four things affect the strength of an enchantment. The first is how well suited the item is for its intended purpose. I mean you don't enchant an anvil to sail fast across the water. The second is how well crafted the item is. The third is how neatly the enchantment matches the nature of the user. And of course, the skill of the Binder who is enchanting it matters."

"Wait, is that a magic sword?" Dern said.

Stan threw a mutton bone across the table at him. "Of course it is! Sorcerers got to have magic swords. Regular swords burn right up in their hands. Don't you know anything?"

Desh nodded at Stan. "Thank you. In physical form, this weapon is as purely designed to kill as is imaginable, and I've never seen a more beautifully crafted sword. Bib, you are the most death-focused person I've ever known. And I admit to being a damned fine Binder." He took a big breath. "From an enchanting point of view, this sword wants things to be really, really dead."

I thought about that for a moment but couldn't come up with anything to say.

Pil helped me by asking, "What does all that mean?"

"It's a bit vague at this point." Desh pursed his lips. "Bib will need to experiment. At the very least, nobody should stand between Bib and something he might want to kill."

"Something?" I said. "What does that mean?"

"Like a bear. Or, I don't know, a unicorn, or an imp. Who knows what it might kill?"

I put a hand on Desh's shoulder. "Thank you, and I mean it sincerely."

"Now . . ." Desh announced, "not that you would do such a thing as this, but I feel the need to say it." He leaned in as if to whisper but didn't lower his voice a bit. "Don't leave it lying on a bench in the tavern. I put a shocking amount of power into it."

"I won't," I said. "Now, back to what I was about to say. Does everybody remember Dimore?"

Ella sat back. "Who?"

"Somebody that owes you money?" Stan asked.

Pil said, "I think only sorcerers can remember him."

I shrugged. "Fine. You all remember Dabbs the butterfly, right?" Everybody nodded.

"Dabbs and Dimore are the same being."

They made some interested comments.

"And he's a Void Walker."

Nobody said anything. Stan cocked his head. Dern reached over and smashed a bug on the wall.

Desh cleared his throat. "He told you that? Do you believe him?"

"I do. Could any mere sorcerer cripple you that way, Desh? Or any spirit? Plus, he took me to his realm, or at least to one that's different from this."

"What's a Void Walker?" Ella murmured.

Pil frowned at me. "Say he is a Void Walker, what does that mean to us? He can go off and turn oceans into steam and ice into blood, or whatever Void Walkers do. I don't care."

"He gave me a task," I said.

"What, like a bargain?" Desh asked.

"More like a command. Do this or else." I lifted a wine cup off the table, but it was empty, so I set it down. I glanced around the table, but every other cup and all the bottles looked empty too. "I have to go northeast and kill somebody he wants me to kill. Otherwise, he'll destroy thousands of people—including every one of us."

"Who must you murder?" Ella asked.

"He wouldn't say. Sorry."

Pil put her elbows on the table. "Do you have a plan for dealing with this?"

"I do. I plan to ride northeast and kill whatever person he says to kill."

Pil let out a big sigh.

"You're going?" Ella's breath caught. "Don't go!"

"I think I've got to," I said. "And I'm asking all of you to go with me. We'll save all those lives, and I suspect there are useful things to learn about sorcerers and Void Walkers. They have a lot more to do with each other than we think."

Stan raised his hand. "I'll go. Meaning no disrespect, but the new king stinks like a mule's asshole. And he wants to make me a guard again."

"Great!" I said. "Dern, what about you?"

Stan cut in. "Hell, he won't go. Dern's got a wife and six kids."

Dern stared at the table.

"Congratulations, Dern, I understand. Pil? Desh? Ella?"

Desh said, "Sorcerers and Void Walkers? That sounds like new knowledge." He rubbed his round, bare chin. "All right."

"Yes," Pil said as soon as I looked at her.

"Don't go." Ella stood up. "I cannot go with you. After everything . . . I just can't go."

"That's . . ."

"Bib, it doesn't matter what you say. I cannot go, not now. Wait with me here instead."

"How long?" I asked, but I knew the answer.

Ella's chin trembled when she opened her mouth, but she didn't say anything.

When I didn't speak either, Ella shouted, "I love you!" and threw a heel of bread at me.

I had been waiting a long time to hear that, although I had imagined it with fewer hurtling objects. It looked as if Ella didn't hate me after all, which meant Lutigan would call on me to betray Pil someday. I swallowed and glanced at Pil before I turned back to Ella. "Darling, I love you too, and if I don't go, then you'll be killed. I have to go."

Ella ground her teeth. "I murdered my son to save you." She sat down and turned away from us.

After one of the most uncomfortable pauses I could recall, Pil said, "Let's take tomorrow to prepare. Equipment, spare horses, food, water. Desh and I got rewarded."

"No reward for me?" I asked without much interest.

"Should have gone to the coronation," Desh said.

"We'll leave the following morning, assuming the weather's not awful. Some of us don't have cloaks that shed water." Pil smiled at Stan, and he wriggled as if she had scratched him behind the ear.

"That's fine." I was distracted watching Ella.

Desh and Stan agreed. Everybody straggled out, saying thanks and laughing as they went.

When they had gone, I said, "Ella, are you going to bed?"

She didn't answer me or move.

I snuffed out all the candles except one. Then I dragged a chair over and sat beside her. If she sat there until morning, I would too.

After a few minutes, Ella turned to me and I made out her face in the candlelight. Her cheeks were slack, her eyes dull, and her brow crushed. Her face was as broken as if somebody had hit it with hammers. I wondered whether she'd ever pick up another sword.

She leaned against my chest, and I held her until it was late.

Once Ella was in bed asleep, I examined the little copper cup in the candlelight and considered its engraved tree. Then I dug down to the bottom of Ella's big pack and left the cup there. I hesitated before stuffing Pil's water-shedding cloak down there too. Then I carried my new sword outside.

The lantern at the inn's doorway threw dim light. I practiced thrusts and cuts under the big elm tree across the lane. I had always believed that every well-made sword was about the same in a fight, even enchanted ones. After five minutes with this sword, I didn't think that anymore.

I yearned to go find somebody and kill them, preferably someone who deserved it. I wanted to do it right now, and the sword wanted it too, which was a foolish thought. The sword wasn't alive, because no damned sword in existence was alive. Maybe the blade and I matched so perfectly that it reflected my desire back into me. I should ask Desh about that.

I made a whistling cut at the air, and my sword sliced through something that squeaked. I scanned the ground, but the light was weak. After fetching the lantern from beside the inn door, I found three dismembered fisherman bats in the dusty lot.

That led to the first curiosity. Why were these fisherman bats flying around miles from any lake or ocean?

The second curiosity then arose. How had I killed all three in a single cut without knowing they were there?

I set those questions aside to discuss later with both Desh and Pil.

Back in our room, the candle had gone out. It wasn't worth lighting again, so I slipped off my clothes and went to bed. Ten seconds later, I was scrambling around the room in the dark, hunting for Ella. She and her pack were gone, but not her sword.

I went out in my trousers and boots and ran circles around the inn calling for Ella. That was stupid. If she had wanted to talk to me, she wouldn't have left. The innkeeper padded out in a nightshirt and told me to shut the hell up. Had I been holding my new sword, the man would have died for certain. Instead, I grabbed him and cursed him to be smashed for eternity by the gods' flaming members.

He peed on himself and ran back inside.

Back in my darkened room, I planned my search for Ella. I also told myself how stupid I was to search, since she had run away from me and didn't want to be found. Besides, if Ella had waited one more day to leave, I would never have known. I would already have been galloping off to the goddamn northeast.

I jogged to the stable to saddle my horse and hunt for her. I made myself honestly answer a hard question: Had I expected Ella to sit in that room until I came back? I couldn't imagine anything less like her. I was behaving like a madman. I stopped myself before I threw the saddle onto my horse's back, and I accepted that hunting for Ella was foolishness.

Ten minutes later, as I trotted my saddled horse out of the stable yard, I pondered which direction to search first. Once I picked up her trail, I could track her as far as any ocean. And then what? We could die together when the Void Walker wiped out thousands of people, horses, and dogs, all because I was being a petulant whiner.

That finally stopped me. I realized that the only way I'd be catching Ella was if she rode straight northeast. I put my horse in a stall and unsaddled him.

A smudge of light was showing in the east. I grabbed my sword and walked out to lean against the elm tree and watch the sunrise. The sword and I pushed down the urge to go kill everybody who was aggravating me. Of course, we wouldn't do that.

We'd just kill the ones who deserved it.

Bib's Adventures Continue in *Death's Collector: Sword Hand*

A KILLER WITH DOUBTS. **A ruinous war.**

A couple of stupid decisions.

When the great war of empires comes, Bib the sorcerer doesn't expect to throw in with a bunch of horrid peasants. In fact, he hates the idea and would gladly trade them for a sock full of sand. But this war has caught him in a transitional period.

Although he's killed scads of people, Bib has never thought of himself as evil. Now his friends tell him to wake up and smell the evil coffee, and the whole idea vexes him.

Saving helpless villagers sure sounds like something a good person would do, so Bib decides to give it a shot. But with two armies slaughtering thousands of people all over the countryside, how not-evil is he prepared to be?

Purchase at: https://tinyurl.com/billmccurrybooks

ABOUT THE AUTHOR

Bill McCurry blends action, humor, and vivid characters in his dark fantasy novels. They are largely about the ridiculousness of being human, but with swords because swords are cool. Before being published, he wrote three novels that sucked like black holes, and he suggests that anyone who wants to write novels should write and finish some bad novels first. You learn a lot.

Bill was born in Fort Worth, Texas, where the West begins, the stockyards stink, and the old money families run everything. He later moved to Dallas, where Democrats can get elected, Tom Landry is still loved, and the fourth leading cause of death is starvation while sitting on LBJ Freeway.

Although Dallas is a city that smells like credit cards and despair, Bill and his wife still live there with their five cats. He maintains that the maximum number of cats should actually be three, because if you have four, then one of them can always get behind you.

CONNECT WITH THE AUTHOR

BMcCurryBooks.com
Facebook.com/Bill.McCurry3
Instagram.com/bfmccurry

Sign Up for Bill's Newsletter!

Keep up to date on new books and on exclusive offers. No spam!

https://www.bmccurrybooks.com/contact-us-2/

PURCHASE OTHER BOOKS IN THIS SERIES

Book 1 - *Death's Collector*
Book 2 - *Death's Baby Sister*
Book 3 - *Death's Collector: Sorcerers Dark and Light*
Book 4 - *Death's Collector: Void Walker*
Book 5 - *Death's Collector: Sword Hand*
Book 6 - *Death's Collector: Dark Lands*

Companion Book - *Wee Piggies of Radiant Might*

Shop at: https://tinyurl.com/billmccurrybooks

LEAVE A REVIEW

Please leave a review on the platform of your choice!

https://linktr.ee/reviewvoidwalker